THREE WELLS
OF THE SEA

Three Wells of the Sea Book 1

THREE WELLS OF THE SEA

Three Wells of the Sea Book 1

Terry Madden

DIGITAL
FANTASY
FICTION

DIGITAL FICTION
PUBLISHING CORP

Edition 3 © 2016 Digital Fiction Publishing Corp.
Story copyright © 2016 Terry Madden

ISBN-13 (paperback): 978-1-927598-32-0
ISBN-13 (e-book): 978-1-927598-33-7

For those I love who've crossed the well,
until we meet again.

The Five Quarters

Chapter 1

"Druids claim that they alone know the workings of the gods and the secrets of the stars. Living in deep forests, they teach that the shades of the dead do not descend to the silent, colorless underworld of Erebus, but that self-same spirit inhabits other bodies in other worlds. . . Death is but a point of change in the midst of continuous life."

— Lucan, "Pharsalia," 61 C.E.

Connor focused on the painted blue eyes of the Virgin Mary. The statue was perched on a corner pedestal in the principal's office between bookshelves and windows striped with blinds that let in slices of sky. Mary peered over Father Owens' shoulder, deaf to the principal's tirade describing in detail Connor's lack of character, moral compass, humility. Connor was about to confess that his failings were far more substantial. Instead, he distracted himself with wondering how many Mary statues there were in the world. He imagined an assembly line of plaster Marys—same sky-blue cloak speckled with stars, bashful smile, northern European skin tone. Probably made in China.

Father Owens pushed his chair from the desk. When he stood, his red face eclipsed Mary's. "Mr. Quinn, have you heard a single word I've said?"

"I heard the part about me being a disgrace to St. Thom's, sir."

"Have you anything to say for yourself?"

"No, sir."

Connor was halfway out of his chair when the office door swung open. Dish, Connor's English teacher, rushed in. He pulled up a chair beside Connor and held his tie as he sat like some hotshot lawyer.

"I thought someone should speak on Connor's behalf," Dish said.

Connor took his cue from Father Owens and sat back down, saying, "I can handle this myself, Dish—Mr. Cavendish, sir."

"It's time we sorted this out," Dish said.

"There's nothing to 'sort,' Cavendish," Owens said. "It's all crystal clear. This young man confessed. He acted alone, correct?"

"Just me and my phone, sir."

Owens deposited the device on the desk in front of Dish. "Father," Dish said, "there are things you need to know—"

"It's all right, Mr. Cavendish." Connor raised his hands in surrender. "I'm ready to accept the consequences of my actions." He tried to stand, but Dish's fingers dug into his shoulder.

"This is rather hasty," Dish said. "Wouldn't it be wise to consult Connor's parents before such a weighty decision is reached?"

"I think my mom is in Vegas, and Dad is probably on a business trip somewhere."

"I don't see that there's anything to discuss," Owens said, "other than setting a time for them to collect their son."

"It was a prank!" Dish said. "Expelling him for something like this—"

"He made a mockery of the Bishop. The Bishop, Mr.

Cavendish." Father Owens spread his palms on the glass desktop and ratcheted to a standing position.

"But there are circumstances—"

"I don't deserve special consideration," Connor said. "I planned it. I did it. I'm glad."

"For Pete's sake, Cavendish, he wants expulsion."

"Indeed..." Dish sucked in his lower lip and gave Connor a long look. "May I ask that Connor wait outside whilst you and I speak?"

Owens rolled his eyes and dismissed Connor with a flutter of his doughy white hands.

Shit.

Connor shut the door behind him and slumped into a chair, his back to the wall of Owens' office. He rubbed the worn knees of his navy-blue pants, hitched halfway up his skinny shins. At least his mom wouldn't have to buy a new uniform.

The school secretary raised her eyebrows at him and answered the ringing phone, "Saint Thomas Aquinas Preparatory School."

A freshman stood at her desk pinching a wad of tissue around his bloody nose. The receptionist pointed to a chair opposite Connor. The boy sat and tipped his head back to the wall while holding his nose. From this position, it was clear the boy was trying to steal glances at Connor. The freshman had witnessed, with the rest of the school, Connor's masterful work with the sound system.

Connor felt like a rock star.

Leaning back to stare at the acoustic ceiling tiles, Connor pressed his head to the wall of Owens' office and discovered he could make out pieces of what they were saying inside.

"... a mockery of the sacrament." Father Owens.

Don't forget, I'm failing three of six classes. He'd forgotten to add that part. He'd been trying to fail religion, but discovered it wasn't possible.

"It's been one year today since his brother…"

Dish knew what day this was? The man had a memory like a machine.

Dish's voice grew louder, drawing the attention of the freshman.

"If you expel him, this school will have failed him." Connor raised an eyebrow at the kid.

"Mr. Cavendish," Owens' voice boomed, "your quixotic tactics have proven ineffective in at least three cases I can think of—"

"Connor is quite different…" Dish's voice dropped again and only murmurs seeped from the office, then the squeal of Owens' executive chair.

The office door burst open and Connor stared at the carpet as Dish strode past.

"Come with me."

Connor shot to his feet and kept pace, past the reception desk and out the door.

"You have running shoes, I presume?"

"Yeah, I guess," Connor said. "But, why?"

He had to jog to keep up with Dish. They crossed the courtyard, passed the fountain, and headed back toward the dorm. "I'm expelled, right, Dish?"

"That's Mr. Cavendish, and no. Not yet. When you're not in class, you're with me. All your privileges are revoked, if you still have any. Where I go, you go. Be at the van promptly at four." He glanced at his watch. "That's fourteen minutes. If you don't show, I'll find you. Welcome to the cross-country team, Connor."

It took Connor thirteen minutes to stuff his backpack with anything worth anything. He headed out his dorm room and through the common lounge, rehearsing in his head what he would tell his mom when he got home. He wished it were true she was in Vegas; it would make running away from school easier. He decided the old anger and abandonment scene might work on her.

Trudy, the cook, was the only one in the kitchen when he went through.

"No ice cream before dinner," she said.

"No worries." Connor headed for the back door that opened past the chest freezer. He eased the screen closed without slamming it, bounced down the stairs, and almost tripped over Dish sitting on the bottom step.

"You don't look ready to run," Dish said, nodding at Connor's jeans and skateboard shoes. "Or perhaps you do." He stood and tipped his chin toward the school van parked a stone's throw away.

"I'm just..." Connor sighed. "I'm ready."

"Right. Off we go, then." Dish brushed eucalyptus leaves off his butt and strode toward the van without even a glance over his shoulder.

Connor could make a run for it. His grandma's old Audi was parked just behind the maintenance shed.

"I'll be needing your keys," Dish said.

Jesus, was he psychic?

"What keys?"

"The ones that fit your car."

"Isn't that illegal or something?"

"Not here." Dish pulled the handle and the door of the van slid open.

"You can't do that, Dish, Mr. Cavendish, sir. C'mon. That's my car!"

The cross-country team appeared around the corner of the dorm. The boys ambled toward the van in running shorts and shoes, whispering behind their hands, their eyes flitting to Connor. Then laughter.

"Your keys." Dish held out his hand.

"That's bullshit. You can't do this—"

"Watch me."

Connor dug the Audi keys out of his pocket and slapped them on Dish's open palm. He'd only had the car for two weeks. "Shit."

He slid across the bench seat, his backpack between his knees. The team tumbled into the van after him.

Aaron, his roommate, jabbed him with an elbow as he took up most of the seat. "Since when are you on the team?" He pointed at Connor's jeans. "How you gonna run in those?"

"I thought you'd be on your way home, D.J.," Kyle said. One of the guys in the back started wailing, "In the jungle, the mighty jungle, the lion sleeps tonight…"

Connor jabbed his middle finger over his shoulder.

These guys had no taste. It was a classic prank. All Connor had to do was pop the mic jack out of the mixer board during the all-school Mass, replace it with a 3.5 millimeter male-to-male audio jack that converted his phone mini jack into an old-school plug, and voilà, The Tokens' ball-busting falsetto had rung out through the gym like an orgasm.

"I hope you like running, Connor." Dish eyed him in the rearview mirror. "You've got an additional mile."

"I love it, Mr. Cavendish, coach, sir."

The eye wasn't amused, or even angry. Just watchful.

Yeah, but the lion sleeps tonight.

One of the perks of Malibu was the beach, at least for most people. Connor hated the beach almost as much as he hated running. The fog would be surely be rolling in when they got there.

The van spun down the long estate drive and through the gates of St. Thomas Aquinas Prep, an old Spanish-style mansion the Church had salvaged and converted into a boarding school. Its nickname had been "The Foundry" for the past eighty years, the perfect symbol of a place where a person's essence and intellect were melted down and poured into an obsolete mold to harden into Dark Age self-denial. It was nothing more than a slag heap for the offspring of doctors, lawyers, and corporate execs with enough money to pay a school to fix what they broke.

Dish's eye flitted to the rearview mirror, then back to the road. Not only was he Connor's English teacher, he was also his dorm counselor, and one of the few teachers who lived on campus. Connor had been wondering long before today what a young, slick, Oxford-educated Brit was doing at The Foundry. Dish didn't fit the inquisition theme.

The boys spilled out of the parked van and headed down the path that wound from Pacific Coast Highway to the beach. Connor shaded his eyes and scanned the coastline. Far below, breakers roared and reached for the toes of a string of beach houses, all teetering on struts and pylons, waiting for the next big storm. Mist from the surf smudged the distant cliffs of the point. The autumn days were getting shorter and the beach was totally devoid of bikinis.

With a sigh, Connor set out after the others, but had to stop to re-tie his shoe.

"Do you always make people wait?" Dish asked.

The other guys were almost to the sand when Connor hitched his jeans over his skinny ass and jogged to catch up to Dish.

"I try," Connor said.

Dish was waiting for him, which could only mean one thing.

He was going to give Connor "the talk."

Once on the beach, they fell into an easy rhythm, side by side. Dish set a slow pace, as if letting the others go ahead. The wet sand gave way just enough to make Connor stumble. It wasn't long before his jeans were soaked to the calves and dragging to a low-rider position. He felt blisters coming on. He started to sweat. He finally took off his shoes and left them on the beach.

Again, Dish waited for him, but still no talk.

Connor rolled up the cuffs of his pants. It felt good to be barefoot, pure somehow, like he could feel every grain of sand through the tender soles of his feet. His stride matched up with Dish's and the shadows of their legs looked like stilts dancing over the sand. Connor wiped his nose on his T-shirt and ran faster. They passed the colony of beach houses and headed out toward the point where the cliffs rose straight up from the sand.

Connor couldn't take the silence any longer. "How'd you know? That today was the day?"

"I remember."

"Aren't you going to tell me to get on with my life? To let go?"

Dish looked from the beach to Connor. "Would you like me to?"

Dish wouldn't talk about the rage that rotted in Connor's gut, or the waste of his brother's life. Connor shook his head and ran faster.

The rest of the pack had grown small ahead of them. Water filled their footprints with the red shimmer of the setting sun.

"Okay," Connor said at last. "I'm your shmuck, I got that. Make me run, make me do homework, keep me out of trouble." He glanced at Dish. "Don't you have a life?"

Dish wiped at his mouth with his sweatband and gave Connor a look. "I'm doing my job, but it doesn't mean I don't care about you."

His job? Connor was just a job? He pushed the burn deeper into his legs, faster, faster, flying over the wet sand, trying to leave Dish behind.

Dish's voice trailed after him, "Your brother is dead, Connor, but you're not."

Connor lost himself in the rhythm of his legs, imagining he'd left Dish far behind. In his mind, Connor opened the door to his brother's dorm room and saw. Nothing could make him quit seeing. The vomit and blood, the sweaty canvas smell of the firemen's yellow suits, the garbled voices on their walkie-talkies, his brother's pale surrender to OxyContin and coke.

When Connor finally turned and looked behind him, he saw that Dish had stopped about a quarter mile down the beach. With hands on knees, Connor panted, then headed back, his jeans making a whoosh-whoosh of chafing denim.

Dish was standing at the base of the sandstone cliff. Waxy gray plants, plump with stored water, grew from cracks in the rock, their flowers nothing but shriveled stalks. They got their water from the sea mist that dampened the sandstone and darkened it to golden tones, layers of ancient sediment stacked and sculpted by the pounding of the sea. At Dish's feet, a depression in the sand formed a still pool of water where the sunset reflected blue and orange.

Dish ran his hands over the rock face and as Connor drew nearer, he saw that water seeped from somewhere behind the cliff and ran out to form the pool.

"Hey, there's fish in there." Connor pointed. Two silver minnows swam circles around each other and vanished under the overhang of the cliff. "How can they swim behind the rock?"

"The pool goes under it, a wellspring," Dish said. "I've run this beach a hundred times. It's never been here before." Connor followed Dish's glance at the purpling sky. "Dusk," Dish said.

"Yeah, so?"

"The threshold of night."

"What's that supposed to mean?"

Dish emptied his pockets of keys and cell phone. "I can't explain it," he said, pulling off his socks and shoes.

"What are you doing?"

Dish waded into the shallow water and scooped up a handful and put it to his mouth. "It's fresh."

"Well, don't drink it, it's probably full of sewage from that strip mall up on PCH."

Dish sat down in the water and gave a shout.

"Bloody cold." He pushed his legs under the rocky ledge, just his head showing above the water. "And deep," he said, "very deep."

"You're outta your mind. That's like sticking your legs under your bed in the dark." Connor looked up to see the rest of the team heading toward them. "It's getting dark, Dish. We gotta go—"

"Christ!" Dish pulled his legs back, tried to stand, but stumbled and fell on his ass in the pool, arms planted in the sand behind him. He exploded in a jubilant hoot. "I can't believe it!" Dish said. "Here? In Malibu?"

"What the hell?" Connor said. "What was it?"

"Something's alive in there."

"Yeah, we saw two fish go under the rock—"

"Bigger." Dish was grinning like a kid who'd found his friend's hiding place. "A bloody guardian…"

"A guardian of what?"

Then Connor saw it. Where water clung like pearls to Dish's goose-prickled wrist, the faintest trace of blue began to appear, like some invisible person was drawing on him with a blue pen. At first, the lines looked like they followed the veins of his arm, then they twisted, thickened and darkened. An image began to bloom. It looked like a tattoo.

"Dish!" Connor was on his knees beside him. "Your—your arm…" He pointed.

Dish pulled off his wristband and traced the image with a quaking finger. His breath came faster and faster.

"Bloody hell…"

He scrambled to his knees and thrust his arm into the pool, frantically scrubbing at it with wet sand. When he finally held his arm up to the fading light, his skin was red and blotched, but underneath, the image was clear. It had a long tail that knotted around itself. A dragon? No, it looked more like a horse, but with a fish tail.

16

Dish traced the design again. "It's not possible..."

The team would reach them in minutes.

Dish looked right into Connor's eyes. "It's the cold."

He crawled out onto the sand and struggled to pull shoes on his wet feet.

"Cold doesn't make tattoos, last I heard," Connor said.

"I don't know, all right?"

"Maybe a jellyfish stung you," Connor said. "What's a guardian?"

Dish's eyes met his for a long moment, but held no answer. He took the sweatband from his left wrist and pulled it over his right. The two bands covered most of the mark, but not all of it. Connor could hear the other guys breathing hard and coming up behind him.

Dish clutched Connor's arm. His eyes overflowed with confusion, but there was something else, a spark of wonder like you only see in little kids.

"This is between you and me, Connor."

"Sure." His answer was mechanical. Connor felt like he should be waking from a dream. Fog condensed on his skin and he could sense every drop. His mind raced. Dish was hiding something... something incredible, impossible, maybe. Dish's look said he knew what Connor was thinking. He let go of Connor's arm and dragged his quaking palms down his face saying, "Let's go," then took off down the beach.

Connor followed, but glanced over his shoulder more than once at the pool behind them.

The insides of Connor's knees were chafed raw from running in wet jeans. He lay on his top bunk, trying to read the assigned pages for Dish's class. He'd stopped reading a week ago, certain he'd be expelled by now. There was going to be a quiz in the morning. He thought he should try to pass it, but the words on the page blurred and the only thing he could see was the tattoo on Dish's wrist. What was the guardian Dish was talking about? And what did it have to do with that tattoo?

Connor's roommate, Aaron, was busy uploading pictures of his new "Bathing Chimp" sweatshirt to Facebook.

"Check it out, Connor." Aaron tipped his laptop so Connor could see the page from his perch on the top bunk.

"That's just fuckin' stupid."

Aaron launched his dirty boxers at Connor. "At least I don't go running in jeans."

Hours later, Connor was wide awake. Aaron was talking Chinese in his sleep and Connor was thinking about the pool on the beach. He had tried to convince himself that Dish had had an old tattoo removed and what Connor saw was the shadow of it, visible only because of the cold water. But the mark he had seen was sharp and dark blue. The head of a horse, the tail of a fish. Connor had watched it appear like the disappearing ink he used to make when he was a kid. Maybe something in the water brought out the image like lemon juice did with disappearing ink. That didn't explain why it was there in the first place, or why Dish came unglued about it. Connor had seen something he shouldn't, and sooner or later, Dish would have to explain.

Connor stared at the ceiling and the glow-in-the-dark stars left by the last inmate. They brightened as his eyes adjusted to the darkness. Their green glow tricked him into feeling that a vast expanse of space opened before him. He was a cliff diver, falling into nothing.

He jerked awake.

Down the hall, a door closed and a key turned in a lock. He heard footsteps. Connor checked his phone. 4:19 a.m.

He eased down from the top bunk and cracked the door just in time to see Dish slip out the emergency exit at the end of the hall.

Connor followed.

Standing on the cold steel grate of the fire escape, he

watched Dish's car head through the fog and out the school gates.

Where you go, I go. Wasn't that the deal?

His breath fumed in the cold night. "Where you going, Dish?"

Chapter 2

Lyleth pulled her hood close and jostled with the crowd. Through the narrow lanes of Caer Ys, tradesmen, fishermen and farmers flowed toward the walls of the keep that crowned the island city. Lyleth was but a droplet in this river, and the multitude would carry her on, nameless as rain. It was worth the risk, for today the grieving queen would address her people, still mourning the death of Nechtan, a king they had loved well. Whatever the queen's proclamation, it would certainly be crafted as proof of her innocence in her husband's murder, or perhaps to support the charge that it was really Lyleth who had killed Nechtan. Either way, the informer Lyleth had come to meet would have to wait.

Caer Ys was unchanged by a summer of grieving for its murdered king and Lyleth's exile hadn't tempered the aroma of peat smoke, roasting chestnuts and oyster stew. Pipers appeared on the walls of the keep, calling the crowd to the square below with a somber rendition of the Battle of Glen Ardach.

The smell from a fishmonger's basket confirmed the haddock he carried might have been fresh yesterday. Lyleth tried to slip between him and a woman bouncing a babe, but someone called out and the fishmonger and his basket swung round, sending Lyleth into a pile of grain sacks.

"Ah, forgive me, lass," he said. "Oaf, me wife calls me."

He offered two meaty hands to pluck her up, but as he did,

his eyes went to her wrist. She tugged at her sleeve to cover the mark, but it was too late. The man's eyes flashed from the tattoo to her face.

She held his gaze and he held her hand fiercely while people eddied around them like snags in a river.

"If you loved your lord," she whispered to him, "you'll let me pass."

"Loved Nechtan well, I did." But he glanced at two guards leaning against a nearby wall.

"The queen offers four fifties in gold for me, aye," Lyleth said, "and I've nothing to offer you but the blessing of the green gods."

The fishmonger snuffed and pursed his lips. "I'd take two fifties and let ye be on your way."

Lyleth wrested her hand free, and taking hold of his tunic, pulled him so close she could smell last night's ale on his breath. "Look at me," she demanded through clenched teeth. "Is it a murderer you see?"

His eyes softened. Trapped as they were by Lyleth's, he had no choice but to see the truth, for she willed it to pass between them like a conjured breeze.

She released him slowly and he yielded, showed the respect of his palms and stared at his boots. "I've seen no one here, solás."

Touching his shoulder in passing, she whispered, "Stars and stones keep you."

Her blessings were as impotent as her curses. It hardly mattered now, for as closest advisor, solás, to a murdered king, she found herself in hiding. And this fishmonger would be loyal only long enough to raise the guards.

High on the wall of the keep, the pipers finished their tune and were replaced by guards carrying baskets from which they showered fists of coppers on the crowd below.

A mad scramble followed, sending a tumble of men into a turnip stall. Blows were traded before guards could stop it and

Lyleth took advantage of the distraction to vanish down a web of alleyways.

A blacksmith stepped from his shop and wiped soot from his hands, saying, "She'll name us a king today, that's what she's about."

Beside him, a 'prentice boy squinted into the sun. "Who'd that be?"

"It matters not to me, long as she leaves me in peace. I've no time for a throne." The smithy belched and laughed and slapped the 'prentice so hard the boy fought to keep his feet.

No, a smith certainly had no time. A fortnight ago, the queen had ordered every smith in Ys to work till his steel ran out, forging spearheads, axes and blades. Did no one else see what she was about? By law, the throne of the Five Quarters would be ruled, not by a man named by the queen, but by a man named by the judges of the wildwood.

The queen, however, clearly had other plans.

On the battlements, the pipers trilled a short tune and the queen materialized. Ava spread her arms wide in a mock motherly embrace while her unbound yellow hair billowed as if she would take flight. This woman who had come to Caer Ys as Nechtan's bride, a frightened girl from the northern wastes, now held the crowd in a hushed thrall.

"She's broke her grieving," an old woman said, pointing at Ava with a palsied hand. "It's been no full turn of the sun's wheel."

Indeed, Ava had cast aside all signs of mourning. She wore a gown of deep ruby with a cloak of sheerest mousseline that fluttered with her hair.

A hush fell over the crowd as two soldiers hefted a large basket before Ava's feet.

"Your king is chosen!" Ava shouted. The wind dampened her words, but could not kill them entirely.

The crowd grumbled and hushed.

Ava reached into the basket and struggled with a thick chain. She braced her feet and lifted the head of an enormous eel, a head as big as a man's. She took two steps to the edge of the wall and extended both arms. The thing at the end of the chain spun slowly, the gills splayed under feathery feelers that wagged in the breeze, the mouth agape to show a yellow throat and needle-sharp teeth the length of the queen's fingers.

"Behold a guardian!" Ava shouted. "Slain by my hand!"

The crowd erupted and passed the queen's words to those out of earshot.

"In the name of all mothers…" The smithy made the sign against evil.

The eel's head was fresh, not a preserved oddity. It splattered pink blood down the battlements, its leathery flesh bunched around a white eye.

To those with eyes to see, there was more to this creature. Lyleth hid in the shadow of a hay cart and watched the spiny feelers of the eel grow into hair, long dark tresses that streamed in the breeze. The white eye turned blue and human, but still dead and staring. A well guardian. Ava would have people think she took its life, that the green gods had made a sacrifice of one of their own, and in so doing, the gods had chosen Ava as king. How was that possible?

Lyleth glanced at the blacksmith.

"I seen nets bring in stranger beasts," he said with some diffidence. "Makes it no guardian."

"It's the biggest sodding eel I've set me eyes on," the 'prentice said.

Lyleth still saw the gray flesh of a bruised girl. The eyes, muddy with the film of death, fixed on Lyleth and the lips curled. She mocks me.

"Our mourning for Nechtan is done," Ava proclaimed.

"It's not done," Lyleth said aloud.

Behind squinty eyes the blacksmith took in Lyleth's features. "I know ye…" he said. "Nechtan's own solás."

Lyleth slipped down an alley and lost herself in the tangled crowd at the edge of the square. Even if the smith called the guards, she would reach the city gate before they could close it. She envied Nechtan his slumber in the Otherworld, and as she pushed toward the gate, she wondered if he remembered anything of the troubles he'd left behind for her to right.

The gatekeepers were busy with a cotter who'd not enough coin to pay his tariff. Lyleth passed through the gate in the shadow of a manure wagon. She had to believe that Rhys still waited for her at the tavern on the quay, and that he'd brought what she'd asked for.

Chapter 3

Connor opened his blue book and tried to answer the essay prompt on the board, but he couldn't help watching Dish who sat at his desk by the window, his red pen tap-tapping on someone's essay, his eyes on a storm building over the Pacific. The blue stain of the horse-fish tattoo still peeked from under the cuff of his dress shirt, reminding Connor what had happened on the beach two days before had been real. He'd rehearsed several casual approaches he might use to bring it up to Dish, but the look in his teacher's eyes always stopped him, and Dish was acting stranger every day.

Pencils scribbled over blue books. Every now and then Connor looked up from his own blank page and caught Dish staring at him. The strange thing was Dish didn't look away, as if he didn't even know he was staring. Connor went back to his doodle.

The past two mornings, Dish had slipped out of the dorm about 4:15 a.m. The second night, Connor tailed him all the way to the school gates and finally realized there was no way to follow on foot. Dish could be going anywhere.

This morning, Connor had set a trap.

He got up before 4:15, listened for the emergency exit door and the sound of Dish's car as he drove off. Stationed in the bathroom right across from Dish's room, Connor fell asleep on a toilet. At 6:13, he heard the emergency door rattle shut and footsteps in the hall.

He timed his stumbling out of the bathroom perfectly so he ran right into Dish.

"You're up early, Dish."

"As are you." Dish unlocked his room and started to slip inside. He was soaking wet.

"Went for a beach run?"

"See you in class, Connor." No eye contact, just a closed door in the face.

So, Dish was going back to the beach every morning. What the hell was happening to him?

Connor looked up from his essay-doodle as the bell rang.

After the other kids had stacked their blue books and filed out, Connor opened his and placed it on the desk in front of Dish.

Dish's eyes flitted from Connor's lame sketch of the horsefish tattoo to Connor's eyes. Dish bit his lower lip and handed back the drawing.

"I googled 'threshold of night,'" Connor said. "Dawn and dusk are considered important times of day for magical rituals. Something about a thinning of the veil between the worlds."

"Yes." Dish leaned back in his chair and exhaled. "Especially for the Celts, did you find that as well?"

Connor leaned on the desk and pointed at Dish's arm. He whispered, "What is that thing, Dish?"

"I want to explain if I can. But there's something I must find before you'll believe a word of it."

The door to the classroom opened and some giggling girls swarmed in, asking Dish for help on their essays.

"We'll talk later," Dish told Connor.

The day plodded on. Three o'clock bell, then four o'clock run. Dish led the cross country team up a fire road that wound into the Santa Monica Mountains, and by the time they got back to campus, Connor could barely put one foot in front of the other, but he couldn't wait for dark.

A long shower was followed by dinner. Study hall came and went, then lights out. Connor set his phone alarm to vibrate at 4:00 a.m. and put it under his pillow.

He startled awake from a deep sleep, pulled on his running shoes, and lay in wait. 4:08, Dish's door clicked open. From the fire escape, Connor watched Dish get in his car. It was parked at the far end of the overflow parking lot, probably so no one would hear him come and go.

As soon as Dish drove away, Connor shoved a piece of binder paper into the emergency exit, bounded down the fire escape, and hit the pavement at an easy jog.

The moon overhead gave him plenty of light.

He took off as fast as he could without taking a header on the winding road that led down to Pacific Coast Highway. Maybe Dish was into some weird cult, or kinky sex or something. Either way, Father Owens would fire him in an instant if he knew about all this.

It was only about a mile and a half to the highway, then less than a mile to the path to the beach.

PCH was empty and Connor hit a sprint down the southbound lane until he passed Dish's parked car. Stopping to breathe, he looked down over the moon-flooded beach. The tide was way out and a figure was walking north. Connor picked up an easy jog and set out after him.

By the time he reached the sandstone cliff, there was no one in sight. A pile of stuff sat at the edge of the pool: clothes, phone, wallet, keys. Where was Dish? It was like an alien abduction or something.

Connor's lungs burned. He sat down in the wet sand and let his breath warm his bare legs. Then, from behind the rock wall, a rippling glow spread through the water of the pool. It came from behind the cliff face. There had to be a cave behind the wall, and Dish was inside.

Connor got to his feet and paced circles.

"Dish? Mr. Cavendish?" He called as loud as he dared. What if someone else was in there?

He collapsed back to the sand, his arms around his knees, and watched the green light flicker and dance in the pool. He should go in, find out what all this scary shit was about.

The sky started to warm in the east. What was he going to tell Father Owens? Mr. Cavendish got tattooed by a pool of water he visits every morning to do something I was afraid to see?

Finally, he got up and started back down the beach. He'd find out what Dish was up to some other way.

He was halfway to the path when he looked over his shoulder. He could still see the green light, rippling, like something was in the water. What if Dish was in trouble? He could drown in there. "Shit."

Connor ran back, pulled off his shoes and waded in. The icy water stopped his breath. He sat down and pushed his legs under the rocky ledge, and the sandy shelf fell away into a bottomless well.

Holding his breath, he dove under the rock. His panic forced his eyes open, but they didn't sting in this water. He swam toward the light coming from above. The bubbles streaming from his arms and legs like jewels in the light.

He surfaced.

Dish was perched on a narrow shelf of gravel and shells, his knees tucked up. He was buck-naked and held a flashlight aimed at the walls of a cavern. The air was moist and stagnant like the inside of the earth's lungs.

"What—the—hell?" Connor pushed wet hair out of his eyes.

Dish wore the face of another man, a scary man. He looked confused and wrung out, or maybe it was just the light.

"Dish?"

He finally looked at Connor, not at him, but through him, then back at the wall above.

"You've no business following me."

"What happened to 'where I go, you go'?"

"This doesn't concern you."

"You said you had something to show me. Is this it?"

"No."

Connor's eyes adjusted to the low light until he could make out what Dish was staring at—some kind of cave drawing. Three red spirals, one winding into the next. Sooty black handprints surrounded the spirals like stars. Shivering, Connor swam toward the gravel shelf and sunk his knees into it.

"What is it?"

Dish dropped the flashlight to the gravel and the spear of light bounced and pointed at nothing. He dragged his fingers through his hair. His voice was a hoarse whisper. "I remember things I shouldn't remember."

"Like what?"

Dish glared at Connor, picked up the flashlight, and switched it off.

The cave went black. Their breathing echoed and Connor's quickened. The sand gave way under his knees as he slid back into the bottomless pool.

"Leave me be, Connor." Dish's voice boomed off the stone walls.

The darkness was absolute, the surf a distant drumming from another world. Connor thrashed about until panic gripped him. Dish had said there was something in the water—something big.

"Dish!"

He flogged the black water until he felt the edge of rock that marked the entrance. He almost forgot to fill his lungs before he dove under and felt his way through the opening. Scraping his side on the rocks, he surfaced, gasping for air.

Outside, the moon had set as dawn took over. He coughed up water, staggered out of the pool, and fell to the sand. Shivering, he looked back to see no light coming from the cave.

His eyelashes beaded with water and tears. He spat out more water and pulled on his shoes, then headed down the beach, leaving Dish to his darkness.

It was raining freaking buckets.

Trick or treating would suck tonight. It made Connor glad he was too old for Halloween. The last time he tried to trick or treat, an old lady told him he should be ashamed of himself, right before she slammed the door in his face.

He waited for Dish, huddled under the overhang of the maintenance shed watching the rain spank the roof of his grandma's Audi. Dish still had the keys. Since the morning in the cave, Dish had spoken half a dozen words to Connor. But today he'd asked Connor to drive him on an errand.

"My battery's dead," Dish had told him. "We'll take your car."

He'd probably left his lights on after his naked, nutcase swim at dawn. So, now chauffeuring was part of Connor's punishment. Dish didn't even seem to notice that Connor was giving him the silent treatment; he was too busy being out of his fucking mind.

Dish appeared from around the corner of the dining hall. He plowed through the squall, the tails of his raincoat blowing behind him. He tossed the keys to Connor, who hit the unlock button and they both spilled into the cracked leather seats.

"Let's go," Dish said. "I found what I was looking for. It will help me explain."

Connor did his best Igor. "Yes, master."

The rain fell harder. Connor turned left onto PCH as Dish instructed and stayed in the right lane. He'd never driven in the rain before, so he slowed and gripped the wheel tighter. Cars passed and sent up curtains of water. The wipers squealed as he drove in painful silence. Was Dish waiting for him to start talking?

Connor couldn't stand it any longer. He blurted, "Aren't you going to threaten me or something?"

"Why should I threaten you?"

"Because I invaded your—your privacy, doing whatever it was you were doing in that cave. You're having hallucinations or something, right? 'I remember things I shouldn't remember.' That's what you told me." The rain nearly drowned out his words.

Dish turned to him, his eyes bloodshot and filled with secrets. "Connor, I need you to understand... there's another world out there, one I remember with painful clarity, and it shapes us no less than this one."

"Another world. Sure. But you probably don't want anyone to know about this... this other world, right?"

Connor stopped at a red light.

"What are you saying?" Dish said.

"I'm just saying maybe Father Owens wouldn't want an unstable person teaching English to impressionable kids. Maybe we can make a deal, is all I'm saying."

"Bloody blackmail?" Dish snorted a laugh and dragged his palms down his cheeks. "And when you're expelled, what will you do? Run home to mum who's too busy drinking to wonder where you are? End up like your brother?"

The red light lasted an eternity. The wipers slap-slapped with Connor's heart and Dish kept talking.

"You know as well as I that running away won't fill the emptiness."

"You don't know jack shit." Connor's eyes clouded with tears.

"But I do."

The light turned green.

The road opened up like an invitation. Connor stomped on the gas and the wheels spun. It felt good to go fast. The car cut a wake through pooling rainwater, and then they were flying. The tires no longer crawled on the pavement, but glided and took their own path. He turned the wheel, but it did nothing. They crossed over the center line and into oncoming traffic.

He saw the van closing in for the longest millisecond in history, heard crushing metal, a frozen car horn, and rain. Through the broken windshield the sky poured in.

He stopped screaming.

Looking down at the bloody man in his lap, Dish's eyes met Connor's before everything went as black as the cave.

Chapter 4

Lyleth found the dockside streets nearly empty, for most of the city was still fighting over Ava's coins. Caer Ys sat like a pearl inside the oyster of the bay, and a great sweep of calm water sheltered a sizeable harbor, trade port to the southern lands, even as far away as Cadurques and the inland sea. Timber, wool and tin sailed out as wine, silks and silver sailed in. A curtain of fog had crept in to cloak fishing scows and trade galleys, but a tavern window spilled light at Lyleth's feet.

Once inside, she skirted a crowd of drunken sailors smelling of sweat and salty wool, their tongues thick with the south.

She found Rhys waiting at a table in a dim corner, his mug more for show than for drink. Rumor said the ale in this tavern wasn't of the same quality as its whores, and judging by the sounds drifting from the rooms above, it was likely so.

Lyleth took a stool across from Rhys and pushed back her hood.

When Nechtan lay dying, it was Rhys who sat with his king through long nights—and it was Rhys who watched Ava's healer apply a stinking balm to a wound that should have healed with nothing more than a good washing with winterbloom.

A barmaid clapped a horn of ale on the table in front of Lyleth. "Two pence."

Rhys dropped coins in her hand.

"Diggin' for gold in the streets, eh?" the barmaid asked him.

Rhys laughed. "A queen with an open hand is a queen I drink to, lass." He raised his mug to the girl.

"Watch your words," he whispered to Lyleth when the barmaid had gone. He nodded toward three men two tables over. "They say she's summoned the chieftains to Caer Ys."

"Of course she has; she'll see who fails to lick her toes." Lyleth leaned in. "And who'll challenge her but me?"

"She's been chose." Rhys glanced over his shoulder at the drunken seamen.

"You know better, Rhys. Ava is the get of reavers."

"I know that no king's been chose by a well guardian since Black Brac, nine hundred years ago and more."

"Ava took this guardian by some guile," Lyleth said, "just as she took Nechtan's life. Now she forces the hand of the green gods. You think they'd choose such as her to rule?"

He leveled a glare at her. "I know Black Brac was chose to push the Old Blood from this land and claim it for us."

"You'd hand over the Five Quarters to Ava's kind?"

"All I knows is we were the murderous reavers once. Guardians pander to none. Perhaps they've a grand design for this she-king." He took a drink of ale and wiped the foam from his mustache with the back of his hand.

"Did you bring what I asked for?" Lyleth asked coldly.

"I've no need of trouble and you bring nothing but to me table—"

"We had an agreement." Her palm met the table hard enough to smart and draw glances from those nearby.

Rhys rolled his eyes, reached into a pouch at his belt, and produced a small horn vial stoppered with a leather plug. He handed it over, saying, "Smells of whale blubber and lavender to me."

She popped the plug with the hem of her cloak and sniffed.

"You're sure this was the balm Ava's healer used on Nechtan's wound?"

"By my life 'tis. I took but a little. If the old crow misses it, I'll be as dead as Nechtan."

With the point of her dirk, Lyleth dug out a greasy bit no bigger than a pea—yellow fat with flecks of powdered root. She sniffed it.

"There's more than whale fat here. Rancid lavender oil to be sure... and black hellebore. It'll stop your heart, sure enough." She replaced the stopper and slipped the vial into her own pouch.

"Stars and stones..." Rhys made the sign against evil and wiped his fingers on his surcoat. "Ava wept great tears over Nechtan. 'Twas that healer's dark work, not Ava's."

Lyleth shook her head. "Don't be a fool."

"What's to be done for it?" Rhys went on. "Nechtan rots, peace find him in the Fair Lands." His hands fumbled with the sign of respect for the dead. "Ava will be she-king. Done's done, Lyl."

"Done's done?"

Lyleth felt rage flush her cheeks. It had taken months for her suspicions to flower full, and now she held the truth in her hand. She'd meant to take this poison to the judges, proof that Nechtan was murdered, not by Lyleth as the queen had charged, but by the queen herself who'd wept such great gouts of tears upon her husband's death. But if Lyleth took this proof to the judges now, they would never see past the well guardian in Ava's hands—her rightful claim to the throne. How could the green gods cast their lot with such as Ava?

Lyleth had been betrayed by the very forces she served. She suddenly envied Nechtan the oblivion of death. But it was not a lasting oblivion. She knew they would all be called back to this world to face their failings.

Rhys started to stand, but she caught his arm. "I ask you for but one thing more, and you'll be done with me."

She felt the muscle of his arm tense. "It's always one more thing," he said.

"The last. There'll be no need of anything else."

"What?"

"Nechtan's harp."

"His harp?" Rhys snorted and plopped back to his stool. "Do you plan to sing Ava from the throne?"

"Help me, Rhys. I'll ask for nothing else, I swear it by stars and stones."

He waved a hand at her as he would a pesky fly. "Ava's assigned me to the kitchen. I've no reason to go into Nechtan's chamber no more, she's movin' everything."

"Then find a way."

A vein on his forehead bulged. His eyes met hers for a long moment. Rhys had a wife and children, after all.

He loosed a weary sigh. "I'll send it."

"When?"

"Two days' time. And I'll not see you again."

He downed his ale and stood as a clutch of castle guards came through the tavern door, tossing fists of coppers to the floor and laughing at the men who fought for them like dogs.

Lyleth saw only their backs on her way out the door.

Lyleth was helping Dunla cover the hives with straw for winter when she glimpsed a wagon on the road. Only someone who had business with the meadmonger would travel this way, for nothing but the Black Wood lay beyond Dunla's holding. Her meadstead lay at the eastern reach of the vale, past apple orchards and flax fields, in the lap of the Felgarths that rose like granite teeth beyond. For these past months, Lyleth had traded labor in the hives for Dunla's silence, but the old woman had come to be a good friend in that time.

"It comes," Lyleth told Dunla. Bees hummed in a cloud around their heads.

"What comes, lass?" Dunla set the smoker aside and placed

a cone of woven straw over a hive, then followed Lyleth's gaze to the wagon.

"Come," Lyleth said. "I mustn't be seen."

She dropped her straw screen under the skeps and started back toward the cottage. If Rhys had done this right, the messenger wouldn't know what he carried.

Dunla came huffing into the cottage after her. "What's all this?" The old woman wheezed and blotted her brow.

"Just agree with him."

"Agree? With what?"

"Whatever he asks of you."

Dunla gave Lyleth's cheek a pat. "He best not be asking for me maidenhead, then."

The wagon rolled to a halt outside.

"I got three barrels of mead here what tastes like sheep dung," a man's voice shouted. "The queen don't like sheep dung."

Lyleth hid between the door and the wall as Dunla stepped outside.

"I sell no sheep dung, fool," Dunla said.

Lyleth heard the chickens protest as barrels rolled off the wagon and bounced in the yard.

"Well, these taste like the sole of a sausage-maker's boot," the man said.

Not until the wagon had disappeared over the pass did Lyleth go out to the yard to find three barrels of mead.

"What in the name of the mothers is going on?" Dunla said.

"It's in one of these." Lyleth ran her hands over the barrel heads and found one that looked like new wood. "This one."

She found a kindling hatchet and hammer and set to work. "If the northern tribes rebel, they stand no chance against Ava and the south," Lyleth said. "They need a king. I mean to give them one."

She looked up from her work to measure Dunla's response.

"Your lord has no get of his own, and he's many months in his grave…" Dunla muttered. Then understanding bloomed on the old woman's face. "What have you in that barrel?"

Lyleth pushed hair out of her eyes. "Ava's father will come to claim what his darling girl has won for him."

"Nechtan's throne?"

Lyleth tapped the hatchet blade into the wood and loosened it. "Aye. The green gods can't give up Nechtan's throne if he sits upon it."

Dunla slumped to the bench by the door of the cottage, fanning herself with her apron. "It's not been done since the days of the Old Blood."

"It doesn't mean it can't be done."

"But… very near it."

Lyleth wedged the hatchet between the planks and popped them free, then reached into the brew and felt the package. As she lifted it, the bundle shed streams of golden mead. She cut the gut that bound it and peeled away a wrapping of oilcloth that fell to the ground in sticky folds.

Dunla struggled to her feet. "The harp of the drowned maid."

It was a simple lap harp, the soundboard made of blackthorn inlaid with shell and tarnished silver in the shape of a water horse.

A song from the time of Black Brac told of the making of this very harp. Two daughters of the high king loved the same warrior, but the warrior loved the younger of the two. The elder sister drowned the younger to have her man, but the maid's body came ashore at the feet of a bard. He fashioned this harp from the drowned maid's rib and strung it with her hair, and when he set it before the king at the sister's wedding feast, the harp played alone, telling all the story of the drowned girl's murder and naming the killer.

The neck of the harp was indeed fashioned of bone, but to Lyleth it looked much larger than a human rib. Porpoise, maybe, or seal. Silver bands held the tuning pegs in place where they were set in the bone. The strings had been cut on the death of every king for generations, as they were cut upon Nechtan's death.

Lyleth would string it once again.

She prepared to leave Dunla's meadstead at dawn, filling a rucksack with bread and cheese. It was important that the old woman know nothing of her destination.

"What you seek, lass, is unnatural," Dunla said. "For you. For your lord. Perhaps you should let this she-king burn bright and sputter out." She handed Lyleth an old cloak and some threadbare trousers.

Lyleth added the clothes to her sack and fetched her bow. "I'll do what I must."

Dunla took Lyleth's face between warm, doughy palms and cooed through missing teeth, her breath spiced with nuts and mead. "They'll ask a price, they will. The green gods are not so free with their gifts."

"I'll pay."

"Though you know not the sum?"

Tears welled in Dunla's eyes and she gripped Lyleth's shoulders as if to plant her in the ground.

"Tell me true," Dunla said. "Do you seek to mend your heart?"

"Some would say I have no heart."

"I know better, lass. Heal your heart and that of your lord, and the harp's work will be true."

Lyleth slung the satchel over her shoulder.

"You've been more than a friend." She touched the old woman's cheek. "I must be gone. Will you help me find a flask of mead worthy of a king?"

Dunla's mead was known not only in the Five Quarters, but even in the vinelands of the south. A fermentation of honey of the finest flowering, it was fed by the elements of an ancient soil, watered by rain and snow that blew off the Western Sea, secreted by the bodies of insects that passed freely between this world and the other.

Lyleth believed there had never been a husband for Dunla. Her story of the widowed bride who inherited this vast swath of hillside and valley from her fine man was all a fancy tale. At this moment, it seemed she had been here for decades, eons perhaps, for there were tales that said a handful of Old Blood had escaped the exile. When the third well was opened, they fled to the northern wilds and there lived on in secret. Children's tales.

Lyleth's goshawk, Wren, perched atop the sod-covered undercroft where Dunla aged her brew. The hawk had followed Lyleth the day she rode from Caer Ys. He was one of Nechtan's hunting birds, and Lyleth had always felt that in this bird, a part of Nechtan followed her.

The air in the undercroft was ancient, cool as winter. Barrels were stacked on plank shelves that bowed with the weight.

"It mustn't be just any vintage," Dunla muttered, working her way through the shelves in the dim light of the doorway. "I have one… 'Twas a year of late winter. The bees fed on the last of the cat's ear lily and fire chalice… ah, here."

The barrel was covered with dust and traced with cobwebs. Dunla produced a decanter from the recesses of the room. Even in near darkness the flask reflected spears of colored light on the stone walls. It was like no flask Lyleth had ever seen.

"Found it buried in here when I put up the shelves," Dunla said. "Fancy that, eh? Such a fine piece left behind. Hold it for me, lass."

Lyleth held the flask while Dunla racked off the pure sweet mead from the dregs, then dragged her finger across the spigot and licked it.

"Aye. 'Tis the one for Nechtan." Dunla gave a short whistle. "My lord won't have tasted any better in the Otherworld."

Grave robbers carry talismans to guard against the bane of the dead they desecrate. Lyleth had no such talisman. Nechtan had cursed her in life, what more could he do in death?

His grave wasn't far now, but which way? The wood grew thick here.

She set Wren to flight above the canopy of oak and beech. The goshawk labored upward, his jesses whipped with the eddy of his wings. He had glided through the ceiling of golden leaves and was out of sight when a long piping cry told Lyleth he moved south and east. She followed, and soon the long barrow that held Nechtan and his ancestors rose from the forest floor.

The Barrow of the Kings tunneled deep beneath a greenwood, the base stones just visible under the heap of earth. A silver hazel tree crowned the mound, embracing it in a knot of roots and fallen leaves.

Wren perched on a bare branch overhead and preened his breast feathers.

"Go get us a rabbit," she told him.

The bird turned a golden eye down on her and shat.

"A fine hunter you are." She knew she would miss the hawk when all was done.

Her kindling axe made a fair wedge, and after some sweat, the portal stone moved a finger's breadth. She shimmed it with sticks of increasing size until a fallen branch would do as a lever. When the huge stone finally rolled, it did so quickly.

A dark corridor beckoned.

She reached into the pouch at her belt to find her store of waxed rushlights. She uncorked a phial of hartshorn, dipped the rushlight and struck it on a rock. A sputtering flame cast sparks of gold down the passage of fitted stones that met and kissed just above her head, leaning at drunken angles, disturbed as they were by the roots of the hazel tree above.

A thousand years of kings lay sleeping in this dark corridor, but Lyleth had come for but one.

She found Nechtan's father in the first recess, and to the

right, his brother. In the next, a slab of granite held nothing but bones crowned by a circlet that had slipped over the eye sockets.

A watchstone marked with runes of red ochre guarded Nechtan's body. On the day of his grieving fresh birch branches had been woven over him. Now, the leaves had dried and fallen to cover his body in a brittle drift.

Lyleth brushed them aside.

"My duty demands this of me—and you." She heard the desperation in her voice and hoped he would, too.

She pulled the branches aside. His form had sunken away, traced by his cloak of farandine pulled close around him, hiding his hands.

The last time she'd seen Nechtan alive, he'd turned his back on her. "Our paths part here," he had said.

Their paths had indeed parted. But he would face the consequences of their mistakes, as surely as Lyleth. She traced his cold lips with her fingers. How cruel of her to remind him of his duty in this world. She leaned close to his ear, whispering, "I am such a fool, my lord."

With her dirk she severed his warrior's braid. The silver bells tied to it rang out like an alarm, but the dead were deaf to her thievery. She tucked the braid in her pouch, pressed her lips to his forehead, and was gone.

The fire Lyleth had built at the barrow's mouth had fallen to coals. Wren napped on his perch in the hazel tree while she twisted bundles of Nechtan's hair, roping three to three to form a string thick enough to pluck. She dipped the ends in a cup of hot beeswax that sat warming at the edge of the coals. By the time she knotted and tightened each string in place on the tuning pegs at the harp's neck, the moon had risen well overhead.

Touching the strings of his hair the harp sang a lethargic dirge, out of tune and muted. She turned the pegs and worked for the notes. The tension on the hair strings slackened quickly and required constant adjusting, but soon she gave it a full trill. At last, the strings trembled like wind in the woods, like Nechtan's laughter.

She drowned in the sound; an old wound bled again.

Beside the fire, the flask of Dunla's mead sat on a flat stone. Cut from a single shard of rock crystal, the flask was big-bellied like a milk pitcher. Veins of imperfections traced rainbow webs in the crystal, brought to life by fingers of fire and moonlight, gold and silver. The mead inside gathered the light into a vibrant chorus of existence.

Lyleth put her ear to the mouth of the flask to hear the light sing.

From a pouch around her neck, she withdrew a pearl. Nechtan had found it while he and Lyleth shucked oysters on the Isle of Glass, their punishment for swimming in the sea rather than working at their recitations. So many summers ago.

"Open your mouth," he'd said.

"It's not even cooked."

"We eat them raw all the time in Caer Ys. Best oysters in the Five Quarters. They're a little better with black vinegar. Open."

She hadn't wanted him to think she was just a shepherd's get who was new to the sea, so she let him cradle her chin with his cold hand. He opened her mouth gently. It slid onto her tongue, briny and sweet, but it wasn't all soft. Something like a rock clacked against her teeth and she spit out a pearl the size of a plover egg.

"Will you have a look at that," Nechtan had said.

Lyleth built up the fire—rowan and ash, oak and poplar, hazel and pine. When it snapped high, she added green salts of calanis, orris root, and moonflower. When she held the pearl to the light, it trembled with its own materiality.

Tonight, the green gods would hear her beg.

She dropped the pearl. It tumbled through the thick mead to the bottom of the flask, leaving a wake of jewel-like bubbles as it sank. Then, like a breath from a fish, it rose up again until it floated at the center of the flask.

Starlight doesn't exist until it meets your eye. Only then is it real. Only then are you real.

She took up the harp and played. Sound and light met and mated in the flask, a tune that would rouse one who lay cradled in the arms of earth.

When dawn finally came, she had sung a lifetime into this mead, memories that shaped a man, both searing and sweet.

For Nechtan must remember everything.

The well was a day's ride deep into the Felgarths. Lyleth pushed the plow horse to exhaustion. She must reach the well by nightfall, for this must be done on the threshold of night when the doors between worlds open.

The narrow trail finally widened, topped a ridge, then dropped down into a hidden meadow. The Well of the Salmon swelled from the lap of three rocky meadows that met and joined as one. Sheer granite faces wept water in black sheets.

Lyleth reined up the spent horse and dismounted, her breath fuming in warm clouds.

The plow horse steamed, and set to cropping grass in the shadows. Darkness was coming, the doors would be opening.

The well was roughly circular, edged with immense gritstone slabs fitted long ago by forgotten men. A standing stone of blue granite stood at due west, marking it as a life well. It was covered with sticky traces of mead, honey, wine and blood, offerings to guardians who guide the dead. A hawthorn grew at the water's edge, its trunk and branches twisted by the scarcity of soil. Scraps of fabric were tied to its branches, prayers left for the green gods.

She picked up a cup that was bound to the hawthorn tree by a rusted iron chain, then hailed the hero who had left it

behind: "Peace find you in the Fair Lands, good sir." The cup
was fashioned from the casing of a man's brain, gilded so long
ago that the gilding had worn away in some places to reveal the
yellow bone of the hero's skull beneath.

She broke the still surface of the well with the cup, and
drank deeply.

It was time.

Dead branches and dry moss made a fast fire. When it
snapped happily, she took the flask from the saddle. Circling
the standing stone three times, she poured a small offering,
then placed the flask at the edge of the well on a stone that
jutted out into the dark water. She unburdened herself of her
bow and quiver, her leggings and boots, and everything else.
Naked, she called Wren to her.

He came after some moments, for he was soaring on the
updrafts that struck the mountain face just at dusk. At her
whistle, he plummeted toward her and landed on the standing
stone with a ruffle of his feathers. She had wrapped her arm
with leather so she might offer her fist as a perch. The hawk
gently grasped her forearm and she took firm hold of the leather
jesses that dangled from his legs. Allowing herself to smooth
the feathers on his breast one last time, she cooed to him softly.

Submerged stones made easy steps into the icy well. Her
feet went numb instantly. Wren flapped and fought against the
jesses, but she held them fast. In an instant she was up to her
waist, then treading water.

The well was bottomless and she seemed to float in empty
space. The hawk fought and tore at the leather on her arm.

She kicked her way to the flask that sat on the edge of the
pool and took one swallow. She filled her mouth again and
pursed her lips tightly. In one swift motion, she wrapped her
free arm around the hawk and submerged him.

Trying to fly, Wren's talons ripped at her chest. She brought
the mass of beating wings back to the surface, then caught his
head and covered his beak with her mouth. The knife-sharp

beak sliced her lip, but she would not let go. She emptied the sweet mead into the bird's mouth and held him. The old words spilled from her. She swallowed the blood in her mouth. She mustn't rush; let the words move into the goshawk.

A fury of feather, beak and talon tore at her. The bird grew heavy, feathers shed and floated, and wings became arms.

Try as she might, she could no longer hold him—then in a heartbeat, he held her.

He cried out in some strange language and took her by the throat. She looked in his eyes and saw only panic. She tried to scream but nothing came out. He plunged her under. Water filled her lungs. He would drown her and all would be for naught. She clawed at the hands around her throat until he dragged her back up.

She coughed up water and sucked in air.

He froze. When his grip slackened, she gasped and made for the edge of the pool.

"It's me," she croaked, swimming away from him.

He took hold of her again.

"Nechtan!" she screamed. He pulled her close and held her flailing arms in a tight embrace. Running a trembling finger over her lips, he seemed to struggle for words.

At last, he spoke in the tongue of the Five Quarters, his voice rough as if from sleep.

"You're bleeding…"

Chapter 5

Ava rode for a day to reach the rough track that climbed to the edge of the Wistwood, a forest so dense not even hunters foraged here. She had stopped for the night at a wayfarer's hut, tucked into a shadow-cool vale. In the morning, the greenmen would come to lead her to the nemeton. Without them, she would never find her way, but fall prey to spirits of root and vine, fang and claw. Or so the greenmen, the druada, would have her believe.

The druada had crowned the kings of this land since the time of Black Brac and the people saw these greenmen as the keepers of earth's secrets, exalters of star and stone. To Ava, they were nothing more than court magicians who used simple tricks to command the loyalty of the people and their king.

Lyleth had controlled Nechtan in such a way, but she had spared him none of her womanly wiles either.

While Ava's guards made camp on the banks of a stream, she inspected the small log shelter. A broken chair, a bedshelf and a musty mattress greeted her.

Irjan waited at the door, her eyes like beetle shells in the dim light.

"The greenmen must be blinded by your radiance, my lady," Irjan said. "The gods of this land have spilled their blood into your hands that you may lift them from their turmoil."

"You think gods suffer?" Ava laughed at the thought.

"Without their suffering, we have no destiny."

"I make my own destiny."

Ava took a blanket from the bed and shook out a cloud of dust.

The brown mud of Irjan's face folded into a scowl. Muttering, she knelt before the hearth and struck a spark to some dry moss. The bells on the corners of her embroidered cap chimed as she fed leaves to the spark and blew it to flame. Wrapped in the pelt of a reindeer, Irjan looked every bit like a man. Ava thought she might be both, one of those aberrations she'd heard tales of. For Irjan was born to a far northern tribe, a people who embrace frozen desolation and sunless winters, a people who feast on whale fat in winter, reindeer and salmon berries in summer. Irjan had never said why her people had left her to die on the open tundra as a child, perhaps she didn't know herself; but Ava suspected they had discovered her imperfection.

"I was suckled by the dead," Irjan had told her once, "and now I taste life with their tongue."

Ava's father had been on his first salmon run when he netted a wild girl who clawed and scratched and left scars on his forearms from biting him. Incapable of words, the girl growled and squawked, and required a stick to the skull to slow her down. Ava's father made Irjan his slave and saw to her training in healing from the best physicians in Sandkaldr. Irjan became a wedding gift to Ava from a father who had won his own kingdom by slaying any man who might have an honest claim to it, a father she grew up calling "the Bear."

When Ava proved barren, Irjan tried to coax a child from her womb and failed. She needed no son now, for she was heir to two kingdoms. Unfortunately, her father had failed to do his part. Unlike Nechtan, the Bear still breathed.

Irjan stood from fanning the fire and took Ava's shoulders in a firm hold.

"You are no longer a child of the north," Irjan said. "No man's sword protects you now. You are an iron lamb."

"You think me weak?"

"You are the spawn of the Bear—"

"My father's seed does not make me she-king in this land. I am anointed by their gods. My father can rot in his frozen hell."

Irjan placed cold, leathery palms on Ava's cheeks and looked into her. "You must not look over your shoulder."

"The greenmen won't decide my fate," Ava said. "That I do for myself."

"Guard your heart. They are not fools."

"I have nothing to hide. Now leave me to my rest."

Irjan bowed and left. But Ava found no sleep, tracing silver spears of light that pierced the ragged thatch as the moon crossed the night, convincing herself she had nothing to hide.

In the morning, Ava found three greenmen ahorse as if they'd waited since moonrise, their moss-green hoods pulled close against the morning damp, the plumes of their breath hanging with the mist. They spoke no word, nor did Ava. It was their way.

Her guards mounted up as if they intended to ride with her, but she knew better.

"You'll wait for me here."

Gwylym, her captain, showed his palms and tipped a grizzled chin. "As you command, lady."

She was tempted to trust Gwylym. For it wasn't Nechtan who came to her the night she awoke bloody and screaming, clawing through her bed to find her dead child in a mass of afterbirth. It was Gwylym who calmed her and reminded her that Nechtan was away. She wondered at Gwylym's allegiance to her now, but saw nothing in his eyes but devotion.

A squire held her palfrey.

"She's feeling the cool air, my lady," the boy said. "Keep a close rein."

She tied the leather satchel and eel spear to the saddle, mounted and dug in her heels. The horse leapt to the bit and she started up the trail in no particular direction.

"The morning grows old, good druada," she called back to the greenmen. "If you won't lead, I shall." She pushed her horse into a trot.

Instantly, they came beside her. Without a word, one of them sidled close and took hold of her reins. She smiled at him as he dropped a grain sack over her head. Knotting her fingers in the horse's mane to steady herself, she bobbed blindly in tow toward the sacred grove.

Past her nose, she could see nothing but her horse's black shoulders and a trail of deep scree at its feet. She let the rhythm of the horse ease her into a dull calm. Guard your heart, Irjan had told her. What was it she feared the greenmen would see there? She was a foreigner, yes, and fathered by a reaver who had ravaged the coasts of the Five Kingdoms for thirty years, but Ava had had no part in it. She bore her father's blood, but she trusted the greenmen to see there was none of his black soul in her.

By midday, the path became a bed of pine needles and fallen oak leaves. Branches whipped at her chest and arms and the air felt cooler, but she could smell nothing but forest and oat dust from the sack on her head.

They halted.

She heard the men dismount to soft ground, then the sound of birds and wind in the trees.

The grain sack came off.

A ring of nine ancient trees watched like mourners round a clearing, each trunk as broad as a cottage. They were of all kinds— oak, ash, hazel. A rowan still bore clusters of red berries high in the canopy and autumn leaves sailed down in silent drifts.

At the center of the grove sat nine greenmen on low stones arranged to reflect the ring of trees. Ava wondered if each druí spoke with the voice of one tree. Her own people, Northmen or ice-born, believed that oracles tended the great world tree, Yggdrasil. Perhaps these Ildana were not so unlike Ava's people after all.

She swung her leg over the horse and slid to the soft ground, untied the sack and spear and clutched them close as she approached the circle.

She had imagined these nine judges would be as ancient as the trees, but only two men were past middle age. The others were men and women of different ages, and one was a dark-haired girl whose breasts had not yet budded. This one gazed into Ava with a disquieting stare.

Stepping into their midst, she tipped her chin in respect.

"What justice do you seek of us, Lady Ava?" the girl asked.

"I stand before you as the chosen of the land, for the green gods have named me High King of the Five Quarters."

"We have indeed heard that the queen has slain a guardian," one of the old men said.

"An impossible task," Ava said, "unless the guardian herself bared her breast to my spear. And so it was. I travelled to the dream well called Mogg's Eye seeking solace after Nechtan's death. Peace find him in the Fair Lands."

"Peace find him in the Fair Lands," all replied.

She fumbled with the sign of tribute to the dead.

"When I gazed into the depths of the well, I saw her there, a water worm. Her eyes held on to mine and she spoke without words."

"You came to the well for solace carrying a fishing spear?" The question came from a woman.

"My slave returned to the inn where I stayed and fetched a spear. And the guardian waited."

Ava cast her spear into the center of the circle and it pierced the ground with a thud. Glancing at the faces of the judges, she chose to hand the sack to the dark-haired girl.

"The guardian waited," Ava repeated, "as if she'd waited for me since the first days."

The girl emptied the contents of the sack.

The eel's head had not completely dried. The eyes had shriveled and it smelled of brine and blood. But as it rolled in the deep leaves it took its true form. What came to rest at the center of the circle was no eel but the head of an immortal, a dark-haired girl, not unlike the girl who held the sack.

These greenmen, the keepers of words, failed to speak, but traded glances. How could they question this? The guardians had slept in the wells long before the Old Blood came to this land. They had chosen the Old Blood to rule, and a thousand years later they chose the Ildana. And now, they chose the daughter of an ice-born reaver.

One of the women crumbled to her knees, her hands raised and her eyes on the ground. "Not in our lifetime have we seen such as this."

"Nor your grandsires' lifetime," Ava said. "Not since Black Brac have the gods chosen your king."

Each in turn went to their knees.

Ava met the trance-like stare of the dark-haired girl while, in unison, the nine rose and pressed so close she could smell the leafy fragrance of their skin. They placed their cool hands on her body, her head, her arms, her belly.

A warm rush moved through her, a quickening. Behind closed eyes, a spinning sky opened before her, and clouds built and streamed and tumbled wildly.

Their hands grew warmer while her heart raced.

When she opened her eyes, the girl's face was inches from her own, her hot palms on Ava's cheeks, and she knew the girl had seen everything. And Ava had never felt so free.

The ceremony was swift. Through a shower of meadowsweet, Ava rode into Caer Ys as the she-king of the Five Quarters. Irjan had fixed a padding of velvet inside Nechtan's circlet, otherwise it would have slipped down to Ava's nose. Still, the simple band of Finian silver pinched like a vice. She would have a new one crafted.

Caer Ys sat on an island, its walls grown from the black stone so long ago it was part of the island now. Brilliant green turf crowned rocky scarps and seabirds rode the updrafts on the bay side. The tide was in and waves crawled up the low banks of the causeway to dampen them. They pushed their horses to a trot, racing the water, which would soon cover it.

Ava was greeted by her seneschal, a narrow man with a slight hunch and balding pate. "I have a pressing matter, my lady."

"I have great need of a bath. What matter?" She dropped her cloak into her chambermaid's hands.

"The harp of the drowned maid."

"What of it?"

"It's gone missing, my lady."

Irjan's skills at divination were no less impressive than her command of spirits. By evenfall, the old shaman had named Rhys the thief. And by morning, Nechtan's bloodied chamberlain told Ava what he'd done with the harp. But the threat of the noose couldn't wring any more truth from him. He had sent it to Lyleth at a meadmonger's cottage in the Long Vale. What could Lyleth want with Nechtan's harp?

Lyleth had been seen in the city on the day Ava proclaimed her anointing, but had slipped away like the thief she was.

Who else in Ava's household conspired with Lyleth?

Ava ordered every man, woman and child in her employ to the outer ward. Rhys was brought from his cell, weeping and begging for mercy while his hysterical wife struggled in the arms of a guard. At the end of the rope, Rhys squirmed for far longer than Ava thought he could. Her father had always said it took careful aim or great force to kill a man. It must be so.

Finally, the twitching stopped and Rhys' piss traced a dark stain down the wall.

Chapter 6

Glass fell with rain. The man tried to shield the boy from impact, but his legs were trapped in a tangle of steel and plastic and the deflating airbag. A blanket of darkness dampened the boy's screams until pain bore the man away.

His body was a kite, and the chaff of his flesh streamed away with the wind to leave bones and then marrow and then nothing but a pulse, the core of a bright, blue star.

Plowing on at the end of a slender string, he was buoyed by his desperation to remember the boy's name, but he couldn't even remember his own and both grew dimmer until he was aware of nothing but this blue pulse of light in a sea as vast as night.

Perhaps he slept. He must have.

He swam a sea of stars until a fire roused his icy limbs, replacing numbness with searing pain, and though his eyes were open, he saw only the inside of his own skull. He tasted mead and blood and fought to breathe, but the sea spilled into his lungs.

He fumbled for something to hang on to. Choking reminded him to breathe. But he was going under. Kick to stay afloat.

"Help me!"

The voice belonged to someone else, surely. His skin pricked with countless needles of returning sensation; his mind was leaden, his tongue thick and foreign, but his flesh struggled to contain an energy that burst from his pores and filled his head with the smell of lightning-seared air.

He tried to rise from this water and fly, but his body was tangled in a new gravity. Blind, he reached for anything solid until his hands found another body and he held on.

"I can't see!"

Fingernails clawed him and, oh god, he was strangling someone. He dragged the person to the surface and the blindness began to clear. Weak firelight revealed a woman. He had her by the throat and she battled him in a pool of black water.

Crying out, she struggled free and lunged for a rock that protruded into the water. Where was this place?

He tried to speak, but his mouth refused to form words, so he took hold of her again and held her tight, afraid she would run and leave him.

"Nechtan!" she cried.

His name was an offering. Nechtan.

She beat on him with balled fists. He wanted to say he didn't mean to hurt her, that she was part of his dream, and they'd both wake soon. The sand of each moment slipped through his fingers, and still he was here, not waking in a warm bed, not squinting into day. He had hold of her bare arms and realized she was as naked as he. Her touch seeped into him like hot honey on bread, and with it, a flood of memories. Were they his or hers?

His name was Nechtan.

The image of the woman sharpened. She stopped struggling and met his eyes. Her hair was as dark as the water, braided and falling over her left shoulder. He knew her well. He ran a finger over her cheek to her lips, and for a fleeting second, he thought they were lovers, then his memory corrected him.

His solás. They thought with one mind, spoke with one voice.

"You're bleeding," he said.

Her terror bloomed into a smile and she took his face in both hands. "You remember me?"

He was drowning in her, the memories coming so fast he tried to drink them down. "As much as I try to forget you, Lyl, I can't."

She spilled a nervous laugh, maybe it was exhaustion, but her look was guarded, changed.

Feathers covered the water, clung to his skin, her hair.

"What is this? Why are we naked in a pool, Lyl, and how is it I don't remember why?"

She climbed out of the pool, shivering, her arms laced around her long-limbed, pale form. She pulled on a waiting tunic and it clung to her wet skin.

He couldn't take his eyes off her.

Feeling like he weighed thirty stone, he stepped from the water into the cold night air where a breeze caressed his skin and fanned a flame inside.

"You can still talk in this dream, can't you?" he asked her.

"Warm yourself." She threw a pair of thin woolen trews at him and set to stoking the fire. A spray of embers danced starward. Without meeting his eyes, she said, "We have much to say between us."

"Don't we always?"

Stepping into the trousers, he wondered if he had ever felt any modesty before her, and it worried him that he couldn't remember.

She draped a moth-eaten cloak around him, hitched up her own trews and buckled a belt around her waist. Blood was seeping through the linen of her tunic.

"Are you going to tell me why you're bleeding? Why you and I were bobbing naked in an icy pool?" He sniffed at the cloak. "And where are my clothes?"

"These are your clothes."

The details of this dreamworld grew clearer. Snowy peaks

surrounded them, just visible in what seemed to be the end of twilight. A clootie tree hung over the water, marking this pool as a holy well. But by the looks of it, they'd been ambushed by a flock of pigeons.

He caught Lyl's wrist and examined her wounds. The gashes were deep, as were those below her collarbone.

"Who did this?"

She took back her arm and handed him a shirt.

"What do you remember?" she asked.

"About a fight? Nothing. I was dreaming. I still am… There was a boy—"

"Who am I?" She asked with a seriousness that made him laugh.

"My solás. And at one point, you used to be my friend—what's going on?"

She fumbled in the satchel for some cheesecloth and started to wrap it around her damaged arm.

"That needs stitching." He tried to help, but she pulled away.

"I'll see to it."

"What's the matter, Lyl?"

"I can take care of it," she said. Her eyes were filled with the defiance of a wounded wild thing. She feared him. And that alone made him hope this was indeed a dream.

"Here," he said. "Take this." He pulled off the shirt and handed it back to her. "This rag'll do me no good against the cold anyway."

She tore a strip from it and fumbled to bind it across her chest and under an arm, and this time, he made no move to help.

His feet were going numb and when he reached down to cover them with his cloak, he found two long leather straps digging into his ankles.

"What's this?" He pulled them off and held them out to her with a quizzical smile. "You tried to tie me up?"

"If I could keep you bound with those, you'd not be worth the waking," she said. "Now, what else do you remember?"

He rubbed at his temples. Even his brain was cold. Images flashed, then faded, memories he wanted no part of. They were like the dead, to be remembered only when they must.

"I remember a meal of Nuala's fine lamb stew and…" He measured her, saw disbelief, so he looked at the fire. "Tell me what happened here."

She offered a flask of mead and it warmed his belly and mind.

"Ava." Lyl spoke the name like a command.

He could hear Ava's throaty laugh in his head. "Do you think I forget my wife? The knock surely wasn't that hard." He felt his skull for a sore spot.

"Irjan."

He could smell Irjan, her salves of rendered whale fat, smudges of herbs that clouded his bedchamber. But why was Irjan tending him? When was he ill?

"Enough quizzing."

"There were no attackers," Lyl said flatly. "I called you back, my lord."

"From where? I must've been drunk for a year."

She leaned close, her teeth chattering, and trapped his eyes, just as she would a poor sot. "Drunk with death."

"What?"

"I called you back from the dead, my lord."

He could only laugh, but she didn't.

"You're the drunk, Lyl," he said. "Let's wake up now, eh? I've seen enough of this dream."

"Oh, you're wide awake, my lord." She couldn't hide the satisfaction in her tone. "It's a summoning only a solás can speak. The Words of Waking Stone. They've not been spoken since the days of the Old Blood."

She knelt beside him, cradled his face in her palms, kneaded his cheeks like a sick patient, and pulled at his lower eyelids.

"You were dead, Nechtan."

"Dead." Repeating it didn't help him believe it.

"Dead and in your barrow."

Her hands travelled down his shoulders, his arms, then she took his right hand and turned it palm up. She ran her fingers over his wrist.

"Your mark," she said. She took his other hand and turned both his palms to the fire. "It can't be."

He should have a binding mark on his right wrist, one that matched the one on Lyl's left. A tattoo of a water horse. He brought his wrist closer to the firelight. His skin was pink with cold, but not even a scar showed where the mark had been.

He felt a sudden need to join her in this inspection of his body. He tossed off the cloak and ran his fingers over his scars—a large one ran from under his ribs to his hip where Gwylym had stitched his guts back in, and there was the arrow in his thigh, his forearms were hatched with cuts, and one thick, fresh scar lay where his neck met his shoulder. He had no memory of taking that wound. Completing his inspection, he found his other parts thankfully intact.

"What game are you playing with me, Lyl?"

"How could I remove your mark?" She huddled beside the fire, her arms wrapped around her knees. For a heartbeat he saw a little girl in a hide coracle, sunburned and laughing with the sea all around, and he knew he had driven that girl far away from him. Now she feared him. Perhaps not fear exactly, but distrust, and something far more bitter.

Her pale eyes were stark as a winter sky, and weary in a way he'd never seen in her before. Her breath streamed from lips split open by a blow he must have dealt her in the pool. He must have been dead. How else could he have forgotten the fierceness of this woman, her relentless loyalty that made him feel so self-seeking? How could he forget what he felt for her? He was sure he had known her since time began, and just as sure this was the first time he'd set eyes on her.

He drew a deep breath and tested his lungs.

"So you plucked me like a ripe apple from the Otherworld. Tell me how. And why?"

"Any druí can call a soul back to this world... as a babe in a mother's womb. To call a soul back whole and grown... more difficult."

"I should think—"

"I took you from the Otherworld, Nechtan. That's the truth of it."

Nechtan listened while Lyleth recounted how she had transformed Wren, his favorite hunting bird, into a body that in all outward appearances save one was identical to the flesh he had last inhabited. He stood and paced. "Then I'm a wraith, like the hobgoblins in the caves of IsAeron?"

"No, you're a man, just as you were."

"Are you certain of that? Why am I unmarked?" He thrust out his arm.

"I don't know."

This was far too much to take in. Circling the fire, he watched his shadow, a dark reminder of his reality, and it made him wonder if he cast a shadow in that Otherworld, and if he did, were they one and the same. How could any of this be real? He dragged his hands through his hair and yanked at it, feeling the resistance of his scalp and the skull beneath. He was a jumble of impulses, and his memories were nothing but painted doorways in an endless hall.

"It's been how long since my... death?"

"Five months."

"When you took me away, I was but a babe there in that Otherworld."

"Time is a trick of the flesh," she said, "woven by the wheeling of the stars. A heartbeat in one world can span a lifetime in the other. You might have been an old man, or a babe at the breast."

A horrible disquiet spread through him. It was no dream.

The boy was still screaming in Nechtan's head. A trumpet wailed while ice that wasn't cold flew everywhere and covered them both.

"You've taken to playing god now," he said. "Tell me why."

"Ava murdered you."

He laughed. "Ava? She's little more than a girl."

"Perhaps when you married her."

"How?"

"Irjan is no healer. She's a soulstalker."

He sat down beside her and poked the fire to flame. "Soulstalkers were invented to frighten children into being good."

Lyl dug through her satchel and pulled out a small horn vial and tossed it to him.

"Black hellebore root," she said. "It stopped your heart. You took a blow in the practice yard while sparring." She touched the new scar at the base of his neck. "Here."

He popped the cork and sniffed the acrid stuff. He knew nothing of poisons. In truth, there was a dark curtain drawn around his last days, maybe even weeks. They were jumbled with memories of the Otherworld and a wide, endless seashore.

Lyl had brought sausage, bread and hard cheese and Nechtan ate like he had indeed slept for five months. She told him that Ava killed the guardian of Mogg's Eye with nothing but a fishing spear, and now she called the chieftains to swear fealty to her as she-king.

"Why would you let Irjan treat me?" he said. "It's you who puts me back together every day."

Lyleth looked into the fire. "I wasn't there."

Something in her tone told him he would not want to hear why.

"Do Marchlew and Pyrs come at Ava's call? Marchlew would surely protect Talan's claim." Nechtan's nephew was all that was left of the blood of Black Brac.

"The rumors say they raise an army."

"And you've called me back to make certain they do?"

"I called you back to lead them," she said. "Irjan has put the Bear's game piece into play. Ava commands your men."

"You think the Bear sent Irjan to murder me so that Ava could take the throne for him?" He washed down the bread with mead. "You've granted the old bastard brains he doesn't have, Lyl."

"When did you stop trusting my instincts?" She started packing the remains of their meal in the satchel. "Emlyn and IsAeron join their forces with Ys. Would these men follow Ava if they knew you lived?"

He tried to read her. He wanted to see in her eyes another reason for this desperate act. But Lyleth was never miserly with the truth.

"I died once for this land," he said, "wasn't that enough?"

"Your life belongs to this land no less than mine—"

"What of the land beyond the well? What of that land? What of those people? You murdered me there no less than Irjan murdered me here."

"Aye. I murdered you in the Fair Lands that you might set right what you left undone," she said. "I consider the fate of the Five Quarters more pressing than your happiness, my lord, for this is my duty, a burden you laid upon me."

He kicked at a bundle beside the fire and knew by the sound it was his harp inside, and not just his harp, but something more. It spoke to him in a discordant hum.

"What choice do you leave me?" he said.

Her eyes offered no hint of the affection he thought they shared. She turned away, poked at the fire, and sent a shower of sparks into the night.

"None," she said at last. "And I will suffer your curses till the end of my days, but this fight is no less yours than mine. We leave for Cedewain at dawn."

From behind them, a chatter of loose rock sounded from

the cliff. The horse startled and Lyl was on her feet. Nechtan swept her behind him.

"I see you brought no weapons with these trousers," he said.

He suddenly found a dirk in his hand, and glancing over his shoulder, said, "I love fighting with a meat knife, Lyl."

She had already nocked an arrow and drawn, and it occurred to him that his span of days in this world might be shorter than Lyl had planned.

Chapter 7

With three fingers ready on her bowstring, Lyleth crouched beside Nechtan in the long shadow cast by the offering stone. She scanned the edge of the clearing, just within light's reach, to see the plow horse spook at something. Night had fallen hours ago, and the moon wouldn't rise for some time yet. They would be easy prey for highland rogues here, with steep mountains at their back and only one trail out. Perhaps what they heard in the woods weren't rogues at all, but Ava's men who had followed Lyleth to the well.

"How many?" Nechtan whispered.

She tried to feel a subtle disturbance of the air, but it had been many years since she had used her skills of far sensing. A trodden blade of grass, the ceasing of cricket song, wings in flight, all could be sensed by one who shared the earth's skin.

The horse's panic stirred the still night and drowned the footfalls of those in hiding. But the horse's ears were sharp.

"The horse hears only one," she whispered, "on the north side."

"Stay here." Nechtan moved out of the firelight and stole into the trees.

Beside the well, the fire flared and coughed embers into the night, and by its light, Lyleth saw a shadow dart from one tree to the next, then a rock burst against the offering stone inches from her head.

Nechtan glanced back from his position in the trees, and even in the dim light, she could see him smile. It was doubtful Ava's soldiers would be slinging stones.

Lyleth spied the figure again, moving from tree to tree at the base of the escarpment. She buried an arrow in a tree as another rock caromed off the stone. Showing herself for an instant to draw another shot from the rogue's sling, she allowed Nechtan to close in.

The sound of a scuffle and curses echoed round the glen, and Nechtan stepped into the firelight carrying a boy under one arm like a sack of grain.

"Our assailant." He set the child on his feet, and the lad wiped his nose on his sleeve.

Lyleth relaxed the draw on her bow and felt the warmth of fresh blood seeping through the makeshift bandage. She adjusted her cloak to hide it.

"Alone, are you not, lad?" she said.

"I'm no lad!"

The child stepped nearer the fire. Not a boy; it was a girl-child. The tangled mat of hair might be sun yellow when clean, and her skin was the color of new cream beneath a blanket of freckles. She couldn't be more than twelve summers old. She wore the rags of a shepherd boy and smelled no less fragrant.

"My apologies," Lyleth said, "but lad or lass, you'll come to a bloody end as a robber. I came near shooting you."

"Why'd ya think I was here to rob ye?"

"You were flinging stones at us," Nechtan said.

"Maybe I jes wanted to scare ye." Even through her mighty lisp, Lyleth heard the accent of Arvon, or perhaps it was the isles north of there. Either way, the girl was a long way from home.

"If your rocks had found our heads," Nechtan said, "you'd have done more than scare us."

"You rob pilgrims?" Lyleth said. "Is that how you live in these mountains?"

"I don't rob nobody. Pilgrims leave offerin's. The guardian don't eat much, and truth be, she don't eat nothing a'tall, as I can tell."

"There's not enough food left here to feed a bird, much less girl," Nechtan said. "What are you doing in these mountains alone, lass?"

"Same as you, maybe. Samhain offerings to the green gods. But sure I wasn't workin' old magic, like ye." She nodded at Lyleth. "He was a bird and now he's a man." The girl grinned at Nechtan. "Can ye fly, too?"

What could be done? The girl had seen everything. Rummaging in the satchel, Lyleth found the remainder of a loaf, which she held out to the girl, saying, "What you saw must be kept between us."

The girl's eyes flitted between Lyleth and Nechtan, waiting for the snare to spring. At last she said, "O'course it does," and snatched the bread like a starving dog. Sitting on her heels beside the fire, her eyes darted about like one who's been alone in the wild for some time.

Lyleth cut some sausage and the child took that too, biting first into bread, then sausage until her cheeks filled like a squirrel.

"What else have you seen, lass?" Nechtan asked.

"I come up from the village at Kirkaveen." She took another bite of sausage, and measured them both while she chewed. "There's soldiers there," she said, "asking after the dead king's solás. And there's a druí here looking much like the dead king's solás to me eyes. And she's about raising to life the dead king. Fancy that."

Nechtan turned to Lyleth. "You passed through Kirkaveen?"

"I did," Lyleth said, "I bought that sausage—" A hole opened in her gut. "Rhys… it's the only way she could know." Ava would have sent men to Dunla's meadstead as well.

"We must go." Lyleth struggled to her feet, the wounds on

her arm and chest throbbing. She stuffed the food back in the satchel. "Now."

"You'd be going north, I should think," the girl said.

Lyleth tried to read the girl's intentions, but food was her only focus. "It's best you not know where we go, lass."

"Any fool knows you'll take the dead man to Cedewain where Marchlew raises his army."

"It's half a day's ride back to the glen below," Lyleth said, "then another day east to the main road—"

"We can't take the road." Nechtan was pacing again.

"There's no other way."

"Oh, but there is." The girl grinned.

Her name was Elowen. She'd been living alone in the highlands for a year, or so she said, and she knew a way through the mountains that most others didn't. If they could reach the northern slopes of the Felgarths, they were only three days' ride to Cedewain and Marchlew's forces.

Before she'd left Dunla's, Lyleth had hired a messenger to ride north. Once there, he was to plead with Marchlew to hold any attack until Lyleth arrived. "I told him I had information that would change his plans," she told Nechtan.

"But you didn't know if your old words would work, did you?"

"I didn't know they'd work until you tried to drown me."

Marchlew bore Lyleth little more love than he did Ava, and the hope that he would stay a revolt at her request was unlikely. He might have moved south already in an attempt to plead his case before the judges, for Marchlew's son was also Nechtan's nephew, and by Ildana law, the boy had a rightful claim to Nechtan's throne. If it was true and the forces of the north made ready for battle, it mattered not whether this man Lyleth called back from death was Nechtan or some demon wearing his body. There would be war just the same. But Lyleth would see to it the northern tribes had a king to lead them.

She adjusted the quiver on her back and the bowstring cut into the wounds on her chest.

"You'll come with us," she said to the girl.

"Nay, not I. You'll be needing your big horse on t'other side. You've far to travel, she won't fit where you go."

Elowen pointed to the edge of the firelight where Dunla's mare cropped grass. The plow horse wasn't alone; there was a pony beside her, smaller than the ones that work the tin mines in the summer country, its coat the color of wet slate with a mane and tail of cream.

As if hearing her thoughts Elowen said, "That's Brixia. She comes and goes as she pleases. Perhaps she'll go with ye, she knows the way."

Elowen set to rummaging through Lyleth's satchel.

"What are you after?"

"This." Elowen pulled out the crystal flask, uncorked it, and poured the mead out on the ground. It was done before Lyleth could stop her.

"The mead—"

"You don't need it no more. Your man's here." Elowen nodded at Nechtan as he snatched the sack from her.

"You trust her?" he whispered to Lyleth.

"Do we have a choice?"

"You told me I have no choice in any of this, remember?"

Elowen scampered to the edge of the well and waded in. Lyleth could hear water glugging into the flask.

"I'll take the well," Elowen said, carrying the water like a prize. "We might need it. And I'll take the big horse, too, and meet ye at the fork of the River Rampant."

"You'll bring our horse and our goods?" Nechtan laughed. "You're a child, how can you know the road to the Rampant?"

"I know lots o' things, dead man."

Lyleth felt hot and chilled at once. The bleeding hadn't slowed. "We have no time to argue."

Nechtan caught her arm, whispering, "What if she sends us into an old mine shaft where her thieving brothers wait?"

"Then it's good we've nothing left to take, now, isn't it?" She gave his shoulder a light punch. "C'mon. We've no time."

His grip loosened, and she felt his anger soften to confusion. He gave her a brief flash of a smile. She had forgotten how much she missed his smile, forgotten he once gave it so freely. The hurt they had inflicted on each other was far away from this man's memory. If it wasn't Nechtan's soul inside that flesh, it was a fine forgery. But it would be a girl's mistake to trust in a smile.

Elowen put two fingers to her lips and whistled for the little horse she called Brixia, and the plow horse came too.

"If you're wrong," Nechtan said to Lyleth with a waggish look, "it'd be a terrible waste of my good hunting bird."

He set to work fixing their bags to the saddle.

"I hope you have strength enough to call fire, druí," Elowen said, kneeling beside Lyleth. "The words weakened you. Drink." She uncorked the flask of well water and held it out.

Lyleth caught the girl's hand and held on. Elowen didn't try to pull away, but gripped Lyleth's hand in return.

"Ye think I'm thievin' ye," Elowen said. "Have a look all 'round at me insides, druí."

With the first wave of emotion that coursed from the girl's hand to her own, Lyleth understood. Elowen was the get of a May Eve's revels, just like herself, a greenwood babe, and the girl could see with touch, just as well. And now, they both peered into the empty box of each other's heart.

"You're not certain," Elowen said.

"Of what?"

"That your dead man is king."

Lyleth pulled her hand away.

"You touched him, surely, felt his heart beat," Elowen said. "Why would you doubt this man ye breathed back to life, druí? Perhaps he just doesn't remember what he done."

Lyleth looked at Nechtan, just out of earshot. He was fixing a makeshift bundle to the plow horse's saddle, but he was also watching them.

Elowen's face filled her view. She whispered, "Ye should tell him."

Lyleth put the flask to her mouth. The well water was sweet and moved through her veins like light. She handed it back to Elowen, saying, "Show us the way."

Through the darkness, Elowen led them beside a stream that spilled from the up-swell of the pool. Reflecting the feeble light cast by their makeshift torches, the stream meandered through a meadow thick with moss, where late autumn ferns and gooseberries grew, until it slipped between two massive rocks that leaned together like drunken giants.

"You must crawl through to the other side," Elowen said. "The way opens farther on."

Lyleth heard the stream cascade into the darkness beyond the opening.

"Stay to the left as far as ye can," Elowen said, "then cross over. Brixia knows." She hung the crystal flask of well water on the plow horse's saddle. "Ye won't need this for now."

Nechtan lifted Elowen into the saddle and she looked like a doll astride the big horse.

"What will you do," he asked her, "if you meet the she-king's men on the road with that harp of mine?"

"I'm just a robber, as ye said."

"And a fine one, at that." He gave the horse a gentle slap to the rump and Elowen was gone, with nothing but the rising moon to guide her.

Nechtan waded into the stream, then disappeared between the rocks. Lyleth heard him splashing in a cavern below.

"It's not deep," he called. "Come."

She handed down the bag of food, her bow and quiver, and

slid through. He caught her ankles, then her waist and eased her into the frigid water.

Elowen's pony, Brixia, was indeed coming with them. The size of a wolfhound, she got on her knees and kicked through the opening until she splashed through the shallows. The pony gave a wet shake, and hooves and feet churned up mud that smelled of roots and worms and silt deposited for millennia.

The cleft in the rock let in the moonlight, but Lyleth couldn't see farther than a spear's length. Beyond that, she heard the sound of falling water. The pony walked past them as if she'd come through here a hundred times, then vanished up a dark embankment.

"It's unfortunate you brought no ball of string," Nechtan said.

"Ponies in the tin mines know the paths in the dark."

"You looked into the girl," he said. "Does she send us to our death?"

"She told us true, this cave leads out."

"If she told us true," he said, "then Ava's men are right behind us."

"They're your men," she said, fumbling in her pouch for a rushlight.

She struck the rush on a wet stone. It sputtered alight to reveal a cavern that sparkled with a moist golden sheen. Water dripped from fingers of stone that reached from the ceiling. The air was sodden and ancient, like the last sigh of a forgotten past.

"Brixia's gone ahead. Come." Nechtan took the rushlight and led the way after the pony.

Lyleth couldn't take her eyes from the man who walked before her. The rhythm of his gait was perfect, the breadth of his shoulders exact, even the unconscious dance of his right eyebrow when he argued was just as she remembered. Yet he lacked the mark that bound him to Lyleth as king to solás, as body is bound to soul. Why would the green gods give him back to her without his mark?

"Tell me what you remember," she said as they walked, "of our time on the Isle of Glass."

"So I can remember who am I, is that what you mean?" A glance over his shoulder said his fury at her had ebbed. Some. Maybe it was the quieting of the stream that calmed him as they moved deeper into the cavern.

"Do you remember the time we were caught in the storm?" he said.

For a moment she wondered which storm he referred to, there were many. "We'd caught at least five perch when the wind came up," she said.

"The sky opened to swallow us." His voice had a tender, sentimental tone. "We couldn't row against it, neither you nor I, and I think you were the stronger between us then. We let go." He looked over his shoulder again, as if reassuring himself she was still there. "The wind took us and we landed on some strange headland leagues from Dechtire's hive."

"So many years ago," she said.

"We turned the coracle over on the sand and slept under it."

"It rained so hard, it was like sleeping inside a drum," she said.

"I can sleep through anything."

"I remember." She found herself smiling, and when the darkness disoriented her, she reached for the cavern wall to steady herself.

Nechtan turned. The rushlight cast a warm veil over his features as he placed a cool palm on her forehead.

"You're fevered. Come," he said, taking her hand, "the little horse leads on."

But a rush of warm air touched the fine down on Lyleth's face. She laid her palm again on the wall of the cave and felt the scrape of steel on stone, felt the tremor that had traveled for miles through the earth's skin to her fingertips.

"We must hurry."

Chapter 8

Connor opened his eyes to find his arm in a nurse's firm grip. He tried to pull away, but she held on and never took her eyes from her watch.

"Eighty-three. Nice to see you, son." Her voice was a tired monotone as she planted a hand on his forehead and flicked a penlight in his eyes. "You've been out longer than I thought you would."

He was in a hospital, by the smell. The skin on the right side of his face was stretched tight and his eye was almost swollen shut. He reached up to feel the stiff tails of stitches over his cheek. There was blood under his fingernails.

"Just relax now," the nurse said, and fiddled with the tubes coming from an I.V. bag to his arm.

His head cleared enough to hear his mom and dad arguing in the hall, Mom blaming Dad for giving Connor the car, Dad blaming Dish for letting Connor drive in the rain.

He bolted upright, and the room tumbled.

"Where's Dish?" he asked the nurse, "Mr. Cavendish? The man who was with me?"

"He's getting the best care possible." She eased him back to his pillow and gave his arm a warm pat. His other arm was in a sling and he felt a sharp pain shoot from his collarbone to his fingertips.

"I need to see him."

"He can't have visitors just yet, and you need rest," she said. "I'll get your momma."

Before he could protest, his mom was storming through the door. She sniffed back tears and gave him a quick air kiss, sat down on the bed and stroked Connor's hair.

"Thank God." The crying started, followed by a string of sentences that made no sense, something about tires and rain and irresponsibility, interspersed with stink-eye looks at Dad.

Dad thumbed his smart phone.

"I should have kept you home this year." Mom sniffed. "You could have gone to San Marino High." There was something about insurance, calls from lawyers, and Connor stopped listening.

Dad slipped his phone into his pants pocket, crossed his arms and opened his mouth once as if to add something, but changed his mind.

"We'll be back in the morning," Mom said. "Get some rest."

"What about Dish?" Connor managed to ask.

His parents shared a look.

"We'll know more tomorrow," Dad said. "Your job is to get well." He held out a fist for a knuckle-bump and Connor hesitantly offered his sore fist.

Then they were gone, and it felt like someone had pulled the plug on his soul.

He slept.

When he opened his eyes, Brother Mike was coming through the door, hiking up the skirt of his Friar Tuck outfit to position his bulk on a chair. Brother Mike was in charge of the dorm, which he liked to think of as the Von Trapp house, but he wasn't humming any show tunes today. Connor could see the worry bubbling underneath all those freckles.

"Such a relief to see you awake," he said.

"What about Dish?"

Brother Mike took a deep breath. "Mr. Cavendish was badly injured, Connor."

"The nurse says he's getting the 'best care possible.' That usually means it's bad."

"Dish is in intensive care." Brother Mike paused, letting the full weight of it sink in. "The doctors here are top notch. You need to focus on getting back on your feet, so you can go home and heal up."

"Go home?"

He felt his foot on the gas, felt the tires leave the road.

"But, Dish..." Connor said.

"Mr. Cavendish won't be leaving the hospital for some time." Brother Mike's look said what his mouth didn't.

"He's going to live, though, right?"

"They're doing tests now. I can keep you informed while you're at home—"

"I want to go back to school." The words were loose before he could take them back. What was that Dish had said? Running away won't fill the emptiness... Connor couldn't be emptier than he was at this moment.

"I thought you wanted out. Planned your whole escape—"

"I did." How could he possibly explain? "But—"

"It can happen to anyone, Connor. It wasn't your fault."

Connor knew better.

Mike pursed his lips and poked his glasses back up his nose. "I'll talk to your parents about it. And Father Owens."

"When can I see Dish?"

"Just as soon as the doctors give the okay."

On his way out, Brother Mike left a stack of cards from Connor's classmates who were probably forced to make them in art class. Iris McCreary had drawn a bunch of smiley suns all over hers. When he turned it over, he found a microscopic F.U. written in the center of one of the suns. What a bitch.

He flung the stack of cards upward. They sailed back to his bed and the vinyl floor like oversized confetti. For the rest of the afternoon, he timed the I.V. drip. One drop every 3.5 seconds. Running away won't fill the emptiness...

When the hospital was quiet, which was in the middle of the night, he got up and dragged his I.V. pole to the elevator and rode it to the third floor where the directory said I.C.U. was located. The halls were deserted. Cold air rushed under his hospital gown. Beside double doors that warned "Intensive Care Unit—authorized staff only," he punched an intercom and talked to someone on the other side.

"I'm here to see Mr. Cavendish."

"I'm sorry, he can't have visitors."

"But it's really important. I have to talk to him."

There was a long pause, then the voice said, "Mr. Cavendish is in a coma. I'm sorry."

"A coma?" That couldn't be right. "But you don't understand. I need to see him."

"I'm sorry."

He pressed the button again. "You have to let me see him."

Static hissed in reply.

He collapsed into a chair in the waiting room and stared at the glow of a muted TV. It was dawn when the nurses from his own floor finally found him.

Brother Mike told Connor he could skip class those first days, but sitting in his room playing Plants vs. Zombies didn't help the waiting, so he went back to class. During break and lunch, he called the nurse's desk at I.C.U. One of them was really nice. Holly was her name. She must have thought Connor's calls were pathetic because she finally took his number and promised to call as soon as the doctor gave the okay for visitors.

The first day back to school was like standing in front of a firing squad. People actually stared at him when they passed in the hall. He couldn't blame them. One eye was almost swollen shut and the bruises under the stitches were starting to turn green. He looked like one of the undead.

The looks they gave him weren't pity, but blame. A teacher everyone admired was lying in a coma because of Connor.

He fell asleep in chemistry and made spit wads to shoot at the sub who'd taken over Dish's class.

From across the aisle, Iris McCreary cast a predatory stare. Her uniform blouse looked like she'd slept in it and all the empty holes from her collection of facial piercings made her look naked. With or without hardware, she looked like a cocker spaniel. When Mr. Cavendish had first started teaching at St. Thom's, it was Iris who started calling him "Dish." She pointed out that "dish" meant a person was hot, back in the day. How she knew this, Connor couldn't guess; she probably lap-danced a baby boomer or something.

Iris had strange taste in guys; she hooked up with the stoners and anarchists and even dated a guy who was into the cult of Cthulhu. The fact that she was leering at Connor from across the aisle confirmed that he'd sunk to a new low.

She licked her lips. While the sub wrote on the board, Iris folded up a scrap of paper and sailed it over to Connor.

The miniature printing read, you look hot with those stitches. When can we see Dish?

Connor just flipped her off.

She blew him a silent kiss. Her red lip gloss was perfect.

That afternoon, he called the I.C.U. one more time. Holly sounded a little ticked off and he realized he was making a pest of himself. But he couldn't stand it anymore; he had to do something. He pulled on his shorts and running shoes and slipped his cell phone in his pocket just in case Holly called.

Dish would go for a run if he could, so Connor would run for both of them.

He had about an hour until dinner. Steep cliffs dropped off the school drive to patches of prickly pear and sagebrush, and far below, he could see Malibu Creek snaking black toward the ocean. On the other side of the creek, the walled and guarded fortress of Don Ziegler, the writer/producer/director of Avalanche and Falls the Night sat like some medieval castle. His guards made regular visits to the school on the occasion of potato cannon test runs. In general, the boys aimed for his swimming pool/lagoon/ waterfall.

The air was cool and fog rolled up the canyon from the beach far below, beading on Connor's face and hair. From Ziegler's castle a trail crossed the canyon and hooked up to a fire road that wound up the far ridge. It was a tough run, just perfect.

The sling yanked at his neck, so he took it off and tossed it in the bushes. His collarbone ached, his arm felt like it weighed a ton, and the skin on his legs turned blotchy with cold.

A crescent moon brightened as the sun dove into the Pacific. Threshold of night, Dish had called it. In between day and night, dusk was both and neither. Connor had replayed that day on the beach a million times. Dish had looked at the pool, then out at the setting sun. Connor recalled the look on his face. It wasn't wonder exactly, but a fear-laced adrenaline rush. Dish didn't know exactly what that tattoo was all about, but it had something to do with the pool, the beach and dusk.

The trail looped back and forth up the ridge.

Connor's lungs burned, but he forced his rubber legs into a mechanical rhythm until he accepted that they were long gone a quarter mile back. He let himself walk, hands on hips, each breath a searing reminder of his broken ribs and collarbone.

Stray cactus grew onto the trail, past a fallen chain-link fence that had once contained the garden of a deserted mansion. Built in the thirties for some film starlet, the Spanish hacienda had started sliding down the hill on a gentle slalom to Pacific Coast Highway. Whoever owned it when the ground gave way just boarded it up and left it to rot.

He planted one hand on his knee, bent over and huffed. He was studying his sweat as it dripped from his chin and splashed into the powdery dirt when he heard a loud hum overhead. He looked up, and there, hanging from a huge white yucca bloom, was the biggest swarm of bees he'd ever seen. They bent the bloom over and hung from it like a dark, boiling sack.

They moved together like one thing, forming a shape, then unforming, like clouds building. Connor backed away slowly, watching the bees' hypnotic motion. First they formed a spiral, then an ogre's face. Then... he stepped on a rock and stumbled.

And the bees were on him.

"Shit!"

He plowed through cactus, swatting at bees. They were caught in his hair, down his shirt. He peeled it off.

Finding the break in the chain-link fence, he hopped it and ran through the remains of landscaping to reach a patio of tumbleweeds and broken plastic garden furniture. In the fading light, he saw the swimming pool was empty, but the dark water of the fishpond he remembered lay just past it.

A burst of stings pierced his scalp, then his back and neck, and his calves burned with cactus stickers.

He ran straight off the edge of the deck and went under. He flailed, shaking off the remaining bees. Remembering his phone, he pulled it from his pocket and tossed it on the deck.

His broken collarbone resisted his attempts to stay afloat so he kicked harder. At least a dozen bees treaded water beside him.

"Shit!"

He pushed the bees away to the edge, and went under again, letting the water wash the bees from his hair.

But when he surfaced again, the water was crystal clear, not murky with carp crap and algae. It soothed his stings and felt cold, tingly, like a bathtub filled with Perrier. Weeds dangled from the edge of the cracked deck and bubbles streamed from somewhere at the bottom, drifting up with a distant light.

If this is a fishpond, it's freaking deep. And where's that

light coming from? His feet found no bottom, just a swirling current. Just like the pool on the beach.

Taking a breath, he dives under and swims straight down, but still finds no bottom. He stops swimming, thinking he'll float back up to the surface, but a whirlpool takes hold of him and pulls him deeper. He forces his eyes open to see streamers of bubbles trail from his skin. The tingling thrill possesses him with a weightless euphoria. All desire is bleeding from him, even the need to breathe.

He sinks straight down, leaving the last glow of twilight behind.

I must be dead already. The conviction fills him with the deepest relief.

Spears of moonlight pierce the water, but the light isn't silver, as moonlight would be, but gold. He has no sense of direction and swims toward the yellow light.

But maybe it isn't really light at all, for the water is alive with a million silver minnows. They circle left, and he surrenders to them, countless flashing points of fish, their scales reflecting, magnifying this new light. They are the vortex taking him down. Or maybe it's up.

They move like the bees, like they have one mind. No, not a mind; they share something else entirely.

He holds out his arms and the fish flow around him like water around a snag. He feels eddies, the cold snap of a tiny fin and there is nothing left to existence but this, for he is one of them, and all of them.

The fish pack tight as armor, lifting him toward the new light.

He breaks the surface.

His breath spews forth in colors he's never seen before.

It's the cave on the beach. Or is it? Did he swim through some underground channel from the hills? That's impossible.

He squints against a blaze clutched in a woman's fist that lights up the bowl of the cave. She thrusts it out before her, dropping embers in the pool, but the flame is something more. He can hear the fire speak.

The woman is soaking wet and blood seeps through her ragged shirt. A long dark braid snakes over one shoulder and her eyes are as wide and blue as the sky and teeming with as many secrets.

The sound of feet sinking in wet gravel draws Connor's attention to a man. He wears a heavy cloak like the woman's. His hair is long and darker than Dish's, but his eyes are green and so familiar. This man has no lithe runner's body, but one of a warrior, dense and calloused with a face that has watched others die at his hands, graceful and yet confused, regal yet dressed in rags. But as Connor looks into his eyes, all doubt vanishes.

"Dish? Dish, it's me!"

Waist-deep in the water, the man sweeps his arms in the air before him. He can't see Connor.

Connor's heart pumps faster. "I'm right here!"

He laughs and it sounds like birdsong. He reaches out, but his hand passes through Dish, through bone and tendon and deafening rush of blood. Dish's eyes lock on his, and for a moment, Connor is certain Dish sees him.

"Hey!" he calls. "Can't you hear me?"

The woman wades in, her hand on Dish's shoulder like she's known him forever. They talk in the same language as the flame. Dish points and the woman's gaze follows. She holds the fire out over the water, and it's then Connor sees the tattoo on her wrist. A horse with a fish's tail.

"Dish! It's me! Connor!"

The woman is very close, her pretty face just inches from Connor's, her eyes blindly looking through him. But words move from her mind to his. Give him time, her mind says, I beg you.

Voices echo from somewhere behind Connor, but none of them are his own.

The woman drops her light in the pool and the cave goes black. A familiar terror overtakes him, a blind weightless panic that assures him there are things below the water waiting to devour him.

"Dish!"

Only Connor's echo chimes in answer.

"Dish! Please!"

A vice-like grip hooks under his arms and Connor's body cuts through the water as if he plows through syrup. It takes him down. And the vision of the man who must be Dish and the beautiful woman recedes like heaven in a rearview mirror.

Chapter 9

Nechtan and Lyleth followed the pony over smooth boulders, skirting the fall of the underground stream. They could go no faster, and neither could the men who pursued them. Lyl said there were at least three of them, a mile or maybe more behind them. Nechtan had never known her to be wrong in such things, but he wasn't as willing to trust the greenwood babe, Elowen. If they found themselves trapped in this cavern, Nechtan's men would meet their dead king face to face. He almost hoped for such an outcome.

The water tumbled down into utter darkness, but Brixia didn't hesitate. The pony was forced to sit on her haunches in places and slide down the steep path. Nechtan followed, one step after the other, Lyleth behind him. If she slipped he would catch her, and maybe Brixia would catch them both at the bottom.

Clenching the rushlight in his teeth sent embers up to scorch his hair, but he needed both hands. The torrent beside them killed all sound and its cool breath threatened to blow out the light altogether. He reached up for Lyl and helped her along. Her trembling had grown more violent. She was fevered and had lost much blood, and Nechtan half-carried her to move quickly.

They reached a level passage at last and followed the stream for what seemed like miles, though in this darkness it was hard to determine. Here, the water quieted to a murmur, which allowed them to talk. Lyl made him recite the Battle of Cynvarra, all five hundred lines. He doubted he could have recited the whole thing even before he died, but she helped. He passed the test in bawdy songs and had Lyl laughing with I Have a Pretty Thing to Give My Lady.

He sang drinking songs, love songs, epics, and he remembered. He remembered the first woman he bedded, the first man he killed, his first hunt, his first battle, his first swim in the sea. His life came flooding back. But an enormous void loomed over the last span of days. It was silent, empty, and as cold as Lyleth.

"What do you plan to tell Marchlew when we reach Cedewain?" he asked. "That you found me curled in a log like a woodsprite?"

"Probably not the truth. You have no mark."

"You expect him to hand over command of his armies to a dead man because I was so well-loved? Or because I have magical powers you've failed to tell me about? I do have magical powers, don't I, Lyl?"

"I was certain you had magical powers when last you lived."

He had to look at her to measure her meaning. There it was. The teasing smile he knew long ago.

He returned her smile. "In truth, Lyl, you'd best have an argument for Marchlew. He might be half a fool, but he's a grasping fool."

"The truth, my lord, is that Marchlew is vastly outnumbered. Fiach's men alone could take Marchlew down."

"Do I bring an army of the dead with me? How is it I'm to improve Marchlew's chances? Tell me that."

"You must win back the men of Ys, Emlyn and IsAeron."

He stopped and faced her, her words echoing through the vaults of the cavern. "You're mad. They'll think me a ghost, nothing more."

"The men of the Five Quarters will gut each other,

Nechtan." She snatched the rushlight from him, pushed past him, and kept walking after the little horse. "If I tell Marchlew the truth," she said, "and he sees your wrist... we're done before we begin. The Bear will come."

"How is it you're so certain of that?"

"It was you who asked me to serve as your solás. I recall you trusted my instincts at one time."

His voice carried into the dark miles of cavern before them. "I recall your instincts led me to marry Ava. Your instincts led me to trust in this peace you built."

"We built." The rushlight had burned to Lyleth's fingers. She cursed and dropped it, then fumbled in her satchel for another.

"You'd best have something more substantial than instinct when you talk to Marchlew," he said.

She lit the next rushlight. He took it and followed the little horse.

"I think you're wrong about Ava," he said. "She's still young. She can produce a son with some bullish chieftain, and stand up to her father."

"Then you're a bigger fool now than when last you breathed," she said. "Why do you think she never bore you a child?"

"The gods want no ice-born princelings? Ava bore me no love? Take your pick."

She stopped walking and faced him. "Irjan was sent to kill your babes in the womb. To kill you. Ava's father will come. And the tribes of the north cannot hope to hold out against both the Bear and Ava."

"Ava despises the old bastard. She'd never give over something she's won to the Bear of Sandkaldr. That I remember." He kept walking. "I'm worthless to you, Lyl. I'm nothing but a dead king without a mark. Maybe less than that, maybe a conjuring of your own failings."

She seized his arm. It wasn't just anger he saw in her eyes, but an outright reproach. "Tell me, my lord," she said. "What do you remember of my failings? Are they as grievous as your own?"

He had banished her, but he couldn't remember why. How long had it been? Feelings stirred that he thought were sealed tight. She was not always such a creature of duty, not always the stern voice of truth who led the Ildana as Nechtan had never wanted to. No, he remembered the girl he had known on the Isle of Glass, the summers they spent together as they grew into their bodies and their burdens, a girl more reckless and rebellious than he, a girl who showed him the secrets hidden in the flight of a damselfly, a girl who led him to swim naked in the sea.

It was he who had changed her. How he wished it was the other way round.

A sphere of light pulsed from the waxed rush between them.

"Perhaps it's best," she said. "Memories mean nothing now."

The last thing he remembered of this world was that he opened his eyes from a fevered sleep and looked up into Ava's eyes, red and raining tears. In that instant, when he knew those eyes were not Lyleth's, he had let go. Of everything.

"I well remember Nuala's lamb stew," he said, and kept walking.

Nechtan followed the rhythmic chatter of the pony's hooves on stone. His thoughts turned to the start of all this, Lyleth's proposal of an alliance with the man who had, for the last thirty summers, beached his longships on the northern shores of the Five Quarters, taking what he wanted and burning the rest.

Lyleth had sent greenmen to negotiate Nechtan's safe passage to Rotomagos, for she had met the Bear on a tiny island far north of the Bloody Spear and negotiated an alliance with this man, Saerlabrand, the Bear of Sandkaldr. The man who had taken the head of Nechtan's father and hoisted it on the point of his sword like a banner while Nechtan watched from the bottom of a pile of dead men.

Three summers of death followed until Lyleth convinced Nechtan to make this peace.

She stood beside him on the deck of the warship, sailing through ice floes loud with seals into the long firth of Rotomagos. They pulled their dories ashore to be met by an army of thegns... and Irjan.

"It was Irjan who met us on the strand that day," he said. The cavern repeated his words.

"Aye, so she did," Lyl said. "She's been there from the start."

"Perhaps she was the only ice-born at the Bear's court who spoke Ildana."

"Your wife learned more quickly than she should for one who had no lessons. Irjan was whispering to her even then."

The memory was clear. Even at table, Saerlabrand wore a bear's head fitted to his helm, the beast's teeth strung from its shriveled lips like a solstice garland.

"Because you bade me," Nechtan said, "I sat at table with the man who murdered my father and my brother, and the fathers and brothers of a thousand other Ildana. And I asked this reaver, as you schooled me to, I asked him for his daughter as my wife."

"And so you know my sin, my lord." She said it with a flourish of her hands.

Nechtan remembered the consuming urge he had felt to slit the Bear from groin to sternum. But Lyleth's steady purpose had stayed his hand, that and the sight of the girl who served him.

"She serves you," Lyl had whispered.

He looked up into Ava's face just as she purposefully spilled ale down his chest, only to take her time at wiping him clean. A maid, not much past her flowering. How could any man fail to find happiness in one as fair as Ava?

That night, he and Lyl had talked until dawn. He remembered searching her eyes for something other than duty. He wanted to know the secrets of her heart as she knew his.

"What do the clouds tell you, Lyl?" he had asked her that night. "Am I to know any joy in this life my father left me?"

She set her fingers to his lips, saying, "Your mistress is old as time and young as spring, and she favors you with sovereignty. You have no other love but the land."

"I didn't choose it."

"Ah, but she chose you."

Nechtan followed the dim bounce of the pony. The path narrowed and became a slippery defile at the edge of the underground stream. At last, the water pooled and eddied as it waited to pass through a narrow channel into the earth.

He held the rushlight out to survey the chamber, a domed cavern hollowed by eons of rolling water. The stream must run through veins of the mountain and exit in the valley of Elfael to become the headwaters of the River Rampant. The left-hand trail they'd been following for what seemed like days ended at a weeping wall of sandstone.

Brixia didn't pause. She waded into the water, her pony legs kicking like a dog, the current pushing her toward some unseen narrows, her creamy mane and tail spread like a cloak on the water.

"Get on my back," Nechtan told Lyl.

She did as instructed, her legs locking around his waist and one arm over his chest.

"'Tis a good thing we learned how to fight a rough tide in the sea," she said.

"I used to have to carry you then, too," he said.

"You remember?"

"I remember."

He shifted Lyl's weight and stepped into the pool. The bottom fell away and he sprang forward, trying to extend his reach across the water. The current dragged at his legs and threatened to pull him under. The pony had almost reached the far shore, but her tail streamed behind her. He grabbed hold of it, and the little horse gave him the heave he needed to pass the churning torrent below.

Lyl hung on with one arm across his chest, her fingers digging into his ribs. For a moment, they were submerged. Nechtan clung to the pony's tail and Lyl kicked behind him for some thrust. He finally felt gravel beneath his feet and fell forward. Taking hold of Lyl's wrist, he dragged her from the water. The rushlight was out and his eyes fought the utter blackness. For the space of three deep breaths, Lyl gave in to his arms. He held her fevered body and she shivered violently.

His eyes fought for any stray glimmer of light as Lyl dug through her pouch for a rushlight.

"I might be able to light this. I need something to strike it on," she said.

He helped her to her feet, his arm around her waist. His feet sunk deep into gravel as he reached out for a wall that must be close. Finally, his knuckles scraped stone. "Here."

He took her hand and laid it on the cool stone and the light sputtered awake. Water beaded like worry on Lyl's face and lashes. The light wavered in her trembling hand and the fabric of her linen shirt was soaked with fresh blood.

"Lyl, we need to see to those wounds."

"I've no herbs, no dressings."

"We've got to be close to the way out. Come. Rest for a bit." He found a ledge of gravel along one wall and sat down. He took her hand and tried to convince her to sit.

"We have but one more rushlight," she said. "We must find the way out."

A bowl of smooth, flesh-colored walls bloomed with light. "Have a look here," she said.

The rushlight exposed a subtle symbol. Three interlocking spirals trickled down the wall, carved into the stone and painted red. They flowed one into the other, like water making its way to the sea. Around it, black handprints of long-dead men were scattered like dark stars.

The image was as clear as a vivid dream.

"I've been here before," he said. "I remember, things I shouldn't remember…" He laid his palms on Lyl's cheeks and looked into her eyes. "You." He turned back to the pool. "And a boy. There, in the water." He knelt beside it, trying to see into its depths, but saw only the rushlight dancing on its surface.

He waded into the swirling blackness. "I feel him here."

Lyl's hand was on his shoulder as her rushlight sent infinite ripples of light into the blackness. It spewed embers that dropped falling stars on the water.

Nechtan reached out like a blind man, believing he could touch the boy, willing his eyes to see him.

He pointed to a gentle eddy that disturbed the smooth surface, and in that moment, he saw him. The rushlight danced over the image of a boy, a distorted reflection in the watery mirror.

"I see him," Nechtan said. A boy with copper eyes and a desperate defiance reached out and tried to take Nechtan's hand. Nechtan reached to meet him, but his fingers dragged the water and broke the reflection.

Lyl's hand squeezed his shoulder.

"I put out the light," Nechtan said. "I left him in the dark." But the truth was even clearer. "I left him."

As if in answer, Nechtan looked across the pool and saw vague motes of torchlight coming from the depths of the cavern, and with them, the echo of voices.

Lyl dropped the rush in the pool, and darkness took them.

Chapter 10

It was well before dawn when the judges of the greenwood arrived in Caer Ys. From the battlements, Ava watched them stream across the causeway, unmindful of the storm that sent waves over the land bridge. Even their torches burned with a wind-troubled green glow that brought fireflies to mind, gnats of the night, stealing into her city. The last ceremony to consummate her marriage to this land would be done in secret, at dawn, "beneath no roof and upon no floor."

Irjan helped Ava into a plain linen shift, fixing a simple brooch at her shoulder. The greenmen had been clear: she was to wear no adornment, to dress as a pilgrim in search of the blessings of sovereignty. She should be reflective, preparing a tranquil exterior to present to the gods of this land. But while Irjan adjusted a belt around her waist, Ava could think of little else but Gwylym's search for Lyleth. Yesterday, she had sent her captain of the guard with enough men to comb every village and holding from Caer Ys to the moorland of IsAeron.

Irjan's thick fingers worked at the knots in Ava's hair.

"What can Lyleth want with Nechtan's harp?" Ava caught the distorted reflection of the old shaman in her silver mirror.

"A sentimental token perhaps," Irjan said, "for the woman that sleeps inside Lyleth."

"She needs no keepsake of Nechtan's devotion. She already owns his soul." No, there was some other reason Lyleth had contrived for Rhys to steal the harp. "You really think there's a soft woman inside that cold armor of Lyleth's?"

"Lyleth has grown scales because she must," Irjan said. "So must you."

"What did Nechtan see that he found so desirable in that druï?" Ava gave up the mirror and turned to give Irjan a challenging look, as if it was the first time she'd asked such a question of the old witch.

A faint shrug was all Irjan offered, as usual.

"You know," Ava said, "Nechtan once told me that he would have given himself over to blind rage, bled out on some battlefield if not for Lyleth. He said that Lyleth knew him. What did he mean, Irjan?"

"The throne was his burden, not his prize. He didn't choose it as you have, my Iron Lamb. When we see ourself as a slave, death is our only savior, be we king or thrall."

Ava digested this for a moment. "Is it so for you? Death is your salvation?"

"Some slaves come to respect their shackles, to use them to remake themselves."

How had Irjan's chains remade her?

Irjan poured rose water into her palms, then ran her fingers through Ava's hair, saying, "Lyleth convinced Nechtan to wear the armor of his duty as she wears hers."

"And today I will don that armor." Ava's distorted image looked back from the silver mirror.

"So it is, my Iron Lamb."

Ava had spent every waking moment of the last five years trying to know her husband. His armor was made of mail and leather and the blood of the battleground, and when he peeled it off, he was nothing but a man. It was just that failing Ava had loved in Nechtan. She had loved him with the naïve passion of a young girl spared the wasteland that was her home by this well-made and affectionate man. She knew now it wasn't love at all, but a maid's infatuation. Ava didn't know the difference then.

"How shall I grow this scaly armor?" she asked.

Irjan tied a plain ribbon in Ava's braid, and coiled it into a knot.

"You must surrender to the ways of these people as you've surrendered to their gods," Irjan told her. "Learn to command them."

"Command by surrendering? Your riddles are no less vexing than the greenmen's."

"They will bind you to your solás. You must surrender every action, every thought to this man. Through him, you will learn to rule."

"Then Nechtan learned from Lyleth to be such a fool." Ava smiled.

Nechtan had surrendered not only his thoughts but his soul to Lyleth. Ava would make no such mistake.

The binding of the solás to the king was a strange custom indeed. The word solás literally meant 'light' in the tongue of the Old Blood, that ancient race who ruled these lands long before the Ildana drove them through the third well. Ava knew the ritual she was about to experience was as old as the Old Blood, that she would wed the land in the form of her solás, for the fertility of the kingdom depended on the king's mating with the forces that bestowed fecundity. Those forces were embodied in a druí who had proven herself, or himself, in the arts of the old race. Any half-wit could see it was simply a means by which the greenmen controlled the throne. It was a clever scheme, and Ava admired their ingenuity, if little else.

In the days of the Old Blood, the king actually bedded his solás in a ceremonial mating. The Ildana had removed that aspect of the ritual after a jealous queen murdered her husband's solás. After that, the judges forbade the physical coupling of king and solás, claiming to do so would curse the land.

It made Ava smile to think that when Lyleth received

Nechtan's spiritual seed, she'd given birth to nothing but death and war.

Beneath no roof and upon no floor. Let the future be conceived.

Below the city of Caer Ys, a rocky cove had been carved out of the steep cliffs by the sea. This place, where water kissed land, met the requirements of the greenmen, and before the sky opened its eyes to dawn, a small retinue of druada led Ava from the fortress walls to the cliffs of the ragged shore. They lit the way with bundles of rushlights and Ava followed, feeling her way down the jagged rocks until she stood ankle-deep in black sand.

Traditionally, kings were men and so their solada were women. In keeping with this, the greenmen would choose a man as Ava's solás.

The chosen one pushed back his hood.

Ava could just make out his features in the swelling light, austere and cold-eyed with a narrow face and hair as fair as hers. Perhaps the judges expected her to see this man as a brother, revealing their incompetence entirely, for Ava's brother had been as much a beast as her father. This man was not much older than Ava, but had the look of one who deprived himself of the pleasures of this world, and Ava feared he would expect the same of her.

He showed his palms in respect, and Ava returned the gesture. He would be the only man before whom she would bow, for the king and his solás were equals.

"I am Jeven," he told her.

"So you are. What is required of us, Jeven?"

"You know as much as I."

His smile was mouse-like. It made her thankful there would be no coupling of the she-king with her counterpart. No, the Ildana were not of the same barbaric stock as Ava's people. In Sandkaldr, her father had mated with a white reindeer hind, which he then slaughtered and ate its heart, or so the skalds told it.

"Come," Jeven said, and held out a cold hand to her.

Beside a fire, two druada heated cups of woad mixed with lard. They threaded needles with linen and soaked these in the woad.

An old woman handed Ava a cup, which she drank down— henbane and poppy in sweet wine to kill the pain. "You'll lie here, my lady."

"Lie down?"

The old woman's chin bounced with her nod.

The sand's dampness reached through Ava's linen shift and chilled her back and buttocks. Jeven lay down beside her, his feet to the south as hers were to the north, like the points of a geomancer's earth needle.

The poppy worked quickly. A needle pierced the skin of her wrist, but it felt as though it belonged to someone else. She watched the thread pull through and leave a line of dark blue woad under her skin.

The riot of a dawn sky rolled over her and Ava had to close her eyes. When she opened them, clouds raged like horses across the pastures of the sky. They beckoned her to leave her body behind, leave the dull pull of thread stitching her future into the tender skin of her wrist.

Irjan had taught her to fly, so she did, and left this pain behind.

When next she opened her eyes, she turned to look at Jeven, his face dusted with black sand. The sun had scalded his face for it was near mid-morning.

"It's done," he said.

He held out his left arm, and she raised her right. Beneath beads of blood, the image of an eel coiled around their wrists, as if this alone could bind them.

Another day passed without word from Gwylym. In that

day, Ava had learned that Jeven was a druí of some recognition, though she suspected he'd been chosen for his sharp eyes and ears. If he was an informer for the greenmen, as she suspected, she would make sure he sent the right information.

Jeven had presented her with a list of pressing matters. As expected, Marchlew and Pyrs would resist her claim to the throne and had called up their retainers, preparing for battle.

Ava was breaking her fast with boiled eggs and oatcakes when Jeven arrived at her chamber, his branch of silver bells giving him away long before he reached the door. She thought milk goats had been turned loose in the keep when she first heard him coming. He showed his palms, the binding mark on his left wrist still pink and probably as painful as her own.

"Sit." She motioned to a chair by the fire. "You have news for me?"

"I do, lady." Jeven's manner was one of constipated serenity, a quiet sponge that soaks up information and squeezes it out only when the proper pressure is applied.

He removed his grey cloak and sat, elbows on his knees. He leaned toward her as if eager to divulge a tidbit.

"Well?"

"Fiach left the keep last evening and I thought it wise to follow. I need not explain why." Jeven had the senses of a hunting hound, it would seem. Fiach, the chieftain of Emlyn, had arrived in Caer Ys just yesterday, the first of the chieftains to come to pledge fealty to their new she-king.

"Go on," she said.

"He went to a smithy, I suppose to make some repairs."

"This is your urgent news? He repairs his greaves?"

"When he left the blacksmith's shop an old woman accosted him, pleaded with him to listen. He stepped into an alleyway and I presume he heard her out."

It was Ava who leaned forward now. "And what did the old woman say to him?"

"I couldn't hear. But Fiach laughed and walked away with

the woman hanging on his cloak. The only words I heard were, 'she calls him back.'"

"She calls him? Who?"

"I fear she was a messenger from Lyleth," Jeven said.

"Bring Fiach to me."

Jeven stood, showed his palms, and left the room. If Lyleth sought to aid Marchlew with his rebellion, she would try to enlist help from Fiach, of course. He'd been Lyleth's lover, had he not?

Fiach came in and crossed her chamber in long fluid strides. His eyes never left Ava's while he showed his palms, suspicion playing in his look. There was much to like in this lord of Emlyn, primarily, the largest mounted force in the Five Quarters. But knowing he bore a certain fondness for Lyleth... Ava must tread carefully.

"Fiach, thank you for leaving your meal. Please, sit."

"My lady." Fiach settled into a chair with feline grace. At least Lyleth had some taste. He was long of limb, big-shouldered and wore a wary expression that reminded Ava she must win this man's allegiance. She wagged her fingers at Jeven to bring ale and a waiting platter of cold meat and cheese.

"As you know," Ava said, "my guards search for Lyleth in the highlands as we speak." She measured his response.

His eyes flitted to hers, then away. He cut a chunk of cold goose. "So I understand." Fiach bit into the meat.

"It is my belief that she works to divide this land, set quarter against quarter, and, if you can forgive my bluntness, I fear she may try to draw you into this rebellion that brews in the north."

He chewed slowly, no doubt hoping it would give him time to think of an answer. "I've not seen Lyleth since before Nechtan's death."

"You've received no messages from her?"

The look he gave said he understood completely that he'd been followed.

"If you mean the old woman," Fiach said, "she's as mad as a boar in rut. It was nonsense."

Ava refilled his cup herself. "What kind of nonsense?"

"She was raving. Said that Lyleth would raise Nechtan from the dead, that he would lead an army against you. Not the kind of talk one takes seriously, my lady."

Ava gave a mirthless laugh. "Raise the dead? And I suppose the hag wanted you to throw in your lot with the dead king?"

"My lady…" He leaned close and wet his lips before going on. "You know better than anyone that I would choose death before following Nechtan, even if the First Mother raised him."

Ava leaned even closer, her eyes locked on his. "Forgive me," she whispered, "but I am ice-born and must tread carefully in this land. Know that I trust you completely, Fiach."

She reached out and placed her hand on his. His eyes flashed with secrets and she vowed silently to know them.

When Fiach had gone, Ava held a cup of mead out to Jeven. "Tell me," she said. "Do the druada teach their students to raise the dead?"

A smile broadened his narrow face. "To call a soul back, aye, to be reborn, not to return to the flesh they left behind. Only the Old Blood were said to have done such a thing."

"A babe at the breast could scarce lead an army," she said. "What's required to accomplish this conjuring?"

"It's not my place to speak of it."

"It's your place to serve me. If our rule is so threatened, it's your duty to tell me of it."

His eyes went to the fire and he pursed his mousey lips.

"You're sworn to me as I am to you, Jeven."

"It's only vaguely known," he said at last.

"What would Lyleth know of it?"

"More than I, I should think, but she would never try it." He shook his head.

"Why not?"

"She's taken the same vow as I. We serve stars and stones; the seasons of life and death are not subject to our desire—"

"Then I see you've never met this sister greenleaf. Lyleth would sell her own soul to stop me. Tell me what she knows of this spell."

Jeven sighed and leaned heavily on his knees. "The only reference to it is a fragment of an epic found carved into a foundation stone in the ruins of a fortress built by the Old Blood. It's far from complete."

"Come, come. I am no necromancer, you can tell me."

"It must be cast on Winter's Eve."

"Which passed just days ago. Samhain Eve." Winter was the night of the year as summer was the day. The Ildana didn't bother themselves with spring or fall.

"It's the threshold of night, the dusk of the year," he said. "The veil between the worlds thins."

"Tell me, what does this fragment say?"

"A solás breathes, or implants—the translation is unclear— the memories of her lord into a living vessel of some kind. That also is unclear. But she must have an object of his, something favored, and she must be submerged in a life well."

"An object? Like a harp?"

Jeven moved to set his cup on the table, but it fell to the floor and rolled away.

"Like a harp."

Chapter 11

Water thick as honey dissolved the rough edges of Connor's panic. Something or someone was hauling him toward the sky like a hooked fish, leaving Dish and the dark-haired woman far behind. Surreally calm, Connor surfaced in the fishpond behind the deserted mansion. It was still dusk, though it seemed he'd been gone for hours. He coughed up water and breathed the inert air of a world he could have so easily forgotten.

"What the fuck..."

"What the fuck is right, dude." A man sat perched at the edge of the fishpond, shaking his mane like a dog. "You got no business here."

Connor clung to the rock coping, coughed some more, and focused on the owner of the hands that had pulled him back. A pair of too-short shorts with holes in the wrong places puddled on the flagstones and a faded wet camouflage shirt barely buttoned over a beer gut. The goatee was classic Shaggy.

The guy picked up a pair of cast-off sunglasses that looked like he'd stolen them from a teenage girl in some mosh pit. It was almost dark, but he put them on.

"Make me save your sorry ass from drowning in my Jacuz," the guy said. "What the hell?"

"Jacuz? I mean, sorry, or... uh, I don't know what I mean."

Connor thought he'd just slipped from one wild dream into another. He started to shiver. Failing to find any steps out of the water, he vaulted out and flopped onto the deck. His collarbone screamed in pain, so he rolled to his butt and sat up.

"Bees were swarming me… I think." He pointed at the trail. "I'm really sorry."

"It's cool, man. It's cool. Good thing I was here, or phfft, you'd be a goner."

A goner. Then why did Connor feel so crushed by the very act of breathing again? He felt like he was still underwater, like every movement was in slo-mo, his voice distorted in pitch and rhythm. His heart was a landed fish.

He wiped at the water that ran out of his nose. "How long was I under?"

"Eh, no more than a few minutes, I'd say. I heard splashin', come out and found you face down."

Connor glanced at the pool. Black and still. Wasn't it a fishpond? He heard the hum of a pool filter from somewhere. He glanced at the walls of the mansion, lit by some kind of tiki torch. The windows were covered with plywood and the walls so thickly tagged it looked like an inner city cave painting.

He looked back at the guy and tried to see past the sunglasses.

"Kinda hard to drown in a hot tub," Connor said.

"Truth be told, happens all the time. A little noggin bump or too much booze, whatever, all it takes. A human can drown in six inches of water, ya know."

"Well thanks. For pulling me out I mean."

"CPR certified, dude."

Connor struggled to his feet and started to walk off, water squishing from his Nikes, his legs trembling so much he thought he'd collapse.

"Bees, ya say?" the man called after him.

Connor turned.

"Yeah, I was running the trail and they swarmed me." He could feel the ache of the stingers in his scalp and the small of his back. The sound of wet buzzing came from his shorts. He did a little dance, opened his pocket and a bee flew out.

"Hey, you didn't see anyone else out here, did you?" Connor asked.

"Like who?"

The world started tumbling and Connor staggered into some shrubs. Then the guy appeared at his side and had hold of him.

"Maybe you should chill for a minute. You're gonna fall on your ass."

"I'm cool. Just don't like bees much."

"African killer bees maybe. They interbreed with our honeybees. Fuck 'em all up." The dude pulled a plastic chair over and Connor slid into it. Reaching behind an overgrown shrub, the guy flipped a switch. "You could be allergic to the venom."

The hot tub frothed and steamed in the cold air. Just a few minutes ago it was icy cold, and now it was hot? Not possible. Maybe the guy was right; maybe Connor was having some weird allergic reaction that made him see shit that wasn't there.

"I gotta get back. Thanks for..." Connor waved at the water and tried to stand, but his legs wouldn't let him.

"Back to what? School?" The old guy coughed, or maybe that was a laugh, and lit a cigarette.

"Well, yeah."

"You know the kids from your school come around here all the time, leaving beer cans and rubbers all over like it was Woodstock or something. I get kinda tired of it, truth be told."

"Sorry. I'll tell them." Connor succeeded in standing and started away. "My phone."

He scanned the deck. The very thought of a cell phone seemed ridiculous to him right now.

"Hey, you were in that accident," the guy said in the high-pitched voice of recognition. He wagged a finger at Connor. "I'm sorry about your teacher."

Terry Madden

Connor froze. "What?"

"I was there, man. Just coming up from the beach with my board and wham, it was all over." The old guy pulled his shades to the end of his nose and looked over them, saying, "You were driving. You hydroplaned. Fuckin' scary shit."

The scene came back in full detail, like someone had hit rewind in Connor's brain. He swallowed hard. "Yeah."

"That's tough, losing somebody that way."

"Lose? No. He's in a coma." But all Connor could see in his head was Dish in that cave, alive and awake and reaching for Connor's hand.

"No shit?"

The dude handed Connor his cell phone and replanted himself in the plastic chair, water dripping from his shorts. He crossed one skinny leg over the other and spewed a stream of smoke.

"Name's Ned, by the way."

"Connor." He thought about making up a fake last name, but wasn't fast enough. "Connor."

"Connor Connor, nice to meet you. What's the prognosis for teach? They think he'll come to?"

Connor couldn't read Ned's eyes behind the girlie sunglasses. Probably a druggie. Why should he care what happened to Dish?

"They don't know."

But Connor's mind was still stumbling over what he'd just seen. He jumped into a fishpond and came up in the cave on the beach. At least, it sure looked like the cave on the beach. He glanced out at the ocean, lit by the last pink of twilight. He must have swum through some underground channel and come up down there. But that was insane. The beach was a good mile from here, maybe more. And even if it was the same cave, what was Dish doing in there? He was in the hospital for chrissake.

Images started to strobe through his mind—the tattoo on

Dish's wrist, the same as the one on the woman's wrist, the look in Dish's eyes, like he knew Connor was there, but was blind. Dish's eyes... Connor was certain the man was Dish. He had seen a man and the man had seen him. The recognition was mutual. But in spite of that, Connor had to admit it wasn't physically Dish. It was just his eyes that gave him away. What was it the woman said? Give him time. Time for what?

"Ya know," Ned said, leaning forward in the plastic chair. "Your teacher could use some help about now."

"He's in a coma." Connor said it with all the conviction of a sane person.

"A coma, shit, your body's breathin' and pissin' and you're a million miles away. That would suck ass. All I'm saying, ya know. Sometimes people decide to pull the plug, don't give 'em a chance. Ya know what I mean?"

But give him time was all Connor heard in his head. "Even if he wakes up, the chance that he'll be a vegetable is 68.7 percent. Even higher if he sleeps longer." He wiped his nose on the inside of his wet T-shirt.

"I'm just saying, we're always playin' god with people like that—"

"You don't know anything about it." It came out more sarcastic than Connor intended. "It's just... I got to go."

"See ya around." Ned took a drag from the cigarette and snuffed it on the pool deck.

Connor limped to the chain-link and slipped through. Maybe Dish was already dead or his soul had moved on, to that other place where Connor could hear fire sing.

It was getting dark, so he forced his legs to jog, but the downhill slope carried him faster. Water squished from his shoes as he picked up speed. He stumbled a few times and finally fell. His chest grated over the ground, and he lay there, smelling dirt. It felt good to cry. The ground didn't try to comfort him; it just took his tears like it takes the rain.

Connor decided to be sick the next day and spent the morning searching the Internet for people who had had the same experience he had—near-death drowning. At least, he figured he must have been near death to see the stuff he'd seen. Other people had seen weird shit too: mermaids, subs made of shells, aliens. So Connor was a nutcase just like the rest of them and his appointment with his shrink wasn't till Friday, not that Dr. Adelman ever helped anyway.

Give him time. Dish and the woman were running from something. She was bleeding.

His cell phone rang. "Hello?"

It was Holly, the nice nurse from I.C.U. "Mr. Cavendish can see a limited number of visitors. I'm not sure how long—"

"I'll be right there."

Connor couldn't wait for Brother Mike to take him. He tucked a wad of binder paper in the fire escape jamb, then walked the quarter mile down to the school gates and met the cab there.

"You can pay, kid?" the driver asked.

Connor waved his mom's Visa card and eased himself into the back seat.

In the waiting room on the third floor of the hospital, the TV was playing infomercials to no one. In the corner, a large woman slept in a chair made for average humans. Her mouth hung open and her thick legs were splayed in a disturbing way.

Connor buzzed the intercom on the wall and waited. Finally, a female voice said, "I.C.U."

"It's Connor Quinn. You called me. I'm here to see Hugh Cavendish."

"He has two visitors right now. We'll let you know when you can come in."

Two visitors? Connor slumped into a chair in front of the TV. The lady in the infomercial was selling a face exerciser while the large lady in the corner had slid further down, hiking her flowery muumuu way too far up her thighs.

He flipped the channel to Oprah. Flipped again.

The electric doors finally buzzed and swung open.

A younger woman blew her nose and walked beside a tiny old lady pushing a walker. She was no more than five feet tall, with a hunch in her back that forced her to look straight down when she walked.

"I can't bear to see him this way." The British accent set off an alarm in Connor's brain. Dish's relatives. Shit. What could he possibly say? Maybe he wouldn't have to. Just let them go by.

They inched their way toward Connor. A black nylon pouch hung in the front of the old lady's walker, overflowing with scraps of paper and a few wilted flowers. A faded bumper sticker plastered on the front announced, I brake for gnomes. The garden gnome in his green jumper and red cone hat was almost worn off.

As they walked by, the old lady turned and looked at Connor with eyes that were so young, eyes that didn't fit the body they were in. She wore a purple- and white-checked blouse with bees embroidered on the front. The trail of their buzzy path from one flowered pocket to the other was stitched in black dot-dot-dots.

"You're a fine lad," she said, and patted Connor's shoulder. "I've missed you."

"Forgive us," the younger woman said. "My aunt's confused, she's had a bit of a shock—" Her eyes went from Connor's sling to his swollen, stitched face.

The old lady had taken Connor's one free hand in hers, the heat from his hand radiating into her cold, papery skin. To pull his hand away would be rude, and she was smiling at him with her eyes.

A voice came over the intercom behind them. "Mr. Quinn, you may come in now."

"Mr. Quinn? Connor Quinn?" The younger woman extended her hand. "My name is Bronwyn Cavendish, Hugh's sister. This is my aunt, Merryn Penhallow. My, you are just a lad."

Connor couldn't shake her hand because of his sling, and the old lady had a death grip on his left hand, so Bronwyn recovered with an awkward laugh.

"I—I'm, uh, sorry," he said.

The sister's eyes welled up and she daubed at her nose with a tissue. She looked like a female Dish, model-ish with the same dark brown hair and green eyes.

"I'm sure you are…" Her words carried a hint of bitterness. She took her aunt's hand and gently freed Connor. "You'd best go see him," she said, "but Mr. Quinn? Could I bother you with a few questions after? We can wait here?" She nodded toward the waiting room.

Questions? He'd already told the cops everything he knew in the hospital. "Yeah. Okay."

The women inched toward the waiting room like two snails.

"Mr. Quinn?" said the impatient voice over the intercom.

He went to the wall and pushed the button. "Ready."

There was a pause and the door buzzed. Connor pushed.

"The room on the left." The nurse indicated an alcove with a window that opened onto the nurse's station. "Ten minutes," she said. She must be Holly. She glanced at his sling and bruised face saying, "I'm sorry."

"Me too." He tried to smile back, but failed.

Dish lay in the darkened room, hooked up to six monitors that registered in colorful blips and sine waves. There was a tube down his throat, just like Connor's brother had had. Dish's face was so swollen and bruised that the guy in the cave looked more like him than this.

Connor fought tears and crept to the chair beside the bed.

"Dish," he whispered. "You know you can't go—" But his throat closed around the word. "You just can't."

Except for the tube, Dish looked like he was asleep. What was the difference between a coma and sleep? Just that you can't wake up? He was alive, so he had to be somewhere. As Connor watched his chest artificially rise and fall, he wanted to believe that Dish was in that cave with the pretty woman. But that was insane.

He got up and paced to the other side of the room to find a row of cards sitting on a high shelf. From the same art class, apparently. Probably more heartfelt than the ones they had sent Connor. Hidden behind them he found a small bottle. It looked like one of those miniature booze bottles people collect because they think they're cute or something.

When he picked it up, he bowled over a row of cards and had to set them up again. The label on the bottle read, Two Blind Dogs. In small print at the bottom: Single Malt Scotch Whiskey, since 1607. Sure, that's what Dish needed right now, a belt of Scotch. But the seal was broken and the liquid inside was clear, like water.

He opened the cap and sniffed. Didn't smell like alcohol, didn't smell like anything, really. It looked like water. There was a tiny gift card taped to the bottom. Inside, Happy Birthday, Merryn was crossed out. In a spidery hand two words filled the remaining white space: From Madron's. Was that some kind of liquor store? He put it back on the shelf.

Aunt Merryn had brought Dish a bottle of water? The old lady did seem pretty nuts.

Connor forced himself to sit back in the chair, to really look at what was left of Dish. His gaze travelled to Dish's arm. The tattoo was still there, half-covered with an I.V. bandage. The memory of the woman he had seen in the pool blinded Connor. Why would she have the same tattoo? And how did Dish get this one in the first place?

He reached for Dish's hand. It was cold. He couldn't stop the tears any longer. But with them came the distant echo of

Dish's voice. There's another world out there. That's what he'd said just before the accident.

"There's another world out there," Connor told Dish. "Where?" He wiped his nose on his sleeve and pleaded, "Where are you?"

Connor looked for a flutter of his eyelids. Something, anything. Give him time.

"It's time," Holly the nurse said.

"Yeah."

He wiped his eyes on the sleeve of his sweatshirt and headed out. When he went through the electric doors, he saw Dish's sister and aunt huddled in a corner of the waiting room across the hall. He looked down at the design in the carpet and tried to walk on by, but Bronwyn intercepted him before he got to the elevator.

"I hate to trouble you, I know you've been through so much," Bronwyn said. "But the insurance investigator would like to talk to you."

She guided him back to the waiting room and motioned to a chair beside Dish's aunt.

Connor sat.

"He's just a lad," the old lady said.

"I know, auntie, but it's necessary—"

"I told the cops everything." Connor was sure he was going to throw up.

"I understand, but Mr. Kline, the investigator, has a few questions," Bronwyn said. "Once some paperwork is settled he'd like to ring you up, if it's not a bother. Might I get a number where you can be reached?"

Connor's eyes met Aunt Merryn's. "You left a bottle of water in Dish's room. Why?"

"Oh yes. From Madron's. A holy well."

"What's it supposed to do for him?"

Bronwyn took her aunt's hand and gave it a pat. "My auntie holds to some old superstitions."

But Connor's eyes searched Aunt Merryn's. "A well is a place where water just comes up out of the ground, right?"

"Yes."

"What's so holy about them?"

"Water from certain wells possesses healing properties—"

"You think well water can heal Dish?"

The two women exchanged a look.

"Anything is possible," Aunt Merryn said at last.

Was that what Dish found on the beach? A holy well? Something magical? "There's another world out there. And it shapes us no less than this one." Dish's words just tumbled from Connor's lips.

"Yes…" Merryn replied, and her smile unfolded the soft wrinkles around her mouth.

"It was raining," Connor said to Bronwyn. "I lost control. That's what happened."

The two women were staring at him. Bronwyn's hand went to his shoulder. He pulled away.

"You've been traumatized no less than my brother," Bronwyn said. "I understand."

"310-599-9057."

Bronwyn looked puzzled.

"My number. For your investigator."

But Aunt Merryn struggled to the edge of her chair and put a bony hand on his. "Tell me, lad. What did you see?"

The familiar look in Merryn's eyes unstoppered everything. It came out too fast for his tongue. He proceeded to upchuck everything he remembered about the pool and Dish's tattoo, but couldn't bring himself to confess his near-drowning vision of Dish and the woman.

Bronwyn gave a chortle and crossed her arms. "It would be like Hugh to get a tattoo of that thing."

"I watched it appear!" Connor drew an uncomfortable stare from the large woman, now awake.

He thrust his bare wrist out to Bronwyn. "His skin was as tattoo-less as mine right now. I watched it—grow."

Merryn's eyes said she believed him.

"Let me show you," he said.

Bronwyn's face glazed over with a mocking smile. "We have things to tend to here," she said, "serious things—"

"This is serious. Let me show you. I think Dish thought it was a well, like the well you're talking about."

Bronwyn turned to Merryn with a scowl, saying, "You think Hugh was looking for his threshold on Malibu Beach?"

Connor didn't remember anyone saying anything about a threshold. "Threshold of night. That's what he said."

The way Bronwyn's eyes flitted from him to Merryn said that she'd let something slip. Bronwyn knew exactly what Dish was doing in that cave, and Connor would find a way to get it out of her.

"Let me show you," he said again.

Aunt Merryn's eyes twinkled brightly. "Take me there."

Chapter 12

Lyleth had only felt the boy's presence in the pool, but Nechtan had seen him—thin with copper eyes, he told her. This boy was no specter of a soul lost in the crossing, nor was he the wandering consciousness of a dreamer so often seen staggering between worlds by those with eyes to see them. No, the fact that Nechtan could see him and Lyleth could not meant that the boy had crossed the well by some means unknown to her. Lyleth would be quick to say it was impossible. Yet, three months earlier, she would have said calling Nechtan back from that world was equally impossible.

But there were other, living men in this maze of river-cut caverns. Their torchlight and voices echoed off the cavern walls.

Lyleth dropped the rushlight in the pool and the cave went black.

"We've nowhere to hide," she whispered to Nechtan.

"Then we prepare to fight."

From the darkness came the sound of the pony's hooves scrabbling for purchase in the gravel. Brixia was pulling herself out of the water. Had she been in the pool this whole time? Hadn't she pulled Nechtan out of the torrent? Brixia gave a shake and started to walk away. With her arms out before her, Lyleth followed the chatter of hooves in gravel. Her eyes finally adjusted to the dark and she saw the pony was headed for a weak light seeping from the far end of the chamber.

"Brixia knows," she said.

Nechtan took her hand and they crept after the sound of the pony and the dim shaft of light.

"The path may drop from under us," he said. "Stay close to the wall."

The damp stone chilled her even more, and she fought a sudden shudder of bone cold. The water had soaked through her makeshift bandages and reopened her wounds, and in spite of her cloak, her bowstring dug deeply.

The path grew narrow, but Brixia plowed the deep scree and slid backward. Nechtan planted both palms on the pony's haunches and pushed. Brixia fell forward on her knees then leapt like a fawn to the opening.

From the other side of the pool muffled voices became words, then laughter, and the torchlight swelled.

"It's Gwylym," Nechtan said.

Gwylym had been like an uncle to Nechtan after his father died. He'd taught Nechtan how to fight, how to lead men to their deaths and how to live with himself the next day. Lyleth knew Nechtan had failed to learn this last lesson, and it was this failing that shaped him into the king who had brought peace to the land.

"Gwylym will know you as well as I," she said, "but—"

"We'll go back with him to Caer Ys." She could hear the hope in his voice.

"We'll go back to Caer Ys," she said, "where Ava commands five hundred retainers. Your retainers. Will they believe it's really you, or say you're a conjuring of mine? Ava's offered a price for my head and she'll likely give a bit more for yours."

The voices grew louder and torchlight danced on the skin of the pool. Men clustered on the far side, about ten of them.

"Ava has slain a guardian, Nechtan," she whispered. "When you face her, you'll need men at your back. More than ten."

He drew a weary breath and exhaled. "Aye," he said at last, "that I will."

The light of day beckoned from the narrow opening behind them.

Nechtan lifted Lyleth to the rocky ledge as if he were tossing her on a horse's back. She caught the edge of the opening with her fingertips and pulled herself up, then reached down for his hand.

"Lyleth!" Gwylym called from across the water. "Come with me now and I'll see that no harm comes to ye."

"The harm's done, Gwylym," she called back to him. "This she-king you serve killed your king. She'll let me live? I think not."

Nechtan scrambled onto the ledge beside her. Below, a rope slapped the surface of the water and squealed as it drew taut. They were crossing the water.

"Speak to him," she told Nechtan.

He hesitated. "You serve me, Gwylym, as you served my father before me." Nechtan's voice echoed through the cavern and the sound of ropes and splashing ceased.

"Nechtan? It can't be—"

"If you truly are my man, Gwylym, you'll turn round and go back the way you came."

"My lord?"

Gwylym hushed his whispering men.

"But your lady wife," Gwylym went on, "she's been chosen by the green gods—"

"The same green gods saw fit to breathe life into me. Whom do you serve, Gwylym?"

A long silence followed, then the splashing resumed. "They're coming." She took Nechtan's hand and started through the narrow fissure leading to a twilit sky.

"So be it," Nechtan called. "If you stick your head out this hole, Gwylym, I swear by stars and stones, I'll cut it off."

"Follow Brixia," Nechtan told her. He worked his shoulders

through the cleft in the rock and took Lyleth's offered hand. She pulled and he spilled out beside her onto a grassy clearing. "I'll be right behind you," he said. "Go."

She knew better than to argue, but he had nothing but a dirk to defend himself. She started down a deer track toward a stand of trees where Brixia foraged among dead bracken at the base of an old beech. Lyleth cursed the weakness in her arms but managed to scale the branches high enough to gain a view of the cave entrance.

She slipped the bow from her back and nocked an arrow.

"What is he about?" She could see Nechtan clambering up the granite cliff that rose above the cave. A large boulder began to teeter, and finally tumbled down the cliff. It rolled past the entrance and came to rest in a cloud of dust. "Ah." She smiled.

A second boulder followed, forming the crude footing of a dam of sorts at the base of the cliff. Smaller rocks came down in a loud rumble.

An arm appeared from the narrow opening, then the other arm, then a man's head and shoulders. Lyleth drew and sighted down the shaft to the man's eye. Her arm quaked with weakness, but she let the arrow fly. It skipped over the rocks beside him. She drew again and this time found her mark. Before the man could get to his feet, he fell still. Then a great fall of stone bowled down on top of him. A boulder as big as Brixia finally came to rest, lodged across the entrance and the fallen man.

When Lyleth reached Nechtan, he was inspecting his work, pulling at some loose stones to reveal an arm and the young skin covering it. She read the relief in his eyes when they both saw it wasn't Gwylym.

"Welcome to the land of the dead, lad," he said.

She knew the bitterness in his voice was meant for her. So be it. She was not his friend any longer, but his solás.

A crevice two fingers wide was all that was left of the

entrance to the cavern. Lyleth could hear curses, the rattle of weapons and the churning of scree on the other side.

Nechtan planted his hands on the rock face and she saw he was trembling.

"You're men of my own clan guard," he called into the cavern. "You know me as well as your own mum. I am no demon, no wraith. Gwylym, you carried me on your shoulders when I was a lad, you watched my father die and you sewed my life back into me. You know me."

He slapped the rock and put his eye up close to the crevice. "Look at me!"

"My lord," Gwylym said at last. "Let us out so we might join you."

Nechtan looked at Lyleth as if for permission. There was a sad confusion in his eyes. She had brought him back to a different world, and she saw that unkind truth settling over him. She shook her head. There could be no trust. Not yet. To do so would risk everything. Certainly, he knew that as well as she.

Nechtan wiped at his mouth with the back of his quaking hand and looked back into the crevice. The torchlight from inside cast a bright slash across his face.

"Gwylym," he said. "If you serve me, then do as I ask. Tell my lady wife that my heart beats as strong as her own. She's to take ship with her soulstalker, Irjan, and sail back to that frozen hell that spawned her. If she fails in this—I come for her life this time."

Silence, then a few hushed whispers. Lyleth thought she heard the charm against the Crooked One.

"Tell her, Gwylym."

Nechtan strode away and had started down the trail when he stopped and returned to the pile of stones. There, half-buried with the dead man, a sword blade caught the setting sun.

He kicked off the rocks and picked it up, testing the weight in his fist.

"This will do," he said.

They walked for the remainder of the day, north into Elfael. The sun went down quickly and in spite of Lyleth's protests, Nechtan built a fire. The trees were thick here, so the light wouldn't travel far. There was only a sliver of a moon and it would set soon. If Gwylym decided to pursue them, it would take him a day to retreat through the cavern and another day to make his way north toward the River Rampant.

Even though the fire was snapping hot, Lyleth shivered with fever. She sent Nechtan in search of deer moss to pack her wounds, and he came back with his cloak full.

"I found cobweb, too," he said. "Now, let me see."

When he unwrapped the soaked linen, the cold air stung the three deep gashes left by Wren's talons. She was sliced from collarbone to armpit.

"These need stitching," he said.

"The moss and cobweb will stop the bleeding until we reach the inn."

"Does Wren's skin come with the gift of flight, Lyl?" He gave her a resentful glance and ripped a fresh strip of linen with his teeth. "My time here would be so much easier—"

"I intended to bring you back to stay."

He looked up from wadding the moss and cobweb. "What about my intentions?" he asked. "You think you know what I want. But you're wrong, Lyl."

"If I'm wrong… then I've squandered my life in the service of a selfish, average man and a land that's not worth the spilling of my blood."

He froze, his eyes locked on hers and she resolved not to let go.

"You never were much of a liar," she said at last.

He went back to wrapping the dry linen under her arm and avoiding her eyes. It was an old game he played, and she couldn't blame him. He always told her he deserved to keep some thoughts to himself, and now, she knew he was right.

"The boy in the water came for you," she said flatly. "What do you remember of this lad?"

He looked up from his bandaging. "Pain." He started to add more, but pursed his lips. Finally, he ran the back of his hand across his mouth and looked away into the darkness.

"The boy is hurt," Nechtan said to the night.

"Why is he coming for you?" she asked. "How is he crossing?"

"First you want me to remember this world," he said, "and now you want me to remember the other. There's no pleasing you, Lyl." He lifted her shoulder and pulled the linen roughly around her.

This lad had the ability to cross a life well. What if he could call Nechtan back to the Fair Lands just as Lyleth had called him to the real world?

She had once vowed she would never let Nechtan see the faintest flicker of what she felt for him. To do so would destroy everything they had built. And now their kingdom lay in ruins, and her secret lay like a stone at the bottom of a river, too deep to be retrieved. He needn't know about this fear either. For if this boy intended to take Nechtan back, and if he succeeded, the boy with the copper eyes would end this battle before it even started.

As Nechtan tied the last knot in the bandage, his knuckles brushed her neck. His eyes met hers, and in a voice that was barely a whisper, he said, "I can't even remember his name."

Chapter 13

Ava stood with arms out stiffly while Irjan worked a pin through the sleeve of her gown, an imported barracan surcoat of the palest blue, embroidered with leafy vines blooming with tufts of freshwater pearls. She looked like the earth mother herself.

Her chieftains had been waiting since midday in the council chamber. What was it her father once said? Let underlings wait too long and they'll know you distrust them, not long enough and they won't respect you.

Ava wondered if Fiach had shared with the other lordlings the message brought to him by the mad bee woman, that Lyleth had called Nechtan back from the dead. But even more importantly, did Fiach believe it?

"Has there been word from Gwylym?" she asked Irjan.

"None, my Iron Lamb. But the meadmonger has been seized."

Ava turned on Irjan, pulling her sleeve free of the clasp. "When did you intend to tell me this?"

"Forgive me, I meant no deception." Irjan looked at the floor and showed her hands. "You have the chieftains to attend to, the woman will wait."

"Where did they find her?" Ava asked.

"Boarding a ship for Cadurques."

"You've questioned her?"

"The jailer persuades her now."

"She'll still be able to speak to me when his persuading is done, I trust." Ava thrust out her open sleeve while Irjan stooped to pick up the clasp. "You'll bring her to my chamber and wait for me here. Is that understood?"

Irjan pinned the clasp, then showed the leather of her sallow palms, saying, "As you command, my Iron Lamb."

Jeven was waiting at the council chamber door, staff of the solás in hand—three hammered-silver branches sprouted from the gnarled limb of a hazel tree, each with three silver acorn bells ringing a discordant chime.

He leaned close to her ear. "Arvon sends no one."

"So be it. Open the door."

Jeven lifted the latch and followed her into the barrel of the chamber. Each arching roof timber terminated in the head of a different beast carved so long ago that they had soaked up the hearth smoke of a thousand winters. How many kings had they watched rise and fall?

Seated on one side of the long table was Fiach of Emlyn and Lloyd, the aging chieftain of IsAeron. Some said Lloyd had lost his wits on a battlefield long ago, and merely followed Nechtan's, and now Fiach's, lead in all things. Ava hoped this was so. On the other side of the table sat a doughy old greenman, his torc all but buried in the folds of his fat neck. Beside him sat the empty seat of the chieftain of Arvon, a predictable dissident for he had been a friend to Nechtan as well as an underling.

They all found their feet when she approached and showed their palms in unison. Ava's chair was too tall and her feet dangled like a child's; she would order a footstool made before returning to council.

"The lands of Emlyn and IsAeron," she said, "have my constant protection and the open hand of trade. And you, sir," she said to the soft old druí, "you come as trumpet for which of my absent lords?"

"I am Finlys, counsel to Marchlew of Cedewain, my lady."

His chin rippled when he spoke. It appeared Finlys enjoyed the pleasures of this world as much as his lord.

"Please sit," she said to them. "Finlys, tell me, what has occupied Marchlew so that he cannot join the council table of his king?"

She could feel Jeven standing behind her right shoulder like a guard dog.

Finlys laced his fingers over the bulge of his belly. "Marchlew sends his respect and his hopes to reconcile what he sees as a... a misunderstanding, my lady."

"Misunderstanding?" She tested a practiced, politic smile. "Would you be referring to the get of Marchlew and Nechtan's sister?"

"Talan is the boy's name, my lady."

"And Marchlew believes this boy should be sitting where I sit now?"

"The boy, Talan, is of age and is the nearest living blood to Nechtan and the sleeping kings of the Ildana."

Ava felt her heart pound behind her eyes and her skin flush.

"You sit before me, sir, and ask that I hand over my throne to Nechtan's nephew because of the blood he bears? Has this boy slain a guardian? Has he proven to the people of the Five Quarters that his blood has anything to do with his destiny?"

"To seek such would be foolish indeed, my lady." Finlys daubed at perspiration with a kerchief. "No, what Marchlew seeks is a union between you and his son."

A chortle escaped her. Leaning back in her big chair, her eyes met Jeven's and she tried to read them. Did she see acquiescence written there? Surely not.

"Handfast Nechtan's nephew?" she said at last. "And why, good druí, would I be inclined to accept such a proposal?"

She glanced at Fiach, looking for some support.

"This is an unusual request," Fiach said. "My lady is not in a position that requires bargaining."

"Quite right," Finlys answered. "My lady is in a position to demand, certainly so. But to demand would require the spilling of blood. Ildana blood."

Ava let her gaze linger on the empty seat of the chieftain from Arvon. Finlys' gaze followed hers, and he certainly caught her meaning. Even if she were to agree to this outrage, fully one fifth of the kingdom would still be in rebellion. Arvon took no part in this scheme.

"Am I right to judge that Marchlew withholds his allegiance until I agree to take this boy to my bed?"

"My lady might consider—"

"This reeks of blackmail, my lords." She met Fiach's eyes, then Lloyd's.

"I must agree," Lloyd muttered, as if he'd awakened from a dullard's reverie. "Marchlew seeks to force your hand."

"I will have my answer for your lord in the morning, Finlys. Until then, avail yourself of my hospitality."

She left the table and Jeven followed. When the door had closed behind them, she said, "Place guards at his door and below his window. If he sends a bird, bring it down. If he receives any message, any at all, I want it. If Nechtan lives, then Marchlew will not be leading the northern quarters to battle; Nechtan will."

"If Lyleth has succeeded," Jeven said, "would it not be wise to agree to Marchlew's proposal rather than meet Nechtan in battle?"

They had reached her chamber door. "Leave me."

Inside, Ava found Irjan and a guard standing over a broken old woman. She reeled about on her knees, blood staining her dirty gown.

"What have you found, Irjan?"

"Her name is Dunla and she speaks in riddles, lady, but I found this." Irjan held out a small dagger, saying, "It was hidden in her bodice."

The bone grip was crudely carved into a skull with eyes of rough-cut red gems. But the blade... the blade was knapped from a single shard of a clear green stone. Ava held it up to the firelight, which exposed spidery traces of fractures that looked like runes, unreadable, at least to Ava. The edge was no thicker than a hair's breadth, like ice that forms on a grass blade in a freezing wind.

"Leave us," Ava told the guard. He withdrew and closed the door, leaving Ava and Irjan to the prisoner.

"What is this?" Ava asked Irjan.

"A soothblade of the Old Blood, those who came before."

The Old Blood. Keepers of some lost magic that Lyleth thought to wield.

"Where did you get this blade?" Ava drew it in a mock slice before the old woman's throat. "From Lyleth?"

Ava tested the sharpness of the stone blade on her thumb and drew blood. She let a fat drop fall on the hag's forehead.

Dunla cackled. "There is no truth in your blood, lady."

"It's you who have truth to spill old woman. And spill you shall if your guts spill with it," Ava said. "I've been told that Lyleth seeks to call her dead love to take back his throne. Is this so?"

"Lyleth's love is the land," the hag spat through broken teeth.

"The land? What kind of fool do you think me?"

The witch looked up at last, the words whistling through her shattered teeth, "The most despised of all fools, lady, them what kills her own lord."

Ava's palm stung with the slap she delivered, but the hag didn't flinch. "Nechtan's gods took him from me."

"Did they now?" Dunla tsk-tsked.

Ava followed her gaze to Irjan.

"'Twas but a slight wound my lord received," Dunla said, "treated with black hellebore by your soulstalker—"

"Hush now." Irjan stepped close, reached out and stroked the old woman's sparse hair as she would a rebellious child.

"Show me this soulstalker," Irjan cooed, "and we'll seek out he who would murder a king."

The old woman looked up, seemingly lost in Irjan's eyes, transfixed.

Ava stepped between them, saying, "Where is Lyleth?"

The hag pursed her lips and stared into the embers of the fire while Ava circled her. "You think Lyleth acts with a noble heart, do you not?"

"Lyleth wears the armor of star and stone."

"If you wish to live, you'll not speak to me in riddles."

"A wish is but a passing fancy. Ye might wish with all your might the land be yours, but it's not choosed ye, nay, for the king lives." The old witch's wild eyes danced in the firelight.

Ava slapped her harder this time, enough to make her hand throb, but the hag just smirked.

"Tell me where to find them, and I shall send you back to your bees."

"She takes him to a place where only they two can go, to forge the bond far stronger than that what binds 'em now. Break it? Nay. Take them? Nay. Ye shan't, lady."

The old thing grinned a hideous, broken grin, waggled her tongue and swayed on her knees.

She proclaimed with a spew of spittle, "A curse of crows upon thee. May the sea rise to swallow thee. May a babe lie within thee forever unborn—"

The stone dagger found its home, slipping easily above the old witch's breastbone and into her throat. She crumbled and twitched and Ava backed away. For from the gaping mouth they came like flies from a carcass, pouring forth in a black flood.

Bees.

Irjan swept Ava aside and beat at the bees with her cloak. But still they came until they were in Ava's hair, stinging, up her sleeves and down her bodice. She batted at the air and screamed, then fell to the floor, Irjan's cloak over her head.

When she looked out again, Dunla's body was flying away; bones, flesh, skin dissipating into a humming black cloud, unmaking itself like chaff before wind. The woman's ragged gown fluttered and fell to the floor, emptied.

Irjan gathered Ava under her arm like a child and made for the door. The last thing Ava saw was the swarm of bees spiraling through the fire, untouched, and up the chimney.

Four mounted warhorses were brought out to the garrison yard. Finlys was stripped to his smallclothes, his flaccid body honest in its failings. Ava took her seat beside Jeven, the breeze off the bay playing at the silk canopy over their heads. She was a mass of throbbing bee stings but she would take control of the beast's head now. Rebellion had a price.

"Ava," Jeven whispered, "taking the life of a druí is—"

"Forbidden, yes. But I also know that taking the life of a traitor is within my rights as king. What if Finlys is both?"

Jeven had no answer. The wind just played with his silver bells, sounding an eerie melody that shifted with the wind's direction.

The guards fixed leather straps to Finlys' wrists and ankles. To these they tied rope that was then secured to the girth of the horses' saddles, one for each limb.

"You deem this a necessity?" Jeven asked.

"An absolute necessity. I write no messages on parchment. Until the northern quarters come to their knees, I write them in blood, Jeven."

At her word, all four riders dug their heels into their horses. The ropes went taut. The horses strained more than she thought they would, and Finlys cried out less than she thought he would. He groaned, as if trying to pull against the ropes. The horses churned dirt, casting it back like a wake. Finlys released a ghastly wail. At last, his limbs tore from his body with a pop of gristle and sinew. The horses lurched forward, until the riders reined them back. All limbs popped free but the left leg.

The last horseman moved freely forward, dragging the leg and torso, until he reined up. A guard drew his sword and finished the separation of the leg from the body.

An arm lay before Ava's canopy, the hand still clenching and grasping at the air, twitching at the elbow. The leg on the far side still jerked at the knee, trying to crawl toward her.

Finlys' torso lay in the middle of the yard. His eyes were wide and his head thrashed from side to side.

A low muttering rose from the crowd and a woman retched. These people were soft indeed. Small wonder Ava's people had always taken what they wished from them.

She got up and moved to stand beside the mass of limbless flesh. Blood pumped swiftly from the ragged sockets. Yet he still stared into her eyes.

"A curse of truth on thee," the dying man croaked.

He stopped thrashing and wheezed something incomprehensible.

"This is your truth, Finlys," she said. "Your green soul is mine."

She thought he was still conscious when they tossed him in the fire. But he didn't cry out. Ava went as close as the flame allowed. She watched his staring eyes dry and wither, the fat of his cheeks blister, melt and glisten like butter. His lips curled into a hideous grin.

"Even in death he mocks me," she said.

Jeven appeared beside her, his bells chiming, casting about at the fleeing crowd. They had begun to move away, covering their noses with their cloaks against the smell.

"Have I won their fear?" she asked him.

"I'm not one to judge their fear, lady."

From her belt, Ava withdrew the pouch Irjan had given her. Finlys would not find his freedom so easily. He would serve her in this world for yet a while. She cast the pouch onto the blaze, speaking the words Irjan had taught her. They issued from her lips like smoke and mingled with the grey cloud that rose from the burning corpse. They twined, word around smoke, to form a rope that coiled into the sky. The pouch caught fire and burgeoned into a violet cloud. Bright white sparks cascaded in a great burst.

"Your soulstalker has taught you conjurer's tricks," Jeven said. "What do you hope to gain with this?"

She never took her eyes from the fire, just as Irjan had taught her, but repeated the circle of words and extended her palms to the smoky tether that rose higher. A figure coalesced in the shimmering heat.

"Look!" The remaining townsfolk pointed at the sky.

The figure slowly condensed into a solid form and struggled to rise above the flames. A raven rose on iridescent, blood-red wings, trailing embers and smoke as it struggled free of the flames. It circled the garrison yard thrice, stooping and turning as if learning to fly, before heading out over the open water of the bay.

In Jeven's eyes, Ava saw a flicker of contempt, or was it envy? Perhaps he thought she had traded a part of herself for this conjuring, the part that might have still harbored some innocence. Perhaps he was right. And perhaps the old meadmonger was right, that it was Irjan, not Lyleth, who delivered Nechtan of his sorry life. Ava's conscience told her she was a fool to trust Irjan. But she knew there were secrets yet to command, and one doesn't kill their teacher before the lesson is learned.

She finally answered Jeven, "Everything. I will gain everything."

Chapter 14

Nechtan waited for sunrise. He tossed a pebble through the darkness to plunk lightly in the river. The air smelled of waking pines, and his breath fumed in the cold like a boiling kettle. What or who allowed him to draw breath in this world? Certainly Lyl owned no such powers. She had flooded his mind with memories of a lifetime and left only ghosts from the Otherworld to people his dreams. He trusted no one more than he trusted Lyleth, yet he'd never felt as helpless as he did this morning.

He and Lyleth had made their way down the mountain by following the growing swell of the River Rampant into the rich vales of Elfael. Lyl had grown weaker and Nechtan had spent most of the night watching while she slept. His own sleep was haunted by the fear of not waking to this world, but another, the one he had left behind.

"Nechtan?"

Lyl had slept beneath drifts of leaves for warmth; they still clung to her cloak like a golden veil. She wrapped it tighter.

"Have you slept?" she asked.

"Enough to know the confusion it stirs," he said, trying to smile.

She sat down beside him and draped her cloak around them both. She felt too warm—the fever still had hold of her.

"I dream..." he said. "I'm in a place I can't describe because

it can't exist. Not here, not anywhere, I hope. It smells of…
of lunar caustic and horse urine. There are snakes that—" He
struggled to find words to describe it. "Snakes that pierce my
skin, my veins, crawl down my throat. Their venom turns my
blood to sand. I always find myself in a room filled with light.
Not firelight, nor sunlight, another kind of light. White light so
bright, so cold, I can't see, I can't move, I can't cry out. I need
to scream, Lyl, but then someone holds my eye wide open and
shines that light inside my head."

He could still feel the mute blindness.

Her brow knotted and she looked to the brightening
woods. If he asked her what the dream meant, she would lie,
so he didn't ask, but dragged his palms over the stubble on his
cheeks.

"If that's the 'Fair Land' I'm seeing, I thank stars and stones
you brought me back."

"Is the lad there in your dreams?" Her parched voice was
barely more than a whisper.

"He's there."

"How old is he?"

"Old enough to carry a sword. He just stands there and
looks down on me. 'Wake up,' says he. That's it, Lyl, just 'wake
up.'"

She puzzled over it, her eyes on the sunrise, her cheeks red
with fever.

"Sleeping…" she mused. "Do you recall when Cynfrig
slept without waking for a full winter? His druí fed him broth.
Enough to keep him alive."

"He took a blow to the head when he fell from his horse,
aye. But he didn't wake up, Lyl."

She gave him no reply, just a flash of her eyes.

"You think I sleep in the Otherworld? The way Cynfrig
slept?"

"It's but a thought. But if it's so—"

"I draw breath in two worlds? How can that be? If I wake there, what becomes of me here?"

Not even Lyl could hide the dread he saw in her eyes.

"Then my time here is…"

"Short. Aye, if the lad has his way. The Otherworld has not let go of you, I fear. And it shapes you no less than this world."

As the day wore on, the path grew broader and the river grew fatter, joined by silver races that spilled in falls from mountain valleys. Clouds of mist scattered the sunlight into rainbow sprays of color. If Nechtan was right, they'd reach the inn by nightfall.

Lyleth was weak. They made slow progress, his arm around her waist, half-carrying her. Brixia led them to a trail that at first seemed to take them in circles, but finally dropped down to the plains of Elfael. When they slowed, the little horse waited, when they rested, she rested. From here, Nechtan could see across the plain to the pale blue rise of the mountains of Pendynas, the border of Cedewain.

"Marchlew knows better than to meet Fiach on the open field," Nechtan was saying. "No, there's something else rolling around that man's brain."

"He would try diplomacy first."

"Marchlew? Diplomacy?" He had to laugh.

"You would," Lyl said.

"Marchlew's ways have never been mine. But I agree he would do whatever it takes to put his son on my throne."

He thought about his nephew; the only reason Marchlew would risk war was that he had fathered the boy most people would accept as heir to Nechtan's throne.

"How old is the boy now?"

"Talan is of an age to take the field and the throne," she said. "Perhaps a season younger than you were."

Nechtan hadn't seen the boy since he was playing with sticks and chasing cats with his wolfhound. It had been that long since he'd seen his sister, Kyndra. He felt a pang of guilt at the thought of her. When his father had proposed an alliance with Marchlew, an alliance sealed by marriage, Nechtan had agreed. When Kyndra begged him to persuade the king, their father, to reject Marchlew as a suitor, Nechtan told her it was her duty to wed for the land. He remembered it clearly, standing in her bedchamber while she slapped his arms, his chest, his face, raving that she would kill herself. He'd let her expend her rage until she was too exhausted to strike another blow. Then he escorted her north for the handfasting, and within six years, he suffered the same fate, married to a reaver's daughter, his marriage bed a peace treaty. Justice, some would call it.

"If we reach Marchlew," he said to Lyleth, "what do you plan to tell him?"

"The truth."

"Maybe I'm just a bit of borrowed flesh." He stopped in the road and forced Lyl to face him. "I have no mark, and I'm planted with memories you've selected."

"I don't own your memories—"

"You've given me only the memories you deem necessary. There's a reason I can't remember those last weeks, Lyl. You don't want me to remember. Why?"

He let go of her and ran his hands through his hair. "Knowing changes nothing," she said at last.

"It changes what lies between us," he said. "I deserve to know what it is I should regret."

He watched her test explanations in her head and discard them silently. She wouldn't meet his eyes when she finally said, "You banished me."

The image of Lyleth riding away without a backward glance flashed through his mind. He stood there, watching her go, knowing he was already dead. Remembering why he had banished her could only renew the bitterness simmering behind her eyes, a resentment that had softened these past two days. Maybe she was right. Maybe some things were better left unremembered.

Brixia came back down the road toward them and urged them on with a high-pitched whinny. After a long silent look, Lyleth turned and started after the pony. She'd gone no more than ten paces when she fell into a fevered heap. Nechtan gathered her in his arms and followed the pony.

"You can't die yet, Lyl. We're not finished, you and me."

The road spilled from wooded vales into pasture. Straw bundles waited to be gathered for winter and sheep grazed the stubble of a flax field. They stopped for several hours at midday and Lyleth slept in the shade of a haystack. And Nechtan watched her. He remembered that he had vowed never to set eyes on her again. He remembered Ava's jealous rants, claiming Lyleth and Nechtan were lovers. She accused them of breaking their vow, and now, watching the breeze dandle the loose strands of Lyleth's hair, the even throb of her heart beneath her skin, Nechtan wondered. Had they?

They found the inn where Elowen said it would be, on the north bank of the Rampant where three rivers joined. A weir held back the flow to form a millpond where a waterwheel churned loudly.

The sound of laughter and smallpipes carried from an inn called The Rampant Rooster. A weathered sign bearing the head of a crowing cock swung on rusty chains in the wind.

Beyond a yard filled with racks of drying salmon, Nechtan found the stable.

"Let's see the quality of guests they entertain before we join their festivities," Nechtan said.

Inside, a bay, a black and a sorrel munched hay beside the fat dun plow horse that Elowen had taken. Brixia confirmed it, nickering to the big horse as she sidled up to share its hay.

"Elowen is here before us," he said. "How is that possible?"

"Perhaps she knew another way."

"Or she rode through the night."

The plow horse showed signs of hard travel; dry sweat matted its neck and belly. Nechtan examined the saddles on the others. The high pommels were bossed with the brass sigil of Emlyn, crossed barley sheaves.

"Fiach's men," he whispered. "Scouts looking for Marchlew's hosting."

Lyl stroked the plow horse's neck. "Or they're looking for you. We should move on."

He glanced at the last of the linen they had used to wrap her wounds. Fresh blood seeped through the old. "We'll not leave here without stitching you up."

"It can wait."

"It can't." He met the stubborn will in her eyes. "A king with no mark and no solás. I'd be a worthless man indeed. They'll be drunk anyway. Wait for me here."

"I'm coming."

He would lose this fight. "Then leave your bow, put your dirk in your boot, and cover the blood."

She turned her cloak so the clasp sat on her shoulder, and hid her bow in a haystack. She looked like death walking, pale with dark circles under her eyes. The innkeep would likely think she was ill and throw them out.

He found a length of rope that would do as a makeshift scabbard for his shortsword. "Tie it on my back."

Lyl wrapped the rope over both his shoulders and slipped the blade through. When he put his cloak over it, the hilt rested just under his hood, the blade running down his spine. He tested his reach.

"We're minstrels," he said.

"Very dirty minstrels, with no instruments?"

"Beggars then."

"I have some coin. We won't beg," she said. "But I hope the men here don't know their king when they see him."

"Or perhaps we hope they do."

The common room held a dozen long tables crowded with farmers, slapping the boards for more ale and arguing over several games of hounds and hares. Nechtan found a bench that put their backs to the hearth, affording him a view of the whole room.

The innkeeper was a stout man covered in a pelt of greying hair that crawled up from his chest into his beard.

"Ale, if you please," Nechtan said. "And meat if you have it."

"You have the coin?"

Lyl produced a silver salmon.

The innkeeper snatched it from her and eyed them with suspicion. "For a silver salmon you'll be wanting the whole pig, or a room for the night, or both."

"Both," Nechtan said.

The three horsemen from Emlyn sat across the room, and in the middle, a boy pumped the bellows of smallpipes and worked at a merry tune. A single barmaid danced with a succession of men, weaving hand to hand through a line.

Lyl's elbow found Nechtan's ribs. "There." She nodded past the dancers.

Through the peat smoke he saw Elowen. She made her way through the tables to take a seat on a barrel beside the boy with the pipes.

As the boy finished his jig, Elowen worked the tuning pegs and readied the harp. It was then she saw Nechtan. Her eyes flashed from him to the horsemen.

The piper's tune done, Elowen's fingers moved expertly over the strings made of Nechtan's hair, the harp of the drowned maid. The sound seemed to come from somewhere inside his gut, but clearly, no one else felt it as he did. It awakened him. His senses sharpened. He could smell rancid fat from the kitchen, vinegar and apples on a man across the table, the smell of lovemaking on a young man farther down the bench, tannery lye on the other.

On the horsemen from Emlyn, he smelled blood.

Elowen plucked and his soul hummed like sun on water. The sound became him and with it, he understood why this second chance at living was a gift.

He smelled the coming rain that moved down from the mountains, and with it, Death.

Wake up, the boy cried from the harp strings.

"Not yet," Nechtan whispered.

One of the horsemen openly leered at Lyl from across the room. The tanner eyed Nechtan, his face going white. He whispered to the man beside him and they both got up from the table.

"You don't like our company?" Nechtan asked.

"I—I've work to tend to… sir," the man said.

Nechtan's look told Lyl that the tanner knew, and it would be moments before the others knew as well.

The innkeeper sloshed two tankards of ale before them. "I'll see about the meat," he said.

"Go to Elowen," Nechtan told Lyl. "Tell her to come along now. You two must be gone. I'll find you."

Lyleth got up and slipped between the dancers to the girl. She reached out to put a hand on Elowen's shoulder, but one of Fiach's horsemen took her by the wrist and pulled her onto his lap. He thrust his hips beneath her and laughed.

Elowen's eyes met Nechtan's. He got up and edged around the room toward the warriors' table.

The young piper took up Elowen's tune, The Bride of Darkmyre.

Lyl cozened the horseman, cooing to him and dandling his ears, moving his hands away from her breasts and his eyes away from Nechtan, who had almost reached them.

She tried to stand, but the man caught her wrist again and held it flat on the table, her mark exposed.

"Looka what I found," he crowed. "The dead king's solás. I hear the she-king pays a nice price for ye, she does."

Nechtan edged closer, alehorn in hand. The man who had hold of Lyl wore a red beard, his moustache braided with blue threads. The one beside him was too young to grow a beard and the third was an aging warrior. All three wore rusted mail hauberks and carried long-hafted riding axes on their backs. Nechtan barely had a shirt.

He stepped up behind the old warrior. When the young one met his eyes, Nechtan lifted his alehorn to him in a toast.

"Nechtan's solás, ya say? And I took her for a whore! But she's still mine." Nechtan wagged his fingers to hand her over.

The three men snorted yeasty laughs. "Four fifties in gold feathers and she's yours, beggar."

Elowen's eyes met Nechtan's once again and he thought he saw her smile. She got up from her barrel and took Lyl's hand and that of the redbeard and tried to pull them to their feet saying, "'Tis a dance tune. Come, come."

But redbeard tossed her to the floor and drew his axe.

Nechtan threw the tankard of ale in the young man's face. Before the old warrior could turn on the bench, Nechtan drew his shortsword and brought it down on the man's bare neck. The blade was dull, but cut deep enough.

Two axes came at Nechtan, but he upset the table between them. Redbeard tossed it aside and closed in on Nechtan, wielding the axe with some deftness, but a crowded room was no place for a long axe. Nechtan danced away and caught the axe haft with his sword, taking a splintered chunk from it.

The beardless boy raised his axe to attack from the other side, but Lyleth snatched his hair and drove the point of her dirk through his throat.

Redbeard tried to hook Nechtan's blade, catching it with the horn of his axehead and twisting. But Nechtan went with the motion and slid free. Redbeard only needed to land one blow to open Nechtan's chest. This must be over quickly.

Nechtan worked the warrior back, protecting his chest with his blade until redbeard's back was pressed against the hearth. It was then, in the firelight, the man's look said he knew it was Nechtan.

Redbeard saw a ghost and Nechtan saw his chance.

He hacked fast and short and the warrior's foot met the coals of the fire. He upset a pot of soup that rolled and splattered across the floor. Slipping in spilled soup, redbeard lunged desperately at Nechtan, who caught his arm in a downward slice that nearly severed his arm at the elbow.

Fiach's man fell to his knees, his eyes turned up to Nechtan.

"By stars and stone," the man muttered.

His axe arm dangled from shredded tendons. Nechtan raised the shortsword with both hands and drove the blade point down just above the collar of the man's mail hauberk.

Elowen stood just behind him, a meathook in her hands, ready to finish him if Nechtan failed.

In the far corner, the innkeeper stood frozen, the old warrior crawling toward him, and the beardless boy heaped on the floor at his feet.

The boy with the small pipes dropped his instrument. His jaw hung open and he muttered, "My lord king."

Nechtan's arms and chest were covered in blood. His breath came fast and he felt nothing but shame for the sweet pulse of life in his veins. Never in his last life had he shed the blood of his own. He crossed the room and finished the old horseman, then dropped the sword beside the dead man.

"I've opened a door that cannot be shut," he said to Lyleth. All he had left in this world stood before him, a bloody dirk in her trembling hand. He said softly, "So be it."

Chapter 15

Bronwyn's budget rental reeked of fake new car smell.

Merryn had sunk so low in the passenger seat that Connor could barely see the top of her head. He slid to the center of the back seat to find Bronwyn's eye in the rearview mirror. That eye looked so much like Dish's... and Connor could read it just as plainly. It told him Bronwyn was not too happy about taking her ninety-year-old aunt for a stroll on Malibu Beach.

The car spiraled down the hospital parking structure and Connor pointed the way to Ocean Drive. Bronwyn was explaining Dish's prognosis, clearly hiding the worst of it from Aunt Merryn. If Connor could see through Bronwyn's optimistic speech, he was sure Merryn could as well. The crux of it was that Dish's chance of coming out of the coma decreased exponentially by the day. Connor found himself hoping Merryn couldn't figure that part out. He needed to change the subject.

"This well Dish was looking for," Connor said, "what's so special about it?"

"The ancient Celts believed certain wells, life wells, were portals to the Otherworld," Aunt Merryn said. "When one dies in this world, the soul travels through a life well to be born again in the 'Land of Truth and Beauty.'"

"Why would Dish want to go to the land of the dead?"

"You misunderstand, lad." Merryn attempted to turn in the

bucket seat, to meet his eyes. Connor helped her by leaning between the front seats, his arms around the headrest.

"The well Hugh was looking for wasn't a life well," Merryn said, with a furtive glance at Bronwyn, "but a door through which an entire people crossed from that world to this one."

Bronwyn gave a mocking laugh. "Connor doesn't want to hear about this nonsense, auntie." Her tone was a shade away from a threat, meant for Connor, not Merryn, which made the questions in Connor bubble to the surface all the faster.

"Could a person go through one of these wells if he wasn't dead? Theoretically, I mean."

"There have been stories," Merryn said, "but—"

"But they're fairy tales," Bronwyn stated. "Nothing more."

"Yes, tales." Merryn gave her bony hands a flutter, as if to shoo away Bronwyn's stale reality. "Tales that disguise truth." Her bright eyes turned back to Connor. "Hugh studied these tales at Oxford, did you know?"

"No," Connor said.

"Ancient Irish and Welsh mythology. He compared them, looking for common elements that survived from pre-Christian times—"

"But it is possible," Connor said, "for a non-dead person to fall into a well and end up on the other side?"

"Not fall," Merryn said pointedly. "A person must be taken across."

"Taken? By who? What?"

The discussion was over as the parking lot appeared on the left. Connor instructed Bronwyn to find the closest spot, and once parked, followed her to the trunk of the car to retrieve Merryn's walker.

"Let's be done with this," Bronwyn said, struggling with the contraption until Connor helped. "You've excited Merryn and she's in a fragile state as it is. She loves Hugh very much and this wild conjecturing is more than she can take."

She was right. Once they got to the well, Connor would

show them. But he hadn't quite figured out how to get Merryn into the cave yet.

"It's not far," he said.

But the walker proved slower than Connor expected. The little wheels dug into the sand and he had to hold onto Merryn to prevent her from taking a header, and since he had only one good arm, it was a challenge. Bronwyn took the other side, and together, they steadied Merryn.

With every step, Bronwyn launched eye-daggers at him.

It seemed like hours passed before they approached the sandstone cliff. During frequent stops to catch her breath, Merryn talked about well guardians who prevented lookie-loos from taking a peek at fairy land. Dish had said something about a guardian that day on the beach.

With a determined stride, Merryn plowed forward.

The cliff loomed before them. But as they drew near, Connor saw no sunlight reflecting on water, just sand. He left Merryn and ran ahead. The cliff was exactly as he remembered, even the crack that ran up out of sight. This was the place. But the pool of water was gone. The sand had come in and covered the well like it had never been there.

He ran his hand over the warm stone as the two women crept closer.

"It was right here. Right where I'm standing. I swear I was behind this cliff with Dish." He slapped the smooth stone till his hands stung.

"Dish swam under this cliff!" he said, frantically scooping wet sand with his one good arm. "I swam under it."

Water welled and filled the hole faster than he could dig, until the sand fell in and filled it. "No. No, this can't be. I swear it was—it doesn't make sense."

"Shall we go?" Bronwyn's voice was stern, demanding. "I have an appointment with the neurologist in an hour."

"It's got to be here!" He dug faster.

Aunt Merryn appeared beside him. She took Connor's

hand between her gnarled ones and whispered, "It's moved, lad. 'Tis all."

Bronwyn barely slowed down when she pulled into the circular drive of St. Thom's, reminding Connor the insurance investigator would call soon. He had just opened his mouth to thank Aunt Merryn when Bronwyn sped off.

He had so many questions for Merryn. But it all made some weird sense now. Merryn had said it wasn't unusual for a well to dry up and be found miles away. The well on the beach had moved. To Ned's. And Connor could think of nothing else but going back there.

School hadn't let out yet, and Connor would be back before Brother Mike knew he was gone. He fell into an easy jog, past Ziegler's and up to the fire road.

Merryn said Dish had been looking for a well that led to some magical land. He must have had some kind of clue. You don't just go wandering the moors, or whatever they're called in England, looking for the door to the land of the dead. He must have uncovered something in all his studying of ancient stuff at Oxford. Connor must really be going crazy.

With no sign of the bees that had attacked the day before, he eased through the cactus and chain-link without injury. But when he stepped onto the deck, he took in the sight of the well, now nothing but a fishpond filled with rain water. It stank of rotting leaves and algae.

"That's impossible."

He took off his shoes and waded across; mud and goo squished up between his toes. He jumped up and down, got out, jumped back in, took a running start and nearly broke his ankles when they hit the concrete bottom. You have to be taken across. But who the hell had taken him? And who took Dish?

"Take me, damn it!"

He sat on the bottom, motionless. Water walkers left dimples on the surface.

Maybe the guardian, whatever that was, sensed Connor's hesitation. Did he really want to follow Dish to the Land of Truth and Beauty? Didn't the Greek gods get so bored with eternal perfection they started meddling in the dirty business of humans? You can only drink so much ambrosia, after all. But Connor remembered his brief glimpse of that Otherworld clearly. It was so... different. The sound, and the colors, and fire that sang...

He finally crawled out of the stinky water and followed an overgrown path to the veranda. The windows were all boarded up, so he tested each one in turn to find one that slid open like the lid of a secret box. Inside, the walls of what might have been the living room were covered with graffiti. Stubs of candles sat waxed to boards and upturned tin cans. The remains of a campfire occupied the middle of the tile floor, right there with all the broken glass, empty cans and faded rags. "Ned?"

His voice echoed just like it had in the cave. Maybe Ned was no more real than the well.

"Hey, Ned!"

"He's not here, asshole." The deep, Johnny Cash voice came from the belly of a dark hallway, and the sound of footsteps in broken glass said whoever it was, was coming this way. Connor decided not to find out if the guy was a zombie.

He was almost to the movie producer's house that marked the trailhead before he looked back to be sure no one followed.

Connor lifted the toilet lid, threw the pills in, and flushed. Twice a day. What a joke. He wished Brother Mike would just give him the whole bottle, but no, he might overdose. School policy. So, Bro Mike doled them out two at a time.

Being back in therapy with Dr. Adelman was like having weekly tea with Big Bird. The psychiatrist had reached a predictable conclusion—Connor was having a break with reality brought on by stress. Hence, the drugs. Connor wondered what it would be like to die of an antipsychotic drug overdose. Death by reality?

He had done his homework on the subject of wells and it looked like he wasn't the only one suffering a break with reality. He had searched websites that described everything from fairy wells to puck wells, goblin wells, and clootie wells where people left rags tied to trees, messages, "clooties," that carried their deepest desires to the old gods. At some wells, people tossed in models of body parts they wanted healed, and in ancient times, actual severed heads were thrown in for unknown reasons. Whole cities had been seen under the surface of several wells. There were wells that turned things to stone and wells that turned stones into people, wells where dragons slept, wells that hid magical cups or jewels or swords, wells that blessed, wells that cursed, wells that granted wishes and wells that granted visions. But no well opened, even on rare occasion, to allow a chosen doofus to cross over to the Fair Lands. One had to be taken, just as Merryn had said.

Connor had been flushing his meds for three days when Bronwyn called to arrange a meeting with the insurance investigator, Mr. Kline. Brother Mike thought it best for him to be there too, so they gathered in the dorm office. He called Connor's parents in for the inquisition, but only his mom showed up—twenty minutes late.

Mr. Kline asked a series of questions that all circled back to: "How fast were you travelling at the time of the accident?"

Connor's mother repeated the police report findings for the third time.

"Connor was driving his own car and the police on the scene found no indication of mechanical failure or negligence." She delivered her lines like she was on the witness stand or something. "Their report said he was travelling within the speed limit, which may have been too fast for the road conditions, but was within the law, and considering his inexperience, he couldn't be held liable. I think that covers it."

Kline turned to Connor and cleared his throat. "Were drugs or alcohol involved?"

"I'm pretty sure you've seen the lab report from the hospital," Connor said. "No."

"And where were you and Mr. Cavendish headed at the time?"

Now there was a question Connor hadn't considered before. Where were they going?

"I don't know. He had an errand to run."

"And a teacher would take a student with him? Ask him to drive even, to run this errand?"

Oh God, Kline thought Dish was molesting him or something.

"His car battery was dead," Connor said, making clear eye contact with Kline. "And yeah, I was on probation. Dish was my jailer, so to speak, so I was required to stick with him."

"But you don't know where you were going?"

"No." It wasn't until that moment that he realized how weird this sounded.

"Is there anything else you'd like to tell me?" Mr. Kline jotted furiously on his legal pad.

Connor looked at Bronwyn. He wanted to give her what she came for and Kline's question was like an open door. Connor stepped through.

"When the accident happened, we were arguing," he said.

Kline leaned on the table, making a steeple out of his fingers. "Arguing about what?"

Connor's heart doubled its pace. "About my brother."

"Your brother?" Kline asked.

His mom was out of her chair, her hands kneading his shoulders. "This really isn't something you need to share with Mr. Kline."

"Yes. It is. My brother died of an overdose a year ago.

I knew he was doing drugs. I knew, and I could have done something—"

"This has nothing to do with the accident, honey." Mom's face was too close, her eyes brimming with tears. "Don't," she whispered.

Connor rolled his chair back and stood up, clearing his view of Bronwyn.

"Dish thought he could fix me." He looked right into Bronwyn's eyes and willed all his regret to fall like rain on her heart. "I stepped on the gas..."

At their next meeting, Connor told Dr. Adelman the whole story of the well on the beach, how he fell through something that, at first, was a dirty fish pond but later became a hot tub, how he saw Dish, or a man he knew was Dish. Alive. Awake.

Connor walked out of Adelman's office with more pills.

When he got back from the shrink's office, he was supposed to go to class, but he'd convinced himself the only reason he didn't find the well was because it wasn't dusk when he went last time. Threshold of night. Dish said there was something magical about that time of day.

His dorm room stank of shoes and dust burned on the radiator. Across the quad, he heard the bell ring and knew a flood of kids would stream from classrooms in a few minutes. He locked his dorm room and headed down the hall, hesitating in front of room 21, Dish's room. He tried the door. Why did he think it would be unlocked?

Jogging across the quad, he tried to beat the navy-blue wave of inmates that streamed toward him.

"Hey, loser!" Iris called. "Wait up!"

The last thing he needed right now was a groping by the psycho bitch.

"Later, Iris," he called without looking back.

The trail was slippery with mud from the rain. Connor

fell a few times, sending spikes of pain through his broken collarbone. It took him longer than usual to reach the ridge where cactus grew over the trail.

Wet from the last night's rain, the flagstones of the pool deck looked almost new except for the cracks where the weeds poked through. The storm had stripped leaves from a nearby tree and scattered them over the fishpond. They dimpled the water like yellow river rafts and Connor knelt down to drag his fingers through them. The water was warm, and tendrils of steam rose between the leaves. A hot tub.

"Didn't I make it clear my pad is off limits, dude?" From the shadows of the veranda, Ned sloshed toward him in slippers and a dirty yellow bathrobe.

Connor bolted to his feet. "I just. I mean, I came by a few days ago and this thing was full of algae."

"So? What's it to you. Get the hell off my property before I call the cops."

Connor turned to go, but couldn't do it. Not without knowing why that fishpond was clean and hot. He turned on Ned.

"Basically, you're a squatter."

Ned stiffened and gave a theatrical look of shock. "Correction," he said. "This squatter saved your sorry ass from drowning. Now shoo, asshole."

"I should call the police."

Ned gave a phlegm-riddled laugh. "The police? Jesus H. Christ. So what is it you want from me, you blackmailing bastard?"

Connor wanted the well to open up and swallow him, he wanted to find Dish, to make him understand.

"I fell through this pool," he blurted to Ned, "and came up in a cave. I was taken across. By a well guardian."

"A well what?"

"I need to cross over. To the other side."

Ned's face folded into an origami scowl. He stood there

for a full minute, then reached into the pocket of his dirty robe, pulled out a joint and lit it. He flipped a switch buried in the shrubs and the tub frothed to life. Leaving his robe on the deck, he stepped in and sank to his neck, then took a drag.

"You're a crazy fuck, I'll give you that," he said with the tiny voice people do when they're holding in smoke. "But what do you want from me? You're holding me hostage here."

Connor paced around the hot tub, leaving a wet trail like a snail. What did he want from Ned?

"What did you mean when you said, 'He's a million miles away'?"

Ned looked up through a cloud of smoke. "What?"

"When I was here the other day, you said Dish was breathing and pissing, but his mind was a million miles away. What did you mean?"

Ned stared at him, his jaw slack. "Who the fuck is Dish?"

"My teacher, the one in a coma. The guy in the accident. You said you were there."

"Oh, yeah, yeah. Shit. Calm down. You're gonna pop a vein or something." Ned pressed his palms down over the water, the joint brown between his fingers. "I just meant there has to be someone still inside these guys who are in comas. I mean, it's like you're asleep for months or something. Dreaming about what? Ya know?"

"You think they dream?"

"Shit, I dunno, kid. Do I look like a psychologist? I mean his consciousness has got to still be somewhere."

"Yeah." Connor kept pacing. "He is somewhere. I just can't get there."

Connor looked out over the ocean where the sun was just setting. Threshold of night. This was it.

"Can you just—just turn it off?" Connor said. "And go back in the house, and come out just like you did last time?"

"What is this, some kind of weird role-playing therapy or something?"

"I just want to see if I can swim through again, that's all."

"Swim through what?"

"Please. It'll only take a few minutes."

"Then you'll leave." Ned stared Connor down.

"Yeah."

Ned sighed and hoisted himself out of the water, dripping and steaming. He flipped the bubble switch off, pulled on his robe and headed back toward the house, glancing over his shoulder a few times.

Connor took off his shoes and shirt, walked back to the fence and started running toward the pool. He didn't look, just ran right in like he did the first time. His feet hit the bottom and his head never even went under.

"Shit!"

Ned reappeared, looking down his hairy chest at Connor, the joint twitching between his lips. "You're a crazy fuck."

A desperate emptiness coursed through Connor.

It must have shown on his face, because Ned sighed, flipped on the bubbles and stepped back into the tub.

"I saw him." Connor found the concrete seat and let his legs be buoyed by the jets. "When I was in here, drowning or whatever. I saw him."

"You saw your teacher?"

"Yeah."

"People see all kinds of shit when they're knocked out—"

"I didn't hit my head. I wasn't drowning." It was the first time Connor had let himself admit it. It felt true.

"I beg to differ. But okay, let me hear your theory."

He passed the joint to Connor. Weed wouldn't help him sort out reality. "I see enough shit already. Thanks."

"Suit yourself."

"Before you pulled me out," Connor said, "I was in a pool of water, in a cave. And my teacher was there with a woman. And I finally know what I was seeing."

"And what was that exactly?"

Connor started to sweat, in the water. He reached over and took the joint from Ned and took a long drag that seared his lungs. He tried to hold it in, but coughed out plumes of the stuff. He had no idea it would hurt that bad.

Ned grinned. "Go on. You got me trembling with anticipation."

It came tumbling out, Dish's weird clothes, the pretty woman who was bleeding, Connor's hand passing right through Dish like he was a ghost. Ned listened with his caveman brows all knotted up and his mouth hanging open.

"I think Dish was supposed to die in that accident," Connor said. "And now a bunch of machines are keeping him alive."

"So, you just wandered into this guy Dish's dream? But if he died, he wouldn't be dreaming—"

"It was no dream. It was another world. It was as clear as you and me sitting here. Dish was looking for a well, his sister told me so. And he found it on the beach. Then bam, he's in a coma and the well on the beach is gone. Because it moved. Here. Right here." He pointed at the water around them.

Ned gave him a long, measured look, like he was calculating what he should say to prevent a hysterical breakdown.

"So… where is this well now?"

"That well on the beach was bait." Connor took another hit from Ned's joint. "And Dish took the bait. And now his soul is over there, but his body is trapped here. Just like you said. Besides, the woman told me to 'give him time.' She needs him."

A long silence was followed by Ned saying, "Okay. So who 'baited' this guy Dish? Tell me that."

Connor sighed. "I don't know."

"This might be a little off the Narnia topic," Ned said and exhaled a blue stream of smoke. "But where the fuck were you and teach going when you got whacked?"

"I have no idea."

Startled, Ned looked up at the darkening sky. "Friend of yours?"

Connor followed Ned's gaze to find Iris standing at the edge of the hot tub.

"Oh shit. No chance."

Connor was out of the hot tub faster than he thought possible. The thought of Iris seeing the pimples on his skinny shoulders sobered him up fast. He tried to pull his shirt over his wet skin with no success.

Oh god, she was taking off her clothes. How long had she been standing there?

"I want to hear everything," she said, and stepped into the hot tub with nothing on but her hot pink thong.

Chapter 16

Ava found Irjan in her chamber, a windowless room that had once been an armory. When she first arrived at Caer Ys, Irjan had chosen this room for its darkness. "The sunlight weakens my compounds," she'd said.

The small room was crammed with shelves of unguents, distillates, and rare roots, wings of birds and insects, powdered stone from across the sea, parts taken from badgers and whales, stinging flies and beetles, reindeer and men. From ceiling beams, bunches of herbs and seedpods hung above ochre and cinnabar, ash, lead and silver powder ordered in crocks against the wall. Ava had yet to learn the use of such things, but certainly, in those jars and vials lay the makings of a poison that could kill a king.

The room smelled like vitriol and dead things, but Ava still had the smell of Finlys' burning flesh in her nose. The fire had finally burned out, and the winds off the sea had taken the last of the greenman's smoke to the inland vales and peaks of Ys.

Irjan sat on a narrow cot, a small table before her cluttered with herbs and a mortar which she worked rhythmically.

"You must learn to guide him now," Irjan said.

"Must I?"

"You've tethered a man's soul to yours, my lady. This druí, Finlys, is bound to you far stronger than is your solás, and you must learn to command him before he commands you."

But Ava hadn't come for a lesson. Not this time. She'd come for truth.

Irjan stood and showed her palms, the bells on her hat singing a faint tune. She wore the garb of a shaman of the frozen wastes, a coat of reindeer pelt and a bright blue cap of the four winds. The spirits must recognize her as their taskmaster, servant as she was, of the Crooked One.

Irjan tapped the powder from her mortar into a horn vial and stirred it with a bone. "We have little time if we are to march north as you have commanded."

"Finlys cursed me with the truth before he died," Ava said. "I come to discover it. All of it. The old meadmonger, Dunla, said it was no festering wound that killed Nechtan. It was you."

Ava closed the space between them.

Irjan stopped stirring, a vague smirk playing at her lips. Ava peered into those small black eyes. Perhaps she'd been wrong to place so much trust in one who'd wedded the dead.

"The daughter of the Bear questions her own destiny," Irjan said.

Ava's father had taught her to trust no one, least of all those closest to you. She could still see Nechtan lying on his deathbed, the wound on his neck a stinking mass of corruption, and Irjan...

"You never touched the salve you used to dress his wound," Ava said. "You spread its poison over Nechtan's skin with a wooden butter knife. Then you wrapped it, so careful not to touch it."

"I did what I must to serve you—"

"Which one is it?" Ava ran her fingers over the racks of jars and horn vials.

"Your king had lost himself to drink and desire," Irjan said. "How long would it have been before your father saw Nechtan's weakness?"

"My father is not your concern. I am."

"Your husband shamed you—"

"Then it should have been my hand that took his life."

"Oh, dear one." Irjan gathered Ava in a motherly embrace, but Ava shook her off.

"It is not your destiny to shape mine, slave."

"Is it not?" Irjan said. "A king, even a she-king, who wears the stain of murder is not a king at all, but a tyrant. Would the gods have chosen a tyrant to lead these people? Would the guardian have given herself to your blade? No. I wear that stain. For you, my Iron Lamb."

The woman's brown lips quavered, her beetle-black eyes threatened to spill tears.

"Guards!" Ava called, and they appeared. "Take her."

Irjan looked over her shoulder, saying, "I offer you wings."

Ava didn't sleep that night. The truth of Irjan's words settled like a gentle snow. If Irjan had not intervened, Nechtan would have sunk deeper in the mire of shame he'd dug, and yes, the Bear would have come to deliver him of his weakness. Ava's father would own this land now, and he would have married Ava to one of his thegns. No, Nechtan's drunken spectacle at the Midwinter revel was a dagger he plunged into his own belly.

The Bear had sent Irjan to open Ava's womb to Nechtan's seed, but in this, she had failed. It was a judgment from the gods, for the offspring of such a man would grow into such a weakling as his sire. It was for the best that her babes were born dead.

The fertility spell had been cast in Irjan's musty chamber. It was Ava's first glimpse of the power Irjan offered. That night, Ava had told Nechtan she was meeting with the seamstress.

Once in Irjan's chamber, she stripped and lay on the stone floor. A black hen pecked around her head while Irjan held the hen's egg cradled in her outstretched palms. She chanted in a language unknown to Ava, until her eyes were as savage as a wolf's. She danced with the egg, miming the act of copulation, led by some lecherous spirit. She tore at her shift, her tongue wagged and slaver ran from the corners of her mouth.

The egg was as hot as a coal when Irjan's calloused hand pushed it between Ava's legs.

She lay frozen as Irjan took the hen by the neck and, in one motion, struck off its head. The body ran, flopping, around the room, falling over Ava, scratching her with its talons. When the thing finally fell dead beside her, Irjan picked up the body and sprinkled the blood on Ava's breasts and belly. Still chanting, she drew symbols on her flesh with the bird's blood, and instructed Ava to sit up. She cracked the egg into Ava's cupped palms and bid her eat it.

She did.

Irjan instructed Ava to rouse Nechtan from sleep and mount him. That night, she would command his desires.

She did.

She felt a new power coursing through her. She demanded and Nechtan's body obeyed. It was the first time she'd felt sweet release spread through her, spilling as he did into her belly. Throughout that night, she'd only wanted more of him and he didn't deny her. Whatever magic Irjan had worked, Ava greedily reaped the rewards.

Nechtan planted a child in her that night that grew for longer than the others before Ava expelled it into a bloody bed. It was a boy. Nechtan's child was too small to live in this world, yet his fingers were formed, his body perfect, like one of the Asrai.

Nechtan was away when she lost that child, settling a dispute between cattle lords in Emlyn. She kept the babe in an empty butter crock where it dried. Upon his return, she dropped the thing in his lap at supper.

"Your son," she told him.

She could forgive him for not loving her, for love is not a wife's right, but Nechtan brought her shame and disgrace that Midwinter night.

Within one turn of the moon, Nechtan was as dead as his babes.

Ava pulled open the shutters of her bedchamber and watched the sky brighten over the eastern mountains. What if the Bear knew of Ava's crowning? Of Cedewain's rebellion? Would her father risk a late autumn crossing of the Broken Sea to lay claim to the spoils of Ava's efforts?

She accepted the truth. She had traded Nechtan's life for his throne. Now she had to find a way to hold it.

She called her guards. "Bring Irjan to her chamber, where I shall await her."

Irjan was smiling when they brought her in, as if she'd been smiling all night. Ava dismissed the guards and closed the chamber door, throwing the latch.

"Teach me," Ava demanded.

Irjan showed her palms and moved to pull the cot away from the corner. Ava helped. Behind a stack of crockery, Irjan revealed a hole in the stone wall, large enough for a wolfhound to pass through.

"What's this?"

"In ancient days," Irjan explained, "the outer wards were yet unbuilt, the keep more vulnerable. This armory door could be barred from inside, and the weapons could be taken out through here." She pointed at the hole in the wall.

"What we do, we do in secret?"

"When you fly," Irjan said, "the body you leave behind is as fragile as a babe. You must be protected. I must always watch over you."

Irjan had taught Ava to use herbs that loosen the shackles of the flesh and allow the soul to roam free. But without a strong command of the self, one could be lost in the wasteland between worlds. It frightened Ava at first, but now she only wanted to see more.

Irjan lit a rushlight, got on her knees and crawled through the hole in the wall. Ava followed.

Inside, a narrow chamber opened onto a dark passageway that vanished between the walls of the inner keep. Irjan had placed a straw mattress on the dusty floor. Ava spread her cloak, stepped out of her gown, and lay down on her side. Irjan bound her wrists behind her with a sinew cord, then wrapped the other end around Ava's neck.

"This noose will keep your soul bound to your body," Irjan said, "for if the cord is broken, your soul will have no need to return, it will cross the water and leave this body behind."

Irjan uncorked a vial and dipped a hollow bird bone into the tincture. This she dripped into Ava's eyes, all the while intoning the summoning of that which was bound, the soul of the greenman, Finlys.

Ages ago, the seed of the self was stripped from some forgotten flower; the husk of petals and pollen carried by a north wind to meet the sea. How long could Ava ride the currents of this cold deep? How long could she imagine herself into life? Waiting until the slow drifts of sleep washed her up on a beach of fertile soil only to become a flower once again.

"Just a flower," Ava said to the darkness.

Her voice came from some other where, not from her lips but from her fingertips maybe. Her voice lay on the floor with her body, drooling and convulsing. She slipped into the defiant skin of the red crow, its feathers singed and stinking of burnt flesh. She laughed at Finlys, and flew far away into the dawn and the vale of Elfael.

She would find them.

Chapter 17

Lyleth felt dull tugging at the skin below her collarbone. With effort, she opened her eyes. A sphere of candlelight warmed the room. Then everything started spinning, until Nechtan's face appeared. Oh, yes... he was sewing her soul's cloak back on. She remembered now. She remembered driving her dirk into the neck of a young man from Emlyn, remembered the despair in Nechtan's eyes.

Elowen's face appeared beside Nechtan's.

"Pour the steeped herbs first." Elowen handed Nechtan a pot over his shoulder. "Don't stitch too deep, deadman."

"I've sewn more men together than you've known in your life, lass. Now leave me be."

Wearing a pout, Elowen's face vanished.

Lyleth summoned all her strength and clutched Nechtan's wrist. "There's no time for this." The words were thick on her tongue. "Go."

He peeled her fingers away and went back to work. "Close your eyes and shut up."

A strong aroma of poplar buds and juniper berries wafted from the concoction he poured over her wounds. This she felt, but only distantly. They must have given her sweet wine or maybe henbane. She spun back into numbness, tried to speak, but only her mind said the words, over and over. She could hear the thread pulling through skin, could see Nechtan's hands working the needle.

"Not to be unmade," she heard herself say.

He met her eyes for a long moment, the needle poised in bloody fingers.

"Not to be unmade," he echoed.

Against her will, her eyes closed.

It wasn't the words of their binding vow that convinced her, it was the voice that spoke them. She had refused to allow herself to believe it until now. With or without the king's mark, this man could be no one else but Nechtan. And she had called him back from the dead to kill his own countrymen. Could anything be more heartless? Floating in this painless fog, she admitted, if only to herself, that she had brought Nechtan back to hurt him the way he had hurt her, and today was only the beginning. But he had no memory of those last days. It's hard to punish a man who has no memory of his sin.

Through the narrow slivers of her eyes, she watched him, his brow furrowed in concentration as he pulled and knotted her back together.

This wasn't the man who so wronged her. No, she had raised to life the man she knew long ago, the man who asked her to bind her life to his so they might lead a kingdom together, the man who once ruled the vast wasteland of her heart.

She couldn't hold her eyes open any longer, and fell back down that well of body-less peace.

Was she dreaming? Or remembering? Nechtan took her hands and leaned close, his breath warm on her neck.

"I don't know who I am anymore," he whispered. "Stay with me."

When she forced her eyes open, the spinning of the room had slowed and a single candle began to gutter out on the bedside table. Thinking she was alone, she tried to sit up and saw him slumped beside her, his arm draped over her legs. Asleep. She let her fingers stroke his hair.

"Not to be unmade," she whispered.

Dawn poked through cracks in the wattle and daub. Chickens hunted insects in the thatch overhead, sending faint drifts of dust through shafts of sunlight. She was in the inn by the river, Lyleth reminded herself. The crackling burn of her skin had gone, and a blessed cool filled her.

She sat up, the stitches pulling taut. Was it dawn? No, it was dusk, it must be. She had slept through the day and she was alone. She hoped Nechtan had fled for it wouldn't be long before Fiach missed the men he'd sent here, and he would certainly send more. Many more.

She made her way to the staircase that led to the common room. Voices and the smell of fresh bread met her as, peering over the splintered handrail, she saw Elowen and the boy who had been playing at the smallpipes the night before. A game of hounds and hares sat between them, the boy deep in thought over his next move.

"You cheat," he said.

"I do not cheat. I'm jus' smarter 'an you's all. 'Tis not hard."

As if sensing her presence, Elowen looked up and gave Lyleth a toothy grin.

"You're back," the girl said.

The boy shot to his feet, and taking the stairs two at once, appeared at Lyleth's side, offering his arm.

"Lady," he said, "I'm Dylan, at your service."

"Tell me, Dylan, where is Nechtan?"

"Seeing to the—"

"The dead. He should be gone from here."

She took the boy's arm, still feeling weak as a babe.

"He's jus' been waiting for you to waken. He tol' me to tell ye that he'll be back soon. I'm to see to your comforts."

"Where's the innkeep?"

"Gone to help me lord king. What might I bring ye, lady?"

"The bread smells grand. Have you apples?"

"Oh aye, sweet as light, our apples."

They'd reached the bottom stair. "Milk, as well, if you have it."

"I'll fetch it fresh."

"Thank you."

Dylan disappeared into the kitchen and Lyleth took the bench across from Elowen. The game pieces were indeed positioned for Elowen's red hounds to make the killing move.

"Nechtan should have fled at first light," Lyleth said.

"The deadman won't leave you, druí, ye must know that. He makes ready to go by night."

It was true, darkness would allow them to cross the plain unseen. Perhaps it was best. And they'd have horses; Fiach's men had no use for theirs now. But what must be done with this girl? Take her with them? Leave her here with the innkeeper and the boy?

"You're a greenwood babe," Lyleth said to Elowen, remembering their conversation by the well. The girl was born with more than ordinary instincts, like Lyleth, like all greenmen. "You should be schooling in a hive."

"It suits me poorly." Elowen snuffed as if she smelled something foul. "All that poesy and practice. Bending the knee to gods who care not for me, nor for no one else."

"That's why you live by the offerings left at the wells. You ran away."

"You'd 'ave run too if you weren't so dutiful," Elowen said, crossing her arms.

"And when you got back to your family, what did they do?" Lyleth knew the answer, but she wondered if Elowen had even tried to return home when she fled her school.

"Shut the door on me, they did. Said they knew me not."

Lyleth searched the child's face for the hurt, but she knew Elowen had scrubbed that hurt away as she must.

If Lyleth had left Dechtire's hive and tried to make her way home, the same fate would have faced her. The get of

May Eve revels belonged to the greenmen. Withholding a child would bring the curse of the green gods and no father or mother would call such as this down upon themselves. Instead, the chieftain paid them a yearly blood price in lambs or calves just as he would if he had slain their child with his own hands. Greenwood babes belonged to the land.

"I might have stayed," Elowen said, "if I could study with the great Dechtire, like you've done. 'Tis true, you studied with her?"

"Aye, so I did."

"They say she makes stones speak."

Lyleth smiled. "In a way, aye."

"And she reads the future in the spinning of clouds."

"Dechtire sees with the eye of leaf and stone," Lyleth explained. "You can see much when you rid your heart of desire."

"Become a tattered rag, blowin' about in the wind? Nay, not I."

Lyleth smiled. "You captain your own ship. How envious I am."

Elowen returned the smile.

There was no mothering on the Isle of Glass, only lessons. It wasn't that Dechtire treated her students badly; in fact, Lyleth had been favored by her teacher. No, Dechtire scoured one's soul that it might be filled with the will of the gods, as indifferent to the passions of men as star and stone. But Lyleth longed for her frailties.

"'Tis your loyalty that bleeds you dry, druí," Elowen said, moving a red hound on the game board to take Dylan's last hare. "Like a rabbit in a wolfhound's mouth, ye are."

Elowen snapped up the wooden piece and held it out.

Lyleth took it and turned it over in her hand. Stiffly carved, its ears whittled to long sharp points, its two eyes burnt out by a hot nail. As bloodless as the dead.

"Perhaps so," Lyleth said.

Dylan appeared from the kitchen with a loaf of bread, a pitcher of warm milk and three small apples.

"My thanks," Lyleth said. "Dylan, my lord might have need of another pair of hands. Will you see to it?"

The boy brightened, tripping over his feet on the way to the door. "As you command, lady." And he was gone.

Butter fat floated in yellow spheres on the warm milk. Lyleth poured a cup for herself and Elowen, who broke off a chunk of bread and soaked up the milk with it. The apple was indeed sweet.

"What will you do," Elowen asked, "when Marchlew finds the king has no mark?"

Lyleth stopped chewing. "I don't know."

Elowen popped the sops in her mouth and mumbled on, "You thought you raised a king from the dead, but instead, ye raised just a man."

The melody of truth is hard to ignore.

"Aye," she said at last, "so I did."

"Which one owns your devotions, druí? The man or the king?"

The door burst open and Dylan reappeared, his arms heaped with mail. He dropped it beside the table, and announced, "My lord comes."

Nechtan came through the door, followed by the innkeeper. "We'll need four days' food and clean linen for bandages," he was saying.

"Aye, my lord."

When Nechtan saw Lyleth, his face bloomed with relief.

"But before you do," Nechtan told the innkeeper, "bring a pitcher of ale and sit with me and my solás."

"Sit with you, my lord?"

"I'm no ghost. Drink with me."

Nechtan took the bench beside Elowen and dropped a pair of cracked sharkskin bracers on the table. His eyes never left Lyleth's.

"If you please, Lyl." He held out his arm and she fitted the rough sharkskin around his wrist and began to lace it.

"See to the horses, lass," Nechtan said to Elowen. "We need blankets as well as food, enough for you if you think to come with us. You eat as much as the plow horse."

Elowen scowled, and stomped toward the door.

"You'll take her with us?"

"She knows." He tapped his right wrist. "She'll find a place in Cedewain. Marchlew will see to that."

"If we reach Cedewain," Lyleth said.

Nechtan had replaced the rags Lyleth had brought for him with the redbeard's clothes. The gambeson was stained with the man's blood, but fit Nechtan well enough if a bit tight.

"We must be gone," she said, and finished the lacing.

"With darkness." His eyes were a storm of confusion. She couldn't blame him if the trust he once placed in her had worn thin.

The innkeeper arrived with ale and three drinking horns.

"Sit," Nechtan told him.

The man crept to the bench beside Lyleth and sat like he might take flight any moment.

"Your son?" Nechtan motioned to the lad who worked at mopping up the remains of last night's soup and the blood mixed with it.

"Oh, nay. He's 'prenticed here, seeing I have none of me own." The innkeeper swallowed and worked his empty hands into a knot.

"Where's he from?" Nechtan asked.

"The lad? Oh…" The innkeeper lowered his voice, "from the Silver Marches. His own kin slaughtered by the ice-born, and he, no more than a cricket then. Hid in a grain bin, he did. Or he'd be slave to 'em now."

Nechtan poured a horn of ale and set it before the man.

"I don't expect you to keep silent about what happened here," he said. "I expect you to speak truth."

"Truth, aye, 'tis all I'm able, me lord." His eyes were two blue coins, fixed on Nechtan.

Lyleth knew as well as Nechtan that when you want to know something, ask an innkeeper. No better information could be bought for gold feathers.

"Ava has called up the men of Elfael and Ys?" Nechtan asked.

"That she does, my lord, at least four hundred men of Elfael march to meet her forces, and with those of Fiach and Lloyd, oh, thrice that or more."

"She marches north?"

"So they say."

"Have any of the chieftains of Elfael refused her?"

"Refuse? Ho, I think not, my lord. They've pledged their blood to her." The innkeeper took a deep swallow of the ale, licked foam from his thick lips, and leaned close over the table as if there might be spies in the empty room. "Marchlew offered his son in marriage to Ava in trade for his loyalty," the innkeep whispered. "To spare bloodshed, is what Marchlew was after, they say. I says aye, to spare his own bloodshed."

Incredulous, Nechtan said, "Ava wed my nephew? And what did she say to that?"

The innkeeper grew stony. "She gave him her answer, aye. She pulled Marchlew's greenman apart, she did, legs and arms, then tossed him on the fire, his soul taking flight as a bird, they say."

"She executed Marchlew's druí?" Lyleth said.

"Worse than execute. 'Tis the way of the ice-born to make death a gift. That she did."

"Ava wants this fight," Lyleth said. The realization frightened her. "She's baiting Marchlew."

"Then we must reach him before she does," Nechtan said.

"Before the Bear beaches his longboats to join her," Lyleth said.

"Might I ask you one thing, me lord," the innkeep said with a timid dance of his eyebrows.

"Of course."

The innkeep licked his lips, twice. "How is it you were dead, me lord, and now alive?"

It was Nechtan's turn to lean conspiratorially across the table. "The green gods saw fit to call me back from the land of the dead. For one reason alone. The Bear comes for the throne of the Five Quarters. I'm here to stop him."

Chapter 18

It would soon be dark. Nechtan figured it would take two nights to reach the mountains that bordered the plain of Elfael, longer if Lyleth tired easily. Now that she was stitched up, he could only hope the plaster she had used so many times on him would be effective—pine sap, wine and silver powder. Finding silver powder proved a challenge, and he resorted to having the local smith grind down two silver salmons from Lyl's money pouch.

Regardless of Lyl's condition, they must be gone.

Darkness would have to protect them across the open fields of Elfael, for Ava would have marched north by now, and she and Fiach would snap at Nechtan's heels all the way to Cedewain.

"My lord. I cleaned the armor like you tol' me. 'Tis there." Dylan nodded at a pile of mail and weapons on the floor by the hearth. "I dunno how to put an edge on a blade, I fear."

"Then it's time you learn. Bring a whetstone and some wool grease. We haven't much time."

"Aye, my lord."

Something about this lad haunted Nechtan. He resembled the boy in his dreams. Close in age, sandy-haired and coltish, but mostly, it was the timbre of their voices. Could Nechtan's dreams be not of the Otherworld, but of this boy? The thought nagged him.

Dylan returned with a whetstone and grease and Nechtan took a stool by the fire. The horsemen's axes were well made, and balanced as are axes for mounted combat. With deep horns and long curved hafts, they offered weight and a long reach. Sharpened, they would make a better choice for battle than the shortsword. He would put an edge on that, too.

"The angle is the most important thing," he told Dylan.

"Aye, my lord." The boy licked his lips, his eyes never leaving the stone and blade. "What's the grease for?"

"You don't want your blades to rust, now, do you? When it's sharp as winter, then you rub some grease in. Here, you try."

The boy took the axe and stone and roughed up a ragged burr. Nechtan showed him how to smooth it. But the boy's eyes found Nechtan's.

"You need a squire, my lord. I can keep your blades sharp, your mail clean—jus' let me come with ye."

"I ride to war, lad."

"I'm old enough. I can fight."

Would the dreams stop if he took the lad with him? Could Dylan possibly survive the days to come? Was he meant to?

"Besides, the lass rides with ye, she tol' me so. If she can go—"

"Why do you want to come with me? Tell me the truth." Nechtan studied the boy's coppery eyes.

Dylan licked his lips and worked at finding words. "I dreamt you would come, and here you are." He seemed to be measuring Nechtan's response, clearly waiting for laughter.

"Go on."

"I dreamt it over and over. In some dreams you'd be nary but a corpse what's lost half its skin, but fight on ye did. Slayin' scores before ye. Then, in other dreams... well, you'd be you. Just like ye are now. Sittin' here in this very room. But last night, t'was different."

The lad's eyes flitted away.

"Different, how?"

"You slept, like one of the dreaming kings of old. But instead of being laid out in your barrow, ye were in a gleaming room of frosty light. Pale as the linens, ye were. Sleepin'."

"Go on." A chill passed over Nechtan, raising the hair on his arms.

"I touched yer hand. 'Twas cold as a dead man's. And on your wrist, I saw the mark of the king. Your water horse. It moved and twisted, a'slitherin' up your arm, then 'round 'bout yer neck."

"And then?"

"Then I woke up to the wind playin' at me shutter."

Nechtan was frozen. This lad had seen into his dreams, seen him laid out for a wake in that cold white room built for death. And everyone there waited. For what? Dylan could not be the boy from the pool. He was no ghost, nor was he raised back to life by a druí. Why would this boy dream the same dream?

"Ready your things, lad. And don't make me come after you." Even those words felt like he'd said them before.

Dylan was on his feet, the axe a forgotten task. "Aye, my lord. You'll not regret this."

"I'm certain I won't." Nechtan forced a smile.

They rode out under a setting crescent moon, Lyleth behind Nechtan on the plow horse, her arms wrapped around his waist, her grip weak.

"You don't let go," he said to her. "Not for anything."

"Never."

The warmth of her body was already seeping through the cold mail, through his gambeson, and her breath warmed his neck.

Elowen rode one of the dead men's horses, and Dylan ponied a third that would be Lyl's mount as soon as she was strong enough. Trailing them all was the little horse, Brixia. Her fancy for the plow horse hadn't flagged, and she dashed after them once she realized they were riding out.

Dylan was already proving useful. Three rivers drained the mountains surrounding the vale, tracing watery barriers across the land. Dylan knew the bridges, but most importantly, he knew the fords and ferry tows that Ava's men wouldn't, those used by farmers and huntsmen.

After the moon set, Dylan lit a shepherd's lantern, a cone made of tin punched through with a design of stars all around. The metal cone slid down over a fat candle, and the lamp spilled yellow light in the shape of dancing stars over the ground of oat stubble and stones. It gave them just enough light to avoid badger holes and rocky outcrops. The wind that gathered force and slapped at their backs had no power over the lantern; it just whistled through the holes in the tin like breath through Dylan's small pipes.

Nechtan pulled his hood closer against the wind and Lyleth's hair came with it, for she rested her head on his shoulder. He laced her arms around him more tightly.

They trekked northward, through fields of harvested oat, barley and flax, through apple orchards and sheep pastures. Dawn found them in the hollows of a rugged heath. The birds were awake, and a flock of larks erupted from a stand of gorse, spooking the horses. The birds rolled over them like one great creature.

A dolmen provided the only cover from day. Three giant upright stones held a long, flat slab of blue granite. It was the skeleton of what had once been a barrow of men more ancient even than the Old Blood, men whose name had been lost with their bones and their songs and their tongue. It would be no different for the Ildana. Someday, their barrows would be looted, their blood mingled with that of an invader. If Lyleth was right, that day was coming soon.

She was asleep, her arms limp around his waist.

"It's day," he told her softly. She woke with a start, and he helped her down from the horse.

"Hobble the horses where there's some forage," he told Dylan.

"As you say, my lord." The boy strung the horses along behind him.

Elowen had already found a brambleberry patch. "The birds missed lots o' them!"

"Save some for us," Nechtan called back.

He climbed to the top of the dolmen and scanned the countryside, warming with dawn. They were more than halfway across the vale. To the north, the black woods of the Pendynas Mountains fell like a dark curtain. To the south, the nearest holding was a black spot in the distance that sprouted smoke from a morning fire.

He jumped down and found Lyleth with her back pressed to one of the old stones, her face to the rising sun.

"It's good to live," she said. "Thank you."

He sat down beside her. The stone felt colder on his back after the warmth of her body. "How many times have you sewed me back together?"

The smile she gave him was none he'd ever seen on her before, something between wonder and bewilderment.

"What is it, Lyl?"

"I know now."

"What do you know?"

"You're the boy I knew on the Isle of Glass—the man I was bound to." She proclaimed it like a judgment.

She was talking nonsense. He touched her cheek, checking for fever, and found none.

"You're as full of life as you once were," she said. "Full of truth, strength of will... love." She looked into him with resolve. "I've missed you, my lord."

His heart must have stopped. His face went hot and his tongue fell mute.

"When I lost you," he finally said, "it was like losing my legs."

He wanted to touch her, hold her, but a cold wall lay between them.

"The last thing I remember," he said, "is watching you ride away from me. I need to know why. Tell me."

She faced him squarely, her legs tucked under her.

Her look said that whatever it was would change everything between them. But he needed a chance to set it right.

"I must remember everything," he said. "You told me so yourself. Everything."

She took his hands as she had so many times. She could feel his thoughts this way, a tool of the greenmen. But this time, it wasn't his thoughts she felt for, she let her own flow through her hands and into his mind. Images flared, a landscape lit by lightning flashes.

"I took a lover—" she said.

"Fiach." He completed her thoughts.

Those simple words painted the scene in his mind's eye. "You have the right to take whomever you wish—"

"He came often to Caer Ys," she said. Her voice was even, controlled, as if she'd rehearsed the words. "Fiach was more to you than a chieftain under your protection. He might have been your friend if not for that night."

Her brow furrowed, her eyes brimmed with tears.

"It was Midwinter last," he said for her, seeing it all take form in his mind.

He couldn't meet her eyes any longer, so he watched the sun rise, and with it, the scene he'd forgotten.

"I sit in the revel hall at Caer Ys," he said, "at one end of a crowded table. I can't see anyone but you. And Fiach."

He let go of her hands and dragged his palms down his face. "I was drunk. Oh, Lyl, I remember."

She took his hands again and trapped his eyes with her own.

It was as clear as if it was yesterday. He watched her and Fiach at supper, the way he stole touches—his fingers to her lips, her cheek, her hair. The way he looked at her.

Late that night, Nechtan ordered Ava to her chamber and ordered the guards away from Lyl's door. He took up their post, until he slid down the wall to the cold flagstones, his back against her closed door. The rest of the castle slept. And Nechtan poured more ale down his throat and listened to Fiach make love to Lyl.

They were both asleep when he burst through the door and staggered to her bed. He remembered his fists beating Fiach's face, Lyl screaming. He drove Fiach from the room, naked, at the point of a sword.

He wanted her more than life. And that was what it had cost him, his life, and so much more. It had cost him Lyleth.

He held her down on the bed, fumbling and stupid. He could still feel the tip of her dirk cutting into his cheek; feel her breath coming in fast spurts beneath him.

"I am your solás, my lord! Give me your respect or your life. Which will it be?"

He had wanted her to drive that dirk into his brain. In that moment, he understood he was already dead long before Ava sent him on his way to the Otherworld.

"Grant me your mercy, solás," he'd said to Lyl that night. He repeated the words now. "For I am a lost man."

She had pushed him away, wrapped a blanket around herself, and left him in her bed to drown in the spreading pool of his shame.

Her grip tightened on his hands, her knees met his, just as they used to sit in the bottom of the coracle when they were children, fishing for perch on the Broken Sea. A deep silence stopped time, and he felt much more than warmth flow from her hands to his.

"I called you back to make you suffer the way I've suffered since that night," she said at last. "I wanted you to pay, Nechtan, not with blood but with a will to protect this land we're bound to. But, instead of that tormented king, I woke just a man. The man who knows me as I know him. The man who keeps no secrets from me, nor I from him. The man I once lived to serve as solás and friend."

He looked from the expanse of warming heath back to her eyes. Tears spilled down her cheeks. She turned his wrist up, covered now by a bracer, and dragged her fingers over the rough sharkskin, then over his open palm.

"That's why you have no mark."

His hand closed on hers and he held on tightly. Tears clouded his eyes when Elowen appeared from around the standing stones like a sprite, her face a purple stain. She held out a hand full of fat brambleberries.

"There's more," she said.

Lyleth took one, put it in Nechtan's mouth, and her trembling fingers lingered there.

Under the cool roof of the dolmen, Nechtan watched the others sleep. Clouds streamed from the north, joining hands and breaking again, curling and dissipating like souls in flight. Nothing moved on the horizon but a stag that sniffed the air, and sprang off through the gorse. Though the air was cold, needles of sunlight pricked his skin until he started to sweat. He wondered at this body he wore. He wondered at the wrath that had driven Lyleth to clothe him in it. He could feel nothing but gratitude for the chance to set things right between them, but how to right something so terribly wrong?

The boy on the other side would wake him soon, and the gods would set the cogs of their wheel back in place.

It was nearly midday when he could no longer keep his eyes open, so he roused Dylan to take his place.

"Keep your eyes on the horizon. Wake me if you see anything."

"Aye, my lord."

The shadows beneath the dolmen were icy cold. Nechtan lay down beside Lyl and Elowen. The child was clinging to her, snuggled close so their foreheads touched, their breathing measured and melodic.

He pulled his cloak close and watched them sleep until his breathing matched theirs, until he dreamed of a sea strand where he ran and ran and ran. The boy was there, too, running beside him and smiling. He had a book in his hand, open as he ran. The book was bound in white birch bark, and the pages were green leaves. The lad held it out as if to show him something. From the book, vines sprouted and grew, tangled and knotted to form a water horse, armored in fluttering leaves, its eyes two blazing golden tansy blooms. From the air above the book, it wound around Nechtan's right arm.

He woke with a start, his hand on his dagger hilt. He looked into Dylan's face and for a moment, he thought he still dreamed, thought it was the face of the boy on the other side.

"'Tis nearing dusk, my lord."

He sat up, rubbing the sleep from his eyes, then climbed out from under the stones to see the sun floating near the western horizon. Lyleth was awake and handed him a portion of bread and cheese.

"Your color's come back," he told her. He took a bite of the hard cheese.

"I'm stronger." She smiled.

Nechtan looked up at a rasping sound coming from the capstone of the dolmen. A crow sat fretting its beak on the rock, as birds will. Its black eye met Nechtan's. Its tongue throbbed with the rhythm of its panting.

"Been here for some time," Dylan said, "looking for our bread scraps, likely. Never seen a crow that color. Red like wine from Cadurques."

It hopped to the edge of the stone, its gaze locked on Nechtan as he took a seat on a rock. He broke off a chunk of bread and tossed it up to the bird. It made no move to take it,

Terry Madden

but continued to stare at him, its head cocked. He shooed the thing away, but it just hopped to the other side of the stone. With one last look, it took flight, its wings the color of embers.

Lyleth appeared beside him, watching the bird fly into the evening.

"What is it?" he asked her.

"We must go. Now."

Stars blistered the night. Lyleth had enough strength to ride alone, so they moved as fast as the little lantern would allow. Darkness had fully claimed the land when Nechtan saw the distant flicker of torchlight behind them.

"How far to the river?" he asked Dylan. It was the last to be crossed before they reached the safety of the woods.

"Perhaps a league, but—" Dylan saw the torchlight too. "By stars and stones."

"Take us there. Quickly."

Dylan led the way over uneven, shadowy ground until they reached a bluff that overlooked a black snake of water, winding between swells of earth.

Lyleth rode up beside Nechtan.

"We won't make it across the tow," she said.

"Indeed."

She caught his arm, the horses' warmth filling the space between them.

"You and Dylan go on," she said.

"I go nowhere without you."

"I didn't risk my soul's peace so Ava can kill you again. Ride to Cedewain. Then come back, and cut her down."

"Lyl—"

She pushed her horse close, their legs pressed between two sweaty hides.

"I'll ask nothing else of you, my lord, not in this life or the next."

176

Her hand slid softly around his neck, and she pulled him to her. Her kiss tasted of blackberries, and of forgiveness.

"Hurry," she said.

Then she was gone.

Chapter 19

From school, Iris had followed Connor through the trails all the way to Ned's house and from what Connor could tell she'd heard everything, from Dish's search for the well to Connor's trip to the other side.

"Jesus, Iris, now you're a stalker." Water streamed from Connor's shorts and he shivered. He had one wet arm through his T-shirt and was stuck.

"Dish's soul is in the Otherworld," she said with that perpetual heavy metal rasp. "That is so awesome."

The candy skull tattoo over Iris' left breast couldn't have been more distracting. She sank into the hot tub beside Ned and draped her arms over the edge, her little boobs bouncing in the jets.

"I always knew there was something special about Dish." She eyed the joint in Ned's hand expectantly. "Mind if I have a hit?"

Ned was frozen. He finally handed it over to her.

Iris took a drag. "Who was the chick you saw with Dish?"

"How am I supposed to know?" Connor had succeeded in pulling on his shirt and was lacing his shoes.

"When I went to visit Dish in the hospital," she said, "I saw the tattoo and knew something weird was up. Dish would never get a tat. His ass is way too tight for something like that."

"Good for you, Iris." Connor squished toward the trail.

"You should really leave Ned alone. He doesn't deserve this. Sorry, Ned."

"Everybody just get the hell out of my hot tub. Pretty soon I'll have the whole school over here on a weed field trip. Shoo!" Ned rose out of the water, offering Iris the full glory of his naked form.

She didn't flinch as she said, "No problem. Thanks for your hospitality, douche bag."

For some reason, Brother Mike believed socializing meant watching a bunch of retards paw each other under a disco ball. Connor leaned against the wall and did just that. Watched, that is. It was the Homecoming Dance. The only difference between this dance and any other was that ties and dress shirts were mandatory, and one wall of the gym was plastered with aluminum foil stars, each framing a picture of a St. Thom's student. A big butcher paper banner announced, "Shining Stars."

Connor couldn't stop thinking about Dish's destination the day of the accident. An errand, he'd said. That could be anything: picking up clothes from the cleaners, ice cream, cigarettes. No, there was no way Dish was a smoker.

It'd been two days since Connor smoked weed in the hot tub with Ned, two days of ditching Iris as soon as the afternoon bell rang. He'd failed to convince her that he was writing a short story and that he'd made up everything about Dish and the well.

"You didn't make up that tattoo," was all she said.

Over at the turntable, the D.J. had a weird pelvic thrust going in time with the music. Connor slipped under the bleachers and found a plastic bucket that made a decent seat.

He took the map out of his pocket and unfolded it. He'd marked the location of the accident and done some digging to figure out which businesses he and Dish had already passed, and which lay between there and Santa Monica. Two coffee houses, five restaurants, a ballet studio, a bookstore and a few realtors.

Dish could have been going anywhere. South of Malibu was Santa Monica and L.A.

Connor looked up from the map at Iris.

"Whatcha doin' under here all by yourself?"

"Avoiding you," he said.

"Very funny."

She wore so much eye makeup it looked like somebody had punched her. The fringe of straight blond hair was twice as long on one side of her head as the other, making her look like a cocker spaniel listening to its master. She'd even gotten past the chaperones with her nose ring tonight.

Snatching up his map, she ran her finger over his scribbles and tossed it to the floor with the candy wrappers and loose change that had fallen from the bleachers.

Before he could react, she straddled his lap, one arm around his neck, the other hand sliding down the length of his tie in a very suggestive way. He realized she was wearing a tie too, and a black silk shirt and a pink tutu. The disco ball made weird flashing signals behind her head and her breath smelled like liquor. Her hands wandered to his face, then his earlobes.

"Christ!" He grabbed her hands and looked into her dilated eyes. "What are you doing?"

"I feel like sitting too," she said with a pout. "I never noticed how cute you were before."

"Oh come on, Iris. Leave me alone, huh?"

"Face it, Connor, you've seen the Other Side. You've had a mystical experience. Fate swept you up and delivered you to Dish like it was your destiny."

"Destiny? Are you kidding me?"

"No. I believe it. Our future and our past already exist and there's nothing that can prevent us from acting out the parts we play in this universe." She was so close her face was out of focus. "I believe you saw him. On the Other Side, with the woman he's been searching for all his life."

"How do you know he's been searching for her?"

"It's just… he always had an emptiness about him, a very sexy tortured look, ya know? Like he's lost his soul. He's special. I've always known that."

"Just because you always wanted to jump him doesn't make him special, Iris."

"Oh?" She grinned. "Doesn't it make you feel special?"

"It makes me feel like I need a shower. And hold on, just a second. How can Dish fulfill any 'destiny' if he's lying in a hospital with tubes down his throat?"

"He's not there, and you know it. You saw him yourself. On the Other Side," she said. "You've never heard of 'out of body experiences'?"

Her hands had crept back to his face.

"Dish is having the ultimate out of body experience," she said. "He's in some other dimension. Maybe another planet. Someone there needed him. She needed him."

"You're crazier than me, Iris."

"You're not crazy and you know it. That's why you flush your pills down the shitter every day."

"Who told you that?"

"You live in a dorm, for chrissake. Everyone knows. What are those pills supposed to do for you, anyway?"

"Make me normal. You wouldn't be interested."

Like a snake striking, her mouth clamped on his. She tasted like strawberry lip gloss and vodka and as her tongue probed his mouth, her hands worked at unzipping his fly.

He stood up, and Iris tumbled to the floor with the candy wrappers.

"Dick!"

"See ya, Iris."

On his way past, he picked up the map.

"You can make some money on those things, ya know," she called after him. "What are they? Like Benzos or something?"

Brother Mike bought Connor's nausea story. One side

effect of the anti-psychotic drug was diarrhea and vomiting, but Dr. Adelman failed to mention that it might cause the user to be groped by the likes of Iris McCreary.

The dorm was empty. Connor got to the top of the stairs and started down the hall, but stopped in front of room 21. Dish's room. He wondered if anyone had been in there since the accident. It would be three weeks on Friday.

His mom's credit card slid in between the door and the jamb easily and after a few jiggles, he pushed the door open and stepped into a dark cave. Flipping on the light, he closed the door behind him.

It looked like Dish had just gone for a run.

A pile of unfolded laundry filled the end of his unmade bed, his laptop was open, and three books lay open next to it. Books were everywhere; stacked on the floor and bed stand, overflowing from the bowed bookshelf.

Connor felt his face go hot and knew he'd be pissing tears soon. Shit.

He wiped his eyes on his sleeve, then slumped into Dish's chair. Moving the mouse on the laptop woke it with a static hum. If only it was that easy to wake Dish. The internet browser was still open and Connor scrolled through Dish's recent search histories. The first on the list was a Wikipedia listing for the word "kelpie," which was the Scottish version of something called a water horse. It had lots of other names: pooka in Irish; glashan, nix, ceffyl dwr in Welsh; and a bunch of others. It can appear as a beautiful woman, combing her hair by a pool, a dragon or "worm," or a little horse with its hooves put on backwards, or a horse with a fish tail.

In Irish legend, children might find a horse wandering around, jump on its back and stick like glue. The water horse invariably took them for a wild ride before diving into a stream or pool to drown the kid.

But on the Celtic Twilight website, a water horse was described as: "A shapeshifter that could carry a man to his watery death beneath river, sea or well. Thought of in a less sinister way, the water horse could carry a man across to the other side, to the land of the dead, the Fair Lands."

So, why was the water horse on Dish's arm? Was he marked for transport to the other side?

Connor poked through the open books. One was in a language he'd never seen before, but the subtitle was in English, Early Welsh Poetry. It was open to a page of writing that had too many consonants, but stuck to the page was a hot pink sticky note.

"Ancient Bindings," Connor read. There was a phone number underneath it, so he punched it into his cell phone. It rang forever, then finally, voice mail: "Ancient Bindings Rare Books is closed at this time. Our hours are ten to seven, Monday through Saturday. Thank you for calling."

He spread the map over the desk. There was a bookshop just south of where the accident happened. He'd marked it, but hadn't put a name to it.

He typed the bookshop's name into the search engine and there it was, on Chautauqua Boulevard. "Purveyors of rare and collectible books, esoterica, documents of all kinds."

Dish was going to get a book?

Connor pulled open the top drawer of the desk. A surge of guilt rushed through him. He had no business looking in Dish's desk, but they had to be here somewhere.

Packs of gum, red pens, old postcards, receipts, an AC adaptor, earbuds and some British money. Connor pulled out a flashlight, recognizing it as the one Dish had used in the cave that night. He flipped it on and flashed it into the drawer and finally found what he was looking for under some scratched CDs: Dish's car keys.

Connor didn't sleep that night.

Saturday morning came. At nine a.m., he flushed his pills, and told Brother Mike he was going for a run. He found Dish's old Fiat parked at the far end of the overflow parking lot. The car might have been cool back in the seventies, but now it was rusted and dented. Connor didn't remember it looking this bad last spring when Dish took a carload of kids for ice cream.

Inside, it smelled like old leather and the springs in the bench seat twanged under his weight. He put the key in the ignition, and only then found the gearshift on the floor.

"Oh, shit." It was a manual.

He'd watched people shift in the movies. He stepped on the clutch and pushed the stick around, then turned the key. It barely turned over, groaned and then, nothing. Shit. He had forgotten; the reason he'd been driving that day was Dish said his car battery was dead. So now he had to learn how to shift and jump-start a car. He slapped the steering wheel and took a deep breath.

Brother Mike parked the school van and Connor jumped out. "Make it quick," Mike called out the window. "They're serving egg rolls and teriyaki chicken for lunch."

Connor saluted and headed for the bookshop. He had told Mike he'd ordered a rare book for his mom for Christmas and if he didn't pick it up today, they'd send it back.

The bookstore sat squeezed between a realtor and a frozen yogurt shop. A little bell rang when he opened the door, and a tall stick of a man appeared from a forest of bookstacks, his half-glasses sitting on the very end of his narrow nose.

"May I help you, young man?" His teeth made a yellow log jam in his mouth and his bald head had a few wisps of hair that really needed to be shaved.

"Yes. I believe a friend of mine called here looking for a book. The problem is, I don't actually have the title of the book."

"And where is this friend?"

"He's in the hospital, actually. I thought I'd try to get it for him. A surprise, you know."

The guy grinned. It was one of those grins that said he really didn't like people coming into his shop, really didn't like people at all, just books. "What's your friend's name?"

"Hugh Cavendish."

He snapped shut the book in his hands, saying, "Ah, yes. I almost sent that book back. Thought he'd forgotten altogether."

Behind the counter, he rummaged through a stack of books with white slips wrapped around them.

"You'd be surprised how many people start a search for a book and then never—ah, here it is."

He handed Connor a slim paperback wrapped in a Ziploc baggie. Through the plastic, he saw a black-and-white picture on the cover. A guy stood with his fist on his hip, wearing those poochy old-style riding pants, high socks and cap. The title read: Ancient Monuments of Wales for the Intrepid Wanderer. The subtitle: One Man's Discoveries by C. W. Pritchard.

"Are you sure this is the book Mr. Cavendish ordered?"

The guy glared over the top of his glasses. "You think I could mistake this? Talk about rare." He pulled out a receipt pad. "That'll be one twenty-five."

Connor pulled a five out of his wallet, laid it on the counter and picked up the Ziplocked book. The man's fingers clamped down on it.

"That's one hundred and twenty-five dollars."

"One hundred? Dollars? For this?"

They both had a hand on the book.

"Fewer than five hundred were printed. I doubt more than a dozen still exist. The guy was a legend, apparently. Hope your friend likes it."

"Jesus."

Connor dug out his mom's credit card, hoping he hadn't tweaked it when he carded Dish's door.

The guy slid it through the credit card thingy and the machine started printing. Connor signed and walked out with a worn paperback that was more of a pamphlet than a book. He took it out of the plastic and opened to the title page. Printed in England in 1935. The Pritchard dude looked like he'd just escaped from the nuthouse. He had a crazy grin on his face and his walking stick branched out like antlers at the top with little bells, or maybe acorns, hung from it.

When he climbed back into the van, Brother Mike took one look at the crispy old book, and said, "Your mother collects books?"

"Yeah. Old books on... hiking."

Back at the dorm, Connor locked himself in his room. He turned pages of grainy old black-and-white photos of stones of all sizes, some with designs carved on them, and the crazy guy standing beside them, his hands on his hips in typical British swagger.

In the preface, Pritchard said his goal was to document monuments in peril of being lost due to lack of preservation in the more remote regions of Wales. He gave short descriptions of the stones and any local legends he'd found that applied.

It was on page 73 that Connor found it. The stone was part of a shepherd's cottage, and Pritchard said it must have been moved there hundreds of years before when the cottage was built. It was common practice, he said, to use standing stones as foundations for new buildings.

This stone formed an oversized cornerstone, carved on both visible faces. According to Pritchard, there was no way of knowing where it was originally located.

Around the edge of the stone in a long ribbon was a bunch of scribbled symbols that Pritchard called "Pictish runes." In the very center of the ribbon was a water horse, its tail knotted and twisted, its mouth open and its front hooves striking out.

The image of the water horse on Dish's arm was a perfect match for the one on that rock. But what did that mean? What did this rock have to do with Dish?

Pritchard's description of the stone read: "A classic well

stone, once used to mark a spring that possessed healing or magical properties. This stone has clearly been moved, as it is now incorporated into a cottage wall. A highly unusual example of such a well stone, as the runic inscription was at first, unobserved."

What did that mean? "Unobserved?"

Connor turned another crisp page. There, on the lower right of page 82 was a blurry image of a woman. She looked like she was turning away to avoid the camera, her dark hair braided into a thick rope. She was glancing over her shoulder and looking right into the camera. He had seen those eyes before. She was looking straight into Connor's soul just as she had in the cave. It wasn't the same woman exactly, but whoever looked out at the camera was the woman Connor had seen with Dish on the other side.

The caption under the photo read "Lyla Bendbow."

Chapter 20

The stairwell spiraled wildly and when Ava reached the bottom she had to pause, bracing herself with a hand on the wall. It was taking far longer than expected for her head to clear of Irjan's tinctures. Jeven appeared, silver bells chiming, and took up beside her like a dog to heel.

"They await you," he said.

"As they should."

She touched the fox stole at her neck. Jeven mustn't see the marks left by yesterday's flight. But by his look, the stole hid nothing. Jeven read her like the entrails of a goat.

Weaker than she expected after such a flight, her legs threatened to fail her, so she took his arm to steady herself.

"Irjan is placing you in danger," he said. "A tethered soul can take possession of you as easily as you possess it—"

"The danger is running free in the Vale of Elfael. Is the order away?"

"The bird flew with your message before dusk last night, as you commanded."

"Lyleth is not alone," she said.

Jeven stopped walking and faced her. "She called him?"

"Nechtan lives. He and Lyleth travel with two children toward the Lost Hammer River."

Jeven lifted the latch of the council chamber, whispering,

"You must march without delay, before your chieftains know of it."

"Everyone will know soon enough."

The new footstool made her feel taller. She touched the stole again to be sure her throat was hidden.

Smoldering fear emanated from Fiach and Lloyd. Perhaps they thought they would be next on the pyre. Nechtan had failed to inspire such fear in his underlings. He drank with them, diced with them, laughed with them, whored with them. Without fear, there is no allegiance.

She let her gaze rest on Fiach. "Has your second detachment of scouts sent any word?"

"Not yet, lady. They should have reached Elfael yesterday."

"I have information that says Lyleth makes for the Lost Hammer River," she said, her eyes never leaving Fiach's, measuring his response. His breathing quickened.

"I sent a bird to your men last night," she said. "They will overtake Lyleth before she crosses into Cedewain. You and Lloyd will make for Elfael today with all haste."

She leaned on the table and said evenly, "You will take her, Fiach."

His jaw tightened as he tipped his chin in agreement. He certainly understood her jest. She found herself grinning. What would he do when he found Nechtan with Lyleth? Would he kill them both?

She stood and Fiach and Lloyd did the same as the door flew open and Gwylym spilled in.

Ava's captain of the guard showed his palms, his cloak and leathers dripping on the flagstones. "I have news," he said, glancing at the two chieftains.

"Leave us," she told Fiach and Lloyd.

When the door had closed behind them, she said to Gwylym, "You've seen Lyleth?"

Gwylym cast about the room and found Jeven waiting by

the door. "What I have to say should not be heard by the walls, my lady."

"Come. We'll talk in my chamber. Jeven, see to the preparations to march north."

Ava led Gwylym through the revel hall to the stairs leading to her chamber. She could tell by his face, he'd seen Nechtan. And if Ava lost the allegiance of the clan guard, there would be bloodshed long before they reached Cedewain. Without them, she was fodder for an assassin's blade.

Gwylym opened the chamber door. Ava glanced at the prize waiting in the corner, covered with a sheet of oilcloth.

"Tell me what you saw, Gwylym."

"Lady. Please don't think me addled." He wasn't a young man, but the years had sculpted him with the chisel of war into a man she found intriguing. There was something rough and violent about him. She could own this man.

"Tell me she's dead, Gwylym."

"She lives. As does my lord king, Nechtan." He needed to say nothing else; anguish and confusion were written in his eyes. The story spilled from him like a confession. He needn't tell her that he was torn in two, a man bred for duty and service now serving two masters.

"Your men saw him as well?"

"Saw him, heard his voice, knew it was him."

Tales of the risen king would be spilled over cups in every alehouse in Ys.

She went to Gwylym, ran her fingers up his arms to his shoulders. He smelled of horse sweat and wet wool, still muddy from the road. "How are you certain it was him?"

"I've known him since he was a lad." He took her hands and gently gave them back to her.

"I thought you said he closed the entrance with a fall of stones, how could you see him?"

"There was a space big enough to look through. I could've spat on him, so close was he."

"Lyleth is nothing more than a conjurer. She deceived you with a demon, cloaked in the gossamer of the druada."

"It was him, Lady—"

"His flesh? His blood?"

"Aye. 'Twas."

"And if I can show you that it wasn't?"

She ran her hands up his chest to his shoulders, kneaded them, but they were like stone. He didn't remove her hands this time, so, gently, she pulled his face down to hers and opened her mouth to meet his, but he resisted.

"Lady, I—"

"You what? You would never dishonor your lord? Your lord is dead, Gwylym. And his queen is lonely."

He softened just perceptibly, leaning ever so slightly toward her mouth as she whispered in his ear, "I must show you the truth. Light the candle."

He did as bidden.

Taking his hand, she led him to the corner. The candlelight warmed the stained creases of the shroud, and she detected the faint stink of cedar oil and death.

She pulled the sheet away.

The candlelight wavered, but Gwylym didn't drop it.

The golden light made Nechtan's corpse appear to be sleeping. Yet, when Ava moved closer, she saw the pallor of death, the severed warrior's braid, the shriveled lips that were once hungry for hers.

"My guards found him sleeping peacefully in his barrow," she said. "Fiach will bear him northward, so that every man who pledges his blood to me will see the truth before they meet Lyleth's conjuring. Nechtan's body will be my battle standard, and my men will know the northern clans are led to battle by a wraith."

Gwylym made the sign against evil, saying, "You dishonor him."

"I did what I must to show you the truth, Gwylym. Lyleth

cut his warrior's braid, there in the barrow. Hair of the dead to work her conjuring. Look at his hair."

Leading him closer, the candlelight revealed the truth.

"The man you saw in the mountains was no man. Lyleth will do anything to stop me from ruling this land. Here is your king, Gwylym. Here. Dead and reeking of it."

He fell to his knees before the corpse, his fingers trembling as he inspected the brooch at the king's chest. He tugged at the oilcloth and touched Nechtan's wrist, the king's mark.

Ava stood behind him, her hands on his shoulders. "If Lyleth had raised him from the dead, would he be rotting here on this floor?"

She felt Gwylym's turmoil and ran her hands down his chest, pressed her belly to the back of his head, then sank down beside him.

"You were always with me, even when he was not. In my despair, it was you who stood beside me, Gwylym. When I lost my babes… I was a fool to hope my king would love a girl he traded for peace. It turns a woman to stone under the touch of her lord when her lord wants another. I should have seen you then as I see you now."

She pressed her breasts to the cold brass of his armlet and felt his muscles soften. She tested his lips, brushing them with her own. She was prepared for a longer contest of will, but he surprised her, crushing her in his embrace. He tasted of meat and ale and his big hands fumbled at the laces of her gown. She almost laughed at him, this man who had served Nechtan's father, had sworn his life to Nechtan, couldn't unlace his britches fast enough to fuck his lord's wife.

She'd been a maid when her father sent her to Nechtan's bed. She'd braced herself for the hurt all maids must endure, but he coaxed her into wanting that pain. He gave her time and touches until she wanted nothing else but him. Now, she realized with revulsion how much her body missed his. But she'd never been more to him than a chit that had been traded for peace.

Blinking away the sting of tears, she opened herself to Gwylym's rough thrusts. Looking at the shell of flesh that had been Nechtan, she vowed silently, I will find you and kill you myself, my love.

Chapter 21

High on a bluff above the Lost Hammer River, Lyleth took one last look at the snaking shoreline where she'd left Nechtan, just visible by the light of the setting moon. According to Dylan, a tow barge waited to take them across the river to the cover of the woods beyond, and Lyleth prayed the boy was right. She could only lead their pursuers off the scent for so long.

She hadn't gone far when Dylan rode up beside her. "My lord told me to come with ye."

"Elowen is with me," Lyleth said. "You'll stay with Nechtan and you'll not let him look back. Never. Do you understand me?"

"Aye, lady."

"And you'll not stop until he finds Marchlew."

Taking the bow and quiver from her shoulder, she pressed them into Dylan's hands.

"You'd best learn to shoot fast, lad. And when you're across that river, you'll cut the tow line, do you understand me?"

"Aye. I understand… everything." Even in the strange light of the shepherd's lamp, she could see a steadfast allegiance in the lad's eyes.

"Now, go."

Nechtan and Dylan would cross the river and vanish into the dense greenwood of Pendynas while Lyleth led Fiach's scouts in the opposite direction. This was how it was to end.

Nechtan would do what she'd asked of him, she had no doubt. They had spoken their last words to one another in this world, but Lyleth had so much more to say. A rush of regret filled the hollows of her heart.

The torches were closing in.

She took the lantern from Elowen, set her heels to her horse, and led the way down the bluff. With no time to cover her tracks, she hoped the scouts would follow, for if Fiach's men saw two tracks, they would surely send men after Nechtan.

A clearing opened, and she trotted her horse in furious circles, plowing up the turf and confusing the tracks as best she could. Then, she waited.

Elowen scowled at her from her perch on the back of the plow horse, Nechtan's harp strapped to her back. Fiach's men mustn't see it.

"They're gettin' close," Elowen whispered. "We should go."

"I've got to be sure they see the lantern first."

Voices colored with the lilt of the southern tribes made it clear they were, indeed, men from Emlyn.

"If we wait any longer, they'll think we're chasing them," Elowen said.

Lyleth raised the lantern higher overhead.

"We are. Come. We've got to move fast now."

"We shoulda been moving fast all along."

Lyleth pushed westward through a stand of gorse, making as much noise as possible. She paused to be certain the men followed. It wouldn't be long now till Nechtan was across the river.

When they'd gone half a league, Lyleth halted, her horse blowing hard.

"What are you doing?" Elowen asked.

"Waiting."

"For them to take you?"

"You go on."

"Dylan says there's an ol' bridge a few more leagues to the west."

"Aye," Lyleth said, "and I don't want the men behind us to find it. There's a fine chance they know nothing of the river crossings here."

She slipped from her horse to the soft ground. "Go, lass," Lyleth said. "You owe me nothing."

Elowen circled her on the big plow horse. "Stars and stones watch over you, druí."

"And you."

And the girl was gone.

Lyleth cut a willow branch and brushed out the girl's tracks until they vanished into a streambed. Then she returned to the clearing and waited. She sat cross-legged with her horse's reins in hand, the lantern beside her. The weakness left by her injuries washed over her and the clearing grew small and distant. Hanging her head between her knees, she resolved not to faint.

They came at last, sounding like boars scuffling through the brush to surround her. They'd put out their torches some distance back, doubtless thinking to creep up.

Lyleth held out her arms, palms up, and spoke to the bushes. "I surrender to Fiach, lord of Emlyn, and to Fiach alone."

With weapons drawn, five men stepped from the willows.

"Where is Nechtan?" one asked. So, the rumor of Nechtan's return had spread as she knew it would, from the innkeep, perhaps, or the local men who'd watched Nechtan kill Fiach's scouts two days before.

One warrior was clearly a member of Fiach's retainers by the barley sheaves bossed on his helm. He edged closer until his sword point rested at her throat. The noseguard of his helm was overly long and partially covered his mouth, making his small eyes seem crossed.

"I said that I'd speak to Fiach alone," she said. "Take me to him."

The warrior's sword pressed deeper, slicing her skin.

"You'll tell me where the ghost of the king has gone, or I'll relieve you of your head, sister greenleaf."

"If he's a ghost, why do you give chase?"

"He's a demon, wearing borrowed skin. This we know."

"You know? Tell me, sir, how is it you know the workings of the gods?" She swallowed against the blade and it cut deeper. "He's your king, living and breathing, and he'll be taking your head soon, traitor, and with it, your soul."

She let her eyes wander to the willows at the man's back, as if to signal someone there.

The warrior spun toward the trees. "Come out!" he called to the night, then to his men, "Go look for him."

Before they made move to obey, from the darkness came a faint strain of harp strings, playing a ghostly aire. The men huddled closer, their eyes searching the willows, their hands flying to make the warding sign against evil.

Elowen should have been long gone by now. Lyleth couldn't let the girl be taken, too.

"Take me to Fiach," she said again. "I have a message from his king."

This time, they were only too happy to bind her wrists and lift her to her horse's back.

It was almost dawn when they reached what could only be an appointed meeting place. Here, Fiach's men were joined by others, and from the talk, it wouldn't be long before the hosting from Caer Ys reached them. They tied Lyleth to an old hawthorn tree and left one man to guard her.

"Your king lives," she said to her guard. He was young, and she could feel that he feared her.

He held a waterskin to her lips, his eyes flitting to her bound hands as if she might magically untie them and strangle him.

"You serve Nechtan's murderer," she said, "this 'she-king' as Ava names herself."

"Men don't die and live again, druí," he replied. "I follow my lord Fiach, none other. Just as ye should."

He took a long drink from the skin and wiped his mouth with the back of his hand, all the while looking her up and down as if measuring what Fiach might have found desirable in her. It was no secret, even beyond Nechtan's court, that Lyleth had shared her bed with the chieftain from Emlyn, and it had become the subject of endless rumor. Some even claimed that Fiach had a hand in Nechtan's death. However, the most popular rumor was that Lyleth had defended her honor when Nechtan tried to take her, and he had died of shame, though in some stories, Lyleth had cursed him. But Lyleth shared much of his shame, for in those months after Nechtan's death, she had come to understand that whatever she'd felt for Fiach, and it was much, it was far from love.

The thought of seeing him again filled her with a deep disquiet. Nechtan had held him at sword point when last she saw him. How could she possibly hope he would understand why she had called him back?

Night was falling when the banners of Emlyn and IsAeron led a black snake of horsemen and foot soldiers onto the plain. Fiach's camp grew up around Lyleth and her hawthorn tree, and soldiers eyed her warily and spat on her as they passed.

Finally, one of Fiach's clan guards came for her.

Weaving through a tangle of supply wagons, she saw tents stretched out to the west as far as she could see, and cook fires like golden beads of light. Lyleth hadn't seen such a hosting since Nechtan had fought the Bear at Fitful Head.

The guard took her to a tent marked with the sigil of Emlyn, but Fiach was not there. Beside his cot lay the bow she'd always admired, ringed with bands of Finian silver and inlaid with glass, and his boar hide quiver marked with runes stitched in gold thread. He was more superstitious than a greenman. She glanced at the little table beside his cot and saw his blackthorn whistle. A pang of loss welled in her. She had thought she could love this man; at least, her body had led her to believe it.

The guard bid her sit on a low stool, where he bound her hand and foot once again. It wasn't long before Fiach burst into the tent and stood frozen in the candlelight. He dismissed the guard with a nod.

Before her stood the shadow of the man whose laughter she once yearned to drown in; golden haired and golden tongued. Part of her wanted to hold him again, to unravel the hurt she'd inflicted. But he was little more than a warrior courting death now.

"Tell me the truth, Lyleth," he said. "Where is this man you claim to be Nechtan?"

"Tell me the truth, Fiach. How can you serve a woman who's murdered your king?"

"I waited!"

His rage colored the air between them. He took another stool, his knees to hers, his face so close, she inhaled the fragrance of the man she'd known so completely and it stirred her.

"When Nechtan banished you," he said, "I knew you'd come to me. That our life together could really begin. I waited. And you vanished into the greenwood—"

"If I had gone to you, this land would have been divided—"

"This land is divided! And it's not my doing, Lyleth. Nor is it yours. It's Nechtan's alone."

"Your king was poisoned."

She tried to take his hands, but the rope went taut.

"Take the pouch from my belt, Fiach. You'll find my proof."

He searched her eyes, and she knew what he looked for. He drew so near, his palms cradling her face, his mouth almost touching hers, but not quite. She understood. He wanted her to beg him with her body, to pretend nothing had changed between them. She broke the hold of his eyes and looked down at the trampled sod.

"I have wronged you, Fiach, but rending this land in two is not—"

"I was there the day you came to Caer Ys, eight years ago," he said. "The day Nechtan bound you as his solás."

He held her face in his hands again, and forced her to meet his eyes.

"I saw it then," he whispered. "You walked into the revel hall and stood before him, this boy you'd loved on the Isle of Glass was now a man, a king, and you a servant of the green gods.

"I saw it in his eyes. And I saw it in yours. No law would let him have you, unless he bound you to him as his solás."

"He didn't force my duty on me."

"No? What did he tell you, Lyleth? Did he tell you he would be a wastrel without you? That he needed someone stronger than he to lead this land?"

She wanted to slap him. She remembered exactly what Nechtan had said to her that day. I don't know who I am anymore, Lyl. The only choice I have left in this life is you.

"Neither of you knew what kind of prison you were building for yourselves," Fiach said.

His breath warmed her skin, and his fingers dug into her jaw, forcing her to look into his eyes. But hers were clouded with tears.

Whispering, so close she felt his words strike her face, he said, "I would have poisoned him myself, love, if I had had the chance."

After a long, desperate look, he released her, stood, and strode away.

"You're a man of honor!" she said to his back.

He stopped, dusk showing pink in the sky outside.

"I swear on the love I once shared with you," she said, "the man I summoned is Nechtan."

He turned at last, an amused look in his eyes. "Swear on your love for Nechtan."

She swallowed hard. "I swear to you, on my love for Nechtan, that when the Bear comes, Nechtan will need you, Fiach, to stand beside him and hold this land for the Ildana."

Fiach chewed his lip and paced, then called to a guard outside, "Take her to her king."

The guard untied her and dragged her to her feet. Fiach wouldn't meet her eyes as she brushed by him and out into the night.

The guard led her to what appeared to be a small supply tent. He lifted the flap and pushed her into the darkness. Her hands still tied behind her, she stumbled on what felt like a grain sack. But the air in the tent reeked of death.

A second guard followed the first with a rushlight and Lyleth saw she had fallen, not on a sack, but on the swollen corpse of her lord king, his warrior's braid severed where she'd made the cut.

"Your lord has missed ye," the guard laughed.

When he untied her hands, she made a swift lunge for the dagger at his belt, but he caught her wrists easily. She kicked and thrashed and screamed until the other guard held her. He threw her down on Nechtan's corpse and pinned her there while the other worked the rope.

They left her, hands tied around the corpse's neck like a noose. Her eyes adjusted to the dim firelight that seeped through the oilskin, and she saw Nechtan's purpled flesh. It felt waxy-cold, and his organs swelled his abdomen with the gases of decay so that his mail was stretched tight as a drum. The pale jelly of his eyes had sunk beneath shriveled lids.

"The flesh is but a cloak." She turned away, and vomited.

Chapter 22

Nechtan was almost hungry enough to shoot the goose himself.

"Keep the bow square, don't lock your elbow, and just open your fingers," he whispered to Dylan. They were almost close enough to wrestle the thing.

It was the boy's fifth try and it would be the last. Lyl's bow was light, but Dylan's arm still trembled with the strain of drawing it. He needed some muscle.

Two rabbits, a swan and a duck had been his target practice. Time was precious. The sack of food from the inn had been tied to the plow horse, which Elowen had ridden off with. Wasting time to hunt just slowed them, but even dead men must eat.

The bowstring sang, and Dylan's grin spread the width of his narrow face.

"Will ya looka that!" Whooping, he ran into the pond to scoop up the goose.

"Hunger always improves your aim," Nechtan told him. "A goose is one thing. A mounted man is another."

Nechtan decided a fire would be safe enough in the dense cover of this greenwood. He and Dylan had crossed the Lost Hammer River on a small ferry that nearly scuttled with the weight of two men and their horses. From the northern shore, he'd watched the light from Lyl's lantern until it vanished beyond a bend in the river.

He'd lost her again, and she'd left him with but one task that could right this crooked path he'd cut through this world. There was nothing that could stop him now, for Caer Cedewain was but a few days away.

With one fall of his axe, he'd cut the towline and sent the ferry downriver to be shredded by rapids. Then the greenwood had swallowed him and the boy. They followed a wide stream for a good distance to cover their tracks, then a game trail took them north through the rugged mountains of the Pendynas. It was good to travel by day again.

Nechtan had to remind the boy that singing was as good as sounding a war trumpet. So, Dylan sang to himself, quietly, and asked questions until Nechtan refused to answer any longer. But the questions kept his thoughts from Lyl.

"You must remember something of the Fair Lands," Dylan was saying.

Since Nechtan remembered nothing but pain, he borrowed freely from the old stories in the Cycles of the Sea.

"'Twas just like Cynvarra tells," Nechtan went on. "Colors your eye's never seen, music that touches you like a woman's lips, ships that plow the seas of the sky."

"And flames that sing?"

"Oh, aye."

He didn't tell Dylan about the boy so like him, or the cold white light, or the snakes. Better for him to think the Fair Lands were truly fair.

"I've heard that women in the Fair Lands are more beautiful than the Asrai," Dylan said. "Are they?"

"I've never seen one of the Asrai, and I doubt you have either."

"But they have women, surely?"

"'Twouldn't be the Fair Lands without women, now would it? They're like... like moonlight on the sea, exquisite in their grace and wisdom, and willing to give their love if you possess an honorable soul. But they're just as deadly as those who dwell on this side." Nechtan's lies were worthy of a bard. "Learn to handle the women here first, lad."

The trail broadened, so Dylan rode up beside him. "Can I ask you something, my lord?"

"You've been asking all day."

"There are rumors. About you and your solás."

"This sounds like a question I won't answer."

"It's just that some say you brought a curse upon the Quarters."

Nechtan rode on, pushing through a stand of young fir trees. "Oh, I brought a curse, truly. I cursed the Quarters when I married Ava."

"Then you never broke your bond with your solás?"

Nechtan took hold of the rein on Dylan's horse and brought them both to a halt. He said, "My solás has given her life to serve me. To serve this land. You'll not disrespect her."

There were no more questions that afternoon.

Nechtan plucked and gutted the goose while the boy built up the fire.

"Mounted men don't sit still and wait for you to shoot them like this goose," he was telling Dylan. "And unless you've got bodkin points on those arrows, you'll have only a few hits that'll bring them down." He indicated the locations with the point of his knife. "Armpit, neck, face."

"I'll remember."

"I owe you protection," Nechtan said. "And I fear the day will come soon when I can't provide it. This isn't your fight, lad."

"It was my choice to serve you, my lord, and I don't regret it."

Nechtan knew there was nothing he could say that would change Dylan's mind. He had been the same way once.

Smiling, he tossed a fistful of goose feathers at Dylan and punched him lightly on the shoulder. "You'll practice with that bow instead of sleeping from now on."

"As you say, my lord." Dylan beamed.

The boy on the other side had followed Nechtan too, into a well beside the sea. That event had replayed in his mind a hundred times, for it was the only one that made any sense. On a wide sea strand, he and the boy found a well. Nechtan remembered thinking he'd found the third well, the portal that swallowed the Old Blood so long ago, locking them away in exile in the land of the dead.

When he first awoke here in the real world, he thought he had succeeded and passed through that lost portal. But if that were so, Nechtan should be as powerful as the Old Blood; he'd be able to fly on Wren's wings and call down a storm from the sky. He'd done a bit of testing and found he bled like everyone else, and flying... he smiled at the thought. No, this body Lyl had given him most certainly could die. Again.

But the boy on the other side was still trying to follow; Nechtan could feel him, even see him in Dylan's eyes. What was the boy from the other side trying to tell him?

The coals were still too hot, but Nechtan skewered and fixed the goose above them and took to sharpening his weapons. The fire singed the meat, but hunger would make it taste fine.

"Perhaps they got away." Dylan stared into the fire and wiped at the grease on his mouth. "I told Elowen of the bridge to the west."

"Aye, perhaps."

"I'm glad Elowen's with her," Dylan said. "'Tis good, that. Her sling's not to be trifled with. I've watched her with it." He gave an impressed whistle.

"Lyleth had no intention of getting away, lad," Nechtan finally said, and cut another piece of meat.

Dylan stopped chewing.

"Those were Fiach's men behind us," Nechtan said. "She'll make them believe they caught her and then she'll make them take her to Fiach."

"But why? You need her with you."

"Lyleth might be good with a bow, but words are her best weapon. I discovered that the hard way." He had to smile just thinking of it.

"Would I be pryin' if I asked how, my lord?"

Dylan's face said he'd given the boy a good fright earlier. Nechtan almost felt sorry for it.

"I spent my summers on the Isle of Glass from the time I was ten until I was old enough to go to battle. I learned the history of the Ildana, music, poetry, philosophy, ciphering and weapons. Enough to call myself a literate lordling. But Dechtire's students, those training for a life as druada, they only saw us in the summers, and bore us dullards very little love.

"Lyleth, being Dechtire's darling, was assigned the task of teaching me the poem The Maid in the Crystal Coracle."

"Ah, 'tis one of my dearest," Dylan said.

"Well, then you would have fared better than me. Lyl inserted a verse of her own. I suppose it was a test of sorts, to see how well-lettered I was. When I failed to catch the added verse…" He let out a long sigh. "Well, let's just say the part where the maid returns home in her crystal coracle was far different in Lyl's version. She didn't return as a maid at all. And I, not knowing the true version from Lyl's version, recited it before Dechtire herself."

Dylan's mouth hung open. "Then what happened?"

"I milked the goats for the rest of that summer and made it my sole purpose in life to exact my revenge."

"Did you?" Dylan sucked the marrow from a bone.

"Oh, I tried. Thought I had the perfect trap set. Lyl was working in the kitchen, preparing a meal for a guest, the high druí from Arvon, a rather pompous man. She was preparing a specialty of hers, plover eggs in pastry. I'd helped her gather the eggs that day, so I pretended to be interested in how she prepared this delicacy.

"I noticed she sprinkled the pastry with melted butter, then cracked an egg in the middle and bundled them up like little packages before she set them on the hearthstone to bake. So, while she wasn't looking, I replaced the cup of melted butter with melted beeswax. It was difficult, because I had to keep it so hot."

"Did she find you out?"

"Lyl served Dechtire and the visitor her little pastries. And when the druí took a bite, his teeth stuck in the wax."

Dylan's laughter sounded like music.

"What did Lyl do, you might ask?" Nechtan said. "She convinced the druí that beeswax was a proven cure for baldness, him being in most dire need of it. It was a new cure taken in the southron lands, says she, and she only sought to aid him, as was her duty as a greenling."

"Did he believe it?"

"And, he ate three more. Then after supper, she tried to give me a black eye. At least I'm better at some things."

"Then how did you seek such a scamp as your solás? If I'm not too forward in askin', my lord." Dylan held up his hands in mock self-defense.

The why's of their friendship never seemed to matter when they were young.

"I spent my winters aching for the spring," Nechtan said, feeling tightness in his throat. "I wanted to get back to the island. To Lyl. The girl found the best climbing trees, she caught bigger fish than me, told better stories than I'd ever heard, shot a bow better than me..." His voice trailed off, remembering the secrets that pass between friends, and the laughter.

"And she could speak to the green gods?" Dylan added.

"Oh, she spoke, aye, the question was always did they hear? Lyl never believed the gods bothered themselves with the trifles of men. She thought they enjoyed our suffering. She said the only reason men worshipped the green gods in their groves was to be certain they would look the other way, not meddle in their personal affairs. She was a bit of a rebel in the ranks of the greenmen."

"Then how did such a hooligan become your solás?"

He could never envision anyone else at his side but this wild, willful girl.

"One autumn," he said, "I sailed south from the Isle of Glass, leaving behind a girl, breastless, straight of hip and scrawny as me—my best friend, and when I returned at Beltaine, she was gone. Shapeshifted into a woman, a creature commanding great fear."

Dylan laughed and tossed his bones away. "And what happened then?"

"I felt I'd lost my best friend." He struggled with the feeling even now. "It was different."

"She no longer spent time with ye?"

"It was probably the other way round. She asked me to go swim in the sea, like we always did, but I found excuses not to go."

"But why?"

This was something he couldn't explain, certainly not to Dylan. What if he had made Lyl understand how he felt about her then? What could have come of it? Her father was a nameless man who took the fancy of her mother one Beltaine Eve, planted Lyl in her belly, and was gone. Lyl was a greenwood babe, servant of the land, not a fit partner for Nechtan by all the customs of his people. It was the first time he felt the chains of his birth. And he had accepted them like a whipped dog.

He swallowed hard and looked into Dylan's expectant eyes. "I wasn't meant to be king."

"But ye were," Dylan said with all the earnestness of youth. "And ye are again. For when Lyl gets to Fiach, she'll convince him that you live."

"Whatever Fiach does, he'll do for Lyl, not for me. She'll try to turn him," Nechtan said. "Because if she doesn't, Marchlew and the men of the north will be outmatched."

"Fiach loves her." By the look on Dylan's face, he knew he shouldn't have said it. Yet, Nechtan needed to hear it.

"That he does. But I've given the man more reasons to hate me than most. It doesn't change what she's asked of me, what she's asked of you. Does it now?"

He shook his head. "Nay, my lord."

"Play us a tune." Nechtan tossed the lad's satchel to him.

"Me smallpipes are too loud, I think. And Elowen's got the harp."

Dylan fumbled in the bag and pulled out a small blackthorn whistle, like the ones children learn on. The sound was simple, yet so full of the subtle forces that had shaped the branch it came from. Life is like that, a breath blows through our bones and makes us live again, a touch gives us voice.

Lyl used to tell him that starlight was like music: neither is real unless it touches one with ears to hear and eyes to see. He never understood it until now. In Dylan's music, he heard echoes of his existence, this one and many others, like ripples on a pond that strike a wall and roll back to meet the others still coming.

Nechtan had surrendered to this grand plan of Lyl's. This task she'd set for him would be over in a few days and once again, he'd be rocked in the cradle of death, forgetting Lyl in the deep sleep of another life. He longed for that forgetting. For he had nothing left in his soul worth giving her.

In Nechtan's dream he was weightless. Sunlight drove green spears of light through the water around him. He was swimming with Lyl in the Broken Sea. They were supposed to be working at their recitations for Dechtire, but the sun was so warm, they'd left their clothes on the black sand beach and thrown themselves into the waves. In the dream, she was swimming for the surface.

He kept swimming after her but got no closer. He could

see it, that boundary of sky and water. His lungs felt close to bursting.

Lyleth turned and looked back at him, a smile on her face. She took his hand and led him to the surface where he gulped in air. Between sea and sky, she kissed him and he knew he was no longer a boy. He knew that he was heavy as any stone, and she, weightless as starlight.

Chapter 23

Connor didn't want to join the other students on their hospital visit; he wanted to remember Dish as he was the last time he saw him, on the other side. Connor had replayed that encounter in his mind over and over. The absoluteness of it had dulled, like a dream that's so vivid right after you wake but becomes muted over time. The look in Dish's eyes burned through it all, the certainty they had recognized each other's souls.

"Dish knows you're there even if he's not awake," Brother Mike said, trying to convince Connor to come to the hospital. "His soul will sense you."

On the off chance that Mike was right, Connor climbed into the overcrowded school van. Besides, Bronwyn and Aunt Merryn might be at the hospital, and if Connor could show Bronwyn the photo of the water horse that matched Dish's tattoo, she would have to believe him, maybe even allow him to talk to Merryn for a few minutes.

Connor had called Bronwyn several times after he found the book, but she never replied to his messages. That could only mean she was giving him the crazy guy brush-off, or maybe it was the scene he'd made with the insurance investigator. Either way, Brother Mike said she hadn't gone back to England yet. She was waiting for Dish to "take a turn."

Connor sat in the back seat of a van packed with kids and

tried not to let too many parts of his body touch Iris. She hadn't been very successful at holding her skirt (way too short for dress code) around her ass when she climbed into the backseat, and Connor had already seen enough of her to last a lifetime.

Malibu beach rolled by, a few surfers waited for the tide change and seagulls picked through trash cans. The sky spat rain and drops clung to the van window, making snail tracks that jiggled to bumps in the road. One fat drop merged with another and through the lens of the drop, Connor saw the beach roll by in miniature detail, but inverted.

Sky became sea and sea became sky.

Through the drop, he saw a man working a kite string, backing up to maintain tension and fighting it when a gust came. At his side a little boy reached up, clearly begging for the reins of the dragon fluttering overhead. They must have been desperate to fly a kite in the rain, but it was Saturday, and Connor imagined the man was the boy's dad. He must have promised the boy they would fly it.

The wind was strong enough to whip the dragon kite into sputtering spirals, its tail lashing.

The van stopped at a light.

Dad handed the kite string to the boy and it took off, dragging the boy down the beach. He fought to hang on, until he finally let go and slammed face down in the sand.

The kite raced away, spun wildly, and finally ditched in the waves, far from shore.

The light turned green.

Connor looked at the boy again through the raindrop. Even upside down, he was crying.

Then it struck him. On the other side, Connor's view of the world was like a kite's that sailed, not through air, but through water, far beyond his body, seeing with his soul's eyes, hearing with his soul's ears. Inside out. Like his soul was his skin.

"Dish should have died."

He must have said it out loud, because Iris pulled her ear buds free, saying, "What?"

He stared at her for an eternity. The pupils of her blue eyes (streaked with gold and green and dove grey) twitched in response to the changing light of this world, and he could see his own reflection in the pools of her corneas. Inverted. "Nothing."

Scowling, Iris reinserted the ear buds and closed her eyes. Dish should have died that day. But human nature is programmed to fear death, to outrun the hungry lion, to cling to our body like a favorite shirt, to forget that other world and the fact that our life's span is just one day in an endless journey.

Dish balanced with one foot in this world and one in the other, his soul held fast by a string, by ventilators and tubes. Connor understood just as clearly, that if the string was cut, Dish's soul would pitch into the sea and be carried away by currents he couldn't even dream of.

The nurse in I.C.U. only let two visitors in at a time, and Connor found Iris at his side going through the double doors. She had a teddy bear clutched to her chest.

Nurse Holly smiled at him. "Glad you're back. How's the collar bone?" she asked.

"Good."

"But how are you?" Her look said she thought he ought to be chewing his fingers off or something.

"Good."

Iris was already in the alcove talking to Dish, something about finding his true destiny. She sat on the edge of his bed and wedged the teddy bear under his arm, then planted both palms on his cheeks as if she could will him to open his eyes.

The tattoo was still there, looking more defined now that Dish's skin hadn't seen the sun in weeks.

The ventilator tube went directly into his throat through a

hole now, but the steady rush of air and the rise and fall of his chest was the same—unnatural in a creepy way.

Iris finally looked up at Connor, her makeup running in long black smears down her cheeks. "What if he doesn't want to wake up? What if he wants to stay with that chick forever?"

"He doesn't want anything, Iris. He doesn't even know he's here."

Gently, she took the teddy bear from under Dish's arm and held it like a little girl as she wandered to the shelf full of cards. She positioned the bear in a jaunty pose beside some wilted flowers, but her hand came down with the little whiskey bottle Merryn had left. She had the top off before Connor could stop her. She sniffed it.

"There's water in here."

He tried to grab it, but she was faster than he expected. "What do you know about this water, Connor?"

"I know it's not yours. Put it back."

"It's probably holy water from church." She watched Connor for a response.

He gave her none.

"If it's holy water," she said, "maybe it can help Dish, give him a little god mojo."

Her eyes didn't leave Connor while she poured a splash into her palm and let it trickle over Dish's waxy white forehead. It rolled off and vanished in the pillow under his head.

Connor snatched the bottle and struggled to get the cork back from her, finally succeeding just as nurse Holly stepped in.

"Mr. Cavendish's relatives are here. I'm going to have to cut this visit short."

Connor slipped the little bottle into the pouch of his sweatshirt with the book. There was no way he was letting Iris pollute Merryn's well water.

The double doors buzzed and parted and there stood Bronwyn and Merryn. It was now or never. Connor pulled the Ziplocked book from his pocket and fumbled for page 73.

"Here," he said, thrusting it out to Bronwyn. "I'm not crazy. There's the mark on Dish's arm. Right there." He stabbed his forefinger at the stone. "Dish was going to get this book when the accident happened."

Merryn reached for the book with two quaking hands, saying, "He found it."

"And look here." Connor flipped to the picture of Lyla Bendbow. "I saw her, Merryn. Well, it wasn't literally her, but it was her in another body." He hadn't meant to tell them about falling into the well and the million fish that carried him over to the other side. It just came out. "Remember when you told me you couldn't just fall through to the other side, you had to be taken. Well, I was carried across by millions of tiny fish. And when I surfaced on the other side, there he was. And he was with her."

"Fish, you say?" Merryn's hand was on his arm.

"Tiny fish, all packed together."

"The souls of the dead," Merryn said. "There are tales of women who net fish from pools such as this one, and when they eat them, conceive the child who will bear the same soul. You were carried by the Sluagh, lad, the host of the dead."

"Enough nonsense." Bronwyn snatched the book from Merryn, slipped it back into the baggie and slapped it into Connor's hands. She caught his wrist, her nails digging in, and whispered through clenched teeth, "You'll not come near my aunt again with this insane talk, and if you do, I'll bring it to the attention of the authorities and have you charged with harassment."

He matched Bronwyn in a stare-down, not daring to glance at Merryn.

"Your brother is split in two," he said with all the certainty he possessed. "Don't you see?"

"I've heard enough."

She took Merryn's arm and guided her through the double doors. They swung closed slowly. Iris was speechless for once.

But the last thing Connor saw was worry in Merryn's bright blue eyes peeking over her shoulder as the doors closed.

That night, Connor sat at his desk and stared at his homework. The sound of Chinese hip hop seeped from Aaron's headphones. Connor's roommate was focused on cutting and pasting information from a website into a research paper on the nature of the muses in Greek literature. He noticed that Aaron hadn't bothered to make the fonts the same, and Connor didn't bother to point it out.

Connor turned Merryn's little whiskey bottle over and over and the water inside glugged back and forth. What if the water had magically awakened Dish when Iris dripped it on him? What would become of the man Connor saw on the other side? He felt sure if Dish woke up here, it would mean death over there. And if Dish died here… would he be lost to the sea, just like the kite? Or would he be free?

He popped the cork and put his finger to the mouth of the bottle and let a single, fat drop bead there. Inside the globe of well water, he saw a perfect, upside down version of the poster above him. Ozzy Osbourne in inverted miniature.

Slowly, he swept his extended finger around the walls of his room. Everything was transformed by the bulging surface tension of the drop until it reached his window and the blazing eye of the moon. He looked deeper into the droplet and saw something move. It wasn't the moon at all. It looked like a bird, but the drop was just too small to tell.

He picked up the bottle of water and held it up to the moon, but the label hid the water from the light.

Flinging open the bottom drawer of his desk, he dug around, throwing stuff out on the floor.

"What are you doing?" Aaron dropped his headphones around his neck.

"Looking for something."

Connor found the little glass container, shaped like a

Christmas ornament that came with jellybeans from his mom. After dumping the last of the stale candy onto his desk, he opened the bottle and poured the well water into it.

He shut off the room lights and held the water up to the moon.

"Hey! I'm working here, douche!" Aaron said.

"Just give me a minute."

The moonlight fractured and bounced through the water until it revealed a fire snapping inside the glass ball. And across that fire sat the man who must be Dish. The scene wasn't inverted like everything else, but right side up. Dish sharpened an axe and talked to the water in the ball like it was a person, but Connor couldn't hear anything. Dish smiled and looked into the fire. Then his eyes locked on Connor's. In those eyes stewed a lifetime of struggle and Connor knew the axe in his hand waited for battle. Dish had a score to settle. That's why he had to go back.

He felt the words move from Dish's mind to his own, the same words the woman had said to him.

Give me time.

How could Connor give Dish time? He didn't hold the kite string.

The lights went on.

"I have a paper to write, asshole."

Just like that, the man inside the water was gone and only the moon and fluorescent light remained.

Chapter 24

Lyleth awoke, her face buried in the crook of her arm to stifle the stench of death. It was day again. The tent was crowded with sacks of flour and barrels of salted meats. Outside, the camp clamored with the ring of an anvil, the passing of horses and boots, and as daylight drifted with motes of dust through the oilcloth, she struggled to focus.

Beside Nechtan's body rose the center-post of the tent, swaying and creaking with a passing breeze.

Had Fiach ordered she be left without food or water? Or perhaps it was Ava, for the news Lyleth had overheard from passing soldiers said the she-king had arrived.

Lyleth had spent the previous day looking for something, anything that might offer a way out, but now that Ava had arrived, her desperation to free herself consumed her. She attempted to drag the body, but the rope cut deeper into her wrists until she lost feeling in her hands. She considered kicking down the tent pole, thinking it would bring enough men she might snatch a dagger in the confusion. But even if she could get her hands on one, cutting herself free would take time. No, her captors would have to put the weapon in her hand and help her cut the rope. Once free, she would be faced with a quandary—run, or stay long enough to slit Ava's throat.

She heaved against the rope.

The body was stiff as a tree and just as heavy. She struggled to her feet and straddled the corpse so she could use her legs for leverage in an attempt to drag it. She had to clutch Nechtan's hair to relieve the strain on her wrists, but it was still no good. Frantic, she flung herself against the rope again and again like a tethered beast until she fell, exhausted, on top of his body. The wracking sobs wouldn't stop, so she stuffed the hem of Nechtan's cloak in her mouth and screamed until she was empty.

How long she lay there listening to flies, she didn't know. The hum of their wings filled her belly; the gentle sway of the tent pole lulled her until she imagined Nechtan's chest rose and fell as if he slept.

A beguiling calm came over her.

She measured her breath and with each inhalation, she became more certain. Fiach was right. She'd loved Nechtan long before her soul came to roost in this flesh, and she would love him in other lands, warmed by other suns, where her mind failed to remember who he was. She'd lived every waking day of this life like a tree in winter, storing love in her roots, letting the wind strip the leaves from her branches.

Come spring, sap pulses from root to leaf, marrow to fingertips.

Lyleth had forgotten how to summon sap to green shoot, to call forth leaves and blooms from her heart.

She thirsted for spring. She thirsted.

Drifting at the bottom of a little hide coracle, she rocked heedlessly on an endless sea. Nechtan was fishing with his drop line, his beardless boy's face painted against the brightest blue sky. Or was it the sea beyond him?

Sky became sea and sea became sky.

He was laughing and his laughter sounded like a gull's cry, or was it a crow?

She awoke with a start.

The croak of a crow came from somewhere near the tent opening. She forced her eyes to focus, but couldn't see past a barrel of salted cod. If she could move it, she might at least have a view out the tent flap. She summoned enough strength to sit up and brace her feet against the barrel, her lower back to Nechtan's hip. She straightened her legs and pushed. The corpse moved a hand's width, and the barrel tumbled and rolled away to reveal a view of the sun-dappled ground outside.

Fresh air kissed her face. Boots moved by. The sound of a dice game drifted in and a crow hopped into the tent.

It ruffled its feathers, hopped across the damp ground and perched on Nechtan's foot.

"Go on. Be gone." She kicked at it, but it hopped just out of reach.

A shaft of sunlight gave its feathers a queer ruby sheen. A red crow. Could it be the same bird she and Nechtan had seen on the heath? That bird had unsettled Lyleth, for it watched with a far keener eye than it should. Who wore these feathers?

The bird cocked its head, its beak agape. Then it hopped across the grain stubble, to perch again on the corpse's booted foot.

Lyleth kicked at it again, but it jumped and avoided the blow, and hopped the length of the corpse until it stood on Nechtan's mailed chest, its eye fixed on Lyleth.

It croaked.

"Are you so afraid to speak to me? Come, coward, let me see you."

The crow hopped just out of reach. Lyleth lay still and it wasn't long before it crept back, making its way to Nechtan's face where it set to work on his eyes.

With her limited reach, Lyleth grabbed for the bird's legs, but it took wing, alighted on her shoulder for a heartbeat, and flew out into the brightening day.

But for the bird, no one had come into the tent since she was left there, and her thirst was growing fierce. Lyleth's sense of smell had long since shut down in self-defense and her consciousness ebbed and flowed with the hum of the flies.

Nechtan would be nearing Cedewain. And what then? Every man and woman in the Five Quarters would know there was one living Nechtan and one bloated, rotting corpse of the same man.

By afternoon, her tongue cleaved to the roof of her mouth and she could no longer produce spit. But her ears still worked. She listened to snatches of conversation, blacksmiths and armorers. Ava had indeed reached the camp and they would march north at dawn.

It was late in the day when a figure darkened the entrance to the tent. A druí looked down his grey robe at Lyleth, and it seemed he waited for her to speak. Was it him who had been watching her with the eyes of the red crow?

He put a cloth to his nose, no doubt soaked in flower oils to dull the stench, and with that motion, he bared his wrist. A tattoo of an eel crawled there. Ava's solás.

Lyleth's voice sounded much like the crow's. "You've come without your lady's permission." Ava would never have sent her solás to Lyleth, for nothing but truth could pass between two who served the green gods.

"I am Jeven," he said. "And I cannot let a sister suffer. I must see to your needs."

She worked hard for the words. "What else could I possibly need?" She nodded to her anchor.

Kneeling beside her, he uncorked a waterskin and held it to her lips. The trickle streamed past her throat and into her belly and she swallowed faster than she should.

"What must I trade for this short extension of my life, Jeven?"

"You spoke the Words of Waking Stone," he said with obvious admiration. "And those words bear a price—"

"Because we fear the wisdom of the Old Blood? We think of ourselves as children playing with fire. Children grow up. But the chosen of the green gods, the exiled ones... no, they are changeless, they grow neither older nor wiser, Jeven. They seek only the way home."

"Of one thing, I am certain," he said. "No price Ava can exact from you could equal the price the green gods will demand."

"Ah. You're here to deliver their bill?" She forced a weak smile.

He returned it, saying, "I'm here to see that you live. Nothing more." He gave her another drink.

"You've heard rumors about me." She hadn't meant it to sound like an accusation, but it did. "You wonder if it could possibly be true that a man might be raised from the dead clothed in his own likeness, and you wait eagerly to see me meet my fate, saying to yourself, 'Shall I study such a waking?'"

She lunged against her tether and he nearly fell backward. "You know as well as I," she said, "that the man who rides to Cedewain is most certainly Nechtan, and this travesty, parading his body before his men means nothing. Not to you, not to me."

He met her gaze evenly, and she saw his answer there. "You're wondering why I would risk so much to call a murdered king back from the dead. You must know the answer by now, Jeven. You must know the Bear comes, riding the wake of Ava's battlecry."

His grey eyes flitted nervously to hers. She knew he could offer nothing but silence and remain loyal to the she-king. He shouldn't even be here.

"I am bound to my king," he said at last.

"As am I." Lyleth tugged at the ropes at her wrists. "My king was murdered by his wife and her healer. Irjan had but one task and one task only—to murder Nechtan and see Ava to the throne. To make way for the Bear. And the judges of the wildwood crowned her. Out of fear, Jeven. The same reason you serve her now."

He put the waterskin to her lips again, then took a loaf of bread from his satchel and wedged it between her palms. With one last questioning look, he started away.

"Our lives are not our own, you and I," she called after him. "Our lives are bound to this land. But your soul belongs to you alone, solás. Remember that."

A hand's breadth at a time, Lyleth managed to push Nechtan's body to the edge of the tent. Here, she could lay her head on the ground and take in fresh air. With one eye, she could see under the oilcloth to the camp outside. The sun was setting and men lined up at cook fires for supper.

That afternoon, they'd stripped Lyleth's tent of supplies and loaded a wagon with flour sacks and barrels of salt pork and cod. It appeared they would indeed march at dawn.

Ava wouldn't execute Lyleth. To do so would risk tipping the unsteady scales of her support. No, Ava would simply leave Lyleth out in this open field tied to her king. Wolves and thirst would do the rest.

Nechtan's corpse wore his ceremonial dress, silver gilt mail that had tarnished, a surcoat of polished linen embroidered with a crimson water horse. They had taken his sword belt, of course. But with luck, they'd forgotten he always kept a knife in his left boot. But had they buried him with one?

Lyleth's hands were far from his boot, and trying to double the body over was impossible, for rigor had set like stone. She tried to slip her hands out of the rope, slick with blood from struggling, but it was useless. Nechtan's flesh held her fast.

With the supplies gone, nothing remained but Lyleth, the corpse and a box with one hooked nail head protruding from a slat. After frustrating failures, she finally hooked her boot on the nail and worked the laces loose. Her leg cramped with the effort, but at last, she kicked off the boot with her other foot.

Sliding her leg over Nechtan to straddle him, she felt for his left boot with her bare foot. She caught the laces between her toes and pulled slowly. They came free at last without knotting; now she just needed to loosen them. She pushed out the tongue of the buckskin boot with her toes, and when it was loose enough, it was time to pull it off.

Clamping her hands on either side of the corpse's neck, she rolled quickly to her back, forcing the body to come with her. Holding her breath, her face pressed into the ripples of his mail, she felt for his booted ankle with both feet and, locking her feet around his ankle, she straightened her knees.

The boot barely budged. His feet were as swollen as his guts.

She rolled the corpse back off her and went back to the laces and, very slowly, pulled them out of the grommets. After four tries, the boot slid off his heel.

She pushed the body off her and took another look under the tent. Dirt clung to the sweat on her face and her breath kicked up a small cloud of dust that stung her eyes. Darkness was falling.

With the boot between her feet, she drew her knees up. She tried twice and lost the boot each time, but the third time, it came with her feet and she dropped it on her lap. Peering in, she could just see the hilt of a meat knife.

It was well past dark when she finally worked the boot to her hands. Her body was failing her. Her fingers fumbled the blade in the darkness. She lay there too long, her head on Nechtan's shoulder.

The sound of laughter drifted in from the camp, belches and clattering bowls, steel on whetstone. Firelight made ghosts of passing men. Was this the price she paid for raising Nechtan? To die bound to his castoff flesh?

If someone came in and found his boot in her hands, it would be over.

With fingers sticky with drying blood, she finally pinched the hilt between her fore and middle finger and slowly slid the blade out.

When she had the hilt clutched in her fist, she knocked the boot away with her elbow, and repositioned her body to cover it.

She placed the blade between the rope and the body's neck and worked her fists in a sawing motion. She couldn't shut out the sound of it cutting the cartilage and muscle of his neck. It made her gorge rise, and if she'd had anything in her stomach, she would have lost it.

She was almost through the rope when a commotion erupted outside. Boots moved by quickly and the sound of rhythmic footfalls could only mean guards.

The knife slipped easily beneath the mail collar at Nechtan's throat. Covering the hilt with her bloody fists, she pretended to sleep, but her eyes were open enough to see Ava step into the tent.

Chapter 25

Weary from the day's ride, Ava wrapped herself in a spearman's cloak and pulled the hood low over her face. It wouldn't do for her men to know about this meeting with Lyleth. Fiach led her through camp, bustling with activity as they prepared to move north. She longed to give the command, to march into Cedewain and rend the walls of Marchlew's fortress and remove Nechtan like the meat from a nut. But armies moved as quickly as the glaciers of her homeland.

"I've awaited your command before dealing with her."

Fiach meant Lyleth, of course. He must have shared a tender reunion with his lover, tender enough that he saw fit to tie her to a stinking corpse. Since she left Caer Ys, Ava had been nursing a dark fantasy—she would command Fiach to strangle his lover while she watched, but realized with dismay that she needed him far too badly to test his loyalties in such a way.

"My command," Ava reminded him, "was to capture Lyleth and Nechtan. Without him, she's worthless to me."

"He'll bargain for her."

"He'll do no such thing, and suggesting it tells me you know nothing of Nechtan, nor do you know this druí you've bedded."

He bristled predictably. Trusting him was sheer folly.

"Wait outside." Ava took his lantern and entered the tent, pinching her nose with a cloth soaked in lavender oil.

Motionless, Lyleth lay pressed to Nechtan's corpse as if spooning with her love, her eyes flitting beneath the lids. She pretended at sleep. Ava sat on a box of nails and clucked in mock disappointment.

"You can raise the dead, but you can't sever a simple rope."

"'Tis the simplest of ropes that bind us the fastest." Lyleth's dry croak resounded with a familiar contempt.

Ava held out the lamp to get a better look at Nechtan's love. Shadows circled her eyes and she was pale as the moon, her wrists bloody and raw, but the self-righteousness Ava had known so well burned in Lyleth hotter than ever. Death would cure that.

"Tell me how you took the life of a guardian," Lyleth demanded, meeting Ava's eyes at last.

"With a spear." Ava smiled. "Is it so hard to believe your green gods would choose me to lead your land?"

"Your soulstalker had a hand in the guardian's death."

"Irjan? She left me at the well called Mogg's Eye with a spear and a net, for I saw the well in a dream, saw the guardian herself call to me. Shall I tell you a bedtime tale?"

"Tale indeed."

"Irjan said my dream was a prophecy. So, I waited at the well, alone. As dawn came, so did the beast. A 'water worm,' your people call it, with a head as big as a wolfhound's. It rose from the water, its eye meeting mine, and it waited. It never tried to flee, but gave itself to my spear, Lyleth. Irjan did nothing more than help me cleave its head from its body.

"You can feel the truth in me, druí," Ava said. "I can hide nothing from you in my touch, at least, so Nechtan believed."

Ava knelt down on the stinking ground and placed both palms on Lyleth's face. The truth stained those sallow cheeks, burned away Lyleth's defiance and left the color of despair.

Ava leaned close and whispered in Lyleth's ear, "Your gods chose me."

It was a moment to be most humbly thankful for. But only Lyleth's tears would give Ava the satisfaction she yearned for, and these, she knew, the druí would never give.

"The same green gods who gave Nechtan back to you, gave me the life of one of their own guardians," Ava said. "What can this mean, oh wise druí? Tell me. What spectacle have they set in motion? They've armed us both, and now sit back to watch us bleed each other dry."

"Nechtan will be reaching Marchlew—"

"He stands no chance against Fiach and me. You're sending him to his death."

"None of us stand a chance against the Bear," Lyleth said. "You think he'll sit on his frozen throne while his daughter takes the land he's lusted for his whole life?"

Ava had heard this rant before.

"I should thank you, I suppose. You saved me, Lyleth. Wedding me to Nechtan. It was you who gave me the life of an Ildana. But it was also you who taught me the shame of jealousy."

"You loved him. There is no shame in that."

"Love? You should lecture me on love, druí. You who seduced him. You who made a fool of him, and me. And now you summon his ghost as if the shame I suffered at his hands wasn't enough."

Ava stood and paced the short distance to the tent flap and back, her eyes on Nechtan's bloating body.

Lyleth struggled to her knees.

"So in your rage," Lyleth said, "you will destroy the land that's granted you refuge from your father's brutality? I know what he did to you—"

"You walked into this camp believing you had your talons dug into Fiach, that you could turn him against me—"

"Oh, Fiach will turn. He'll turn when he sees the Bear and

his thegns beach their longships on the shores of his land. Irjan has made straight the Bear's path to Cedewain. She's murdered your husband, seen you crowned, and sent a message every fortnight to your father.

"Rhys saw Irjan in the pigeon house, saw her with the bird keeper. You believe Irjan murdered Nechtan in the name of honor? You are but a girl, aren't you?" Lyleth's sunken eyes blazed now. "When the Bear comes, Ava, who will you fight?"

Ava started out of the tent, but Lyleth's voice followed.

"Irjan gave you the wings of the red crow… but you fail to see why."

Ava glanced back.

Lyleth's look said she'd untangled a puzzling knot; a revelation bloomed on her dirty face.

"You didn't know that Irjan murdered your babes. Your father sent Irjan to you as a gift," Lyleth cried, her voice quavering excitedly. "A slave who taught you to tether souls to your own, to fly on the wings of a red crow, to see with eyes that aren't your own. Irjan seduced you with a power so great you couldn't see what she was really doing."

Ava hesitated, her hand frozen on the tent flap.

"The Bear sent Irjan to kill Nechtan," Lyleth said. "To lead you to this very moment, to cleave this land in two so he can beach his ships and take what you've won for him."

Rage clouded Ava's vision. "We break camp at dawn," she said as evenly as possibly. "I entrust you and your love to the wolves."

Ava's men must have erected her tent by torchlight, a pavilion of oilcloth dressed up in a fluttering eel standard and oriflammes of brilliant silk. Inside, Ava found Irjan laying out a fresh gown, those black eyes perhaps concealing a true purpose. Had Ava failed to see what was right before her? Irjan might have killed Nechtan to make way for the Bear, but she certainly had no power over the green gods. Had the gods chosen Ava solely to hinder the Bear's plan?

If Irjan had come to poison Ava's womb... she made certain no son of Nechtan's waited to assume his throne.

Ava's heart raced. She tossed aside the spearman's cloak and stepped beside the brazier, her eyes never leaving Irjan.

"Fetch me something to eat."

"As you command."

When Irjan was gone, Ava summoned Gwylym.

"Send a man to follow her," Ava told him. "I want to know where she goes, what she does."

"Your slave is untrustworthy?"

"Not as untrustworthy as you." She smiled and gave his cheek a light brush with the back of her fingers. It wouldn't do for Gwylym to know of Lyleth's suspicions. The rock had started its long roll down the hill and neither Ava nor Lyleth could stop it now.

Gwylym ordered a waiting guard to follow Irjan, then helped Ava strip off the ceremonial sword, mail, quilted gambeson and coif that had pinched her head and torn at her hair. Playing the warrior was more uncomfortable than wearing a corset.

Finding a basin of warm water waiting, she splashed her face, washing the road grit from her eyes.

Her tent smelled of linseed oil and sweat, of peat fire and the fine dust of the harvested oat field beneath her boots. The smell brought an intense memory of Nechtan returning home to her after putting down a skirmish in the east. There was a deep sadness on him and, wordless, he had pulled her into his lap and held her, rocking her like a child, his eyes lost in the flames of the hearth beside them.

She splashed her face again, but the feeling wouldn't go.

Knowing nothing of war but the waiting that plagued women, fear quickened in her. The things Nechtan had seen in his short life would empty anyone of hope. And now she would lead these men to meet their king in battle, and if Lyleth was right, to meet a force they hoped never to meet again, Saerlabrand, the Bear of Sandkaldr. Ava's father.

Gwylym hung her armor on a stand with sticks for arms.

As if reading her thoughts, he sat down on a stool, pulled her into his lap and held her, tenderly, even fatherly.

"You'll stay behind the lines," he told her. "I won't let anything happen to you."

She pushed him away and found the gown Irjan had left on her cot. "No king stays behind the lines. I'll do what I must."

"You must stay alive. Leave the rest to Fiach and Lloyd."

"I am the king. Fiach and Lloyd act upon my command."

"And you've led an army before, love?"

"I've watched Nechtan lead this land for the last five years."

"Forgive me, but watching is not leading. You must take counsel from your chieftains and your solás—"

"I'll take counsel from you," she said. "You know better than anyone what Nechtan will do."

She slid back onto his lap, dandled his hair and kissed him, but she could only see Nechtan behind her closed eyes.

"Aye, I know what Nechtan would do," he said. "Not what Nechtan's ghost'll do."

Gwylym was hard.

She unlaced his trousers, hiked her gown to her waist, and straddled him. He groaned and pushed into her, his mail adding a tuneless chime to their coupling. But she could only think of Nechtan... and the Bear, his longships dragging onto the eastern shore, his thegns moving silently through the forest. Why had she not seen them while on the wing? She was looking for Nechtan, not ice-born.

She struggled from Gwylym's lap. He tried to pull her back, his grip more forceful than she liked.

Laughing, she drew the green stone blade from her boot, the one that had been the beewoman's. She held it playfully to Gwylym's unruly member.

"You'll get your fill of me when we've taken Cedewain,

love," she said, forcing a smile. "Until then, a hard cock makes for a savage fighting man."

He laughed. "Did Nechtan teach you that?" He stood and laced up his trousers.

"He taught me many things. He taught me jealousy. He taught me what wild, selfish desire does to a man. So, beware."

"Did you love him?"

His question was like a blow.

She held the green blade to the firelight. "Do you know what a soothblade is?"

"Looks like the work of the Old Blood."

"That it is. Jeven says the Old Blood used it to flay the truth from a man unwilling to give it. They would bleed him into a cup and their greenmen would read the truth there."

She held the bone handle out to Gwylym.

"Perhaps if you cut me, you'll know of my love."

He smiled sadly, took the blade from her, and slipped it back into the sheath hidden in her boot.

"I already know the truth."

Ava found no sleep. She woke long before dawn and stood at the foot of Irjan's cot, but five paces from her own. Irjan's breath came in a musical wheeze and Ava wondered if she dreamt of her reward. What had the Bear promised this slave?

Irjan had taught Ava much; she had taught her enough.

Ava found the green blade in her hand, warm from her boot. Killing Irjan would change nothing of what faced her in the glens of Cedewain, but she would know the truth.

So sharp was the blade that Irjan never stirred while her veins spilled the venom of a thousand snakes, spurting over Ava's hands, sticky with deceit. Her eyes flew open, and Ava gazed into them, saying, "If I can tether your soul, traitor, I shall."

Chapter 26

Dr. Adelman's office looked more like a tea parlor than a shrink's place. There were little lace doilies under the lamps, a bookcase full of thrift store novels, and fluorescent lights covered with plastic photo panels of a perfect blue sky with puffy white clouds. But the light tubes behind the clouds still hummed with electricity.

Dr. Adelman flipped through Connor's file.

"The events that have confronted you in the past few years are more burdensome than most face in a lifetime." He set the file on his lap and churned the air with his hands. "Tell me, Connor, how are you feeling right now?"

When he locked his fingers over his stomach, he looked even more like Big Bird.

"Fine. I feel fine."

"Still having nightmares?"

"Doesn't everyone?"

The laundry list continued: Hallucinations? A craving for drugs or alcohol? Sex? Who doesn't crave sex? Rage that's uncontrollable? An urge to hurt yourself or others?

"How is the Risperdol working for you?" Adelman asked.

"Great."

"No nausea?"

Connor thought about the days he'd missed class due to the side effects of the drug he wasn't taking.

"Some," he said.

"Good, good. Let's try a lower dose for now. And I think an antidepressant is warranted as well." He scribbled out a prescription and handed it to Connor.

"Now, where were we?" Adelman crossed his legs, pen poised over his legal pad. "Mr. Cavendish is responsible for the school retaining you as a student. He negotiated another chance for you after," he glanced back at previous notes, "a situation in which you were acting out and admittedly seeking expulsion."

"That's about it."

Connor couldn't look at Big Bird and talk at the same time. So, he worked at a doodle he'd started on a handout outlining the side effects of Risperdol. A water horse. It looked like the cover art on a Megadeth album.

He kicked back in the recliner and worked at the shading on the water horse, delivering a moving monologue about how Dish was important because he grounded Connor in the real world, a place he didn't like much, how Dish had helped him through some really rough times right after his brother's funeral, yadda yadda, all the stuff they like to hear.

"Dish was a safe harbor for you," Adelman said. "With your feelings of guilt over your brother's death, he offered an objective, non-familial mooring."

Connor was feeling seasick.

He didn't want to talk about this for the thousandth time, and he certainly wouldn't tell Adelman about seeing Dish in the well water. After relating the story of falling into the hot tub and seeing Dish with the woman who looked something like Lyla Bendbow Adelman had put Connor on an antipsychotic drug. To admit that he was seeing shit in globes of water would up the ante, and the next step could only be a psych ward and a straight jacket. Maybe he really was nuts. He had held Merryn's well water to every light source possible—candles, stars, sunlight, even a laser pointer, but it was clearly a one time show, just like the trip through the well, a teaser, making Connor believe he could change a future that had already been written.

Adelman droned on about dream therapy and the need for Connor to start a dream journal.

He let his head fall back on the pillow of the recliner and watched the photo clouds move across the fluorescent light panels. They went from left to right and Connor could swear they curled and evaporated and reformed.

"Okay, so right now I see those clouds moving like they're real."

"Everyone does, Connor. Your brain sees what it expects to see, not what actually is."

Connor digested this bit of double talk for a minute.

"So, my brain's been programmed to expect clouds to move in the sky, so the fake ones do, too?"

"That's about it."

"So, how can we be sure anything we see is real?"

"I suppose, on some level, we can't."

"Then why are you so sure that what I saw in that well, or hot tub, or whatever, wasn't real?"

"Okaaaaay. You saw a man you concluded was Dish, though physically he looked very different than Dish. He was with a strange woman, wearing strange clothing, and they seemed to be in some kind of danger."

"She was bleeding, yeah."

"Tell me," Adelman said, "what could have pre-determined that your brain would choose to see Dish in this situation? Why did you need to see him aiding a woman in distress? Acting chivalrous and honorable?"

"Maybe there is another world. How 'bout that? Maybe there's a shitload of other worlds and some of us are just crazy enough to see them."

"Your need, Connor. Your deepest need right now is to know that Dish is all right. That's why you built that vision of him, real though it may have seemed. You have a deep, deep need to heal yourself of your feeling of responsibility."

"The word is guilt, doc."

Connor kicked the leg rest closed on the recliner and leaned on his knees.

"Dish is lying there with tubes down his throat because of me."

He slapped his chest with a palm, buried his face in his hands, and willed the tears to stay where they were.

Maybe Adelman was right. Maybe Connor's brain had made up all these visions to put the blame on someone else, on Lyla Bendbow, or whoever called Dish back to the other side. But deep down, Connor didn't believe that for a second.

A long heavy silence made it worse.

Adelman handed him a tissue, saying, "Are you still angry with Dish?"

"I was just a 'job' to Dish."

"As your teacher and mentor?"

"Yeah."

"How so?" More air churning.

Connor had never really thought about what Dish's goal was in saving him from expulsion. "I guess he thought he could 'tough love' me into accepting my life. Myself."

"And you think that Dish befriended you solely because he was doing his job as your teacher." It was a statement, not a question.

"I know so. He told me so."

"Do you also believe that the reasons for initiating a relationship often don't change the outcome?"

"What does that mean?"

Dr. Adelman pushed his glasses up his nose. "Just that Dish may have been asked to look after you as part of his job, but, he may have developed a genuine bond with you, nonetheless."

Nonetheless. Connor liked that word.

He looked back up at the clouds racing across the lights. They made him feel like he was flying. "I suppose so."

"Before our time is up," Adelman said, "I have something to tell you."

He set Connor's file aside and forced the solid eye contact; his heavy brows tucked like bird wings. This could only be bad.

"I've had a discussion with Mr. Cavendish's sister, Bronwyn. I believe you've met."

"Yeah. She told me I couldn't contact her anymore."

"Yes, I'm aware of that. That's why she asked me to tell you the decision has been made to remove life support from her brother."

Connor was on his feet. "You mean pull the plug?"

"She thought it was only right to let you know—"

"When? When is she going to do it?"

"As soon as the last tests are complete. They're looking for specific brain activity—"

"When?"

"Connor, Dish's quality of life is ebbing by the day—"

"When?"

"The end of the week, most likely."

Connor grabbed his sweatshirt and headed for the door. "Our time is up, doc."

"Connor." Adelman met him at the door and caught his arm. "I want to help you let go."

"Dish would never let go of me."

Brother Mike drove silently while Connor stared out the window and chewed his nails. At least Mike didn't ask him any questions. Because he knew, that's why. They all knew.

It was only ten o'clock when he got back to school. Connor couldn't find a reason not to go to class; he'd played the nausea card a bit too much lately. So he came in halfway through English and slid into his desk. The sub gave him a sour look, an ancient lady with lipstick that seeped into the wrinkles around her mouth making her look like a pink sea anemone.

Dish's classroom was just like he'd left it—fallen stacks of books on the floor and posters of dead writers. Connor recognized one poster as a picture of the Irish poet W. B. Yeats, author of one of the books Connor'd found on Dish's desk. Yeats wore big old-school glasses and a bow tie. The quote on the poster said:

Come away O Human Child!
To the waters and the wild
With a Faery, hand in hand,
For the world's more full of weeping
Than you can understand.

"Hand in hand," Connor heard himself whisper.

Iris gave him a scowl from across the aisle, the long side of her hair swaying. She handed him a sheet of paper and a pen and nodded to the essay prompt on the board, something about the use of the chorus in Greek tragedy.

To the waters and the wild…

That's where Connor wanted to go.

He gripped the pen, his knuckles going white, and started moving it over his paper. It wasn't words that emerged, but twisting, writhing coils of scaled muscle. The ballpoint rolled right off the paper, up and over his soft white skin, leaving a glistening blue trail. He couldn't have stopped if he wanted to. The image grew from the spot where his wrist met his palm, up and around the tendons and veins. The horse's mane knotted into an impossible design, entwined with its tail, its front hooves striking out.

Connor wanted to slip onto its back and let it take him down, take him away, take him to Dish.

The bell rang.

Iris was standing over him, her backpack slung over one shoulder, her eyes on his wrist.

"Shit. That's awesome."

Connor spent the afternoon watching every online video there was on how to drive a stick shift. According to Bluesnooze, an apparent authority on carjacking, to start a manual car with a dead battery, one had only to put it in neutral, get it rolling, and then execute something called "popping the clutch." But it was imperative you keep the engine going to charge the battery; otherwise, you'd have to do it all over again.

Slipping out of the dorm and driving around the overflow parking lot was something that could only be done in the dark. And night was slow to come.

Connor waited till after bed check, which was about ten, and then headed out with Dish's car keys.

The overflow parking lot was nice and isolated. There were only a few lights there that worked, and it was on the terrace level below the school itself. Connor couldn't turn on the headlights—no battery.

Leaving the car door open, he inserted the key and turned it to "accessory" just like the video said. With the gearshift in neutral, he got out and started pushing. It took a bit to get it rolling across the open parking lot, but when he had some speed, he hopped in, forced the gear into first and let the clutch out.

The engine turned over, the car leapt forward, then stalled.

After the fifth try, he was soaked with sweat, and he'd reached the lower end of the lot.

He slapped the steering wheel and rested his forehead on it. "Shit."

Looking up, he saw a shadow flash across the window. Iris' face would make anyone piss their pants. She tapped the dirty windshield with her nails, and after Connor started breathing again, he rolled down the window.

"Scared ya, huh?" She snapped her gum. "Who said you could drive Dish's car?"

"What the hell, Iris?"

"Where you going?"

"To hell. Leave me alone."

"Okay." She started away. "Brother Mike would like to hear about it, I'm sure."

He leaned out the window. "So what do I have to do, give you my pills or something?"

"Just take me with you."

He slapped the steering wheel again and sighed. "Shit. Okay, get back there and push."

By one o'clock in the morning Connor was shifting into fourth on his way to the hospital and Iris was adjusting the radio. They'd only had to push it twice on the way.

The main entrance to the hospital had closed at ten, and only the emergency entrance was open. Connor led the way through the emergency waiting room, down a corridor marked "Radiology" to a bank of elevators. The TV was still going in the I.C.U. waiting room.

"Just wait for me here," Connor pleaded with Iris. "I need some time with him."

"I got that part. Really." Iris plopped down on the couch in front to the TV, saying, "He can hear you, ya know. He might be in a coma, but they say the last sense to go is hearing. Make it count, Connor."

He buzzed the intercom at the door.

The nurse's voice wasn't as nice as Holly's. "It's late for a visit," she said.

"I promise I won't wake him up." When she didn't respond to his stupid joke, he added, "Please, it's important."

The door buzzed open.

The nurse scowled and nodded toward Dish's alcove. "Ten minutes," she said.

He sat down on the molded plastic chair and swallowed hard. Dish's lips were raw and cracked and he smelled like antiseptic and plastic tubing. His hair looked longer. Connor'd read somewhere that even after you die, your hair grows for a while because the follicles don't know they're dead yet. What other parts don't know they're dead? Someone had shaved him. He looked pale, almost transparent.

Connor took the little book by C. W. Pritchard from his pocket and held it out.

"I got the book you were looking for."

The nurse was watching him from her desk and he felt a self-conscious wave wash over him, like when someone catches you talking to yourself. Screw that. He opened the book to page 73.

"There it is. Just like the one on your arm."

He held the picture next to Dish's arm. The I.V. had been moved to his neck and the tattoo looked even creepier on his pale skin.

"You were taking me to the bookstore to buy this book, Dish. Because you knew this picture was in it. You knew it. You remembered it. And here," he flipped to the picture of Lyla Bendbow. "I saw you with this woman. You know her. Who the hell is she, Dish?"

The hussshh-husssshh of the respirator answered. He slapped the book closed.

The nurse gave him an "I'm watching" look.

"I really, really need to talk to you, Dish."

He felt emptiness well in his chest.

"I need you to talk to me. Please. They're gonna pull the plug. Do you hear me? They're going to let you die unless you open your eyes, and I don't think I can make it—"

He hung his head and stuffed his hands in his pockets. He found the little whiskey bottle there. Maybe Iris just didn't have the right touch.

He uncorked it and poured a little of the water into his hand, then sprinkled it over Dish's forehead and chest. When nothing happened, the tears wouldn't wait any longer. He spilled them too, but they didn't have the power to wake him either.

Connor locked his fingers with Dish's and squeezed. He tried to warm Dish's hand with his own and only then noticed that the water horse he had drawn on his left arm matched up with Dish's on his right.

"Like a mirror," he said.

His voice cracked and fell into pieces.

"I know you're in another place, I saw you there. And you saw me. I know it. If they pull the plug, your life will end, in both worlds. You need to do something, because I can't."

Then he felt it, a tingling just like the water had felt when he fell into the well, like his skin was more than alive, more than just flesh. It was light. It surged with his pulse from his wrist to Dish's, moving, like roots through soil.

The skin where the two images met began to burn and Connor could swear he saw a faint green glow flicker and dance between their wrists, sparking just like phosphorescence in the waves.

He closed his fingers tighter and Dish's hand got so, so warm. And finally, just perceptibly, Dish's fingers closed on Connor's.

Chapter 27

Sheltered behind a maze of steep ramparts and ditches known as a ráth, the stronghold of Caer Cedewain safeguarded Marchlew's lands, a web of highland glens and forests carved by rivers, mountain brooks and tumbling falls. Home to shepherds, weavers and miners, Cedewain was said to produce the most handsome people in the Five Quarters due to the land's nearness to the sky. Indeed, Nechtan felt he could touch the race of clouds streaming from the peaks behind Caer Cedewain.

From the west end of the glen, Nechtan could make out the snake of a curtain wall. The Ildana had extended the fortifications of the ráth, built a thousand years before by the Old Blood. It sat on a headland, its back pressed to the teeth of the Pendynas Mountains. Caer Cedewain guarded Maiden Pass, an aptly named parting of the mountains which no invader had penetrated since the fortress was built. From here, the range of the Pendynas drove through Arvon like the spine of a great serpent crawling northward to the Isles called the Bloody Spear, where the granite beast dove to the bottomless depths of the Broken Sea.

Marchlew had clearly raised the standard of war, and as Nechtan rode closer, it was clear this battle would happen with or without him. A sea of men were encamped outside the ráth. Looking out over the growing swell of soldiers, he found himself wondering why Lyleth needed him at all.

He led Dylan up from the vale, to the outer earthworks. Nechtan saw tartans from west Arvon, hosts of archers from the north coast with their longbows of starwood, spearmen from Ynys Keldean, even men from the outer islands of Sun's Rest and Ynys Gall.

Nechtan pulled the cowl of his cloak closer as they rode through the turns of ditch-work leading to the main gate.

"Act like a lordling," he told Dylan.

"Pompous and full of hot air?" Dylan smiled at him.

"You already have the hot air."

A crow caught Nechtan's eye, hopping from a wagon to alight on a stanchion. As Nechtan passed beneath it, the bird spread its wings and gaped at him, croaking with a rhythmic jig of its head. He looked up at feathers tinged blood red, its eye cocked to take in Nechtan's passing.

"Looks like the same crow," Dylan said.

"Aye, so it does."

Lyl had said it was a tethered soul, watching with borrowed eyes. But who watched? Nechtan would lay a feast for this crow soon enough.

Once at the gate, they dismounted at the request of the guards, and gave up their horses to stable boys.

"I bear a message for Marchlew from Lyleth," Dylan told the guards, "solás to the king."

"And who might you be, lad?"

Dylan glanced over his shoulder at Nechtan standing behind him as a servant would. Dylan stuttered, "I'm uh…"

"My lord is 'prenticed to Lyleth," Nechtan offered.

"Aye, so I am. 'Prenticed. Dylan, I'm called."

"My lord prepares for war," the guard said. "This message best be important."

"Very," Dylan said with some authority.

The guard opened a small wicket door just big enough for

one man at a time to pass through the massive gate. The chains on the gate wheel chattered and the inner portcullis opened.

A guard escorted them through the inner bailey thick with armorers and the smoke from several forges, then on through an empty revel hall, down a narrow corridor, to the gallery, a long chamber with shutters that opened onto a garden. Dylan craned his neck at the carvings on the barrel vault of the ceiling and tapestries that hung between arched doorways.

"Close your mouth," Nechtan whispered to Dylan. "You'll catch flies."

"'Tis so grand."

Outside the gallery, Kyndra, Nechtan's sister, had planted a garden with flowers that bloomed only white. She called it a moon garden, and Nechtan imagined it as Kyndra's refuge, glorious in the spring and magical on a summer's moonlit night. Kyndra preferred to take her meals here rather than the hall, especially when the seasons turned cold, for the gallery faced south. But now, the flowers of her moon garden had faded; a few yellowing petals clung to swollen seedpods, ready to burst and scatter themselves.

The gallery was somewhat small to hold chieftains from all reaches of Cedewain and Arvon. They crowded one long trestle table, Pyrs and Desmund and chieftains Nechtan had fought beside since he was old enough to carry a sword.

Flanked by Kyndra and their son Talan, a spidery boy close in age to Dylan, Marchlew labored to breathe. He had grown larger since Nechtan had last seen him, and Kyndra more wraith-like. He knew she would prefer to seep into the soil of her garden, to be reassembled by root and leaf into a flower of brief beauty. Perhaps she already had.

"Dylan, is it?" Marchlew bellowed. "What news do you bring from that reckless sister of the green, eh? Animator of cold flesh, I hear, and cogwheel of insurrection. I suppose I'll have to thank Lyleth for that."

Dylan stepped aside, and Nechtan came forward. He showed his palms and pushed back his hood.

"I am Lyleth's message."

The chieftains fell silent. Then, as if waking from a dream, they got to their feet and moved toward him until they formed a circle, seeming afraid to come any closer.

But Nechtan couldn't take his eyes off his sister, knowing it was she who would decide if he was real. Kyndra was on her feet, clinging to Talan's shoulder. Lines of disquiet marred a face that once worried over nothing more than knots in her hair. Nechtan should have considered what he would say to her, but instead, he found himself wondering if she'd ever really loved a man. When he brought her north so many years ago, had Nechtan taken Kyndra from a lover to wed this obscene excuse for a chieftain?

Nechtan realized the only sound in the room was Marchlew's wolfhound chewing a bone until Dylan cleared his throat.

Nechtan held out his hands to Kyndra, but she wouldn't take them, she just gave him an ashen stare. He stepped into the sunlight that streamed from the high windows. Let them take a good look.

"It's me, Kyndra."

"It can't be." Marchlew hoisted himself to his feet and drilled Nechtan with bloodshot eyes. "Ava parades Nechtan's dead body through the streets of Caer Ys. Nechtan's as dead as Black Brac himself. So tell me, who in the name of the mother's dugs are you?"

Nechtan would let these people decide who he was. He looked from face to disbelieving face until his eyes returned to Kyndra's, ready to spill tears.

"You're my sister. Look at me and tell me you know your little brother."

He moved from man to man round the circle, and looked

each in the eye. He took Pyrs by the shoulders; the man seemed frozen under his touch.

"Pyrs, you know me well. I held your newborn son at the last Beltaine fires. You named him for me. Your wife is Nest, daughter of Maddoc, there." He pointed at the warlord from Ynys Keldean, a bull of a man with a neck as broad as his head.

"And Griff and Desmund, you hold the land from the Gannet's Bath to the Bloody Spear, and your ports have been plundered, your women raped, your sons slain by the reavers from Sandkaldr."

He paced the circle and stopped again before Pyrs.

The chieftain of Arvon had arms like willow branches, his brows swept over brooding eyes. He'd been more a friend than liegeman to Nechtan.

Pyrs hands went to Nechtan's shoulders where he tested the meat in a strong grip. "My lord, men return from the dead only in tales of the Old Blood."

"I left much undone, Pyrs. By the will of the gods I've come to finish it."

"Was it the gods' will? Or Lyleth's?" Marchlew asked.

But Kyndra was floating toward him. He took her trembling hands as her legs gave way; he caught her and eased her to the flagstones, then knelt beside her.

"Then it's true," she said. "What she told me is true."

"Who told you?"

He followed Kyndra's gaze to a serving woman who stood in the doorway holding a platter. When she saw Nechtan, the platter crashed to the floor.

"By stars and stones, my lord does live indeed. Where is she, my lord? Where is my Lyleth?"

"Taken," Nechtan said to the woman, "by Fiach. How do you know Lyleth?"

"Served her, I did, me lord."

Nechtan helped Kyndra to her feet. She laced her fingers

in his and said to the serving woman, "We'll discuss this with a meal. See to the table, Dunla. My brother has a great hunger."

Nechtan oversaw the distribution of weapons to the men who poured into the vale of Cedewain. When word reached the more remote mountain valleys that Nechtan had returned, the numbers began to swell. He'd emptied Marchlew's armory, and still more men came. They'd have to fight with sickles and staves, he told them. "We'll fight with our fists for ye," was the reply. The more visible he was to these men, the more real he was, not only to them, but to himself.

When night fell, his thoughts turned to Lyl. When Ava reached Fiach's camp, what would she do to Lyl?

Dylan trained with the bow and ate at every opportunity, and was proving his talent at both. The serving woman, Dunla, delivered to table platters of boar stuffed with hazelnuts and honey, wild sloe cakes and baked apples, mountain trout wrapped in pastry, blood sausage, mead from the Long Vale and coal-roasted partridge.

Dylan never slowed in his battle against the table.

Nechtan had stolen short exchanges in the kitchen with Dunla, who claimed to have given Lyl refuge after Nechtan banished her.

"She didn't go to Fiach when you cast her out, my lord," Dunla stated flatly, as if he needed to be convinced of it. "Nay. Distraught was she. Mightily. And then, well...then you were dead."

She wadded the apron at her generous waist. "I seen into her with the eyes of a tired ol' woman, aye, 'tis true. I see her heart, me lord, her heart. Lyleth thinks her love for you is a blemish on the duty you laid upon her." She gave a harrumph of disbelief. "'Tis this that troubles her."

He tried to speak, but ended up staring at her. What was the old woman saying? And how much of this had she fancied in her own mind? When he left the kitchen, he could think of nothing else but wonder if Lyl really felt anything for him other than duty? Had he forced the role of solás upon her? If she had refused, he would likely never have seen her again. Had that been the reason she accepted?

It smelled of vanity to even think it, and worse, it distracted him from the task she'd set before him.

Dylan attacked his food with dire intent, licking his fingers and slathering his cakes with honey butter and exchanging rapturous glances with Nechtan.

Marchlew had protested when Dylan was seated beside Nechtan. "Servants eat in the kitchen," he'd said.

"My servant eats with me."

Nechtan tapped the meat knife in his hand, and raised his eyebrows at Dylan. After a stricken look, Dylan took up his own knife and cut away at the boar rather than tearing at it with his fingers.

Across from Dylan sat Kyndra's son, Talan, who picked at his food and openly gawked as Dylan behaved like a starving hound. The light fuzz on Talan's lip said he'd come of age. He was no longer the lad with squirrelish cheeks, but had grown into a long-limbed creature with a brooding scowl. Nechtan wondered how much Marchlew had to do with that scowl.

Kyndra wore the distant mask of one who'd given up joy long ago. Still beautiful, she looked more like their mother than Nechtan, which was a good thing, for their mother had been sculpted from a pale, brittle stone and colored with the sky.

Kyndra had given Marchlew the required son as well as a daughter, now at the court of IsAeron as a ward of Lloyd. The girl had been betrothed at five to Lloyd's heir, a man of seventeen years then. Nechtan wondered how long it'd been since Kyndra had seen her daughter. She worried for her now, certainly, for Lloyd of IsAeron marched north with Fiach and Ava.

No other children had filled his sister's belly. He imagined that she saw her duty fulfilled and preferred to send Marchlew to his whores rather than suffer the sweating, drunken sod in her bed.

Nechtan caught Marchlew's stare and held it. His rebirth certainly couldn't please Marchlew who had, according to rumor, sought to bargain for the throne by wedding Talan to Ava. Nechtan was certainly a serious inconvenience.

"Fiach commands more spearmen than archers," Pyrs was saying. "But his mounted troops number far greater than Arvon and Cedewain combined."

Nechtan took a bite of sloe cake. Dylan was right. The food tasted like sin indeed.

"What of our numbers, Pyrs?" Nechtan asked.

"We have twice their archers and far more war dogs."

"The reality is that Ava commands three of the Five Quarters against our two," Nechtan said, "and if Lyl is right, the ice-born wait to run up our ass as well. The only way we can succeed is to use what we have at the right time in the right place. And if they know we're coming, it will mean our death.

"We set the dogs on Fiach's horses," Nechtan said, "Archers against spears in the initial push."

"My men in Sandkaldr say the old Bear lies dying," Marchlew said. He spat and his wolfhound got up from his slumber and licked it off the flagstones. "If this is so, how is it he can be floating out on the Gannet's Bath waiting to beach his longships?"

"Lyl thinks he would still send his thegns even if he is near death."

Marchlew rocked back in his chair and ran his hands over his belly. "Ah yes, the leafy counselor who thought it great diplomacy to marry you off to your killer. Why would I listen to Lyleth?"

His eyes flashed from Nechtan to Talan.

"This bird that shits upon us now," Marchlew said, "took wing years ago, Nechtan." He leaned across the table and wagged his meat knife. "From the moment you walked into the

Bear's hall at Rotomagos and asked for that little ice bitch for your bed, he planned to murder you."

"What's done is done."

"Ah, but that's the thing, brother. 'Tisn't done. You've left us to clean up the mess your druí made."

Kyndra set a hand on her husband's arm. "This is not the time—"

"There's never been a better time. Nechtan, or whoever he might be, bids us ride out and die with him, woman." He sniffed.

"The Five Quarters would have fallen to the Bear years ago if not for Lyl," Nechtan said.

"That woman has brought you nothing but disgrace!" Marchlew sprayed spittle. "And now you tell me she's brought you back from the dead. For what? To salvage your honor?" He gave a fat snort and tossed a bone to the wolfhound.

Dylan's hand was on Nechtan's shoulder. His eyes were the anchor Nechtan needed.

"She brought me back," Nechtan said evenly, "to see that we prevail."

Marchlew rumbled to his feet, saying, "No, brother. I lead this army. No ghost. But a living, fuck-loving man." He pounded his chest. "I say we prepare for a siege. If you wish to join me, I can use your sword. If not, go back to the hell you came from."

Dylan had gone to fetch more water. Nechtan lay back in the wooden tub and stared at the rib vaults in the ceiling, each terminating in a creature's head, wagging stone tongues, baring fangs or lecherous grins. The dance of firelight made them appear to come alive. The mind sees what it thinks it should, not what's really there. Maybe this entire world moved only by the hand of a shifting light. Maybe this was the land of the dead and nothing was real. Not Lyl, not Ava, especially not Nechtan.

Real or not, Ava's army marched for Cedewain and if

Marchlew had his way, they would sit behind his walls and wait. The hot water melted the knots in Nechtan's flesh but all he could think about was that Lyleth had given her life for him to roll over at Marchlew's feet like a bad dog.

He closed his eyes. One way or another, he would do what Lyleth had brought him back to do, and this overmatched army of the north would slice Ava to pieces. But he sorely needed to talk to Pyrs.

The door opened and feet crossed the room. He heard a bucket rattle to the floor.

"Dylan, fetch Pyrs. I need to speak with him."

He opened his eyes and started to sit up, but hands caught his shoulders and pressed him back into the water, massaging his shoulders with an expert touch. He turned to see a serving girl.

"Where's Dylan?"

"My lady Kyndra sent me. To see to your shaving, my lord."

"Shave?" He rubbed at the thick stubble on his chin. "Be quick about it."

He let his head rest on the edge of the tub while the girl soaped his face. The thought struck him like a blow—one slice of the razor and Marchlew would have no more contention over his battle plan and Talan would still be heir to the throne. Nechtan would be just as dead as he had been a fortnight ago.

He caught the wrist that held the razor.

"I don't know what you've been told, lass, but if you cut me, you'll be dead long before I will."

She froze, the crescent-shaped razor dripping soap on his chest.

"I'm quite good at this, my lord. I shave my lord Marchlew." Nechtan doubted that was all she did for Marchlew.

She set the blade to his throat and dragged it up to his chin.

It felt good to be rid of the itch of beard stubble. But his mind was on the narrow glen that opened out from the gates of Caer Cedewain. Ava would come up that glen, one way or another, for taking that many men through the mountain passes would be impossibly slow and leave her open to ambush. Nor would she move at night, not with thousands of men. But Nechtan figured Ava would reach Morcant's Roost at the neck in another day.

The serving girl dipped a cloth in the water and wiped stubble from his cheeks.

"Thank you," he said, and sat up.

But her hands were on his chest, sliding under the water. She hitched up her skirt and stepped into the tub with him.

He caught her wrists and stopped their groping as she lost her balance and splashed into the tub on top of him, grinning.

"I was in need of nothing more than a shave, lass. Now, fetch my serving boy."

Her grin trickled away. "Yes, my lord."

He glimpsed his own exposed wrists holding hers. It was clear from her face that she'd seen his lack of the king's mark as well.

If he were another man, he would offer her gold for her silence, and others still would drown her. He continued to hold her wrists and she began to struggle, fear flashing in her eyes. He held her gaze, willing the fear to build.

"You need not speak of it," he said.

"No. I'll not speak of it. Thank you, my lord."

He held her still, tightening his grip on her wrists.

"Please, my lord! I swear on my life, I'll say nothing of it."

When he released her, she was frozen for some seconds, and then spilled out of the tub into a puddle. She scrambled to her feet, showed her palms, and was gone. And so was his secret.

Nechtan dressed in a surcoat and trousers Kyndra had sent. Smelling clean was something new for him in this lifetime.

Dylan laced up his bracers and chattered on. "Do you think I can carry a bow with the archers from Arvon, my lord? They can shoot the eye from a grouse a league away, they say. Is it true that some are women?"

"The best are women, and yes, I think you can fight beside them. But hitting a grouse from a league away..."

The boy grinned and tied off the laces.

"Now go fetch Pyrs for me and get cleaned up," Nechtan said. "You stink."

Dylan disappeared and Nechtan poured a cup of mead. If the tactics for this ambush came from Pyrs, perhaps Marchlew would agree to them.

A knock came at his door.

It wasn't Pyrs. It was Kyndra.

She closed the door quietly as if she feared being followed.

"What is it?" he asked.

She stood carved out by the firelight, her hands fretting with her belt.

"Kyndra?"

"Let me see your wrist," she said at last.

"Whatever you've heard—"

"Show me!"

"Lyleth doesn't know why—"

She slapped him, hard. Then her trembling hands went to her mouth.

He held his right arm out to her. She pulled at the laces frantically and peeled the bracer away. Her gaze went from the pink-white skin of his wrist to his eyes.

"Who are you?"

Chapter 28

Across leagues of grain fields and moors, Lyleth and Elowen followed Brixia northward in darkness. The little horse's direction didn't waver any more than when she'd led Lyleth and Nechtan through the mountain. When the wheeling night brightened to blue, clouds streamed from the east, joined and parted with the wind, and dawn gifted the land with the hues of heather and frost-rimed gorse, with white drifts of thistle down that followed unseen currents of the sky.

Lyleth took a deep, thankful breath and felt tears well. She had so far to go.

Long before dawn, she had finally succeeded in cutting the rope that held her fast to Nechtan's corpse. She lay there for a long time, trying to imagine the camp that had grown in the past few days. How far was it to the edge?

Glancing under the tent, she saw the guard slumped over, and beside his bulk a pair of dirty, bare feet.

She scrambled back to the corpse, clutched the knife between her palms, and pretended to be bound and sleeping.

The tent flap opened.

"Wake up, druí."

Elowen held a rushlight in one hand and a bloody dagger in the other. "We must be quick."

"You were supposed to run," Lyleth scolded as she took the girl in her arms.

Elowen smiled, showing her missing teeth. "I never do as I'm told, ye should know that by now."

She ducked outside and returned with an armload of weapons: a bow, two quivers packed with bodkin-tipped arrows, and a swordbelt. Her skills at thievery commanded admiration.

"How'd you find me?"

Elowen touched her nose and made a face. "Easy, that."

The little horse stood in the doorway and nickered.

"Truth be, 'twas Brixia," Elowen said, helping Lyleth to her feet. "She wouldn't go south. I said to meself, 'she's got someplace to take me to,' but nay. I finally figured it—she's got someplace to take the druí."

Elowen had two horses tied in a thicket just north of camp. She'd walked right through Fiach's men and convinced them she was the get of a camp whore, begging for food, doing chores for copper. Who would ask questions of a ragged girl?

Lyleth stripped the cloak of farandine from Nechtan's corpse and wrapped herself in it, and, concealing the arsenal Elowen had stolen, the two walked right out of camp, a whore and her child.

Dawn had come now, and a dark forest beckoned no more than a league to the north. They followed the river until they found Dylan's bridge. Lyleth dismounted, drew her sword, and crept down to the water's edge. A bridge was a fine place for an ambush.

She took the opportunity to drink and wash, for the smell of death clung to her like peat smoke. When she scrambled back up the embankment, Elowen was scanning the southern horizon.

"There." She pointed.

Through the thick of dawn, Lyleth saw them too. Fiach's men weren't far behind.

Once across the bridge, Lyleth pushed her spent horse towards the woods not far away. Stands of oak and beech had long shed their leaves, offering little cover, but a dense copse of golden willow welcomed them as Fiach's horsemen reached the bridge.

Thrashing through the underbrush, branches lashing her face and catching her cloak, Lyleth broke free into an open meadow, then wove back into a heavy stand of fir. Tracking them would be easy in this soft ground, so she found a game trail that wound up to a limestone ridge. The only soil here clung to cracks and pits in the great slab warming in the morning sun, but the horses' iron shoes left a trail, even here.

Rejecting the obvious route, Lyleth crossed the stone shelf at a trot and took a steep descent, which plunged into a glen so thickly wooded a deer would struggle to get through. But a stream sliced through the middle and Lyleth rode into it, her horse stumbling over moss-slick rocks and making far more noise than she intended.

She reined up.

"Did you hear that?" she whispered to Elowen.

The girl listened, eyes wide. "Aye."

Lyleth pointed upstream where faint voices drifted through the trees.

She put her fingers to her lips, dismounted, and handed her reins to Elowen. With bow nocked and ready, she waded upstream.

The woods gave way to a pocket meadow, deep with highland grass covered in a dusting of morning frost. There, at the meadow's edge, was a camp of perhaps fifty men, maybe more hidden by trees.

Lyleth made her way as close as she dared, close enough to hear the guttural tongue of the ice-born. These men had built no morning fires, travelled in trackless woods, spoke in hushed voices. Ava didn't know they were coming. But she would soon, and so would Fiach.

Lyleth found Elowen planted in the middle of the stream where she'd left her.

"They're comin'," Elowen said, and handed the reins to Lyleth. "Fiach's men. Comin' down the cliff, I heard 'em."

"Stay with me."

Lyleth mounted, turned, and headed back downstream, directly toward Fiach's scouts.

"Are ye daft?"

"Just stay with me."

Lyleth finally spotted Fiach's men as they reached the base of the cliff. Certain they saw her, she fired an arrow, spun, and trotted back upstream, heading straight for the ice-born. But before reaching the meadow, Lyleth left the stream and flanked the ice-born camp on the west.

Elowen followed close behind.

Dense trees swallowed them, and here, Lyleth reined up. The horses were blowing plumes of hot fog, even little Brixia, wedged between them.

"We should run," Elowen whispered.

"Not yet."

Through the thicket, Lyleth watched the ice-born scramble for their weapons. They'd heard Fiach's men splashing up the stream and as they burst onto the meadow, there was a heartbeat of indecision on both sides.

Spears launched from the ice-born camp and brought down half of Fiach's dozen men. The rest fell before they could reach the safety of the woods.

No, the Bear's men weren't ready to be found out.

Lyleth and Elowen would crest the next ridge before the ice-born were done looting the bodies, and if Lyleth didn't reach Nechtan soon, he'd march right into the lap of two armies.

Brixia had a nose for good oats, and after riding through that night and the next day, the little horse led them to the outer edge of Marchlew's war camp. Warriors from the north country covered the fields from the ditchworks of the ráth all the way to the river.

It was night again. The walls of Caer Cedewain were lit by a hundred torches.

Lyleth showed her mark and they soon had an escort of five horsemen to see them to the fortress.

She found Nechtan in the forge.

"We need two hundred spearheads by morning," he was saying to the armorer. "We have little time—"

"We have less time than you think," she said. "And I have much to tell you."

The room spun.

Lyleth could see nothing but the rise and fall of Nechtan's chest. He breathed. And she wanted nothing more than to hold him, warm and alive against her own body, to feel the air move in him, to feel the flutter of his heart. When he crossed the space between them and took her in his arms, she knew she'd never heard the music of blood moving through flesh before, not until that moment, not like that.

It was all she could do to say, "He's here."

"Who?"

"The Bear."

How long had it been since Lyleth had been warm? Dylan banked the fire in Nechtan's chamber and she reached for it with numb hands.

Elowen had gone to the kitchen and fetched a tray of cold meat and cheese. With the smell of food, Lyleth realized how hungry she was.

"How many?" Nechtan asked her, filling her cup with ale.

"At least fifty. All thegns," she said, her mouth full of greasy meat.

Nechtan paced. "They'll try to bargain with Ava."

"They just killed Fiach's scouts."

"They're buying time. Waiting for the Bear." He took the chair beside her and laced his fingers, his brow pinched. "Would Fiach side with the ice-born?"

Fiach would do anything to bring Nechtan down, but would he sacrifice his own land for it?

"I don't know," she said at last.

She took a bite of sloe cake and washed it down with ale.

"But I do know that Ava was never part of the Bear's plan," Lyleth said. "Ava placed her trust in Irjan and was betrayed." Was that sympathy she heard in her own voice?

The food started to fill the void in her gut, and her body felt heavy with the meal and weariness, but Nechtan was intent on the map he had spread before them.

"You saw them here." He placed a cup on the spot. "But leading a sizeable number of men through these mountains would be madness. They can only bring longships up the river to here." He pointed to the falls at Balaclun, at least fifty leagues away from the glens of Cedewain.

"No. If the ice-born come in numbers, they'll come from the sea." His finger moved across the map, tracing a path from the broad bay known as the Gannet's Bath to the valley that led directly to Cedewain's back door, Maiden Pass.

"They'd beach their ships and ram the gates."

"There's something else." Lyleth rubbed at her throbbing temples. "Ava watches with the eyes of the red crow."

Nechtan got up and paced, dragging his hands down his face.

"Have you seen it again?" she said.

His eyebrow jumped. "Aye. Here."

"Then she knows your numbers."

The room began to recede, the walls closing in, as if she fell into a barrel. All she could see was Nechtan's decaying flesh holding her fast to the ground. She realized she was staring at him, lost in the perfect, breathing replica before her.

"Lyl? You need sleep."

"There's no time."

"I didn't tell you that part," he said, his pacing making her dizzy. "Kyndra knows I lack the mark, and she fears for Talan's life on the open field. The boy's never ridden to battle before. If I fail to agree to Marchlew's siege, she'll make certain my chieftains know I'm not who I seem."

Lyleth eased back into the cushions of the chair. "So she'll ruin us all to save her son. What did you tell her?"

"I won't concede to a siege."

"Then they'll all know soon that the king has no mark."

"You would have me concede to the siege? Not even these walls could hold against Fiach and the Bear."

Every muscle in her body hurt and her mind begged for sleep. "I can't think anymore, Nechtan."

His arm slid around her waist and he helped her to her feet. "You smell terrible," he said.

"You smell a sight better than last time I saw you." He returned her smile, and helped her to the bed.

"Dylan will see to drawing a bath. Not even Marchlew could stand this stench." He picked up the edge of her cloak like it was a dead thing, his cloak, and looked from it to her eyes. "You'll tell me some time."

She nodded and felt his lips on her forehead, and sank into the deep sea of the feather mattress. His last words came from the bottom of that sea.

"Sleep now," he was saying. "I'm going to need you soon."

She awoke to the sound of splashing water. Startled, Lyleth sat up, reaching for a weapon that wasn't there. She was no longer in a tent of death, but a large chamber. Fingers of morning light spotted the floor and Dylan looked up from the hearth. He poured water into a waiting pot, and then swung it over the fire.

"Good, you're awake," he said. "My lord's been asking for ye."

She dragged her hands down her face, then examined them, brown with dried blood, her wrists crusted over with scabs.

"Aye."

Her head began to clear as she got out of bed and looked at the wooden tub half full of steaming water.

"Lady Kyndra sent those." Dylan pointed at a moss-green gown and chemise draped over a chair. "I took your armor and gambeson for cleaning."

"Thank you, Dylan. Where's Elowen?"

"Gone to see to Brixia. She feared the little horse'd run off again, seeing's how she won't be tied. But I think she's looking for more food, if ye want to know."

Lyleth smiled, but felt numb. What use would she be to Nechtan in such a state?

Dylan poured the next pot of hot water into the bath, saying, "My lord's seen wondrous things in the Fair Lands, lady. Things I long to see for meself."

"Don't long for it overmuch."

"My lord says I'm going to fight beside the archers from Arvon." He grew a few fingers in the telling.

"And you'll do as they tell you, and never leave your cover."

He nodded and started for the door.

"Promise me," she added.

"I promise." He grinned and crossed his lips with his thumb to seal it.

She unlaced her dirty trousers, and saw the lad still standing by the door. "Is there something else, Dylan?"

"I just... I need to say... My lord set out to do what ye brung him back to do. He wants it more than anything, to set things right, says he. He has a great sadness on him. I'm just not certain he'd tell you hisself's all."

She forced a smile. "Thank you, Dylan."

The doorlatch fell behind him.

On a table beside the hearth sat the harp of the drowned maid. Lyleth let her fingers taste the strings and from them, a lament sang out as if to echo Dylan's words. The tune soaked into the stone walls and Lyleth stepped into the tub with its whispers still in her ears.

In the mirror, Lyleth inspected three stripes of stitching on her chest. The poultice Nechtan had applied came off easily in the bath water, and the stitches were healing cleanly with no sign of festering. He was a better seamstress than she'd thought.

The gown Kyndra had left felt bulky, but warm. It had been a long time since Lyleth had worn anything but leather hunting trousers and a surcoat of homespun. She braided her hair quickly and took one last look at the druí in the hand mirror: not exactly a courtly lady, with a row of neat stitches above her bodice. It would have to do, but she hoped she wouldn't put anyone off their meal.

Starting down a narrow spiral of stairs, she nearly collided with Dunla.

"Oh, 'tis true!" Dunla took Lyleth in a bosomy embrace. "My lord says you were here. But I had to see ye with me own eyes, lass."

"I thought you taken," Lyleth said. "How—"

"Oh aye, I told that ice queen nothing, then flew away." Her hands fluttered before her round face. Another embrace and a squeeze of the cheeks. "Your lord awaits you. There's much haste, lass. I'll take ye to him."

Dunla led her through a maze of halls and rooms, gossiping the entire way about the workings of the fortress and, in hushed tones, Marchlew's capriciousness and the sorrow of Kyndra. It sounded like the lyrics of a weepy ballad.

"A slave to that man, she is," Dunla whispered. "My heart feels it."

Kyndra wasn't the only one to suffer a loveless marriage for the good of her kingdom, nor would she be the last. At least Marchlew hadn't murdered her. Yet.

Before they reached the council chamber, Dunla took Lyleth's arm and stopped her.

"You'll fit the pieces one to another. He's a broken jug. 'Tis what you called him back for, is it not?"

Lyleth's mouth hung open stupidly. "What?"

"He's the only man's been called from the land of the dead. And why'd you think the green gods granted ye such a favor, eh?"

"I'm needed within," Lyleth managed to say, and after a long look at Dunla's resolute red face, opened the council chamber door.

A long table was crowded with men. Marchlew sat at one end and Nechtan at the other. Just the arrangement itself meant discord. They couldn't afford a battle here at the table.

"We could move tonight to Morcant's Roost," Nechtan was saying. He put a stone on the map that lay before them. "And Marchlew would wait across the river here." Another stone marked Marchlew's position.

"This is utter suicide," Marchlew bellowed. "You're dead already, Nechtan. We have no desire to join you. I say we wait for them here, with archers, scorpions and burning pitch. Let them try to come through these walls."

The clamor quieted when they saw Lyleth. Pyrs rose and took her hands, and leaving a kiss on her cheek, he whispered, "Please help."

Pyrs would die for Nechtan in any lifetime and the look in his eyes confirmed it. He made room for her on the bench beside Nechtan. But Marchlew's fish eyes said something very different.

"Sister greenleaf lives," Marchlew grinned. "Nechtan claims you've seen ice-born in the mountains."

"If you think to cower in this fortress," Lyleth said, "you'll have Ava beating at your gates while the Bear breaks through Maiden Pass."

"None's ever fucked that maiden." Marchlew chuckled.

Kyndra appeared in the doorway. Her eyes met Lyleth's, and it was clear what she'd come for. Kyndra would settle this now. But Lyleth got up and met her in the doorway, whispering, "Your boy must become a man, Kyndra."

"What do you know of a mother's love?" She pushed past Lyleth and lay a hand on her husband's shoulder. But as Kyndra moved to whisper in his ear, Lyleth said, "Marchlew, I must speak with you. It's of some urgency."

"As must I," Kyndra countered.

"Alone," Lyleth added.

"Sister greenleaf has a proposal." Marchlew winked at the men, tugged at his belt, then hoisted his bulk to his feet. "Kyndra, love," he said, "see to their cups."

Kyndra looked as if she would spill what she had to say that moment, then her eyes met Nechtan's, and something passed between them, the truth, perhaps.

Lyleth followed Marchlew down a narrow corridor to a small anteroom. The door closed and she looked at this man who held the fate of the highland tribes. He'd wasted himself even further since Lyleth had last seen him.

"Speak," he demanded.

"When Nechtan returned to this world," she said flatly, "he bore no mark of the king."

"No mark?" He huffed in clear satisfaction. "So, the man is a wraith, just as I've said."

"He's no wraith."

"But he's no king, either." Those jaundiced eyes held hers for a long moment. Perhaps that was exactly what she was saying.

Marchlew paced a circle around her.

"A siege will bring certain death," Lyleth said. "To you. To Talan. To the Five Quarters."

Stepping in front of him, she brought his pacing to a halt and met his eyes. "Tell me, Marchlew, what is it you want?"

Chapter 29

Connor begged the nurse for more time with Dish, but she threatened to call security if he didn't leave. He couldn't bring himself to let go of Dish's hand, feeling the warm pulse of life between them, the green fire that arced from his wrist to Dish's.

"It's 2 a.m.," the nurse said. With a fierce grip on Connor's arm, she dragged him toward the exit of I.C.U.

"But he moved his hand!"

"Young man, patients with injuries such as Mr. Cavendish will show unconscious reflexes. It's normal."

"Not this. He heard me!"

The nurse slapped the button and the automatic doors swung open.

"I'll make a note of it on his chart." With a wooden soldier wave and a hand on Connor's back, she gave him a push through the doors.

Connor's hand was still on fire, and when he looked at the water horse drawn in ballpoint pen on his wrist, he could see random flashes, like fireflies dancing from his veins. He sucked in a lungful of air as if he'd forgotten to breathe.

In the corner of the waiting room, Iris was asleep, curled like a cat in a corner chair.

"C'mon." He shook her awake. "Let's go."

She gathered her patchwork hippy bag and stumbled after him.

"Go where?"

"Bronwyn told me where she was staying. She's probably still there." He checked the time on his phone. 2:53 a.m.

Shit.

Connor stalled the car again as he pulled into the entrance circle of the Marriott, but finally got the thing parked. As he expected, you needed a passkey to get into the hotel at this hour. He put his face up to the window. Nobody at the front desk. He rapped on the glass. The manager was probably asleep in the back room, sandbagger.

He got back in the car, his body heat steaming the windows. You'd have thought he and Iris had been going at it in here. But his body was a furnace. He cranked the window down (too old for power windows), pulled off his sweatshirt, and glanced at his wrist again.

In the electric cold of a streetlight, the drawing of the water horse smoldered. Static images flashed before his eyes. He saw the stone with the water horse carving rising from the center of a pool in a dense forest. Moss softened its edges and the exposed roots of ancient trees wove a bowl to contain water so clear he could see through it to the other side. Clouds raced across the sky there. A crow cocked its head to look at him, there on the other shore, then dipped its beak into the still water and fractured the vision.

"What's the matter?" Iris was staring at him again.

He balled up his sweatshirt and wiped the inside of the windshield with it. "Nothing."

"You look like you've seen a ghost."

"I'm just tired." The voice that came out of him wasn't his own. He'd lost his somewhere. "They have to come out sometime," he said.

"Who?"

"Bronwyn and Merryn."

"You mean you're going to stalk them?" Iris said. "And when they do, you're going to do what exactly?"

"I need to talk to Bronwyn."

"Why don't you just call her? You have her cell number, right?"

"Why would she answer a call from me?"

"Maybe to scream at you for waking her up at 3 a.m., dumbass."

Connor dug his phone out of his pocket, scrolled to the number, and hit "send." It rang and went to voicemail. "It's Connor." The pause was way too long. "You have to listen to me. Dish moved his hand. He could hear me. Just let me talk to you." He shut the phone.

"Dish moved his hand?" Iris' face was too close.

He gave her the abbreviated version, without the crazy talk, and moved the car to a parking place that offered a strategic view of the entrance. Iris was talking about how some psychic healers feel hot after they do whatever it is they do to make people well. But Connor had stopped listening. He was trying to reconstruct the scene of the pool in the woods, trying to hang on to the overwhelming urge he'd felt to step into that water and fall through to that other sky.

After fifteen minutes, Connor decided to send Bronwyn a text. Even if she didn't pick up the voicemail, she might not be able to avoid seeing his text.

He thumbed the keypad. dish moved his hand. please talk to me i'm right outside hotel. He hit "send," closed his phone, and tossed it on the dash.

It felt like someone had opened his veins and bled him out. Fog tumbled over the parking lot and through his open window, cooling this insane fever. Iris was cocooned in his sweatshirt, music stuffed into her ears, and he couldn't keep his eyes open any longer. Even the thought of Iris acting as lookout couldn't keep them open.

"Don't go to sleep, Iris. Please."

He was gone before he heard her reply.

He sank into a dream worthy of Dr. Adelman's dream journal.

Ned gave him an aquarium, the typical pet store type, rectangular with plastic plants and hot pink gravel. But the cool thing about this aquarium was it had no glass, none at all. The water stayed in that shape.

Connor watched the fish, and they watched him back.

A few mottled goldfish and a big black one with pop eyes twitched kite-like tails, sailing the water in meaningless circles. The black goldfish moved closer, hesitated at the division between water and air, and then swam right out of the aquarium to hover before Connor's face. Sure the fish would die in the air, he pushed it back with his index finger, which penetrated the water as easily as the fish. Surface tension left a deep dimple where his finger went in and it tingled, like when he fell into the hot tub, like when his arm touched Dish's arm.

The little fat fish eyed Connor just at the edge of water and air.

He woke up sweating, his left arm asleep and tingling.

Color was just coming into the sky. He looked over at Iris. She was asleep, using her bag as a pillow.

"Shit!"

He fumbled for his phone. No message from Bronwyn.

He wiped the windshield again and looked across the circular drive and through the double glass doors. He could just make out the foyer lit by a big ugly chandelier, and there was someone walking across it. Very slowly.

He stumbled out of the car and jogged across the drive to the door.

Wearing pink sweats and slippers, Aunt Merryn pushed her walker toward the entrance at what Connor knew to be her maximum speed. When she got close the door opened, and Connor charged in.

"Where's Bronwyn?"

"In the loo. Have you a motorcar, lad?"

Connor folded the walker and put it in the backseat beside Iris.

"You're kidnapping an old lady?" she whispered.

"Not kidnapping."

He helped Merryn into the passenger seat and took off. On the way out of the parking lot, he saw Bronwyn in his rearview mirror, coming through the glass doors of the hotel lobby.

He just drove. Clutch, shift, gas, go.

"He took my hand." He was talking faster than his mouth would move. "Bronwyn can't pull the plug on him. Not yet. It's like…" He wasn't sure how to explain it. "Like he has something to finish on the other side."

"Oh," Merryn said, "Sure it is. Don't we all. Look, a Tastyburger. They make splendid chips. Shall we have some chips?"

Connor pulled into the parking lot. Good thing Tastyburger was open all night. It wasn't until they were almost inside that Merryn noticed Iris.

"I'm sorry," Connor said. "This is Iris McCreary, unwanted appendage."

Iris grinned and talked loud like Merryn was deaf. "I'm Connor's girlfriend."

Shit.

The fries, or chips, were super greasy and salty and Connor realized he was starving. In between bites, he explained to Merryn why she couldn't let Bronwyn pull the plug, at least not yet.

"She won't listen to me," he said, "but maybe she'll listen to you. Remember the book I showed you?" He wiped his hands on his pants and pulled the book out of his sweatshirt pocket and handed it to Merryn.

She reached for it with reverence, her bright blue eyes igniting.

"Oh yes," she sighed, and made a crooning sound. With shaky, gnarled fingers she traced the figure of the man on the cover.

"It's Clyde. Hugh found this book?" When she looked up at Connor, her eyes were filled with tears.

"He ordered it at a special bookstore. We were going to pick it up when… anyway, he had just said he had to show me something. And look. I tried to show you the other day." Connor reached over to the book and flipped to page 73.

Merryn stared at the picture of the water horse carving.

"It's the design on his arm," Connor said.

Merryn's breathing quickened, and her eyes darted about like someone might be listening.

"I took this picture," she blurted.

"You?"

"I was fourteen. Oh my, but Clyde was a comely man. I was smitten with him, of course."

"Of course," Connor echoed, lost already. "So, you knew this guy? You helped him take these pictures?"

She flipped to another page and pointed to a young girl with braids posing beside another strange rock. "Me."

Iris moved from the other side of the table and slid onto the molded plastic bench beside Merryn.

"That is so awesome," Iris said.

"Tell me about this stone," Connor said, flipping back to page 73, "the one with the water horse on it."

Merryn talked without taking her eyes from the picture. "Clyde Pritchard came to my little village to document ancient monuments, inquiring after standing stones or wells that might be less well known or even forgotten, for he was writing a book, he said. Well, you know what kind of excitement that stirred up in my little corner of Brecknockshire."

Connor nodded, pretending he did.

Merryn's eyes twinkled with the memory.

"He was so dashing. The ladies lined up to tell him of stones here, there and everywhere."

"And you knew of some?"

"Not only did I know them, I spent my days in the highland vales with my sheep. I could take him right to them."

"So, you were like his guide," Iris said.

"I suppose I was. I'm surprised my mother let me go. I think she was as taken with Clyde as everyone else. He told us tales of druids and spirits that lived in trees, stones, water."

"It was you who took him to this rock, the one with the water horse?" Connor asked, trying to get the train back on track.

She nodded wistfully. "I knew the woman who lived in the cottage. We traded lambs often. Lyla was her name. She was a bit queer, but very beautiful. She lived alone, sheared her own sheep and took the wool to market all herself. She took no husband, though she had plenty come a-courtin'. Until Clyde came to her door."

"Lyla," Connor repeated. He flipped to the page with her picture and pointed at it. "Lyla Bendbow."

"This sounds like a Disney movie." Iris dipped her fries in a gob of ketchup.

But all Connor could think about was Dish and Lyla, or somebody who seemed to be Lyla, there in that cave.

Merryn's eyes roved from Iris to Connor. She pursed her lips. "I have told few people of this day."

"But you told Dish. I mean Hugh."

"Oh, yes. Bronwyn believes that's why Hugh got the tattoo. She says I filled his head with nonsense when he was a boy."

"Dish knew about this picture?"

"Clyde gave me a photo of Lyla and himself with the well stone. I kept it on my dressing table. When Hugh was about your age, I found him standing in the middle of my room, the photo in his hands. When he looked at me, there were tears in his eyes. He said nothing, merely placed it back on the table, and walked out. Not long after, I had an electrical fire in my cottage. My bedroom burned and so did the photo. But Hugh remembers it. Most certainly."

"Why would Dish be crying over an old picture?"

"I didn't ask, lad." She gave his arm a gentle pat. "There are things we'll never understand about ourselves, and speaking of them invites a longing back into our hearts."

"This stone obviously means something to him," Connor said.

"Or maybe it's the girl, not the rock." Iris glared at him with mascara-smudged eyes.

"The girl didn't appear on his arm. The water horse did. What does it mean?" Connor pulled a photocopy of the stone from his pocket, one he'd enlarged, and spread it out on the table. "You can see it better here."

After a pensive silence, Merryn said in a low voice, "Lyla said the stone was far older than her family cottage; it was moved, ages before. She said the water horse marked a well." She ate a french fry and met Connor's eyes. As she chewed, she was clearly weighing whether she should go on. "The third well of the sea."

"There are so many wells, I can't keep track," Connor said.

"Lyla said, 'Three wells feed the sea, the moon's flood tide, rain that falls from the stars, and flinty veins that bleed the mountain snows.'"

Connor digested this bit of nothing. "What sea? What does a riddle have to do with Dish and his water horse tattoo?"

"Ha, well," Merryn said, dipping another fry in the ketchup. "According to Hugh and his folktale research, the third well of the sea was opened for one purpose only."

"What purpose?"

"There were once a people known as the 'Old Blood,'" Merryn said. As she spoke, her face took on a faraway look as if she were recalling a scene in her mind's eye. "Caretakers of a land called the Five Quarters. They were pitched into a terrible battle against an invading tribe, the Ildana, who'd come to take their land. The king of the Old Blood, a young man with a heart too tender to watch his people slaughtered, sued for peace."

Her story stopped and she examined Connor as if to measure his response.

"And what happened?" he asked, impatient.

Merryn glanced at Iris, as if she was about to share a secret and Iris shouldn't hear it. "My tea's a bit cold, love, would you mind?"

Iris' mouth was hanging open, but with a venomous stare at Connor, she took the paper cup from Merryn's quaking hand and slithered toward the counter to freshen Merryn's tea, looking over her shoulder as if she could lip-read.

"The king of the Old Blood bargained for peace," Merryn explained. "He asked the invader to share the land with him, but in his youthful naiveté, he agreed to take the land beneath the land."

"Land beneath what land?" Connor couldn't lean any closer to Merryn. He wanted to snatch the words as they fell from her lips.

"In ancient times, they believed that when the sun set, it travelled to a land beneath the land, to another world that can only be reached either through the wells or through the old fairy mounds. The king of the Old Blood agreed to take that land as his own, to leave the Five Quarters to the invaders and be exiled to a country on the other side of night."

Her lower lip quivered, and Connor worried that Merryn would start crying over these Old Blood guys.

"Where is this country they've been exiled to?"

Iris set a steaming cup of tea in front of Merryn.

"Why, here."

"Here, as in the United States?"

"Here, as in this reality," Merryn said.

"So the Old Blood came here from another dimension?"

"The Celts believe that when we die, we are reborn on

the other side of night." Merryn held her palms together like she was praying. She indicated the back of one hand, then the other. "Wells link the two realms." She splayed her fingers and opened the way between. "We are born, live, and die in one world and return once again to the other side, there learning lessons that can't be learned here. And then back we go again. But the souls of the Old Blood are reborn in endless night. For what the young king didn't know when he sealed the peace was that when he led his people through the third well, it would be slammed shut. They were cast forever into exile."

"So, they're all here." Connor pointed to the orange tabletop. "But what does that have to do with this rock and the mark on Dish's wrist?"

Merryn squinted and brought the photocopy close to her face. "I'm not sure, really."

It was something in the timbre of her voice that told Connor she was lying. The look she gave him confirmed it. There was more to this story than Merryn was willing to tell. But why? What could she be hiding?

Connor pushed on with his questions anyway. "You found the stone and Clyde Pritchard translated the runes?"

"The runes weren't there before."

"Before what?" He strained to see the stick-like symbols Merryn pointed at, circling the water horse.

"I was readying the camera," Merryn said, "a cumbersome contraption in those days, and Clyde was setting up a flash, battery powered, of course, for there was no electricity at Lyla's cottage. We were ready to shoot the picture when Lyla stepped in front of the stone and ran her fingers round the water horse like this."

Merryn's two quaking fingers slowly traced the symbols on the photo.

"As her fingers passed over the stone, the runes appeared. And I opened the shutter on the camera." She made a popping sound like a flash, startling both Connor and Iris.

Connor closed his gaping mouth. Iris was frozen with a fry dripping ketchup.

"They just appeared?" Connor said. "Like the tattoo on Dish's arm?"

"Precisely. And within moments, they were gone just as surely. Clyde asked Lyla to try again, and she did, over and over until it was dark, but the runes never showed again."

Merryn handed the photocopy to Connor, saying, "This photo is the only record of them."

"Was this Lyla some kind of magician or something?"

"That's a story of its own, I suppose. Clyde fell madly in love with her. They married and moved to London. People in the vale say he died soon after in the war, but Lyla never returned to the vale. She auctioned her flocks and her land and vanished."

"But what do these runes, or whatever they are, mean? Is it writing?"

"Certainly it's writing. Clyde spent years trying to translate it, according to Hugh. He searched Clyde's old notes and publications, but found it matched no known script."

"So, no one can read it," Connor said.

Merryn shrugged.

"Great. And the writing itself is gone, vanished?"

"Possibly the stone, too."

Connor spread his arms and cried out to the stained ceiling tiles, "What does this mean?"

Tastyburger employees leaned over the counter and stared at him.

Connor was at a dead end, chasing after a lost well that might or might not have something to do with what he'd seen in the hot tub. There was nothing in Merryn's fairy tale that could bring Dish back, or give him more time. The only thing Connor could say with any confidence was Dish thought he'd found this third well on the beach, and the tattoo on his arm seemed to link him to the woman Connor saw on the other side, a woman who might have once been Lyla Bendbow if all this world trading was true.

He looked up from the photocopy to see two cops come through the door, their eyes on Merryn in her pink sweats. It was hardly likely they could make a run for it. Connor stuffed the book and the photocopy into his pocket before the cops got to the table.

Merryn held up a fry. "Chip? They're jolly good."

Chapter 30

Nechtan watched the chamber door close behind Lyleth and Marchlew. He was on his feet, his arm around Kyndra, who wore a look of utter ruination. Her knuckles were white from gripping the arm of Marchlew's empty high seat. At the council table, the chieftains shared words behind their hands, but every eye was on Nechtan. If Kyndra told them he was unmarked, Nechtan would be judged a wraith, or worse, a demon, and when Ava came to batter down the gates, she'd be met by his borrowed body hanging from the walls of Caer Cedewain. How did Lyl hope to save either of them?

Nechtan forced Kyndra's weepy eyes to meet his. "Don't do this. For the sake of the land—"

"The land! It was you who delivered me like a sow to market, Nechtan. 'A marriage to strengthen the land,' father called it. Remember?"

"Of course I remember." He tried to take hold of her, but she struck out wildly, beating his chest until he caught her arms and held her close, whispering, "If letting Ava and the Bear tear down these walls and slaughter the lot of us would give us our souls back, you and me, I would do it. But you know better. Talan can die inside these walls as easily as outside. Let him fight, Kyndra."

He searched her eyes for agreement, but found none. She shook off his embrace and turned to address the men at table.

"Kyndra, please."

Their chatter ceased, and they looked to her, all but Pyrs.

"Your kind feeds on boys like my Talan," she said to them. She clutched at her skirt, her wild eyes roving from one man to the next, saying, "Tomorrow, their blood will water the earth, and from it, more death will grow, and mothers will bring forth more babes to die for this land." Her eyes were spears into Nechtan's heart. "My brother died last summer—"

The squeal of a door announced Marchlew's return. "Hold your tongue, woman," he wheezed. "These matters are not yours to meddle with."

He waddled into the room and settled into his seat. But where was Lyleth?

Marchlew stroked his wolfhound's head, saying to Nechtan, "Tell us what part we're to play in this ambush of yours... my lord."

Nechtan understood Pyrs' suspicious look, and while explaining his strategy, he could think of nothing else but what Lyl had traded Marchlew for this grasping bastard's compliance.

"When we've engaged here," Nechtan pointed out the abandoned watchtower at the west end of the vale, "we'll know what we've got our hands on. Then, we send three, maybe four hundred back to guard the pass. What news have the scouts from the bay?"

"They've not returned," Maddoc said.

"Then we assume the beachhead is gone. The Bear should be at our door by midday tomorrow."

Nechtan looked to Marchlew for a response. A calm, compliant shrug was all he offered. He stroked his dog's head, saying, "My son will ride with you, Nechtan. For I know well you'll keep your nephew safe. Heir that he is."

Marchlew's beetling eyes said far more than his words.

With a glance at Kyndra, Nechtan said, "His mother has requested he be among the swords protecting the fortress."

"A king must show his worth in the field or he is no king.

You should know that better than anyone, Nechtan," Marchlew said. "You'll see to it that Talan lives out the day, for you'll put Talan's life above your own. And then I'll know you're the man you claim to be."

"We leave at moonrise," Nechtan said, "and hope the red crow doesn't fly by night."

Nechtan found Dylan alone in his chamber. Lyl had taken the harp and gone to Kyndra's garden, he said. Nechtan followed. A cold wind kicked at the fallen leaves and stripped the last flower petals to sail like snowflakes. A distant harp tune led Nechtan to a path that wound through a maze of ancient garden walls where thickets of holly branches, heavy with dark red berries, had breached the purity of Kyndra's moon garden.

He found Lyl with his harp in her lap, the hood of her cloak pulled up against the evening breeze. Her back was pressed to an old starwood tree, bare and gnarled, its white blooms long blown away.

"I told Marchlew you lack the mark." She said it without looking at him. She strummed the harp a full trill.

"What did you trade, Lyl?"

She finally looked up at him and set her palm against the harp strings to still them. "Something you never wanted in the first place."

"No riddles, tell me."

"Your throne."

At first, he was stunned, but gave in to a wave of confused laughter. "You'll put Talan on the throne? But Lyl, you brought me back to save it."

She gave him a sidelong look. "Did I?"

He sat down on the leaf-covered turf beside her and hugged his knees, because if he didn't, he might shake her.

"Let me get this right. If I survive the day, I'll step aside and Talan will be crowned in my place."

"Yes."

The weight of a kingdom rolled from his shoulders like rainwater. "What kind of king will such a boy make, eh?"

"You were no older."

"No, but I was more... humble."

She laughed at that. "Humble? Maybe in the Otherworld."

"If that's all it took to win that fat bastard," he said, "I should have offered him the throne when I first arrived."

But Lyl wasn't laughing anymore. Her hands closed tightly on his.

"The green gods are capricious as children for they never grow old, never die," she said softly. "They play us like game pieces, grow weary of us, then tip the board and spill our blood.

"They wanted me to call you back, Nechtan. And just as surely, they gave up a guardian to Ava's spear. They made her she-king. They set all this in motion. They want tomorrow to come. Why?"

"Perhaps they want the Ildana to perish, tribe against tribe, brother against brother."

"They're jealous of us." She said it with surety, as if it was a revelation she'd just come upon. "We live, we die, we change. We take our heart's lessons from one life to the next, from one world to the next. But the green gods... they will be children forever, changeless as star and stone, and we seek only to appease them, to avert their eyes from our daily struggles so they won't toy with us."

"Perhaps it's not the doing of the green gods," he said, "but the Old Blood."

A light flashed in Lyl's eyes. "From beyond the roots of earth? The Old Blood have ways unknown to us, aye. But to sacrifice a guardian?"

Nechtan knew the stories. When the third well swallowed the Old Blood, it swallowed their magic as well.

"Ava slew a guardian," he said. "But you raised a man from the dead. No servant of the green gods has ever done such a thing."

"The Old Blood... the green gods," Lyl mused. She touched the harp strings. "Or the Crooked One."

"He's nothing but a tale told around winter fires."

Nechtan absently touched the bracer that covered his wrist. The look in her eyes betrayed a fear he understood completely, perhaps better than she did.

"Whoever, whatever used us, Nechtan, it was for some purpose."

He let his fingers trace her chin and cheek, so red with the cold.

"You don't always have to understand," he said. "I would gladly have them use me again, to have this chance."

She wiped tears away. "The green gods will ask a price," she said. "Know that I never meant for you to pay."

"I pay gladly. But Lyl, I need to know one thing." He had rehearsed the question in his mind, but the words always dribbled away into selfish coddling. He finally said, "Why did you bring me back? If not for the throne, why?"

She set the harp aside and took his arm in her lap. She unlaced his bracer and ran two fingers over the sensitive skin of his wrist. "If you're not the king," she said at last, "then I'm not your solás and we're not bound now, you and I. Death will unmake us again soon enough, Nechtan."

Her fingers brushed the tender skin inside his elbow, slowly, then down to his open palm. His breath stopped. The breeze touched the strings of the harp where it leaned against the tree, playing the faintest of tunes that spread through his skin like Lyl's touch, playing at the deep strings of his soul.

"Let him guard truth and it will guard him." Lyleth spoke the charge of the king, words he'd not heard since his crowning.

"Let him strengthen truth, and it will strengthen him."

As she spoke, her hands moved up his shoulders to the soft depression at the base of his throat and lingered there. She traced his brow, his cheekbones, his lips, like a blind woman reading his features with her fingers.

He was a frozen pool in winter, melting under her touch.

"Let him exalt truth," she declared, "and his land shall not wither."

She kissed each of his palms in turn, then pressed them to her cool cheeks.

"I brought you back to hear the truth from me, my lord. But I was too afraid to speak it." She was so close. "Listen, now."

Her eyes streamed into his and touched him where soul and bone meet. She brushed his lips with hers, and then tasted his mouth fully.

His body answered for him.

She pushed him down to the dying moss and he pulled her with him, knowing that having her could never be enough.

Her lips parted his and she whispered into him.

The dark veil of her hair hid them while he freed himself of his laces. She slid her leg astride him, and beneath the folds of her skirts, he found her hips and pulled her to him and in three thrusts, he'd broken the chains of their duty.

"Not to be unmade," he whispered to her.

The day had died, and night stole over the eastern fingers of the Pendynas before they'd spent themselves completely.

Nechtan held her, her head tucked under his chin, his breath playing at her hair. He felt the hot wet of her tears on his neck as she whispered, "The moon rises."

Clouds raced before the eye of night, and like petals from a starwood tree, snow began to fall.

Chapter 31

In single file, Ava and two thousand warriors of the southern tribes passed between rocky crags fondly called the Ballocks. Marking the pass into the highland vales of Cedewain, the route required a thorough scouting before Fiach agreed to move forward. No doubt he thought Nechtan would leap upon him from the rocks, for at this point, confusion and distrust reigned.

Certainly, Lyleth's escape smelled of treachery, though Fiach claimed she'd cut the ropes that bound her with a knife she found in Nechtan's boot. The only evidence that protected Fiach from suspicion were the prints of bare feet beside the dead guard. Small feet.

Fiach had sent men after her. The fact that they had not returned was more than suspicious. Lyleth could not have killed a dozen men, but Fiach could have ordered them to spare her, aid her even, and see her all the way to Marchlew... and Nechtan.

The rumor had spread, with some coaxing from Ava, that Lyleth was the one who had slit Irjan's throat, mistaking her for Ava in the darkness of the tent. But Fiach knew the truth. He was no fool. And Ava suspected he understood just as well her reason for killing the old woman.

The road widened into a valley specked with sheep. Fiach, as if feeling her distrust, rode up beside her.

Testing her theory, she said, "If they're coming, they're here already."

"I agreed to fight the northern tribes, not the Bear." He was as clever as she predicted.

"Will you just bend over and present your ass to him?" She examined Fiach, looking down the length of her nose.

"My swords are already shaken," Fiach said. "They're spinning tales—that Nechtan will sow dragon's teeth and call forth a host of the dead to fight beside him, that he'll free the Old Blood from the greenwood and waters—"

"Then your men will piss themselves when my father takes their rear."

"How many ships would he bring?" Fiach asked.

"The autumn seas are treacherous, even for their longships. How many would he risk to take the land he's always lusted after? What do you think?"

"Then we take Caer Cedewain before the Bear does," Fiach said, "and hold it against him."

"And if Nechtan and Marchlew wait for a siege?"

"Then we draw them onto the field," Fiach said.

Cedewain was comprised of a maze of river valleys that trickled down from the great spine of the Pendynas range. Scattered pastureland divided vast forests, all prime for ambush. Caer Cedewain, Fiach said, sat at the eastern end of a long narrow glen bordered to the north by a river and to the south by a nearly impenetrable greenwood. Once they passed the Ballocks, scouts took to the woods, flanking the main body of troops.

The Bear would be beaching his longships to the east now. If Lyleth had made it to Cedewain, then Nechtan would know the Bear was coming, and he wouldn't want a siege any more than Fiach.

Evening made stilt-like shadows of their horses' legs. Ava leaned toward Fiach, saying, "I know a way to assure you Nechtan will leave his walls and meet us on the field."

Fiach raised a pretty eyebrow.

"Burn every shepherd's hut," she said, "every hunter's hovel, every millhouse and pigsty. Slay their flocks and put their children to the sword. Leave nothing standing between here and Caer Cedewain. Nechtan will come for you."

Fiach's face paled. "You would kill your own?"

"They are not my own, nor yours. Do you serve me, Fiach?"

Here was the test, and the struggle was written on his face. She watched his throat work as he swallowed and gazed at the horizon; he dragged the back of his hand over his mouth. Were his fingers quaking? She liked to think so.

"As you command," he said at last. He wouldn't meet her eyes, but dug his heels in and burst away from her at a trot.

It was nightfall when riders approached the camp bearing fir branches, a sign of truce.

"Ice-born," Jeven said.

Ava felt the blood drain from her face.

They were indeed ice-born, all thegns of some renown by their arm rings. Jeven talked quickly, informing her that a thegn named Rua wished to discuss terms. Ava's men had yet to lift a sword in battle and the ice-born wanted her to surrender.

She knew Rua too well. Named her father's "Thegn of the Wastes," Rua had eaten the Bear's scraps for a decade. As was the custom, Ava was betrothed to the beast before she was old enough to marry, for Rua had proven his brutality in countless summer raids of the Five Quarters. His prize was to be Ava... until Nechtan had arrived in Rotomagos.

Ava had often wondered if that slight had turned Rua against the Bear. And now, he brought demands, most certainly, but were they his? Or the Bear's?

Rua was accompanied by thirty men. Ava could slay them all easily. But Jeven warned her these might be a fraction of the men who had landed on the beaches or pushed upriver, deep into the woodlands of the Five Quarters. Killing them would start this battle far too soon.

Ava dressed in a blue damask gown trimmed in fox. Her serving girl, a dirty thing found among the camp whores, held a mirror. Ava ran her hands over the form beneath the bodice and skirt, but the distorted image of a royal cunt mocked her. What was she trying to do, seduce the man? She couldn't seduce them all. She must command them. She was done with this game. Rua would treat with a she-king. And he would either submit to her, or make his way back to his longships with Ava slashing at his back.

"Unlace me," she ordered the serving girl.

"My lady?"

"I said, unlace me."

The girl did as bidden. Ava slipped the gown from her shoulders and let it fall to the ground. Candlelight washed over her sallow skin, revealing her protruding hipbones, the soft blonde forest between her legs, her withered breasts, and pink nipples hard with the cold. Her flights with the red crow had ravaged her, and she felt she looked upon another woman's body. She'd freed herself of its demands and no longer had need of it, just as her body no longer needed her soul.

Naked, she stepped out from behind her bed curtain into the outer room of her tent. Fiach, Jeven and Gwylym froze at the sight of her.

The silence was thrilling.

"I am your king, and you shall arm me," she said to Jeven. She glanced at Gwylym and saw red flush his cheeks. He moved toward her with a cloak in his hands.

"No, Gwylym. It's the duty of my solás to arm his king."

She challenged Jeven with a look and motioned to her rank armor that hung from the stand at the entrance to the tent.

Jeven didn't hesitate. "As you say, my lady."

The others busied themselves, stealing glances, while Jeven took Ava's smallclothes from her extended arm. He knelt, like a dutiful servant, holding out her britches. With one hand on his shoulder, Ava stepped into them. He made no move to avert his eyes, a thing she admired in this greenman.

He pulled them up around her hips and tied the drawstring. The trousers followed, then the gambeson and mail. Finally, he buckled her sword belt.

Draping the heavy dreadnought cloak around her, he whispered, "Your crown."

"Yes," she said.

He took it from the box and settled the circlet on her head, then offered his palms. She should have placed her trust in Jeven rather her father's slave, she thought. For Jeven's loyalty was bought by the green gods. He owed Ava his soul.

"Bring him in," she told Jeven.

Before she saw him, she heard Rua and his man approach, for a skald was singing a runo immortalizing Rua's feats of brutality. In fact, as he drew nearer, she understood the song, describing the beheading of Nechtan's father in the Silver Marches. Other than Ava, Jeven was the only one of her counselors who understood high Skvalan, or Rua would have been dead before he reached the tent.

Jeven's eyes met hers, saying clearly, Beware.

She stood tall as the flap opened and a granite block of a man darkened the doorway.

Rua's scaled hauberk of walrus ivory chattered when he moved. Hair the color of iron rust was knotted at the back of his head, exposing a pink scar that ran above his left ear, across his eye, to his mouth. His left eye was milky and likely blind from the blade that sliced it. His beard failed to grow around the twisted flesh, and she couldn't help wondering what Ildana warrior had left that scar. It was enough to make her smile.

"You've travelled far from the sea," she said. Her native tongue felt thick as cold fat on her lips.

Rua's eyes openly worked up and down her armored form

as he paced a circle around her, measuring her like a heifer at a fair.

"Behold, the she-king, spawn of the Bear," he finally said. At last, he offered his palms, dropping his chin to his chest but bending no knee.

She wanted no ears but hers to hear what this man had to say.

"Leave us," she told the others.

When the golden-haired skald balked, she said in Skvalan, "Go. I'll care for your lord."

Jeven hesitated, honest concern in his eyes. Did he think the man would murder her with a thousand Ildana outside the tent?

"Go," she said to him, and he and the ice-born lad finally followed Gwylym out. "I assume there are more than your thirty warriors in the forests of Cedewain," she said.

"Is that a question?" He locked his hands behind his back and took up pacing again.

"Not one I think you'll answer. Tell me… what news do you bring from my loving father? Does he gain any ground against the wasting sickness that plagues him?"

Rua stopped pacing, poured himself a cup of ale from a waiting pitcher, and took a deep swallow. "The Bear will not rest in death until this land is his."

"This land is mine."

He bellowed a laugh, making the little bells in his moustache tinkle. "And you are his, woman. The spawn of his loins."

"I belong to no man, thegn."

"Do you not, warrior queen? I've heard that your husband wanders the moors like a wraith. You failed to kill him properly and he crawled from his barrow, alive."

She forced a laugh. "What would you know of my husband's death?"

"I know the gods didn't choose his hour."

No, the Bear did. Through Irjan.

"My father waits for me to put down Marchlew's rebellion," she said, "so he can claim this land for himself. Or do you come offering his assistance?"

"Not assistance, exactly."

"Tell me, then. Exactly. What brings you to creep through the woods of Elfael? Speak plainly, man."

"He sent me to feel your muscle, girl."

He squeezed her arm and she shook him off.

"A queen without a king," he proclaimed, "is worthless as teats on a bull."

"I may have no cock to measure against yours, thegn, but I am the king no less. My father doesn't count the green gods among his slaves, and it was they who made me king. In this land, I need no man. Nor cock."

"The Bear's reach is quite as long, my queen." He drew out the word 'queen,' dróttning in high Skvalan. "Your green gods favor you, and the Bear is in their debt. But he wills that you rule this land as our gods command, with a man in your bed."

Anger throbbed behind her eyes. "The only men I need serve me. My chieftains."

Rua sniffed and sucked at his scarred lips. "Some of your chieftains would prefer to hack at you with their swords, I'm told. And they've raised a dead king to lead them. It would seem you have a… problem. If you accept this proposal, this ghostly king who haunts you will die for good."

"If I do not accept?"

"The Bear will take what he wants and offer you no protection."

"Two thousand men outside this tent could make certain you bring back no answer to my loving father."

"Do you threaten me, little queen?"

He drew a dagger and, with a rhythmic jangle, ran the tip over the mail between her breasts.

"After all, who'll plow your field and plant it well, eh?"

Laughing, he gave his crotch a clutch.

Ava had forgotten the disgust she felt for her own. "Tell the Bear he'll have to kill me for this land."

"As you wish."

This time Rua bent the knee, before he and the stench of home vanished into the greenwood.

Chapter 32

With eight hundred warriors snaking through the woods behind her, Lyleth could just make out the figure of Nechtan riding ahead. Snow fell with purpose, dimming the moonlight and forcing them to feel their way through the woods.

Talan rode between her and Nechtan, for his safety was the price she'd paid for the bloodletting to come. She would likely regret it as she regretted so many bargains made for the sake of this covetous land.

Before they rode from Caer Cedewain, Kyndra had tied a garland of autumn leaves and holly to her son's helm. She had kissed him, not as a mother would kiss a son, but as she would a lordling, softly on each cheek. But her eyes had met Lyleth's, saying she was resigned to her son's fate, for they were dry and distant as the eyes of one who's lost everything.

The forests of Pendynas were dark even during midday, but tonight the moon reflected feebly from the growing drifts of snow. Without torch or rushlight, Nechtan led the way, following huntsmen west and south from Caer Cedewain. The game track they followed required archers and dogmasters to move single file, and those who were mounted slowed them even more. Nechtan had split the northern forces in two, with him leading Pyrs and Maddoc and the bulk of archers and dogs along the southern edge of Glen Rannoch while Marchlew, Desmund and Griff took the mounted men north of the river called the Hag's Gossip. Once they reached the bridge at the narrows, they would await Nechtan's signal.

The barest defenses were left behind to guard Caer Cedewain and the towers of Maiden Pass. Lyleth knew as well as Nechtan that their number was insufficient if the ice-born came, but there was no other way. They must win the field first before they could defend the fortress from the ice-born.

They had travelled a league at best when the first scout returned.

"They're burning people out," he told Nechtan. "Killing women and children."

"Fiach wants us to come to him," Nechtan told Lyleth.

"Surprise is not to be ours," Lyleth said.

"No. Not entirely."

They rode as fast as possible in darkness. The fall of snow grew so heavy that Nechtan's dark figure would momentarily vanish in the flurries. But his touch lingered on Lyleth's skin, his voice still sounded in the deepest part of her. They had drowned in each other, and nothing could come to pass this day that could change it.

She shifted the weight of four full quivers on her back. The fletchers at Caer Cedewain knew how to craft triple bodkin points with perfect balance, good spine, and fletched with the tail feathers of barnacle geese. She had taken all she could carry.

She glanced over her shoulder at Dylan riding behind her. The boy carried as many or more quivers, and his new starwood bow peeked from his back. Even beneath the shadow of his hood, she could see him grinning.

Elowen rode with the armorer, a concession Lyleth had made. The girl said she couldn't stay back at the fortress and wait because Brixia had insisted on following Lyleth. Elowen declared it a portent of victory, and the men had festooned Brixia like a warrior, with battle braiding of ribbons and holly berries. The little horse was a sight indeed.

Tonight, Lyleth had armed Nechtan for the last time, as

was her duty as his solás, yet she wondered if her words of warding could strengthen his steel as it always had. What was it they had broken and built between them? It was stronger than any steel, that she knew.

Marchlew had sent Nechtan a hauberk of scale mail. It was too heavy, Nechtan said, and went back to the rusted mail he'd taken from the dead man at the inn. It was fitting for a man such as himself, he said, who'd suckled at Death's breast not so long ago.

"No matter what the outcome," Nechtan told her, "you will take Talan and the remains of Marchlew's retainers to the judges of the wild wood."

She laced his bracers. "What if Ava lives? The druada will not name another king while one lives."

"You brought a man back from the dead, Lyl, they'll listen to you. Everyone will listen to you."

He stood and held out his arms while she buckled the axe belts across his back.

"I'll do what I can," she said.

He took her in a firm hold. "No. You must do exactly as I ask, or the blood spilt tomorrow will be just the beginning. The Five Quarters will tear itself to pieces. Fiach and Lloyd will both move to take the throne and Marchlew and Pyrs will try to stop them."

"I understand," she said.

"Promise me you'll see Talan to the throne."

She gave him a sad smile, dragged her thumb across her lips as a pledge, then touched his lips. "I promise."

He took her hands and kissed them, and she read in his touch a knowing that was far beyond the sight she possessed.

"I am a bird that swims," he said softly, "a fish that flies."

She opened a carved yew box and removed two arm rings of Finian silver, a matched pair of water horses with eyes of carnelian. She unpinned the hinges and fitted them around his upper arms.

"But today you are king of the Five Quarters."

She finished the words of warding, her hands moving over each of his weapons, "I arm you with the light of Sun, radiance of Moon, swiftness of Wind, depth of Sea…"

Chapter 33

Connor and Iris rode back to school in a cop car, because, in spite of Aunt Merryn's protests, Bronwyn had decided to press charges. Connor was not just a lunatic; now he was also a car thief.

Father Owens called both of their parents, but Iris' family lived in Portland, so she would be alone in her defense.

Within the hour, Connor's mother had arrived and they gathered in Father Owen's office, listening to a lecture that sounded more like a Sunday sermon, something about maturity and responsibility and accepting the trials of life without lashing out at the establishment. Connor found the perpetually forgiving, painted eyes of the Virgin, and stared back. He didn't need forgiveness anymore.

"Congratulations, Connor," Father Owens said, "you've succeeded in your quest for expulsion."

"I talked Iris into coming with me. She didn't have anything to do with it."

"God gave Iris free will."

"Not really, sir." Connor tried not to look at Iris.

Father Owens looked up from the paperwork in front of him. "Excuse me?"

"Free will," Connor said, "implies that the future is fluid and changeable. But that's not really the case, except maybe on the other side."

Father Owens rocked back in his leather executive chair and glowered. "Has Cavendish been filling your head with this existentialist garbage?"

"Dish? No. I didn't choose the accident. Neither did Dish."

Owens leaned back over his papers. "You'll be better off at home, surely. I'll consider your request regarding Miss McCreary, but now I think you have belongings to gather, farewells to say."

Owens gathered the stack of papers and tapped them square, the cue to get out. Connor's mom had her hand on the doorknob.

"Please let me stay," Connor said. "Until it's over."

Owens glanced at Connor's mother, then said, "You mean until it's over with Mr. Cavendish."

"I'll be too far away to get here if Bronwyn—I mean, Ms. Cavendish—decides to call me."

Was that compassion in Father Owen's eyes? He stated clearly, "She won't call you." No, it was loathing.

"You believe there's life after death, don't you, Father?"

Owens straightened in his chair, his pale eyes narrowed. "Of course. Everlasting life. And it will belong to Mr. Cavendish as well as you and me."

"Let's pack your things, Connor." Mom's hand was on his shoulder.

"I've seen the other side." Saying it was like taking a lung full of mountain air. "It's alive, more alive than we are. Alive with fear and love and colors so real they hurt. And choices." He heard his voice dribble into silence.

Iris was giving him the stink eye, and his mom was dragging him by the arm toward the door.

He turned back just before the door closed behind him, calling, "No angels and harps!"

Connor's mom daubed at her nose with a tissue, and headed past the receptionist's desk. Connor followed.

Iris must have convinced Owens she needed to say

goodbye because she ran from the office and caught Connor's arm, saying, "See ya." As she shook his hand, she slipped him a tiny origami star of binder paper. Her eyebrows bounced under bleached bangs.

"Are you coming?" Connor's mom was holding the door to the courtyard.

She marched beside him and when he gave her a long, questioning look, her tears finally came.

"Why are you doing this to me, Connor?" she demanded. "Don't you think I've been through enough with Dylan?"

At the sound of his brother's name, something bitter congealed in Connor's gut. He had no answer for that. No one did. She must really believe that everything he and Dylan had done wrong in life they had done solely to punish her.

Brother Mike met them in the dorm lobby with more paperwork for Connor's mom.

"I'll go pack," Connor told her.

He went upstairs and stood in his dorm room, frozen. He was headed back to the home Dish said was no home, leaving Dish to die in a hospital bed, falling between this world and the other, like falling between a train and the platform.

He unfolded the origami star and read Iris' note. Get your ass over to Ned's, jerk. Bring the picture.

Iris had already started up the fire trail when Connor caught up to her. He had left through the fire escape, knowing it would take a few minutes for Brother Mike to realize he was gone. No one knew about Ned's place but Iris.

"We're going to get you over to the other side," she was saying, "and you're going to warn Dish. Maybe if he knows, he can make some kind of choice."

"I've already tried to get back."

"Then you haven't tried hard enough. If Ned didn't pull you out last time, what would've happened?"

"I suppose I would have drowned, I don't know."

"Then maybe you just need to drown again."

Connor had stopped listening to Iris a half mile back. They made their way up the snaking trail into the foothills. Connor was trying to talk himself into going along with Iris' plan. But drown? What if she didn't pull him out? He would be as lost as Dish. Between the two worlds where the roots of trees meet.

He glanced up at the sky. Creamy clouds rolled by and he thought of the clouds in Dr. Adelman's office. None of this was real. And all of it was real. Someone decided so. Lyla maybe, or maybe it was Connor all along, his personal universe balled up inside his head and he pulled at the string and untangled the truth he'd made.

Connor took Iris' hand and helped her through the crumpled chain-link. It was the first time he noticed a "no trespassing" sign, and it occurred to him it was new.

"What if Ned throws us out?" Iris asked.

"If we're lucky, he won't be here."

Connor knelt down beside the hot tub and peered into the water. He couldn't see the bottom because the plaster was painted dark blue so it looked like a natural pond. But the plaster was peeling in places, leaving dull grey pock marks. He slipped his shoes off.

"Let's do this fast."

Iris pulled a lipstick from her hippie bag. "Let's just do it right."

"What do you mean?"

"You have the picture, right?"

Connor fished in his pocket for the photocopy of the stone and spread it out on the pool deck. Iris handed him the lipstick. It was so red it was almost black. He read the name on the bottom, "Nearly There?" He had to laugh. "What am I supposed to do with this?"

"Write the runes, just as they are in the picture, around the hot tub."

"You're kidding, right?"

"Do you have a better idea?" Iris knelt beside him and started sweeping cigarette butts away with her hands. "Maybe the runes can open the well."

"And if I really do drown in there, I'll be as lost as Dish."

Iris looked right into his eyes and said, "Connor, you're already lost."

She gave him a quick kiss on the cheek and went back to clearing the deck. "Start drawing," she said.

His recreation of the stick-like runes was less than impressive, the crossing hash marks weren't perfectly straight and some were too small. It looked like the work of a first grader.

The lipstick was just a nub when he drew the last rune. The circle of strange words fit perfectly, the last one meeting the first back at the beginning.

"Okay," Iris said. "I'm ready."

Connor figured he should be ready, too. He was about to dive into a shallow hot tub and possibly break his neck or drown. Death was just a slip down this waterslide to another world.

"Okay." He stripped to his boxers and walked to the fence.

Iris was positioned just outside the ring of runes.

"Okay." He knew there was more to existence than what he could see and smell and hear and feel. He had seen it on the other side, felt his true self quake with the longing for it.

He didn't want to be lost any longer.

"Okay." Dish already knew there was no land of the dead, no Fair Lands. Because everyone is dead. And all lands are fair. Iris was right. Connor was already dead.

He took off, bare feet slapping the hot flagstones, but as the surface of the water came into view, he saw it boil, just for a second, like the jets were on.

Something was in there.

He kept on running well past it, stopping before he reached the porch. He jogged back to the hot tub and knelt at the edge.

"What's the matter?" Iris knelt beside him.

A flash of sunlight reflected from something deep and moving. "There's something in there."

The sunlight cut bright shards through the water and revealed the unmistakable shimmer of scales.

"Jesus... there it is." It must be the water horse. He should jump in.

But Iris was already heading for the shrubs. "Piranhas!" she cried. "I knew it! Fuck!"

The beast was as thick as his leg and lots longer. He watched it ripple and glide like a ribbon at the end of a stick. It spiraled toward the surface; the sun caught its dorsal fin and shimmered with every color. Crimson gills pumped at the side of its head and feelers fluttered from its snout. Its yellow eye twisted in the socket until it locked on Connor.

"Yeah, that's not the water horse."

Finding his feet at last, they took him at a dead run to the cover of the bushes.

He clutched Iris' arm. "Stay still."

"Like hell," she demanded.

As if in answer, the thing rose from the pool, a waterfall in reverse, shrouded in a dense, shimmering, golden fog that spiraled with the creature. When the fog cleared, Ned stepped onto the pool deck. He shook water from his hair, glanced down at the runes under his wet feet, and then turned those glowing yellow eyes on the bushes.

"What the fuck, Connor?"

Chapter 34

The snowfall had slackened and the moon was overhead when Nechtan glimpsed the watchtower through the trees. Built in the time of Black Brac, Morcant's Roost was nothing more than a square stone tower rising from an outcropping that overlooked the glen. Since the binding of the Five Quarters into one, the watchtower had been home to soothsayers and ravens. The battlements had begun to crumble and the bartizan had fallen down the cliff a long time ago.

The moon came and went behind a bank of purple clouds, and Nechtan hoped both the clouds and the snowfall would hide them long enough to take position at the edge of the woods.

He called for the snaking column behind him to stop.

Archers and hound masters had their orders. The dogs were muzzled, and they spread through the trees as silent as sand through fingers.

Nechtan dismounted.

"Fetch dry kindling and tinder," he told Talan and Dylan. "Quickly."

Lyl moved to follow the boys, but he called her back. "Let's go to the top for a better look. Come."

The new snow was dry as barley flour and made the climb over the rocks slick and slow. When they reached the tower base, Nechtan found the door hanging from its hinges. Lyl lit a rushlight and the sputtering flame revealed a damp, low room. It smelled of molding leaves, wet ash and urine and they stepped around mounds of bat droppings.

"My family's holding wasn't far from here," Lyl whispered. "When I was a girl, an old soothsayer lived here. She taught me to read clouds."

"And what do this night's clouds tell you?" He took her hand and led her to the stone stairs that spiraled up the wall.

"That the battle's already been won."

He turned to her, to measure her meaning, and saw what he hoped to see in her eyes. The Five Quarters might fall into oblivion, but nothing could change what they shared.

Taking the rushlight, he made his way up the stairs. The floor on the second level was buckled, for the weather had come through a hole in the roof. He kept going up to find a wooden hatch swollen shut. He was able to force it open with his shoulder and heft the snow away.

He put out the rushlight, climbed out onto the wall walk and found it stable enough, at least the side that faced the glen below. Seeing Dylan and Talan, he motioned for them to come up.

The boys climbed the steps with dead wood bundled in Dylan's cloak.

"Put it there." Nechtan pointed at the ribs of the exposed roof joists.

They obliged, and shivering, Dylan pulled his cloak back on.

"Stack it for proper burning, and douse it with this," Nechtan said, tossing a skin of walnut oil to Dylan. Marchlew's failure to maintain this tower was unfortunate, but it would make a fine torch.

Nechtan searched the glen below. A shepherd's holding of some size lay tucked between the watchtower and the big sweep of the river bend. He could just make out the bridge and the darkness of the forest on the other side where Marchlew's horsemen would be waiting. Far to the west, he saw the flicker of burning holdings. Ava's brutality would mark their movement eastward very clearly.

"Fiach baits me like a fish. How long till dawn?" he asked Lyl.

She leaned on the wall and, with her fist extended, measured the moon's height above the horizon. "Little more than an hour until first light." She pointed at the circular enclosure of wattle that surrounded a herd of sheep outside the holding below the cliff. They bleated restlessly. "The sheep smell our dogs."

"Then we'll have to engage Fiach long before he reaches that holding."

Snowflakes caught in Lyl's eyelashes, like cold stars they hung there; and then melted on her cheeks. He would miss this woman beyond measure. He had missed her for untold ages until she called him back to this moment. And if he believed her now, they would not be parted long, but would wash up on a new shore, and look upon each other with new eyes.

As he always had, Nechtan chose to believe her.

He walked to the western side of the tower and looked to the wood below where Pyrs awaited his signal. Pyrs' dogmasters were some of the best in the Five Quarters. The war dogs of the Ildana were trained to serve a single master, not starved before a fight as were the dogs of Cadurques, but trained to voice commands from one man. They killed to please their master, not to fill their bellies. Nechtan had learned that men kill for much the same reasons, and pursue both rewards with equal fervor.

From the eastern side of the tower, he saw Maddoc at the base of the steep scarp, shaking his shield to indicate he could see Nechtan.

Everyone was in position.

He paced the short square of the wall walk. Even if Fiach thought to skirt the glen and take the north bank of the river,

Marchlew waited. But where would they hold Ava during the fight? Surely she wouldn't take the field.

At last, the eastern sky kindled to sapphire and pink. And at last, he saw them. They must have stopped to rest where the snow gave them cover.

"There," he pointed. "Maybe a league away, close to the river."

Lyl followed his finger to where the horses and men appeared like dirty smudges on the fresh snow. They'd cleared the mouth of the glen during the night.

Lyl's breath streamed in the cold air. "I see them."

As the sky brightened, so did the snow. Birdsong echoed through the woods. Nechtan roused Talan and Dylan with a kick to their feet. "They come, lads."

He never heard Lyl nock and draw the shaft, just the song of her bowstring slicing the air as she released. He looked up at her target and watched a crow spiral into the trees below.

"The red crow," she said. "Ava."

When they reached the place where they'd seen the crow fall, it was no crow they found. War dogs leapt at the trunk of an oak, barking and snapping through their muzzles. Wedged high in the branches was the grey flesh of a man, an arrow through his neck. Without arms or legs, his back was broken on a branch, the flesh blackened and seared and falling from the bone as if he'd hung there since summer.

"I know him," Talan said. The boy circled the base of the tree and stared up at the dead man. "He's my father's man. Finlys."

Dylan vomited in the snow.

"The druí Ava executed," Lyleth said.

"But how is he here?" Talan asked.

"It's dark work," Lyleth answered. "Ava tethered his soul, trapped him in the body of a conjured red crow. She's been watching us."

"Is it the work of a druí?" Talan asked her. Nechtan saw a morbid exhilaration flash in Talan's eyes.

"Not the work of one who serves the green gods," Lyl said flatly.

Nechtan met Lyl's eyes, and he took the meaning in that glance—she had tethered his soul no less than this. But Nechtan was thankful for his chains.

Talan set aside his spear and swordbelt, and took to the branches with the agility of a squirrel. When he reached the corpse, tendrils of red vapor curled from the ragged sockets of its absent limbs. With wide eyes and a trembling hand, Talan reached out to touch it.

"You mustn't," Lyl warned.

But Talan paid her no mind.

Nechtan watched the boy's fingers pass right through the rotting flesh. Before Nechtan's eyes, the breeze gained strength and unmade the corpse. It dissolved into fine blood-red chaff that eddied about, catching in Talan's hair and cloak. Within moments, the cloud had blanketed the oak's trunk and Talan with it. Instantly, the rough bark soaked up the stuff, leaving no trace of Finlys or the crow.

Nechtan thought he saw the tree swell and writhe, like a snake that's swallowed a rat.

Talan looked down from his perch, his eyes wide as if he'd awakened from a nightmare.

"Ava," Nechtan said.

Dylan appeared at his side. "Is Ava dead, too?"

But Nechtan was already running. He bounded back up the snowy cliff to the tower. Once on top, he struck a rushlight and tossed it on the pile of brush and timber. It was time.

Dawn drove the clouds to the south and day broke blindingly clear and cold. The storm left drifts of snow up to the men's knees. Behind them, Morcant's Roost shoved a hot spear of fire into the morning sky. The remainder of the roof collapsed with a fountain of sparks and flames, and snow fell with cinders.

As if in answer, the bridge over Hag's Gossip billowed smoke and flame. Marchlew was across. And as Nechtan had instructed, he burnt the bridge to ensure that there would be no escape northward for Ava, nor for Marchlew if he decided to seek the safety of Cedewain's walls.

Nechtan must press hard and fast.

He raised an axe to signal Pyrs, and the dogmasters' horns bellowed. Freed of muzzles and harness, the war dogs lit out across the snow in a snarling surge.

Once in open ground, they set out to cover the snowy bowl of the glen quickly.

Ava's footsoldiers had seen them. Good. Nechtan would draw them to him while Marchlew closed from his position across the river.

Nechtan reined up and measured the movement of his men to the west and east. They closed like a scythe from the borders of the shepherd's holding. He had sent a bank of archers to take position behind a long wattle sheep fence, and now the first volley of Arvon arrows blackened the sky.

Talan rode up beside him. "Shouldn't we follow the dogs, uncle?"

"The dogs will soften them for your spear, lad."

There was something changed about Talan, anticipation of the fight perhaps, or the memory of something he'd seen up in that tree. The boy's lips had gone blue with cold. Eyes just as blue were wide behind a silver-gilt face piece that extended from a helm of filigree and gemstones. One blow from the butt of a sword would dent the work beyond repair. Nechtan hoped there was some steel under that silver.

"Come. You'll stay behind me as we agreed."

"I'm a man, uncle. I don't need you as a shield."

Nechtan couldn't help but smile. "And if I fall, your spear

will be all you have, lad. And I doubt it's as experienced as your cock."

By the battle standards, Gwylym and Lloyd had taken charge of Ava's van, their foot soldiers forming a shield wall while Marchlew slammed into their northern flank. Fiach's horsemen trailed farther down river, no doubt planning to use speed to cut Nechtan's forces in two.

But where was Ava? After the red crow fell, would she even live?

Nechtan pushed through snowdrifts and closed ground to see war dogs meet Fiach's horsemen. The archers had already dropped a good number of them, but now the dogs leapt and ran up the horses' haunches to pull men to the ground. Growls mixed with screams, the whine of bowstrings and the sound of battle horns from the river.

"Now your spear has a task," he told Talan. "Finish what the dogs started."

Nechtan glanced at Lyl. She needed no orders. She and Dylan dismounted and took a stand with a score of archers behind an abandoned wagon, a position that would allow her to guard Talan.

Nechtan spurred on, leading his small party of horsemen toward the southern flank where he would tighten the noose.

He rode straight for a man he recognized as one of his own retainers.

"Man of Ys!" he called. "You swore your life to me. Now it's mine to take." He would not hesitate, for if he did, this day would never end.

The man froze, his shield tucked tight to his chest.

Nechtan wheeled his horse and swung an axe. The man didn't even lift his shield as his helm and skull split like a rotten log.

No king should have to kill his own men.

Nechtan leaned over his horse's neck and caught the long

haft of the war axe, retrieving it before the next man was on him.

But this man reined up and made the sign against evil. "Stars and stones... you're dead."

"Not as dead as you'll be if you don't join me now." Nechtan rode at him.

But the man spun and spurred his horse back through the confusion.

"Tell them!" Nechtan yelled to his back.

He turned to see a rider come at Talan from his blind side. Nechtan called out, but an arrow found the attacker before Talan could test his spear. Lyl. But within a few strides, Talan found a fallen rider crawling away from two dogs and drove his spear home, his expression as calm as if he threw against a quintain. He glanced over his shoulder at Nechtan and smirked.

Perhaps Talan was indeed the king this land needed, one without mercy.

Nechtan hacked his way deeper into the men of the Ildana and the sun crawled higher. Fiach's men attempted a shield wall, but the dogs needed only take down two men to open it like a gaping wound. As he'd hoped, many turned and fled when they saw him, but his axes bit the flesh of too many who should have fought beside him, not against him.

Then he saw Fiach's standard, the crossed barley sheaves of Emlyn.

He was less than a spear's throw from Nechtan. No other target mattered now.

The snow was a slick stew of frozen blood and entrails, and dying men's wails drowned out shouted orders.

Nechtan pushed toward Fiach, but when he looked back, Talan rode in pursuit of a man who fled the field. Nechtan glanced to Lyl's position behind the wagon. Talan was moving out of her range.

"Talan! Let him go!"

The words had just left his mouth when a spear caught

Talan's shield, upsetting his balance. A foot soldier took advantage of it and pulled him to the ground.

Nechtan rode down the foot soldier, hacking at his shield until Talan could find his feet and join him. But a horseman rode past and regained a cast spear. He rode at the lad, now without a shield.

Nechtan sent his axe end over end. It struck the horseman's chest hard enough to unseat him, though the blade didn't break the mail, just bones.

Sliding from his horse, Nechtan drew his second axe. The foot soldier from Emlyn hammered at Talan's sword.

"Keep your feet," Nechtan yelled to Talan.

Nechtan took on the horseman.

Just the right angle of parry and Nechtan had the blade trapped in the deep horn of his axe. He twisted until the sword popped free of the man's fist, then he buried the axe where the man's neck met his shoulder.

Talan was backed against a dying horse, his feet tangled in its thrashing legs.

Nechtan's axe bit cleanly through the foot soldier's leather hauberk and the man fell forward into Talan's arms, both of them collapsing onto the horse.

Nechtan pulled the man off Talan, not a man at all, but a boy no older than his nephew with red down on his upper lip. Nechtan wanted to beat Talan himself.

"You'll ride back to Lyleth now."

"But he was getting away—" Talan's breath pumped fast.

"I have a mind to send you back to suckle your mum—"

"No, please, uncle, I'll do as you say, I swear it."

Nechtan pointed at the wagon in the distance. "Then ride back to Lyl and you'll not leave her side. Ever."

Nechtan retrieved the axe he'd thrown and wiped the blood from the haft with his cloak.

"Ride," he said to Talan.

The boy mounted up and headed across the field.

Nechtan mounted up as well. Scanning the melee near the river, he warmed his hands on his horse's steaming hide, and started back to where Fiach's banner fluttered.

Chapter 35

With a score of archers, Lyleth and Dylan held their position behind the wagon. In the distance, Nechtan assaulted Fiach's southern flank with foot soldiers, dogs and a handful of horsemen. No sooner had Fiach's shield wall formed than it collapsed, and now Nechtan split Fiach's forces in half, but the fighting had moved well out of bowshot, and so had Talan.

Lyleth looked at the holding behind them. She must either move her band in range and search for Talan, or fall back in case men broke from the woods, a tactic she would expect from the ice-born.

"Come," she told the archers. She prepared to mount when she saw a lone rider coming toward them from the melee.

"It's Talan," Dylan said. "But where's Nechtan?"

When the boy reached them, he slid from the winded horse, hurled his spear into the snow, and planted his hands on his hips.

"Where is he?" Lyleth asked.

"Going after Fiach without me."

"Fiach would eat your heart for supper," Dylan said.

Talan shoved Dylan, who returned it, and suddenly the boys were scuffling in the snow. Lyleth took hold of Dylan by the cloak and dragged him off Talan, who stood up, drew his sword and held it to Dylan's throat.

"You'll not speak to me ever again, minstrel boy."

"Not if I'm lucky—"

"Sheathe that sword," Lyleth said, "before I take it from you."

Talan stared at Dylan for a long moment, spat, then sheathed his sword. He showed his palms to Lyleth with an impertinent scowl. "Yes, mum. Do we flee?"

She glared at him. She had to take him with her, what else could she do?

"We're riding to the holding."

"They're behind us?" Talan's face brightened. "Why haven't they attacked yet?"

"That's what we go back to know." Lyleth hitched her quivers on her back and swung onto her horse. "We can use a sword with us. But you'll do exactly as I say."

"You command me, druí, or so says my uncle." He wiped a bloody hand over his mouth, but Lyleth saw that hand tremble, just perceptibly.

Dylan bristled, his pride clearly bruised. It was unfortunate Dylan wasn't Nechtan's heir. How easy it would be to see him to the throne.

Lyleth led the way across snowy pastures to the holding's sheep pens. From the fence line, she could see an open gate through the stockade. The sheep would tell her more.

Leaving their horses tied to a withy fence, she led them through churned snow. The sheep bunched and flowed away, bleating, but as they parted, Lyleth saw the body of a man, not a soldier, but a shepherd. His throat was slit. She opened his mouth and inserted two fingers. The back of his throat was still warm, telling her he'd been dead since dawn, possibly earlier, but not much. Whoever killed him had either fled, or hid inside the holding.

Lyleth looked for the answer in the whites of the sheep's eyes. They sniffed at the air and so did she, smelling little more than the smoldering tower on the crag above and the blood of the dead man at her feet. But a ram was staring at the open gate.

"Come."

She scanned the timber walk that ran along the top of the stockade, and saw no one.

Keeping to the fence, she led them forward. It had all the markings of a trap. "Archers take the wall walk. Talan and Dylan, come with me."

The barnyard was silent. The bodies of a woman and two children lay where they fell, while chickens pecked for grain between their fingers.

The door of the house stood wide open.

"Stay behind me," she told Dylan and Talan.

"What if they're in there?" Talan's breath was rapid and shallow.

"Watch the door." He didn't argue this time.

She touched Dylan's arm and he followed. She drew her dirk and Dylan a shortsword.

The dying embers of a fire barely glowed in the hearth, and Lyleth's eyes struggled in the dim light. Crumpled beside the fire lay a man wearing the cloak of a druada. Planting her foot on his shoulder, she pushed him over.

His hand went to her ankle and Dylan's sword went to his throat.

"Ava's solás," she whispered. Jeven was his name.

He let go of her ankle, his arm losing strength for he bled from a wound to the belly. He convulsed and clutched at her cloak. Who would have done this? Fiach's men? That made no sense.

Ava would not be far from Jeven, and Irjan, not far from Ava. "Where is she?" Lyleth whispered.

She followed his gaze to the timber ceiling and the ladder on the far wall.

Lyleth placed her fingers on Jeven's temples to draw out the pain, but he seized her wrist, his eyes wide and frantic. He tried to speak, but failed. Then his will let go of him, and so did

Lyleth, freeing him of his flesh. She whispered the words of passing and closed his eyes.

Dylan's eyes were on the ceiling, where tiny streams of dust came through the floorboards. She touched his arm and motioned for him to wait here.

She dropped her cloak and led with her dirk.

The ladder was narrow and bound to creak, so she became a mouse and placed her feet where the rungs met timber braces.

Slowly, she climbed until her eyes were level with the loft floor. Spears of daylight shone through seams of a shuttered window and fell on the unmoving body of Ava. But for her boots, she lay naked among fleece bundles and racks of dried fish. She was bound in the manner of Alamit seers, a primitive method used to prevent the soul from wandering too far. The bindings served to shock the body into dragging the spirit back, but one always had another keep watch in case of strangulation. Where was Irjan?

"The queen." Dylan's head poked up beside her. He repeatedly made the sign against evil.

"Watch the ladder," Lyleth told him.

A stoppered horn vial lay beside Ava. Lyleth uncorked it and smelled the black liquid. Poppy and henbane, and probably nightshade. Ingested, the contents would kill, but used sparingly in the eyes or nostrils, it would allow one to fly, and in Ava's case, share the body of her conjured red crow. Irjan had abandoned Ava, it seemed. When Lyleth shot the red crow, Ava's soul had crashed back into this wasted shell of flesh.

Ava lay flat on her stomach, the tether so tight she wheezed. Lyleth pushed a stray strand of hair from Ava's face, and lifted an eyelid. Her pupils were wide and black, and a stream of spittle trickled from the corner of her mouth. Lyleth rolled Ava to her back against a fleece bale, and laying a palm on her chest, detected a shallow breath and a sluggish heartbeat.

"Ava." Her head lolled, and her eyes moved rapidly behind the lids.

She was a frail shadow of the girl who'd sailed from Sandkalder as the wife of a king. Lyleth had stood beside her on the deck and watched Ava's face as the frozen shores of her homeland grew small on the horizon. "Gone," she'd said, testing her new language. "I am gone from here." She laughed into the wind and salt spray, "I am gone!"

Ava's skin felt icy and goosefleshed.

Lyleth patted her cheeks. "Where is Irjan?"

Ava's eyes tried to open, but it seemed even the dim light was blinding.

Dylan's voice came from the top of the ladder, "Found me that greenman's killer."

"Irjan?"

"Nay, just a lad round 'bout Elowen's age," Dylan said. "Hid himself in the kitchen cupboard with a meat knife, he did. The druí must have spooked him, and he give him a good stick in the belly."

"See to the boy, Dylan."

Lyleth turned back to Ava, her eyelids fluttering, her words an incoherent wheeze.

"Your men die for you," Lyleth said, "while you fly on borrowed wings. What was it like to fall from the sky?"

She pinched Ava's cheeks and trapped the lolling, bloodshot eyes with her own.

Ava just smiled weakly, and laughed, rolling to her side on the pile of fleece until the cord around her neck tightened. She croaked past the noose, "Did my husband please you?" She went into a fit of choking laughter. "What's it like to rut with a dead man?"

Lyleth shook her. "Irjan left you here to die. Where is she?"

Ava looked into her for a long moment. "Feed me death, druí." Her eyes went to the vial of poison. "Do what you've come to do."

Ava was close enough to death already. Lyleth took her dirk and cut the cord around Ava's throat and hands.

Sitting up, Ava rubbed at her wrists.

"Your death is Nechtan's decision," Lyleth said, "not mine."

Ava pulled her knees to her chest, and in one motion, drew a blade from her boot. She stabbed wildly, but before she connected, Lyleth caught her wrist and squeezed. The knife dropped to the floor.

Lyleth picked it up and pressed it to Ava's throat, a blade of green lightning glass, a soothblade of the Old Blood. How did Ava get such a weapon?

"You're a coward," Ava said. "Do it."

"Your life is Nechtan's." It took the sum of Lyleth's will to stay her hand and slip the ancient blade into her belt. She bound Ava's hands with the cast-off cord.

Rolling into a pile of vomit-soaked fleece, Ava keened. Lyleth had never felt such sorrow spill from another. Death was a gift she would not give Ava. It would come soon enough. She draped her cloak around the shivering, wasted woman and stuffed the hem in her mouth to quiet her. Who knew Ava was here? And how long would it be before they came for her?

A low whistle came from the archers on the wall walk.

Lyleth opened the shutter and looked east.

A bright lick of flame curled from the towers of Maiden Pass and Caer Cedewain itself burned.

Lyleth squatted beside Ava and looked into those lost eyes. "Your father comes for you, lass." She stroked Ava's hair. "He's been coming since your wedding day."

Chapter 36

From behind the hedge, Connor watched the last of the golden fog dissipate until Ned stood there on the pool deck, naked. Moments before, he'd been a giant eel, and now here he was, examining the runes Connor had drawn around the hot tub with Iris' lipstick.

Iris was tugging on Connor's arm. "Run!" she cried. "Go on."

"Are you crazy?" She was halfway to the fence already.

Ned didn't even glance at Iris; his eyes were trained on Connor, hiding in the shrubs in his boxers. Ned strode toward him like Bigfoot, until he stood on the other side of the hedge, his hands on his hips. His eyes bored a path through the leaves to meet Connor's.

"Hey ya, Ned," Connor said weakly.

"Come out, you pussy."

Connor crept from behind the bush, his eyes scanning the deck for the used-up lipstick, the evidence. The blood drained from his brain.

"I—I just thought I'd try one more time to get through, because I really need to see Dish, just once more, and I didn't know I would be, uh, interrupting." The next words just barfed out. "You're a water horse."

Ned gave him an offended scowl. "A water horse? You on crack?"

Ned found a towel, wrapped it around his waist, and plopped into a chair. He examined the runes on the flagstones, then measured Connor from under heavy brows.

"I won't tell a soul, honest to god," Connor said. "I know it was you who took me through the well the first time and I know you can take me again if you want to. It's really important, or I would never ask, but I suppose you already know that."

Ned's mouth was hanging open.

"First of all, Connor Connor, I'm no stinking water horse. Second of all, I'm the one who's gonna be making the demands around here, not your sorry ass. And third, it wasn't me who took you over the first time. Why the hell would I do that?"

Stories of trading your soul to the devil came to mind.

"Then how did I get through?"

"Fuck if I know. But I do know I should've left you there."

"So, you did pull me out?"

"Of course I pulled your ass out," he snuffed. "You got no business over there. And you got no business here now—"

"If you're not a water horse, what are you?"

"I'm not a what, kid. I'm a who."

How could Connor have failed to see it before? Suddenly, so many things became clear. And Connor wasn't about to let Ned get away with it.

"You're a well guardian! That pool on the beach. You lured Dish there, you tattooed him! Then the crash, and poof, Dish's insides are gone because you took him." Connor was talking so fast he couldn't stop. "You moved the well and I just happened to find your little hiding place here. But why did you take Dish?"

For once Ned seemed at a loss for words, his face all scrunched up. "'Lure' isn't exactly the right word—"

"But you did. Just tell me why."

"I don't owe you an explanation, Judge Judy, but you owe me a few." He nodded at the runes.

"You purposely took Dish over to—to wherever it is,"

Connor said, "and you told me he 'needed a chance.' A chance to do what? What do you need Dish for?"

Ned found some cigarettes behind a dead potted plant, shook one out of the pack, and lit it. He took a long drag, and exhaled a plume of smoke in Connor's face that most definitely took the shape of a water horse.

"Sit down," he demanded.

Connor coughed, and sat.

"You need to take a deep breath, kid." Ned put on his friendly face and leaned close to Connor, but all Connor could see was that lidless yellow eye swiveling in its socket. Ned always did smell a bit like fish.

"Your Dish had a task that needed doing." Ned was clearly struggling to keep his temper. "He would have gone himself if he'd found a way over. Now, where'd you get these runes?"

"Had a task? You mean he's done it already?"

"Let's suppose he has. Where did you get this?" Ned tapped cigarette ash on the runes.

"So, if Dish has done what you took him to do… you don't need him anymore." The pieces fit together now. Dish had fulfilled his role, and Bronwyn was going to pull the plug. What would happen to him when the kite string was cut?

Connor looked at the runes circling the pool. "It says something terrible, doesn't it?"

"Where did you get them?" Ned's friendly face was gone now.

These runes must be more important than Connor thought. Had the words summoned Ned? No, it couldn't be. Ned had been here from the first day. But the only place the runes existed before Connor drew them was in the photograph. He jumped out of his plastic chair and started scuffing at the lipstick marks with the heel of his bare foot.

"I got this. It'll be clean in no time. A little bleach—"

"Cut the bullcrap."

Connor turned to face Ned and the beer gut rolling over

the knot in his towel. Well guardians were supposed to be beautiful women. Connor felt cheated.

"It's some kind of magic spell, isn't it?" Connor asked. "Like druid magic?"

Ned's voice was frayed. "There is no 'magic.'" He made little quotes marks in the air. "Not on this side."

"What are you talking about? I just saw you—you swimming around as an eel. If that's not magic—"

"Don't get your knickers in a twist. Think of this world as the left side of your brain, the other world as the right. Here, you got virtual reality and spy planes, there, we got shapeshifters and shit. When you die, you go back and forth, back and forth." He waved his cigarette side to side. "You build your resume till you can use both sides of your brain."

"Back and forth?" That was exactly what Merryn had told him. "Till you reach enlightenment?"

Ned's mouth was hanging open. "Sure, whatever."

"This well is the way through, it's the third well." Connor said it with conviction.

"This is a well." Ned exhaled wild shapes of smoke from his nostrils. "Not that well. So, now…" Ned stood up, and got in Connor's face. "I'm pretty sure these symbols didn't just come to you, unless you got one hell of a right brain. Now, unless you want to get hurt all over, I'd start talking, dickweed."

Connor scanned the deck for the photocopy, but he distinctly remembered Iris stuffing the paper in her hippy bag.

"It was a photo." His voice cracked into a falsetto.

"What photo?"

Connor wiped his sweaty palms on his boxers. "I know you took Dish over to fight some kind of battle, but they're going to cut off his life support. Let him die. And I know if he dies here, he'll die there, too. So, tell me the truth, and I'll tell you about the picture."

Ned sighed. "His show's over."

"Show? Is that all Dish's life is to you? Some kind of show?"

Ned's eyes ignited. He slammed his bare, wet chest against Connor's, like a batter arguing with an umpire. "Give. Me. This. Photo."

Terror settled like shorted wires in the pit of Connor's belly. Iris would be halfway back to school by now. Connor's eyes must have flashed toward the trail, because Ned said, "Your girlie has it?"

"I—I uh, well, yeah."

In a millisecond, Ned's hands closed around Connor's throat.

"I swear—she has it!" The words croaked past Ned's tightening hands.

"You'll bring me every copy, because you know I'll know if you hold out on me, you little turd."

Ned's face turned red and the world started to recede from Connor's view like a time warp tunnel. Ned let go, and Connor collapsed and sucked air while Ned pulled at his goatee with a trembling hand.

Connor forced himself to his knees, coughing, then stood. This time, it was Connor's turn to get in Ned's face.

"You want the picture," Connor said, "and I need to go through that well because there's no way in hell I'm going to just let Dish die, here or there."

When Connor realized what he was doing, his heart stopped. Shit. Ned was grinning at him.

"Are you trying to make a fucking deal with me?"

Connor thought for a long minute whether the answer should be yes or no.

"Yeah. Here's the deal." Connor swallowed hard. "Let me see Dish one more time. Let me warn him."

"Bring me the pictures. All of them."

Connor stood at the edge of the well, naked. Ned was in there somewhere, all scale and fangs. "Jump," was all he'd said before disappearing underwater.

Connor had gone back for the book and gotten as far as Ziegler's mansion, then called his roommate. Aaron said the cops had already been there for the missing persons report. Connor asked him to give Iris a message: she was to meet him at Ziegler's, and bring the book and all photocopies.

"Photocopies of what, dude?"

"Just tell her."

Ten minutes later, Iris was there, pleading with Connor not to do it.

"What if Ned's a demon?" she demanded. "What if he's going to use this for evil? Open a portal to hell?"

"Just give me the pictures," he told her.

She fished around in her hippy bag and produced two crumpled photocopies and Clyde's book, still Ziplocked.

"See ya, Iris."

He was a few steps away when she ran to him and gave him a long hug. It actually felt good, and he held her for longer than he thought he would.

"Stop crying," he said, and headed for the trail.

When Connor got back, Ned was sitting beside the well eating Chinese food from a carton.

"Here."

Connor held out the pictures and the book. Ned took them with a strange reverence, tracing the runes with his fingers just like Aunt Merryn had. Finally, he glanced up at Connor, like a dog protecting his bone. Whatever this stone was, it was a big deal to a well guardian.

"Now it's your turn," Connor said. "Take me across."

Connor stood with his bare toes gripping the edge of the hot tub. There was no bottom now. The plaster was gone and a deep current sent a subtle curl over the surface. He thought his heart would leap out of his throat. Ned had promised to take him to the other side, but he never said anything about bringing him back. In the old stories, these trips were usually one way.

With both feet, Connor jumped in.

Connor lets the cold take him, forces his muscles to cease fighting, his arms streaming above him like vines seeking sun. His lungs beg for air until he gives in, and inhales, and a concerto of crystal bells fills his head. Every nerve in his body is fully awake, tingling wildly with the touch of effervescence.

He is a black goldfish, and he's swimming right out of his aquarium into another sky.

The heavy burden of his body dissipates slowly and carries him on like a balloon.

Through streamers of bubble-jewels, shafts of distant light dance in clear water. Roiling in and out of the light, a great beast moves. Ned. His scales are hammered silver and the light from another sun sparks his armor with iridescent flashes. But his yellow eye never leaves Connor. He circles, faster and faster, until a breaking wave carries Connor toward the surface.

In slow motion, a sword tumbles past him, end over end. A man follows the sword, his open, empty eyes staring at death, the weight of his armor dragging him past Connor into the darkness below.

Connor breaks the surface and draws a crisp, icy breath.

He's in a river and the current is dragging him away. He slams into a clump of bare bushes, makes a frantic grab for them, and drags himself out into frozen red slush. Up a low embankment, he sees dead and dying scattered across a churned field of bloody snow. When he looks back at the river, the last glint of silver scales disappears below the water. Ned has left him.

Chapter 37

Supported by volleys of Arvon arrows, Nechtan and his men pressed Fiach toward the river. Nechtan had broken Emlyn's shield wall twice, but didn't have the numbers to make a final push, and now he'd lost sight of Pyrs, who assaulted Fiach's line to the east. Rather than protect Lloyd's rear, Fiach had hung back, likely as eager to meet Nechtan as Nechtan was to meet him.

Lloyd and Gwylym had made no move to send out a flanking attack as Nechtan expected. With no stingers in his backside, it was clear the men of Ys, his own men, pressed Marchlew's back to the river. If he was going to engage Fiach, it had to be now.

Nechtan commanded three score horsemen, twice as many foot soldiers, and three hundred archers, a sad remnant of the detachment he'd led at dawn. He'd sent Talan back to Lyleth, and that was the last he'd seen of either of them. He could only hope they were among the archers at his back.

Nechtan plowed through the snow on foot, for his horse had been hamstrung. With fingers frozen around his axe hafts and arms like dough, he sliced his way deep into Emlyn's men until he saw Fiach's yellow hair spilling from under his helm.

Fiach's foot soldiers reformed a meager shield wall, waiting for him.

Then he saw it. Far beyond the wide bend in the river, smoke billowed from Caer Cedewain. The Bear had come.

He pulled off his helm and tossed it to the red mush of the ground.

"Fiach!" Spreading his arms wide, Nechtan strode directly toward Fiach's position.

Nechtan crossed his axes and tapped the hafts together.

The men of Fiach's guard backed away.

"Look to the east, Fiach!" he called. "Caer Cedewain burns. The Bear comes for us. Shall we kill each other? Or the Bear?"

Nechtan closed the ground between them with long strides, his arms wide, inviting a spear, yet no man of Emlyn raised a weapon against him.

"Your men die today for the Bear, Fiach, not to avenge the shame I brought on you, on myself."

Fiach's eyes flashed to the east, then back to Nechtan. "Where is Lyleth?"

"Safe. She's safe." He hoped it was true.

Fiach lunged at him, but Nechtan parried with crossed axes.

"Fiach, listen to me!"

He tossed Fiach back, but the man growled and came at him again.

Nechtan deflected a slice to his thigh, then one to his head. "Kill me, and you still have the Bear," Nechtan said. "Join me, and we bring him down."

Fiach feigned left, and came at Nechtan with a red-faced hack. Nechtan trapped the sword blade between his axes and pulled Fiach close and held him.

"I draw breath for this, Fiach. For this alone: to mend the shame I've brought on myself and those who once served me, the shame I've brought on my solás and yes, even the wife who murdered me."

Fiach thrust Nechtan away and stumbled free, wiping at frozen snot with the back of his hand.

"I have three hundred archers at my back," Nechtan said, "and Lyl's among them. She'd like to see you live, Fiach."

He snorted a laugh. "Lyleth brought you back to raise an army against me."

"She brought me back to join you," Nechtan said.

Fiach drove at him and punched his shield into Nechtan's chest, but Nechtan caught the edge with his axe. He worked Fiach's guard open, and caught him in a strained embrace.

"She's worthy of our love, is she not?" Nechtan said. "The woman? And the land who bore us?"

Nechtan broke his hold on Fiach and tossed him to the ground, then started walking east toward the burning fortress. He fixed his gaze on the sky, waiting for Fiach's spear to bite into his spine, certain he'd be adrift on the sea of death, riding the cold current back to that white light of the Otherworld and the boy who demanded his return.

The sound of hooves in icy mush came from behind him. He would not turn. He spread his arms wide, an axe in each fist, hoping it would be quick. But the horse passed him by and the rider reined up and stood before him. He was a young man of Fiach's clan guard, his nose red and his breath a warm streamer in the cold.

He dismounted, handed Nechtan his reins, and showed his palms, saying, "Take my horse, my lord."

Nechtan turned to see Fiach and a field of horsemen at his command.

"Take us to the Bear, Nechtan."

Snow fell again, but now it came in blinding flurries. Nechtan led Fiach and his horsemen upriver to join Pyrs, and they swiftly brought Lloyd to heel. The battlefield was silent now, but for the wails of the wounded and the dissonant bickering of crows. The men who remained whole, on both sides, turned toward the burning timbers of Caer Cedewain.

Marchlew had already gone east, back to his fortress and his wife.

The battle between kinsmen was over, and the battle for the Five Quarters had begun.

A battery of archers had returned from the south side of the battlefield, but Lyl wasn't among them. Nechtan wouldn't allow himself to think of her. He had only one thought, to finish what she brought him here to do.

He rode over the bodies of the Ildana. It was a waste of life that had won nothing. It was then Nechtan saw Talan riding toward him from the south. He rode alone.

"We have Ava!" Talan called.

Nechtan found Pyrs and told him, "I'll bring Ava back and find you."

"I'll send Maddoc for her," Pyrs said. "We can't spare you. Not now."

"I'll be back before you reach the ráth."

Nechtan rode to Talan. "Does Ava have any men with her?"

"Her solás. But he's dead."

"And Lyl?"

"A dozen archers, no more. And Dylan."

"Take me to her."

The boy led him across a hollow between the river and the withy fences of the holding. As they reached the sheepfold, Nechtan saw the glint of steel from the ridge above, just below the burnt-out shell of Morcant's Roost. Ice-born were making their way down from the crag. It was impossible to say how many. If Ava fell into their hands, there would be no stopping the Bear. Nechtan had no one to hold them but Talan and the handful of archers he could see on the stockade before him.

Nechtan spurred his spent horse and Talan followed.

"Through there," Talan pointed to an open gate in the stockade. Nechtan had started across the sheepfold when Lyl appeared with Dylan clutching Ava under his arm like a broken doll.

From the walls, Lyl's archers opened fire into the trees behind the holding. The ice-born had reached the south side.

"Get to your horses and go," he told Lyl.

He gathered Ava in his arms and started back across the pasture. Her sunken eyes locked on his face. She was a fragile shell of the woman he'd wed; bruised and stinking of Irjan's poisons.

"My love," she croaked, her eyes full of mocking contempt. "You've come for me."

Her hands were bound, but she placed both trembling, icy palms on his cheeks as if she appraised this flesh he wore. He saw something else in her, something she could not mask with spite or venom, and a pang of remorse flooded him. Nechtan had killed something precious in her, no less than she'd killed his flesh. It was for this sin alone he paid with the blood of his kinsmen.

He lifted her onto his horse. "I am deserving of your hatred, as you were deserving of my love."

He looked into her, hoping to see some finality. But she studied him with a distant wonder in her eyes, as if taking in every curve of his flesh.

"By stars and stones," she said at last, "it is you, Nechtan."

His eyes found Lyl's for a long moment. He wasn't sure if the pity he saw there was for Ava or himself, or both.

Another flight of arrows rained from the archers on the wall, and he heard the rhythmic blow of a warhorse at full gallop. He turned to see an ice-born thegn clear the sheep fence on horseback. The man's spear was set and he rode straight for Nechtan.

"Take them and go!" Nechtan said to Lyl. But her eyes refused to say goodbye.

"Go, Lyl!"

She tipped her chin just perceptibly, and dug in her heels.

A cacophony of bleating drowned out all other sound. The warhorse trampled through the flock and bore down on Nechtan. He turned the horns of his axes. He had one chance to hook the rider. As the thegn drew closer, the snarl curling his upper lip became clear. It was Rua. Thegn of the Wastes. A parting gift from the green gods indeed.

As Rua closed, Nechtan lunged right at the last moment, hooking his axe horn around Rua's knee.

Rua's falchion slashed, missing Nechtan's bare head and meeting his shoulder, but the mail held and the big man tumbled down on top of him.

Nechtan drove an axe haft into Rua's gut and rolled him away. A churned mire of frozen dung and mud sucked at his feet, but Rua was up, too.

The sheep formed a ring of bleating spectators.

Rua circled and grinned; his tongue waggled and an old scar curled his lip like a mad dog.

"I never kilt a det man before," he said in broken Ildana.

"The Bear falls to Pyrs while you play games with me." Nechtan saw a star glaive at Rua's belt, a throwing weapon, but not an accurate one. Two throwing spears were strapped to his back, and a seax hung from Rua's shield wrist by a leather thong. That would be a nasty surprise.

"Da Bear comes, det man, ya. And Rua comes for hees bride." He thumped his shield with the hilt of his falchion.

The facepiece of his helm formed the neck of a swan and battered wings wrapped round his head as if in flight. Vambraces covered his knuckles and ivory medallions scaled his hauberk and rattled like bones.

The vambraces would limit his wrist movement for throwing those spears on his back. Quickness would win this.

Nechtan crossed his axes and tapped the heads together. "Come," he said. "You must kill me first."

Rua lunged, his falchion arcing high.

Nechtan slid behind the blow, striking at Rua's thigh, but

Rua crossed his shield to deflect it and Nechtan's axe head glanced off. Rua's ivory scales chattered, and Nechtan tuned his ears to the warning they gave as to direction and speed.

Nechtan's axehead deflected a spear, and he moved quickly to counter, hooking Rua's shield edge with the horn of one axe and wrenching the arm and wrist that held it, pushing him back.

Nechtan tried to bind up the falchion with the other axehead, but Rua hacked at the haft, just missing Nechtan's hand. As Rua cocked the falchion for another chop, Nechtan hooked his leg and the big man crashed to his back. Nechtan's axe buried in the snow where Rua's head had been.

Clattering, Rua regained his feet, casting his last throwing spear, which was off mark. He was agile for such a big beast.

Rua had spent his spears, but there was still the circular star glaive. He would need time to aim and release it, and Nechtan would give him no such time. He kept close and when Rua's falchion sank deep into the haft of one of his axes, Nechtan popped the sword out of Rua's hand and threw the axe and bound falchion into the flock of sheep.

Nechtan looked back in time to see the star glaive snap from Rua's hand in a spinning whorl of blades. It came for his throat, but struck his raised axe, rattling metal and wood, slicing Nechtan's knuckles before it fell to the snow.

Rua was charging him.

Nechtan picked up the glaive and threw with an arcing twist. It found Rua's inner elbow and slashed through to the bone. His sword arm dangled like a broken doll's, the seax falling to the snow.

Rua fell to his knees and Nechtan crossed the ground in two strides, cocked the axe and brought it down and through Rua's neck.

The wolf of the frozen wastes, prince of savagery, slayer of Nechtan's father, fell forward in the frozen muck. It took two more swings of the axe to sever the swan-helmed head from its massive body. Nechtan emptied the helm of its head, the eyes still wide and blinking. He took hold of the red hair and held it out so Rua's last view of this world was his own twitching body, lying in sheep dung.

"May your ship sail an endless sea," Nechtan cursed him, "and your feet never know the earth."

With that, he tossed the head into the boiling froth of sheep.

The archers had left the walls and moved toward Nechtan in a hasty jog. "Another wave comes, my lord," one of them called.

"Go," he told them. "Keep them from Lyl."

At the edge of the woods he saw a handful of horsemen coming. He could hold them for some time, long enough to be sure that Lyl was well on her way to Pyrs.

He collected Rua's weapons and only then saw Talan. The foolish lad had come back. He'd been watching from the fence.

Talan was at his side before the horsemen entered the sheepfold.

"You're supposed to live, lad. Go."

"My father says a king who's not proven his courage is a king who's not respected."

"You must live to be respected."

"Perhaps not." Talan weighed the spear in his hand. A smirk played at his thin red lips.

The horsemen crossed the sheepfold and circled them. One man dismounted and picked up Rua's head, displaying it to the others and bellowing something in Skvalan. He pointed at Nechtan, saying, "Ahhh. The det kink killt Rua. Big man."

The man drew his sword, more for posturing than to actually fight. But as Nechtan watched, Talan's spear sprouted out of the man's chest. The others closed quickly.

"Keep your shoulder to me!" he told Talan.

A second man fell easily to Nechtan's axe before the other two circled one last time and rode on, making for the forest they'd come from.

While Talan retrieved his spear, Nechtan finished the man he'd brought down. It struck him as so peculiar; he saw no fear in the man's eyes as he died. Just laughter.

He extracted his axe from the body and steam rose like a last breath from the cleft in the man's chest. Nechtan stood and inhaled deeply of the crisp air, feeling a bone-deep weariness he'd never known before.

Turning to Talan, he said, "I'm done with death."

His eyes met Talan's, just as the spear left the boy's hand.

The shaft flew for an eternity, spiraling to meet him with the perfect aim of ambition.

Nechtan fell, his hands clutched around the burning shaft in his gut.

Talan stood over him breathing hard, or was he bleating? His eyes darted to something beyond the fence, then he set his foot against Nechtan's chest to wrench the spear free. But Nechtan clutched his ankle and held on with all the strength left him.

"The land is a jealous bitch," Nechtan growled.

Talan fell backward into a clutch of sheep and the spearhead and Nechtan's insides tore free in a surge of pain. The sky dimmed and a searing frost closed down on him.

When he opened his eyes, he looked into his nephew's face; the warrior's braid a snake of dark hair with tiny silver bells tied in it. The bells chimed like rain, like the silver bells on the branch Lyleth carried beside him, like wind through harp strings.

"Finish it," Nechtan commanded.

The lad cocked the spear as if to oblige. But someone was coming, Nechtan could read it on his face.

Talan lowered the spear, muttering, "Peace find you in the Fair Lands, uncle." And he was gone.

Chapter 38

Lyleth had left Ava with Pyrs under heavy guard. Pyrs intended to use her to negotiate with her father, but Lyleth doubted there was anything left of the woman that would be of use to the Bear. They needed Nechtan. But neither he nor Talan had returned from the shepherd's holding. Against Lyleth's command, Talan had turned back before they'd even reached the river, saying only a coward would let his uncle face ice-born alone.

Lyleth feared she'd lost them both.

The boy Dylan had found hiding in the cupboard was another matter. Lyleth couldn't send him into battle, so she told him to hide and hide well. He was to wait the day out, then run to his grandfather's, though Lyleth knew the chance of it being burned out was high.

Her thoughts were on the boy as she and Dylan rode fresh horses back toward the shepherd's holding. Arvon warriors would be following as soon as Pyrs could spare them, but they had just reached the walls of Caer Cedewain, and every man was needed. The longer the Bear held the fortress, the harder it would be to take him.

When they reached the sheepfold, the flock was in a frantic stir. As they drew closer, Lyleth saw something move through the sheep like a mole under a blanket of fallen leaves. It was Brixia—ribbons, holly and mane flying. Elowen trailed close behind her. They had clearly been flushed from their hiding place in the woods and the ice-born would be right behind them.

Lyleth slid from her horse and raced across the muck. Sheep spurted and flowed in all directions, their bleating and bells drowned Elowen's cries. When the sheep parted, she saw where Elowen was headed. Nechtan.

Encircled by sheep, he lay in a muddy pool.

Lyleth ran to him and placed her palms on his cooling cheeks. A spear had ripped through his mail, and his intestines lay strung out in the filth, spilled when the spearman retrieved his weapon. But he hadn't the kindness to finish him.

His eyes saw her, but did his mind?

He fought for words. "You'll do... what I asked?" His words were barely more than a whisper.

"Talan." Lyleth held him, her tears leaving muddy streaks on his face. "Talan came back for you. Where is he?"

Nechtan fought for breath. "I sent him... to Pyrs." He took her face between bloody, quaking palms. But his eyes were hiding something from her when he said, "You promised me..."

A whisper of arrowflight sounded from the walls. Lyleth's archers had turned back with her, and had taken position on the stockade.

More ice-born were coming.

From the woods across the pasture, mounted thegns appeared.

"Ready your bow," she told Dylan.

The boy nodded and pulled his bow from his shoulder, and Lyleth did the same. They took up position behind a low jumble of granite. Blinded by tears, she drew her bow and fired. When she glanced back at Nechtan, his eyes were on her.

I'm coming with you, her heart said to his.

He shook his head.

She read his reply on his lips, for she couldn't hear him now. But it was as clear as if he'd whispered in her ear.

"Call the sea, Lyl."

Chapter 39

Naked, Connor pulls himself from the river to stand on a bank littered with dead men. The wind is frigid; at least, it should be frigid because snow is falling, but he feels no cold. Looking back to the river, there's no sign of Ned's silvery coils. He's certainly long gone, and without him, there's no going back.

The bloody muck of this other earth oozes between Connor's bare toes, but he feels nothing of the satisfying squish. He knows what it should feel like, has indulged in it beside so many lakes, but here, he senses nothing but a dull resistance to his presence.

He's suddenly overcome by a longing to feel this mud, to taste the snowflakes, to grieve for the dead around him. This world is painted with unnamed colors and sings with music too perfect for his ears. But he is deaf. And he wants nothing more than to rend his flesh, to expose his heart to the light of this fairer sun.

But he's come here for Dish.

Taking a deep breath, his alveoli swell with birdsong and the steam that rises from cooling horseflesh. He takes in the landscape.

From the edge of a river in a narrow valley, he looks across a field littered with the remains of a bloodbath. But snow is

Terry Madden

laying down a pure white blanket, covering the heaped bodies of men, horses and dogs.

An arm flails, a dying man sobs. The sight should sicken Connor, but his gut is stone. One of these men is Dish. But there are so many...

He draws another deep breath and smells the faintest fragrance of life, upstream. There, a bridge burns, groans and collapses into the river. The sound of a distant horn tells him the battle still rages there, and if Dish is alive, that's where he'll be.

He runs. His feet feel no impact of bone and muscle with earth, so he tries to fly and fails.

From a pile of broken flesh, a boy stirs and sits up. Not much older than Connor, he stands and looks down at the mutilated remains of his own body where crows pull at the flesh of his cheeks.

Connor takes hold of the boy's arm, saying, "I'm looking for Hugh Cavendish."

The boy speaks in a language that's both music and laughter, his eyes dancing with anticipation. Joy.

Connor shakes his head. "I don't understand."

The boy points at the river, then back at Connor as if he considers trying again to communicate. Finally, he just gives Connor a weary smile, shows his open palms, and with one last look at his cast-off body, heads toward the river.

Connor watches others stand and after a long look at their bodies, they follow the boy to the river. Connor will follow them also when it's time to go. When will he ever need to go? Is he dead? Or just trespassing? As they pass by, the dead mutter a greeting, or show their palms, or just meet his eyes with obvious expectation, as if the world they seek, Connor's world, will be the heaven they hope for. He tries to tell them, "There's death there, too." But they just nod, and move on.

"I'm looking for a man," he begs them, "a warrior, I think."

When they reply, it's always the same; they point to the river and say things Connor can't understand.

Giving up, he turns around to see a boy on a galloping horse, headed upriver. He is a living boy, with helmet and armor flashing silver in the sun.

Connor leaps in front of the charging horse and waves his arms frantically. For a millisecond, this living boy must see Connor, or maybe the horse sees him, because the boy reins the horse hard. It rears and the boy tumbles to the ground. When he regains his feet, he has a sword in his hand and slashes at the air in a circle as if he's under attack in a dark room.

He's afraid of me.

Realizing he's the target, Connor dances out of reach of the hissing sword. Then it catches him, soundlessly slicing through his belly and out the other side, spilling nothing but powdered light.

Unhurt, Connor grabs at the boy's flailing arms, but just like that time in the cave, Connor's hand passes through, sensing every corpuscle, every atom, every proton of this boy's flesh. And something else—the inky stain of fear? Or is it madness?

The boy glances about wildly, blindly, finally sheathing his sword. He walks right through Connor, knocking the breath from him. Molecule passes through molecule, two holograms on different frequencies, never touching, without gravity or friction.

But the boy's flesh leaves a faint trace of Dish's blood on Connor, and he looks in the direction from which the boy came. Another fire burns in the distance, a house, and a tower on the ridge above it.

Connor turns to watch the boy step into his stirrup just as an arrow buries in his back. The boy falls. Riders approach, dismount and with a grin, one man swings an axe. He kicks the boy's head away from his twitching body, then empties the helm of its head. Laughing, he removes his own plain helm and slips on the shiny silver one. It flashes with rough stones.

As quickly as they'd come, the horsemen are gone.

Connor stands beside the body of the boy, waiting for his spirit to rise and head for the river as the others had done. The boy does indeed stand, but not his spirit. His violated body stands, streamers of blood-red powder drift from his severed neck and blow through Connor. As Connor watches, the boy finds his head in the dirty snow and fits it to the stump of his neck. He turns to look at Connor one last time with eyes like embers, then he mounts his horse and rides away.

Over the snowy landscape, Connor's bare feet fly. He should feel terror, but the dull indifference of this dreamworld makes him a distant observer. His body passes through a fence and into a pen of sheep and there's Dish, lying among scattered dead. He's not alone. There's Lyla, and a blonde-haired girl, and... Dylan. At least he looks like Dylan. But it can't be.

As Connor starts across the pasture, mounted warriors break from the woods and charge toward them.

The woman he takes to be Lyla and Dylan fire arrows at the riders, but there are so many.

As Connor draws closer, he sees that the woman is crying. She looks over her shoulder at Dish. He says something to her, then she's holding him, her face buried in his neck, rocking him.

Connor reaches Dylan's side. The boy's jaw is clenched. He's intently drawing the bowstring to his cheek, his dark eyes damp with tears as he sights down the shaft. Dylan's arrow drops a man, leaving a riderless horse to charge freely through the sheep.

Dylan looks over his shoulder at Dish and Lyla, and mirrored in Dylan's face Connor sees everything he feels for Dish, and he wishes more than anything he could feel it now. He wishes this boy really was his brother, that he could make Dylan understand how much he misses him and loves him. But this Dylan is a man here. And Dish is his teacher no less than he is Connor's.

Feeling a surge of desperation, he reaches out to touch Dylan's hand and hesitates. Connor came here for Dish. The reminder blinks in his mind like the remnant of a dream.

He turns to see the blonde-haired girl hand the woman a flask. It's made of light and tears, and the woman begins circling Dish, pouring a stream of luminous water from the flask and chanting words that Connor's soul understands but not his ears.

"She calls the sea," he hears himself say.

She pours the last of the flask over Dish. As if in answer, blood flows from his open belly, a rivulet that seeks low ground, making its way back toward the river that brought Connor here. Blood soon becomes water, spilling from Dish until a torrent bursts from nearby rocks. Not blood now, but water.

The sheep are swept up like leaves in the flood.

Connor is swept up with them. The water flows in a circle, carrying Connor, the sheep and dead men in a whirlpool that begins to form a lake, leaving an island in the middle where Lyla and Dylan are taking up their bows again.

A mail-clad man thrashes beside Connor, but the weight of his armor drags him under. Connor watches Dylan turn, draw, and fire with a fierceness in his eye of one who is fully alive.

Riderless horses swim for the far shore where a timber wall burns and spits hot pitch. Chunks of burning wood fall into the growing lake, steaming. Warriors fight for a foothold on the muddy shore and men with spears race along the water's edge.

Connor swims to the island and drags himself out onto the muddy shore.

A horse no bigger than a large dog, adorned with ribbons and red berries, runs in frantic circles at the shore of the island. It stops where Connor lies in the muck and sniffs at his hair. This, he can feel. He revels in the warm, damp breath of the horse, the velvet softness of its tiny muzzle. He strokes its sleek coat, rests his forehead against its cheek.

Dish, the little horse reminds him. You're here for Dish.

The horse trots away and suddenly leaps into the water and disappears under the surface.

Connor can't take his eyes from the spot where the little horse went under, for a whorl grows of a million tiny silver fish. They move as one, like a flight of birds, turning and twisting and condensing so tightly that it becomes one beast. He knows this beast. The water horse.

It breaks the surface and jumps like a great fish, taking a horse and rider down with it.

Connor makes his way to Dish, and falls to his knees beside him.

Dish looks into Connor's eyes and takes his hand. It doesn't pass through this time, flesh and bone meet, and Connor can feel the trembling man inside. At that moment, from the wound in Dish's belly, downy feathers sprout. The wind catches them and they mix with snow and embers. And just like that night in the hospital, a flash of green fire passes from Connor's wrist to Dish's.

"You have to wake up now," Connor says.

"I'm coming," Dish replies.

Lyla gathers Dish in her arms and weeps. As Connor steps back, Dish's clenched fist opens again to reveal a pearl the size of a small bird egg. A fog surrounds it in the colors of a stormy sky.

The pearl rolls from Dish's hand into the water.

Connor understands and dives after it into the muddy current. His fingers sift silt and pebbles as the rush of water tries to carry him away. He can see only dimly in the churned muck, but the glow of Dish's soul guides him. As he seizes the pearl, the water horse wraps him in its shimmering coils and takes him under.

The hiss of sea foam dragging over sand forced Connor to open his eyes. Silver fish convulsed in the sand around him;

they gasped for air just as Connor did until the next wave forced him farther ashore and took the fish back to sea.

He coughed up seawater and looked back at the waves that had brought him.

The water horse was gone. And this was Malibu Beach.

A knock-kneed kid with a plastic bucket stood over Connor. His blonde hair was on fire in the sunlight.

"Where's your swim trunks?" the little boy asked. His voice moved through water, shrill and distorted, and the words finally meant something to Connor's mind.

He got to his hands and knees and willed himself to stand. His head hammered with the pulse of the sun's rays, piercing his skin with a million needles. Then he opened his frozen fingers to find the pearl nestled there with a fistful of sand.

The kid's mom was running full tilt toward him, and with a look that said she feared for her kid's life, she scooped up the boy and kept running.

Connor followed as fast as his leaden feet would go.

The mom was grabbing a cooler and a second kid was crying, but Connor managed to snatch a beach towel from the little girl before they left him to wade through this honey-thick reality.

He drew a deep lungful of this stagnant world, wrapped the Little Mermaid towel around his waist, and headed for Pacific Coast Highway.

The guy who picked him up was chatty, but a long stare from Connor brought silence. He wondered if this guy could even see him. After all, Connor was just a ghost.

He told the security guard at the hospital his brother was dying and was escorted to I.C.U.

Connor hit the intercom button and was thankful when Holly's voice came on.

"I'm not too late. Please," he said into the wall.

He looked at the pearl once more. It was smaller now, and felt like dry ice in his palm.

The door buzzed open. Connor walked into the cold light of sterile death. The vision of Dish lying on the little island superimposed on top of this one and out of the corner of his eye, Connor saw the little horse flying out over the water with ribbons fluttering.

Lyla held Dish and wept. But no one held him here.

Holly met him at the door of the alcove, saying, "His heart rate's grown erratic. They've decided to do it now." She draped a blanket over Connor's shoulders.

Bronwyn turned at the sound of Holly's voice, her face streaked with tears. She met Connor's eyes and there was so much sorrow there, he had to look away.

It was Merryn who held Dish's hand in this world.

I'm coming, Dish had said.

Merryn sat beside him, Dish's hand sandwiched between hers. She was talking to him, but when she saw Connor, she stopped and looked up at him. "You've come at last, lad."

"Yes, Aunt Merryn."

"Hugh will be pleased."

He extended his closed fist over the wrecked flesh that was Dish. Connor opened his hand. There was nothing there but a tingling chill and damp sand. "Where is it?"

Merryn took his open hand and patted it. He felt the bones like twigs beneath her fragile skin. Molecule met molecule, and the gravity of this world governed them.

"Where did the pearl go?"

"What pearl, lad?"

Dish was fading into the white of his sheets. The bruises and cuts had healed, but his cheekbones were sharp and his collarbones stuck out from under the hospital gown. He was as wrecked in this world as he was in the other.

The nurse powered down one machine after another,

finally flipping the switch on the ventilator and the artificial rise and fall of Dish's chest stopped.

"Come on, Dish." Connor's vision blurred with tears. The rhythmic beating of Dish's heart continued in green sine waves on the heart monitor. Slowly, the line began to flatten out, the rhythm erratic and fast.

Bronwyn sat on the edge of the bed and took Dish's other hand.

I'm coming, a voice whispered in Connor's head and he saw a dragon kite fluttering in the rain, envisioned himself drawing in the kite string. He could feel the tension, the string cutting into his fingers, the buffet of a determined wind.

The green line flattened out and droned a monotone. Alarms chimed and the nurses switched them off.

At the end of the kite string, a pearl the color of a stormy sky pulsed in a void.

"Come on, Dish."

Connor saw Dish's fingers twitch in Merryn's hand. I'm coming.

Standing over Dish, he looked down at this man who had already fled his body on the other side.

"You can't just let him go," Connor pleaded, "fight for him!"

The nurses were unhooking the cables to everything. "Wake up." Desperation took hold of him. "Wake up!"

I'm coming.

He took hold of Dish's shoulders and shook him, his face inches from Dish. "You have to wake up!"

Holly's arm was around Connor's shoulders. "He's gone."

"He's coming."

It was Merryn's touch that drew him away. She took his hand and patted it. "It's all right, lad. He's all right."

"No. He's not."

He collapsed in a chair beside her. It was over. And Dish was swept away in the current between the worlds, waiting for another universe to be born. Connor measured the air moving in and out of his own lungs. He was a machine controlled by something that could never die and he wanted more than anything for someone like Lyla to hold him like she held Dish. And it suddenly became more important than forgiveness to know that she would hold Dish again, and that someone waited to hold Connor in just the same way. Maybe then, he could let go.

Dish gasped.

His arms swung wildly, tearing at the wires that sprouted from his chest and the I.V.'s in his arms, the tube that still went through a hole in his throat.

An alarm chimed outside and the room was suddenly thick with nurses and doctors. The green line jumped on the heart monitor, then went flat as Dish pulled the wires free. He cried out, a deep throaty wail, and the nurses tried to hold him down while Merryn and Bronwyn struggled to get out of their way.

But Connor was frozen in his chair.

When Dish's eyes found Connor's, he stopped fighting, the dislodged ventilator tube clutched in his quaking fist. He looked right into Connor's eyes and said, "Dylan."

Chapter 40

The new boy-king, Talan, had commanded Ava to watch her father's execution as if it would pain her in some way. The spectacle had been set for morning. Lyleth, and three guards, escorted Ava to her father's cell far below the smoldering walls of Caer Cedewain to speak her farewells. These Ildana liked to pretend at civility.

Lyleth left her alone with him, probably hoping Ava would choke him with his shackles.

The Bear was chained to the wall by his ankles and wrists. Stripped of his bearskin and armor, he was nothing more than an old man wearing a surly smirk.

"Come to weep for your daddy, have you?"

How long had she dreamt of this? She had believed a transcendent rage would take her, that she would sink her teeth into his flesh and rip it from his face. But the fury refused to come. No, she would hurt him far more than mere mutilation.

"The new boy-king of the Ildana sees fit to place me on your throne in Rotomagos." She said it with the tone of a gossipmonger to an eager housewife. "And I will see to it that your stench is scrubbed from every stone in the land." She savored the horror in his eyes.

"You are your mother's daughter. She never told me a truthful word in her short life—"

"Because you'd have cut out her tongue if she did. Just like Ilsa."

He chuckled and yanked at his chains, leaning closer, so she could smell his rotting teeth. "She was your 'friend.'"

They were just girls. Ilsa was a low-born herder's daughter, sold into service by her family to act as Ava's chambermaid. The Bear decided to make an example of Ilsa, to teach Ava her place in life. After he raped Ilsa, he cut out her tongue. But within the week, Ilsa had hung herself, for she too was Skvalan.

Ava had learned her lesson, but not the one the Bear had intended.

"May your death be slower than the growing of a great tree." The Ildana curse felt right on her ice-born tongue.

He was laughing still when she left him with a gob of her spittle hanging from his beard.

In the morning, when Talan gave the order to strip the Bear's skin from his body, Ava smiled. And the Bear screamed at last.

The only thing that pained Ava was seeing Gwylym die. His eyes were on her through the fall of the axe and she felt a rush of desire to be taken away from this world too. She was tired of living.

Talan hung the Bear's skin from the walls of Caer Cedewain in the same place he'd found the pale rag that was his mother. While Marchlew and Nechtan engaged Ava's forces in the glen, the Bear had slaughtered everyone left behind in Caer Cedewain. When Talan arrived, he found his mother's body hanging from the walls with the rest like butchered meat, flayed, covered with a rime of hoarfrost, her frozen skin hanging beside her like a cloak. The Bear's skin looked no different now.

Talan kept Ava in a makeshift prison, a room of the fortress that hadn't burned. It lacked a window, so Ava had lost track of the days and the guards would tell her nothing. She passed time watching ants ferry the remainder of her meals along the joints of the flagstones.

At last, Lyleth came to call.

"Let's be done with this," Ava said to the druí.

Without a word, Lyleth took a seat on a stool beside the small brazier. Had she come to chat over warm milk? Nechtan's solás wore her veil of indifference poorly today. He must have died in her arms, for in those shrewd, piercing eyes Ava could see the hollowness he'd left in Lyleth's soul. She envied it.

"You serve a boy," Ava said. "Is it so different than serving a she-king?"

In spite of Lyleth's trained composure, Ava saw a flash of doubt in those eyes. No, Lyleth distrusted this boy, as well she should.

"I serve the judges of the greenwood," Lyleth said. "And I do the will of my king."

"Noble, but tell me, when will you send me after my loving father? I have no patience for these games."

"You told the Bear you would be king in his place, in Rotomagos."

"Now you spy on me, too. Execute me for lies, then, if it please you. Just do it." Ava had to smile at this. But Lyleth's expression never changed, playing her part in the court of a king.

"You will rule the land that has come to you by virtue of your blood. You will work to build peace between our lands."

By Lyleth's tone, this proposal had cost the druí a large sum of pride, something these greenmen were forbidden.

"Do I hear you rightly? You want to send me back to Sandkaldr?"

"He used you, Ava." Was that pity in Lyleth's voice? "You are the only living heir of Saerlabrand, the Bear of Sandkaldr. As such, you inherit his throne by your own laws as well as the laws of the Ildana."

Ava snorted a laugh. "You're afraid. Afraid of who will

win the Bear's throne and sail back to your shores. You've not studied the ice-born, have you, druí?"

"Oh, I have. Without ships, they are as crippled as an archer with no arrows. And more pliant."

"You think burning their ships will stop them. They'll still come. If they have to swim the Broken Sea, they'll come."

"I've burned all... but one. The ship that will bear you back. If you want a kingdom, take your own."

A she-king of the north? Her kin would slit her throat in her sleep.

"The hearts of the ice-born are as frozen as the land," Ava said.

"Not yours."

Lyleth looked at her as if she could see something decent and deserving flickering in Ava's frayed soul. Ava had to look away. Lyleth pulled the green soothblade from her belt and held the hilt to Ava. It belonged to the beewoman, not Ava, but Lyleth needn't know that. Ava's hand closed around it, feeling the weight of truth. She might plunge it into Lyleth's eye and send her after Nechtan. Perhaps it's what she wanted. But when Ava looked up, the door was closing behind Lyleth.

The Broken Sea had begun to freeze in the shallow bay of the Gannet's Bath. Wide stretches of beach were white with snow, without a sign of the Bear's longships that had been beached here. Talan had them burned and their charred skeletons had surely been taken by the tide. Pyrs' fleet waited beyond the waves while Ava and her escort boarded the last longship and launched with the tide.

Men pushed through ice floes with harpoons and hooks and cleared a path for the ship through the shallow waters until they reached the open sea, where they could set their backs to the oars.

The flat keel pitched over hummocks of rolling sea, its dragon masthead diving and resurfacing with every swell.

Ildana sailors made up the majority of the crew. This was no swan ship, and the Ildana fought the single sail's shroud and tack until it bellied steadily and plowed the sea north and east.

Ava leaned over the bow rail and watched green water curl and return to the vast and bottomless sea. The spray washed over her, and the deep beckoned.

She inhaled the smell of salt spray and horse fat from the sail, and the smell filled her with the melancholy of a Skvalan winter, sunless and cold. Nechtan's laugh came back to her for some reason. Perhaps she heard it in the splash of the sea.

She refused an evening meal offered by Lyleth's servant, the boy, Dylan. He watched her tirelessly. But he had the will of a boy, and at last, he slept with the others between the thwarts. The ship had fallen into a still pocket of night air. The sail flapped, limp. A path of moonlight buttered the windless water, and blue icebergs drifted in the distance like cities.

Ava reached into the soft leather of her left boot. The bone handle was warm from her flesh. She drew out the soothblade and wondered how fair the Old Blood truly were. They lay hidden now, in stone and root, star and wind, but they were the only part of this land that had wanted Ava. They had given her the guardian. At least that was true.

She held the green blade to the moonlight. The fractures in the stone ignited with silver fire, but she was blind to the runes of the ancients. What truth would spill? Poison? Bile? The black tar that seeps from under the earth and burns with the stench of the underworld?

Was there any truth left in her at all?

The blade was sharp and she cut deeply. Holding her arm to the moonlight, she examined the truth spilling from her. It beaded and glistened, like the sticky juice from a brambleberry. She caught a drop on her fingertip as it fell to the stinking deck, and put it on her tongue. She smiled, and felt Nechtan's warm fingers on her cheek, wiping away her tears.

While the moon watched, she laid down another cut beside the first. She had much truth to spill. And she did.

Chapter 41

The midwinter festivities in Caer Ys were more extravagant than the usual guise dancing and mummer's plays. The Ildana had crowned a new king and cast the ice-born back into the Broken Sea. The common folk had already taken to calling Talan the Winter King, crowned as he was on the Dark Day. Lyleth supposed it was fitting, since Nechtan had once been called the Summer King, though now the ballads gave him titles he would have loathed—Immortal Guardian, Deathslayer.

Dylan had returned just days ago with the news of Ava's death, and Talan seized the opportunity to remind Lyleth of her wasted effort. "The ice-born are too savage for your treaties of peace, they understand nothing but the sword," he said.

Perhaps he was right. But Lyleth had spent most of this lifetime trying to make it otherwise. The ice-born would return to these shores under another banner; another Bear would rise.

On this day of his crowning, Lyleth rode behind Talan through the city gates. His solás rode to his left, a student of Dechtire's as Lyleth had once been, yet this druí was as fair as Lyleth was dark and some years older than Talan. She carried the silver branch timidly, the boughs hung with holly and mistletoe, hazelnuts and acorns, and of course, silver bells.

The Winter King. It suited Talan, for he was as cold as the wind off the peaks of the Pendynas.

Lyleth had stood at Talan's side when he reclaimed Caer

Cedewain from the Bear. The ice-born couldn't hold the walls for long against the numbers Talan now commanded, for Fiach's and Lloyd's forces tripled the numbers of the northern tribes.

Marchlew had died in battle and Lyleth thought it a blessing, for the sight that met them at the gates was not one a husband should see. Yet Talan seemed unmoved by the sight of his mother's corpse, flayed and hanging from the gate tower. The boy simply said, "Cut her down."

The ice-born had slaughtered all in Caer Cedewain, servant and soldier alike, children as well as women. But Lyleth had never found Dunla among the dead.

Lyleth watched Talan ride before her, shoulders growing broader by the day. His silver circlet had been Nechtan's, for Talan wouldn't allow a new one to be forged, saying it would give him counsel in a way he had not yet divined. Perhaps so, but he didn't strike Lyleth as one who listened to the voices of the dead. No, he needed the allegiance of those who had loved Nechtan, and they were many. He would glean some glory as nephew and heir of the Deathslayer.

The streets of Caer Ys were choked with revelers and those come to glimpse their new king; troupes of Midwinter guisers with chiming ankle bells dressed as stags or riding hobby horses, their faces darkened with soot. Playing blackthorn whistles and goatskin drums, they beat out ancient songs to rouse the sun from his slumber. Lyleth knew the sun could never warm her heart again.

A tall man wore a hide cloak, the skull of a horse fitted over his head. He worked the jaw with cords to mime the words of a bawdy tune trilled by a chorus. But dancing behind him was a hobby horse with fins, a water horse, its scales made of layered oyster shells that rattled when it shook its mane of kelp.

The song he sang was a new one, recounting Lyleth's calling of the sea and the "battle of the water horse." It told of Pyrs' men, how they arrived at the summoned lake to see the tail of the water horse sweep the ice-born under as they tried to claw their way back to solid ground. But the image that had burned into Lyleth's mind was Brixia, scrambling out of the water and shaking like a dog. With a high whinny, the little horse trotted into the woods and disappeared.

"Nechtan's lady, please!" An old woman pushed her way through the crowd to reach out to Lyleth's foot. The woman clutched at her leg, threatening to unseat her, crying, "Exalter of star and stone, she who sings men to life, help me, I beg you!"

Talan's guards had the woman in hand and started to drag her away, but Lyleth stopped them.

"My son," the woman cried, "he's dead not more than a day. Bring him back to me, I beg you, druí."

"I'm sorry. I cannot." Lyleth parceled these words out a dozen times in a day. The look of betrayal always followed, from every mother, husband, brother. She could raise a king; why not their dead, too?

As Talan's retinue reached the outer ward of the fortress, snow began to fall. Lyleth found a warm fire burning in the bedchamber that had been hers when she served Nechtan. Staying here, so full of memories, was like wearing a gown made of stone. She would be gone soon, back to the Isle of Glass and the hive where she had learned to serve the green gods. Dechtire, her teacher, had fallen ill, and Lyleth would see her before the end.

But there was one last ritual she must see to. She sent Dylan to fetch the harp of the drowned maid, now in Talan's treasury. The day they had left Caer Cedewain, Dylan found the harp half buried in snow where Lyleth and Nechtan had left it, lying under the starwood tree in Kyndra's moon garden.

"The wind told me where it was," Dylan said. "It plucked out an angry tune."

"What did it say?" Lyleth asked him.

His reluctance finally gave way. "That Nechtan was to leave us." A distant sadness clouded his eyes.

"Have you ever wondered if the land of the dead is not beyond the well at all, but here?" she asked him. "Perhaps we're the dead, just waiting for another chance to live among the wonders of the real world."

"Maybe there's no death at all."

"Aye, and no rest."

Dylan built up the peat fire to a rosy glow, and Lyleth took up the harp. It was Talan's harp now, and following the tradition of a thousand years, she would cut the strings of Nechtan's rule. She had seen his nephew to the throne, as Nechtan required of her. Now, her thoughts turned only to following him to that other land and the days or years that lay between.

She sat on a stool, took the harp in her lap and thrummed the full range of notes, hearing Nechtan's laughter in the strands of his hair, chestnut, ash and wet oak bark.

She plucked out an aimless tune, and when she looked up, Dylan was closing the door on his way out. She set her fingers to the strings and played a tune that reminded her of the feel of Nechtan in her arms, flowing with the will of water shaping stone. This flesh is frail, he had whispered under the starwood tree, but it's all we have.

"Not all," she said to the stone walls.

When her fingers left the strings, the harp played on. The dissonance of the Otherworld blended with a melody of this world. In a voice like birdsong, it sang in the tongue of the Old Blood, like wind dandling a barley field. A mere whisper. A name, repeated.

Talan... Talan stole what is only given.

The final notes left the strings and surged through the aching skin that held her bound to this world, through the chamber, through the courses of old stone, out to meet the light of the stars.

For no word is uttered that goes unheard, and no light burns without casting a shadow.

Talan's spear had taken Nechtan from her.

She reached into her boot and found Ava's soothblade. A shard of pure green olivine, shot through with dark veins that spoke in runes, the blade that had bled Ava into the hull of a longship.

"Not to be unmade," she said to Nechtan.

No one else would know the truth it had to tell. Not yet.

In one slow cut, she severed the strings of Nechtan's harp, and they sang like silver threads under a bow of spider silk.

The king was dead.

Chapter 42

When Connor and Iris went back to Ned's, the house was boarded up and the fish pond/hot tub was drained. Nothing but a collection of beer bottles and Chinese take-out boxes were left to say Ned had been there at all. He opened the well on the beach to bait Dish, but bait him to do what? Unless Dish remembered his stay on the other side, Connor would never know.

Father Owens gave Connor a stay of execution, probably because he had showed up in the I.C.U. wearing nothing but a beach towel to witness Dish's awakening, or maybe Owens and Dish had a chat again. Anyway, Connor could stay at school with a list of conditions.

He visited Dish twice a week while he was in rehab. But Connor knew there was no therapy for what Dish had been through. Dish spent a month there, learning how to live without the use of his legs because the doctors said his paralysis was permanent.

As Dish's traveling librarian, Connor brought him specific books from his collection, things with ragged spines and hundreds of notes stuck in them. Their talk was all surface stuff, like how Connor's term paper was going, how many miles he had run that week, or what he thought of Don Zeigler's new movie, that kind of thing. Dish never even hinted that he remembered anything about the Otherworld, and Connor began to wonder if his memory had been wiped clean by somebody like Ned. The bastard.

Half the time Iris came with Connor on his visits, because there was no way to stop her. At least with her along, there were no awkward silences because she talked enough for all three of them. At first, her parents decided to send her to a different school, saying she had made some unsavory friends, meaning Connor, but Iris made some promises, and they let her stay at St. Thom's. Connor was glad. He even admitted it to her.

Brother Mike was driving them back from visiting Dish. Connor and Iris sat in the back seat, even though no one else was in the van. On the beach, people were playing volleyball. A kite fluttered past, a fairy kite. It looked sort of like Tinkerbell.

"You still haven't told me what you saw over there." Iris jolted him from his thoughts, as if she knew he was wandering back to that other place.

"It's like…" How could he find the words? It wasn't possible. "Here, we live in a world ruled by the left side of our brain. Over there, the right side rules…"

"You mean like conscious and subconscious?"

"Maybe. I can't explain." The best Connor could do was draw pictures. The images in his sketchpad felt like a shadow of that other place. After all, drawing is a right brain activity.

His eyes never left the beach as he blurted out, "I saw someone who looked like my brother."

Iris' arm slid around his shoulder, and she rested her head against his. "He was okay, wasn't he?"

"He was… amazing."

Iris smiled at him, and he returned it.

When Dish finally got out of rehab, he spent most of his time locked in his room, coming out for meals, and not much else.

More than anything, Connor wanted to talk to him about what happened over there. But Dr. Adelman warned him to wait a while before bringing up serious talk, till Dish came to grips with his handicap. He was suffering from grief, like someone he loved had died. Connor figured he was the only person who understood what Dish had really lost, and it wasn't just his legs.

Bronwyn had tried to convince Dish to go back to England, saying he could live with her family. But Dish later told Connor, "I'd rather live with sixty smelly lads than my sister." After Connor's experience with Bronwyn, he would have to agree.

By February, Dish was back to teaching. They moved his classroom to the lower floor of Austin Hall and built ramps so he could get up and down the steps. They also moved his dorm room downstairs and put Connor in the room beside his.

Connor had become his unofficial "pusher." In fact, Father Owens gave him special dispensation from tardiness because he pushed Dish to and from class, lunch, etc. Dish could really get just about everywhere by himself—his arms were getting beasty. But Connor still came with him, more because he wanted to than because he needed to.

One day after school, Connor was pushing Dish back to the dorm when he raised his hand and jingled some keys.

"I hear you fancy my car," Dish said.

"'Fancy' isn't exactly the right word."

"Let's go for a drive."

Connor could swear his heart stopped for a full minute. Drive Dish? How could he do that?

"Yeah," he said, "Okay."

Connor helped Dish into the front seat and loaded the wheelchair in the trunk. He slipped into the driver's seat and ran his hands over his pants to dry his sweaty palms.

"There's a bike path that runs along the beach," Dish said. "I thought perhaps you'd take me down there."

Connor worked up the words. "I'll take you wherever you want to go."

Dish gave him a wistful smile. Connor knew where he

wanted to go, and he would have given anything to be able to take him there.

The fog was rolling in and felt cool on Connor's face. They didn't talk for the longest time. He just pushed the wheelchair along the path; the rubber wheels gritted over the sandy concrete, and Dish stared out at the ocean. A bright star pulsed on the horizon. It looked like a jewel hanging over the purple tumble of fog. Connor wondered if people in the Otherworld looked at the same stars. Was their day lit by the same sun?

Connor had to say it. "The threshold of night." He knew Dish was thinking it.

A long silence answered him. Finally, Dish said, "So it is."

Another long silence.

"I called the bookstore," Dish finally said. "They told me a young man had come by and purchased the book I ordered."

Connor stopped walking. It was time for the talk. Thank god.

He pushed Dish over to a picnic table and set the brake, then sat down on the bench beside him.

"I was hoping you'd ask about it."

"Connor, we have some things to sort out. You need to understand that what happened to me was completely out of your control. You can't blame yourself—"

"I know that now, but—" Connor had nothing to lose now. But how to ask it? "Do you think they're okay?" He let the question settle between them.

Dish's eyes flitted to the waves, and he pursed his lips as if trying not to answer. "We have to believe they are, don't we?"

"You remember—"

"I remember." The burden of those memories was clear. "And I know why the gods bless us with forgetfulness from one life to the next."

Connor had so many questions he couldn't stop them. "You were looking for that well, because you remember this symbol?" He pointed to the water horse still coiled around

Dish's wrist. "Merryn told me all about it. How she took the picture and all. It's why you came to California, isn't it?"

"It's quite the opposite, really. As I grew up, the only memories I had of that place came like snapshots. From dreams, from poetry. I remembered a longing, and that was about all. When Merryn told me about the stone, I believed if I could find it, I could find my way back there. I would find what I so longed for." Dish squinted against the setting sun. "I came to California to end my obsession."

"But it followed you," Connor said.

"I suppose, for some reason, it did."

"And now you remember everything about your life on the other side?"

Dish nodded sadly. "Everything."

"Ned said they took you back because you had a job to do over there. What job?"

Dish sat straighter in his wheelchair and ran his hands up and down his dead thighs. "I made a perfect mess of my life there, Connor. I got another chance. Let's leave it at that. You have the book?"

Connor launched into a long, convoluted tale about Ned and the moving well and finally admitted he'd traded the book and every photocopy he'd made of it to Ned in exchange for a one-way pass to the other side.

They talked until the sun sank into the sea.

Dish told him about Ava and Lyleth and his nephew Talan. But when he talked about that last day, about leaving Dylan and Lyleth on that island, it was clear that worry was eating him up.

"The water horse was with them," Connor said. "How could they lose?"

When he saw tears in Dish's eyes, it was impossible to stop his own. It felt good to cry.

"Can you take me to the place where you found the well?" Dish asked.

Connor wiped his nose on his sleeve, got up, kicked the

brake off the wheelchair, and pushed Dish down the bike path. It was getting dark. "I left your flashlight in the car."

On the drive to the mansion, Connor asked questions about the mysterious Old Blood that Merryn told him about. They were exiled through the third well, trapped here with no way to get back.

"If these guys are so magical," Connor was saying, "how could the Ildana take them in battle?"

"There's much to be said for steel," Dish said. "The Old Blood saw it as the will of the land when Black Brac killed the guardian. So, they made peace, crossed over, not knowing they couldn't return by way of death. I tracked down some old folktales about a people who swam through a well as silver fish and climbed out as people on the Isle of Anglesey, Ynys Môn."

"That's where druidism started," Connor added.

"How do you know that?"

"I did some reading while you were asleep." Connor pulled up to the overgrown weeds and chain-link fence in front of the deserted mansion and parked the car. Looking over at Dish, lit by the dull interior light, he asked, "Did you think the well could take you back to Lyleth?"

"At the time, yes. Now, I know better."

Connor had to pry the chain-link gates open with a tire iron so he could get Dish's wheelchair through. Dish carried the flashlight and Connor rolled him down the walkway that led to the pool area, leaves crunching under the wheels.

"This well couldn't be the third well of the sea," Connor was whispering, "because there's no stone here, right?"

"This is just a life well," Dish said. "There are many, on this side and the other."

Connor recalled the laundry list of well types he had found on the Internet.

"If the water horse marks the well, why do you have one on your arm?"

"I was—I mean, Nechtan was a king born into a long line of kings descended from Black Brac, the one who convinced the Old Blood to make peace. Every king of his line wears this tattoo." He held up his wrist.

Connor digested this for a bit. "Why did Ned want the picture of the stone, then?"

"To make bloody sure wankers like us don't find it, I should think."

Connor lifted the latch on the rotting gate and dragged it open across the walk. The pool area was just as he had left it, littered with Ned's cigarette butts and beer caps. He rolled Dish across the deck to the edge of the empty fishpond.

"You wrote the runes around the edge?" Dish traced the flashlight beam around the well.

"I used Iris' lipstick—and lipstick has oil in it. Shit!"

"What is it?"

"It's chemistry!"

Connor was on his knees, brushing away fallen leaves, gum wrappers and cigarette butts. "Now, I just need some water."

At the bottom of the big pool, Connor found stagnant rainwater. He scooped some in a beer bottle and brought it back to the well.

"What are you doing, Connor?"

"Lipstick is made of oil. When I wrote on the stone patio, it should have soaked in. If I dampen it, we might be able to see the runes as darker spots, because water and oil don't mix. It's like a negative image."

"Give it a go."

Dish held the light while Connor sprinkled water over the stones. The runes appeared like disappearing ink, the darker outlines of the stick figures barely visible in contrast to the wet stone.

Dish pulled a pen from his pocket, held the flashlight in his teeth, and copied the runes on a flattened take-out carton.

Connor looked over his shoulder as Dish read them

aloud. Speaking the words with reverence, he almost sang in that language of the other side. Connor could hear the snap of flames in Dish's words.

"But what does it say? In English?"

Dish was lost in thought, his eyes fixed on the dark horizon where the ocean lay. He ran his hands through his hair and finally looked up at Connor, worry written on his face.

"What is it, Dish? What does it say?"

"It's a prophecy," Dish stated.

"Prophesying what? You got to tell me what it says." Connor was in front of the wheelchair, his hands planted on Dish's shoulders. "It's me, Dish."

His eyes flitted from Connor to the runes and back. "Maybe it's not meant for us to hear."

"Only Ned would say that. Come on."

Dish exhaled sharply and dragged the back of his hand over his mouth. "It says, 'Cleave star and stone, Child of Death...'" His voice fell to a whisper, "'Call the Old Blood home.'"

The riddle turned circles in Connor's head. "What does that mean? Who's the child of death?"

Dish was staring into the empty well. "It means... there are things not meant for us to understand." He tucked the take-out carton in his coat pocket, clutched the rims of his wheelchair and started rolling back toward the car like he was in the Special Olympics.

Connor chased after him. "You mean it makes no sense to you either?"

"No."

"Why do I not believe that?"

"We'd best get back," Dish called over his shoulder. "It's well past dark."

Chapter 43

Summer had finally come to the Isle of Glass. Elowen thought she'd never feel warm again, but the black sand baked her back and a breeze played in her hair. Dylan had already set to digging the clams Lyl had asked them to fetch for supper.

Lyleth had left Talan's court in early spring, for her master, Dechtire, was dying and the old green sister had asked for Lyleth. And where Lyl went, so did Elowen and Dylan.

Elowen liked this hive, and even decided to learn a few things taught only to greenwood babes—reading a coming storm, coaxing life from long-dried seed. But the thing Elowen liked best was the summer days here almost never ended, for the sun would dip just below the horizon in the southwest and hang there, like it was waiting for something.

"Get off your lazy backside!" Dylan called.

"We can't set to work yet," Elowen said. "We got lots o' time."

"But we've got the Battle of Cynvarra to know in three days."

"You're no fun at all." Laughing, she pitched a fistful of sand at him and led him on a chase down the strand. When she felt him close behind, she plunged into the breaking waves, believing he wouldn't follow because he didn't fancy the cold. But when she turned, he was right behind her.

He caught her and they went under, laughing, water up her

nose, the sea closing over them like the sky, dancing with green sunlight.

Elowen surfaced and fought the drag of the tide back toward the beach.

"Come on," Dylan said, pushing wet hair from his face. He pointed at a figure far down the strand. "Lyl's coming. We best get to work."

Elowen followed him, but her eyes didn't leave the figure moving down the strand.

"I want to tell him," Elowen said. "More than anything, I want to tell him."

"Tell who what? You prattle on like a loon."

"Nechtan. He should know."

"Maybe Lyl don't want him to know."

"O'course she does." Elowen jabbed Dylan's shoulder with a good punch. "She bears a king's babe."

Lyleth had stopped a good way down the strand. Shading her eyes, she looked out at the endless break of the sea, her hand on the swell of her child. In that moment, Elowen knew the price the green gods would ask and she wondered how long Lyleth had known, for she most surely did.

"C'mon," Dylan said. "We've clams to dig."

Elowen watched Lyleth step into the sea foam, a shimmering veil of sun jewels at her feet.

Picking up her clam bucket, Elowen followed Dylan, smiling.

"He knows."

Acknowledgments

There is a commonly held belief that what lies beyond death is something of our own design. I've never been one to hope for a perfect paradise. I think it would be rather boring. So when I set out to write this story I discovered an opportunity to explore my own personal "land of the dead." When I go, I'm going to the Five Quarters.

This story would never have come to pass without the discussions I had with one of my astronomy students about communicating with the dead through internet games. Connor Whitman kept pestering me about writing an outline for the story we had cooked up. Most of the elements of that early story fell by the wayside, but Connor strongly influenced one of my main characters.

My family has been my cheerleaders and my critics, neither of which I could have done without. My daughter, Erica Maulhardt, is always my first reader and a great editor along with Joe Braasch and Bradley Darewood. My husband, Alan Maulhardt, always lets me know when my writing is confusing, and has helped me trim the superfluous. He and my son A.J. have provided encouragement at the times I needed it most.

My friend and editor, John Harten, who crossed to the otherworld before this book was completed, smoothed out the final draft, pointing out the "pedestrian and cliché." Bonnie Blanton was a perfect beta reader. Writer friends who have weighed in on various chapters include Marsha Maulhardt, Christy Bell and Jane Howatt. You guys are the best, as are my Writers of the Future volume 30 colleagues, especially Liz Colter, Megan O'Keefe, Amanda Forrest and K. C. Norton.

The opportunity to learn from such writers as Kevin J. Anderson, Orson Scott Card and Dave Farland was a great gift from the Writers of the Future contest. But the mentoring and encouragement I have received from Tim Powers is what keeps me writing, and I can't thank him enough for being him.

Many thanks to Michael Wills for believing in my writing and to Christine Clukey Reese for her attention to detail in proofreading. Many thanks to Holly Simental for her work on the cover art.

For more information about me and my writing, check out my website: **www.threewellsofthesea.com**

You can follow me on Twitter @**tlmaddenwrites** and Facebook at **terrymaddenwrites**

Join Us

Thank you for reading our novel, **Three Wells of the Sea**, and for supporting speculative fiction in the written form. Please consider leaving a reader review so that other people can make an informed reading decision.

Find more great stories, novels, collections,
and anthologies on our website.
Visit us at DigitalFictionPub.com

Join the Digital Fiction Pub newsletter for **infrequent** updates, new release discounts, and more:
Subscribe at Digital Fiction Pub

See just some of our exciting fantasy, horror,
crime, and science fiction books on
the next page.

Also from Digital Fiction

Digital Fantasy Fiction Anthologies

Short Stories Series One
Uncommon Senses – Book 1
Ignis Fatuus – Book 2
Casual Conjurings – Book 3

Digital Fantasy Fiction Novels

The Black River Chronicles: Level One –
David Tallerman and Michael Wills
The Messiah – Vincent L. Scarsella
Three Wells of the Sea – Terry Madden

Digital Fantasy Fiction Short Reads

Fantasy Short Stories – Various Authors

Copyright

Three Wells of the Sea: Book One
By Terry Madden
Digital Fantasy Fiction Novel: Terry Madden
Executive Editor: Michael Wills

DigitalFictionPub.com

61132072R00208

Made in the USA
Middletown, DE
15 January 2018